Charming Lily

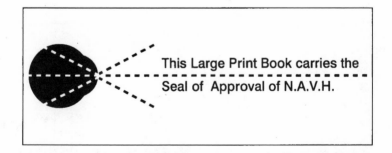

This Large Print Book carries the
Seal of Approval of N.A.V.H.

Charming Lily

Fern Michaels

Thorndike Press • Waterville, Maine

Published in 2001 by arrangement with Zebra Books,
an imprint of Kensington Publishing Corp.

Thorndike Press Large Print Americana Series.

The tree indicium is a trademark of Thorndike Press.

The text of this Large Print edition is unabridged.
Other aspects of the book may vary from the original edition.

Set in 16 pt. Plantin by Rick Gundberg.

Printed in the United States on permanent paper.

Library of Congress Cataloging-in-Publication Data

Michaels, Fern.
    Charming Lily / Fern Michaels.
        p. cm.
    ISBN 0-7862-3451-2 (lg. print : hc : alk. paper)
    ISBN 0-7862-3452-0 (lg. print : sc : alk. paper)
    1. Dwellings — Conservation and restoration — Fiction.
2. Women mountaineers — Fiction. 3. Natchez (Miss.) —
Fiction. 4. Missing persons — Fiction. I. Title.
PS3563.I27 C48 2001
813′.54—dc21   2001034656

For my friend, Pam Nelson

ACKNOWLEDGMENTS

I'd like to thank Pam Nelson who took time out of her own busy schedule to arrange my trip to Natchez and for sharing some of her childhood memories, Betty Lou Hicks, (of the Hicks Chicks) also known as Blue, Rene Adams, the Assistant Manager of Dunleith Plantation for the wonderful tour and seeing for myself those places at Dunleith where scenes from *Gone With the Wind* were filmed, and the equally wonderful accommodations. Thanks also to Don Estes, Civil War Historian of the Natchez Historical Foundation for his guided tour and informative dialogue. I'd also like to thank Yvonne Scott for her kindness and generosity and for sharing her "ghost" with me. My thanks to Charles and Rosemary Hall of Cover To Cover, Natchez's wonderful bookstore.

Prologue

Matt Starr, CEO of Digitech, entered the lush corporate offices like a whirlwind. While the offices were state-of-the-art, Matt himself looked like a vagabond. He flopped down on his ergonomic chair and propped his feet on the glass-topped desk that was virtually bare of all ornamentation. He removed his base-ball cap that said Lulu's Bait Shack on the brim and turned it around. Now he was ready. For what he didn't know.

He eyed the hole in the knee of his jeans. It looked to be the same size as the hole in the toe of his right sneaker. The thought pleased him. He swiveled his chair around so he could look at the long line of pictures on the shelf behind him. Lily sitting on a swing, Lily hanging a Christmas ornament on her tree, Lily and Buzz mugging for the camera, Lily sitting at his side on a park bench. Lily, Lily, Lily. His very own charming Lily. He smiled when he looked at the date on his computer screen. In a little less than three weeks they would be man and wife. His smile stretched into a wide grin. Married. Kids. Dogs. Cats. Maybe a bird. A house. A yard and a lawn mower. The whole damn ball of wax.

The media called him a legend in his own time. Wall Street loved him and his company. Investors loved him because they trusted him. He'd made them all rich. And now he was ready to move on so that all the buttoned-up MBAs and high-tech computer geniuses he'd recruited over the years could run the company.

He was thirty-seven, and he'd done it all. He'd done the Himalaya thing, climbed Everest, chatted with the Dalai Lama, almost got married once, kissed Mother Teresa on the cheek, shot the most dangerous rapids in the world, gone big-game hunting in Africa, almost got married once, graduated at the top of his class at Harvard, almost got married once, was a billionaire several times over. According to the press, he had it all, but they were wrong. He wouldn't have it all until the day he married Lily. But that was no one's business but his and Lily's.

Lily. Sweet, charming Lily. The girl he'd left standing at the altar ten years ago because he was afraid of commitment. At the time he thought it was a fair trade-off as he walked away — actually rode away on his Harley — and started up Digitech on a shoestring. It had been a hollow ride to the top. What good was success and victory if you didn't have someone to share it with? He'd searched for her for years with no success. The detectives he'd hired said she dropped off the face of the earth. They also told him he was wasting his money continuing the search. And then, by chance, he found her. It had been Marcus's idea to plan an Extreme Vacation package for the high-level executives at Digitech. He'd signed on himself at the eleventh hour. It was the best thing he'd ever done in his entire life.

He closed his eyes to relive the moment as his index finger worked at the hole in his jeans. He'd followed his employees out to the center of the campground prior to trekking off into the wilderness. Gear was to be checked, pockets emptied. Nothing was to be left to chance. He was on his knees, unzipping his backpack for inspection by the survival guide when he looked up to see a pair of long, sun-tanned legs wearing Timberline boots. And then he looked upward again to see the face he'd dreamed of for ten long years. Speech-less, he could only stare, and mutter, "I've been looking for you."

It wasn't the Lily he remembered. This was a new breed of cat. She was lean, mean, and hard as nails. She'd only laughed once during the twenty-one-day trip from hell, and that was when he developed a raging case of poison sumac. She'd warned him not to touch the plant, but he hadn't listened. From that point on, she'd worked him like a pack mule and didn't give an inch during the entire twenty-one days. He did her bidding as he itched, scratched, and cursed. He refused to buckle or cave in no matter how miserable he was. Alone at night in his sleeping bag he marveled at the change in her, marveled that not by word or deed did she acknowledge that she'd ever known him, much less slept with him, that she had waited at the altar for him. When he slipped, because he wasn't paying attention to her instructions, and rolled down the side of the mountain, she'd peered over the ridge, and said, "You have exactly fifteen minutes to get your ass back up here or we're leaving without you. Rules are to be obeyed." He'd never moved so fast in his life, but she was as good as her word; they'd left without him. It took him another hour to catch up. She'd called him a prairie flower, a *wuss,* and a few other choice names. Later he realized it was her M.O. as well as the other guides' M.O.

Matt laughed. The whole crew had been a bunch of *wusses,* but at the end of the twenty-one days, every single man and woman on the trek had hugged Lily and promised to stay in touch when they returned to civilization. Everyone but him. He'd wanted to bawl right then and there when she turned away from him.

He'd waited that night until the camp fell asleep before making his way to her cabin. There was no way he was leaving Ozzie Conklin's Survival Camp until he told her what he wanted to say. He heard the rush of wind, smelled the fragrant evergreens, and then he was flat on his back staring up at the stars, the big dog standing guard. He muttered a ripe curse. The big dog growled as he planted a huge paw on his neck. "Awwk," was all he could manage by way of sound.

"It's three o'clock in the morning, Mr. Starr, and you don't belong in this part of the camp. I suggest you get up and go back where you belong. If you don't, I'll fire this gun smack-dab in your gluteus maximus. And if you're facing me, you'll get it where it will do the most damage. Buzz, come."

Matt rolled over and managed to get to his knees. "Okay, okay. I'm going, but before I go you're going to listen to me even if I have to wake up this whole damn camp. What's it gonna be, Lily?"

"I'll give you ten minutes. I have to be up at five to take out a new group. Make it quick, *Mister* Starr."

"Look, I'm sorry. I know those are just

11

words, but they're true. I tried so many times to tell you I wasn't ready to get married, but you didn't listen. I was young, and I wanted my chance at the brass ring. I got the ring, but I lost you. A day hasn't gone by that I didn't think of you. I even hired detectives to find you. I tried, Lily. For years. I never stopped loving you. Not for one single minute. I wish I could say if I had it to do all over again, I would do things differently, but it would be a lie. I'd do the same thing. I wasn't ready to get married, it's that damn simple. I wasn't ready for it. We would have ended up hating each other. I didn't want to work for your father the way you wanted. I tried to tell you that, too. Jesus, Lily, you never listened to anything I said. You were so hopped up to get married, and that's all you wanted. You didn't look ahead to the future. I wasn't ready for kids and diapers and bills out the wazoo. Yeah, I walked away, but you weren't blameless. You changed. You aren't the Lily I remember."

"I loved you so much. I couldn't imagine my life without you. Maybe you're right, and I didn't listen. You should have told me. You took the coward's way out. You literally left me standing at the altar in a wedding dress. My parents spent a lot of money on that wedding. We all looked like fools. The pity was the worst of all. That's all in the past. Now that we cleared that all up, I think it's time for you to head back to bed. The camp bus will be here at seven to pick you up. I leave here at six, so we should say good-bye now. By the way, you did pretty good out there."

"You were magnificent!" He heard her suck in her breath. "I'm really sorry, Lily. Can we be friends?"

"Why don't we just leave things the way they are. You have your life, and I have mine. Our lives are so totally opposite we have nothing in common. I'll send you a Christmas card. Have a safe trip home. Come on, Buzz, time for bed."

"I want more than a Christmas card, Lily. Now that I found you, I'm not going to lose you again."

"Good night, Matt."

Matt's feet thumped to the floor. Hands jammed into the back pockets of his jeans, he stared out at the New York skyline. That year was the toughest of his life as he pursued her with a vengeance. He was relentless and finally, during the Christmas holidays, he'd asked her to marry him. She agreed and said if they still felt the same about each other a year from now, the wedding would go forward. Now that year was up. Three weeks from now he would be married. He knew in his heart and in his gut that he and Lily would live happily ever after. He was turning in his high-tech world for a world of domestic bliss. He could hardly wait.

He watched a light snow begin to fall. His thoughts turned to Christmas and what he was going to get Lily for a present. He was so caught up in his thoughts he didn't hear Marcus come in until he felt his hand on his shoulder.

"Matt, I'm calling it a day. I promised my wife I'd try to make it home early for a change. Don't forget the reporter and photographer will be here first thing in the morning. High-Tech Man of the Year three years running. Now, that's something to be proud of. You gonna wear a suit and tie?"

"Nah. I hate that shit, Marcus. Been there, done that. Isn't it time they picked someone else? You should apply for the job," Matt said carefully, his gaze still locked on the skyline.

Marcus shrugged. Long years of familiarity allowed him to say what he thought and when he thought it. He and Dennis Wagner had been on the right and left of Matt from the beginning and knew the workings of Digitech almost as well as their boss did. "Matt, what are you going to do about . . ."

Matt threw his hands in the air. "I don't know. With all the safeguards we have in place, I can't figure out how he could have done it, and all we have are suspicions at this point. Maybe I just don't want to believe it. He's my best friend. We played together in our sandboxes from the age of three on. The guy's been with us forever. We pay him five times what the others would pay him. I need to know why."

"Big lump sum right up front. Piracy goes on all the time. It's the name of the game. Our security is top-of-the-line. No one said he did anything. Yet. He's being watched. Ten million, possibly more, in some bank in the Caymans would be my answer," Marcus said smoothly.

I don't like this guy, Matt thought.

"If this gets out, and he's innocent, the man's life is ruined," Matt said. "No one will touch him. He's got his whole life ahead of him. He doesn't need the money. He's got all those stock options. I'm having a hard time with this, Marcus. On top of that, he's a friend. Now if it was you, I could almost understand, with that high-maintenance wife of yours."

"You're treading on my personal life, Matt. Don't go down that road. I see the wheels turning. What's your plan?"

"It's not a plan. I've got three weeks till the wedding. Things are running smoothly here.

I'm going to hit the road and see what I can find out. I'll be discreet. Sometimes those detective agencies are so eager to get results they forget they're dealing with human beings. I forgot that once. When you want to know what's in a man's future, you have to go back to his past to see where he's been. I, better than anyone, know that. The new software is safe. You can go home now, Marcus. I'm going to phone Lily and call it a day myself. Give my regards to your family." He listened to his own voice and wondered if Marcus was picking up on his tone.

Marcus clapped Matt on the shoulder. "Happiness becomes you, old buddy. It's hard to believe in just a few weeks you're going to be an old married man like the rest of us. By the way, when are the Christmas bonuses going out. Aren't you late this year? Need any help on that?"

"I've got some catching up to do, but I'm up to it. Married life that is. I haven't decided on the bonuses yet. Do you need yours?"

"I can always use money. Christmas is an expensive time of year. Betsy saw some diamond earrings she wants. It's not a problem. I still can't believe you're not going to be here when we unveil the new software after the first of the year."

"I'll be honeymooning. C'mon, are you

telling me you and Dennis aren't up to this?"

"This is your company, Matt. How's it going to look with us standing there instead of you?"

"It's going to look great because you're going to be wearing a suit and tie. I, on the other hand, would appear as I am now. Go on, get out of here. Tomorrow is another day. I'll be leaving right after the Man of the Year thing. I'll call. Have a great holiday, Marcus, and I'll see you at the wedding."

The buddy-buddy crap bothered Matt. He felt his eyes narrow as he stared at Marcus Collins's back. No, he did not like the man, and he despised his artificial-looking wife. He offered up a small prayer that Lily would never turn into a Betsy Collins. Matt looked down at the hole in his sneaker. It looked like the hole was bigger than it was a little while ago. He wiggled his big toe until it worked free of the canvas. He beamed at his accomplishment. He turned his baseball cap around, adjusted it before he turned off the lights in his office. He'd call Lily on his cell phone. It would make the ride home less boring. God how he loved that girl!

One

"I should have heard from Matt by now, Sadie. I am going to be so embarrassed if he doesn't show up at the rehearsal dinner. How's that going to look? Just tell me how that's going to look? Are you sure he didn't call? Damn, I hate voice mail. I liked the machine with the little blinking red light."

"It's going to look like . . . he's on the way and is late. It's a long drive, Lily. Don't forget, he has to stop and walk his dog, buy coffee, get off the Interstate, and get back on. It's called delays. Think of it as just another dinner. Ten people, twelve counting you and me, all business associates of Matt's. There's no reason for you to be embarrassed if he doesn't make it on time. Things like this happen all the time in this high-tech world we now live in."

Lily stared at her friend Sadie and smiled. She always knew the right thing to say at just the right time to make her feel better. Sadie was her best friend in the whole world, going way back to grammar school and then college and finally Ozzie Conklin's Survival Camp,

where they both worked as survival special-
ists. Sadie wasn't movie-star beautiful but she
was pretty with gorgeous blue eyes, a light
dusting of freckles across her nose, and incredible dimples. Her silky, curly hair had
been the envy of every female at Ozzie's
camp. Sadie hated the curls, said it made her
look like Orphan Annie.

Lily hugged her. "You always say just the
right thing. We should get going. Won't it be
great, Sadie, if Madeline, the ghost at King's
Tavern acts up for our guests this evening?
That would certainly be a memory for them
to take home. Matt is positive it's going to
happen." She loved the stories of the docu-
mented ghostly apparitions of King's Tavern,
the oldest building in Natchez. On rare occasions, Yvonne Scott permitted a disbeliever to
inhabit the room on the third floor for a night,
and always with the same result. Guests
checked in but didn't check out, preferring to
leave in the middle of the night. "You know
what, I'm not going to miss this apartment at
all, nice as it is. I can't wait to move into that
great old house you sold me."

"I hope you're still saying that a year from
now when you see all those ghosts at the foot
of your bed. I swear, sometimes I think every
old building in this town is haunted. Did you
change your mind about living here all year

round? Maybe you should start thinking about Natchez as a home base, so you and Matt can put down roots. If you go from one of his houses to another to another, you'll be transient, and that's no way to start a new married life. This would be the best place, Lily. Natchez is a small town, the people are wonderful and friendly, and it's a great place to bring up kids. Eventually you'll get to know practically everyone in town. The first thing you have to do is join the Pilgrimage Garden Club. Betty Lou Hicks will take you under her wing. We met her last year around Christmastime, remember? She told us to call her Blue. She's one of the Hicks Chicks. There was something in the paper a few days ago about the club. Just give me a minute, and I can tell you what it was. They have 615 active members. You would make 616. They have," Sadie said, squeezing her eyes shut as she tried to recall what she'd read, "55 emeriti, 18 associates, 39 honorary, and 212 out-of-town-members. And, they own a bunch of plantations: Stanton Hall, Longwood, and they lease King's Tavern to Yvonne Scott. How's that for total recall? What's wrong? I can tell by your expression something is bothering you. It's just a dinner, Lily. Don't go down that old road, my friend. That was then, this is now."

"I guess I was thinking about the last time Matt left me at the altar. And before you can say it, I'm aware of my part in that fiasco. You're wrong, though, Sadie. It's more than a dinner. I had to call off the rehearsal. The minister said we'd just enter from the chancery and take it from there. A phone call would have been nice. Did you check the messages when we came in? This just isn't like Matt. I know he's been on the road for a month, and we've been playing telephone tag for so long I'm starting to forget what he looks like. Even though I accepted it, I'm still smarting over the fact that he didn't show up for Christmas. Calling and talking for hours is not the same thing. Christmas is special. I was really looking forward to opening all these wedding gifts with Matt this evening," Lily said, pointing to the mountain-high pile of exquisitely wrapped packages in the dining room. "I'm ready, let's go. You drive. I'm too jittery. It's been raining for two solid days. I hope it isn't an omen of some kind. Are there any messages?" Lily asked hopefully.

Sadie grinned. "Listen for yourself."

Lily brought the receiver to her ear to listen to her voice mail. She smiled at Sadie. "He's on his way, but he's going to be too late to make the rehearsal and dinner. There was a big pileup on the Interstate and he lost two hours, and then there was a detour some-where, and he lost more time. I feel so much better. Actually, I feel a whole lot better. Wonderful in fact. Absolutely wonderful!"

Fifteen minutes later they were headed down Jefferson Street on their way to King's Tavern. "Look at that shepherd those people have. Matt has a dog like that," Lily said, turning to crane her neck so she could see out the back window. "She's so cute and lovable. Kind of like Buzz. I sure hope they get along once we move in together. There's always one who wants to be top dog."

"Okay, Lily, we're here. Put a smile on your face and don't act concerned because Matt isn't here. Prospective brides are supposed to be all smiles. So, smile, Lily. That's a damn order."

Lily worked a smile onto her face as she climbed out of the car. "Sadie."

"Yes."

"I don't really like those Digitech people. They look right through you. It's very hard to hold a conversation with any of them. They make me uncomfortable. I especially don't like Marcus or his wife. I always feel like both of them are trying to take my measure, and I'm coming up short. Dennis is nice, but he's shy. He's sort of like Matt in a lot of ways. If you see me floundering, step in, okay?"

"You got it. Just be yourself. It's one night, Lily. You can handle it. By this time tomorrow they'll all be gone."

Lily looked around. "I guess I'm feeling inferior this evening. They're all so wealthy. They're going to think this is all very tacky. I love King's Tavern, and so does Matt. Yvonne said we could spend our wedding night in the third-floor suite. I can't tell you how excited Matt was with her offer. And, it was his idea to have our dinner here. I'm angry with myself for feeling this way. It's almost as though I have to justify myself to these people. Why am I doing this, Sadie?"

"We said we weren't going down that road. We're going to go inside, we're going to sit down, we're going to smile and smile until our faces start to hurt. The tavern is known for its prime rib, and we are going to gorge ourselves. The wines you chose are excellent. Trust me, no one will be able to find fault with the dinner. Let's go now. By the way, you look stunning. Blue is definitely your color. Just remember to smile and look happy."

"Thanks, Sadie. This is Matt's favorite dress."

The restaurant was small, cozy and intimate with bright red tablecloths that complemented the Christmas tree and the poinsettias nestled along the wall and in the corners. A fragrant garland decorated with red-velvet bows curled around the white staircase leading to the third floor. A cheery fire crackled in the fireplace. Waiters hovered but were in no way intrusive. Yvonne stood to the side, her eyes sharp and alert for any and all mistakes on the part of her staff.

"Hi, everyone. Matt sends his apologies. He got held up on the Interstate because of a bad accident and a detour, so he won't be joining us this evening," Lily said as she took her seat at the head of the table, Sadie on her left.

"It's so nice to see all of you here in Natchez. I hope you had some time today to do a little sight-seeing. I know Matt is going to give you all a quiz later on." The soft murmurings around the table unnerved Lily. She honed in on Dennis. Dennis was Matt's best friend, and now a friend of hers. He looked befuddled. No help there. She turned her attention to Marcus Collins. "How do you like our city, Marcus?"

"For some reason I thought Natchez would be larger. It's *quaint*."

Quaint. Lily could feel the fine hairs on the back of her neck move. Her backbone stiffened. "I'd hardly call it quaint. It's a lovely city. The buildings are beautiful. The people smile at you and say good morning. I'm taking umbrage here, Marcus." *Matt doesn't like you, you stuffed shirt, and that means I don't like you either.*

"You asked for my opinion, Lily. I prefer New York City, as does my wife. I guess it's all in what you get used to. Are we having a toast?"

"Of course. Matt ordered the champagne himself. I hope you don't find fault with it, Marcus."

"Matt's wine choices are about the same as his choice of clothing, terrible," Marcus said as he watched the waiter pour the bubbly into his glass.

"I'll be sure to tell him you said that," Dennis said.

Lily's eyeballs snapped to attention. *What have we here?* she wondered. A minute later, Dennis was on his feet, his glass poised high in the air. "To Matt, the best friend a guy could have, and to Lily, the lady of his choice. Mine, too, now that I've had a chance to get to know her. May all your days be filled with wondrous things."

Lily smiled as she sipped the champagne.

Small talk continued throughout the rest of the dinner, mostly talk of Natchez, the climate, the mansions, and, finally, a description of Lily's wedding gown. She was ready to jump out of her skin by the time dessert and coffee were served.

It was hard not to notice that the elegant, lacquered Betsy Collins barely touched her food. Lily looked pointedly at her plate, and said, "The prime rib here is the best in the state. Didn't you care for it, Betsy?"

"I'm a vegetarian," Betsy responded curtly. Her husband looked surprised at her announcement. Lily shrugged as she poured cream into her coffee.

Lily looked up and down the long table. "Did you all enjoy your dinner? Matt will want to know."

Again, soft murmurings of agreement rushed up and down the table. The atmosphere was so chilly, Lily longed for her coat. She knew in her heart the dinner would have been more festive if Matt were there. Were the others intimidated by Dennis and Marcus? Possibly Marcus, but not Dennis, she decided. She wished she knew what was going on. There were undercurrents here that she didn't like. She hoped Matt would be able to explain it to her.

Lily sighed with relief when the waiters arrived to take away the dessert plates. The others looked at her. She knew they were wondering if they should get up to leave. Suddenly her backbone stiffened for the second time. "This is not a wake. It's supposed to be my rehearsal dinner. That means we're all supposed to be happy and smiling. The only people smiling here are Sadie and me, and my face is starting to hurt with the effort. I'm sorry if this was such a chore for all of you. As I said earlier, this dinner was Matt's idea, and I agreed with him because I viewed it as a happy event. There has been nothing happy about this evening at all. And, by the way, I am just as concerned about Matt's absence as you are. Things happen. Unfortunately, this is one of those times when he has no control over the situation. Having said that, why don't we just finish our coffee and go our respective ways. I'll leave it up to all of you to explain your attitude to your boss tomorrow." She winced at Sadie's hard kick to her ankles.

Marcus stopped stirring his coffee and placed the spoon on the saucer. "I apologize, Lily. Dennis and I *are* concerned about Matt's absence. You're absolutely right about this evening. Our manners are deplorable. If it's all the same to you, I think Betsy and I will head back to the hotel and make some phone calls to the State Police to see what the road conditions are. If I find out anything, I'll give you a call. I'm sorry, Lily."

Lily nodded miserably. It didn't help at all

that Marcus's wife looked at her with such pity she cringed. Dennis's date, on the other hand, looked everywhere but at her. She did mumble something, but Lily couldn't make out the words.

"Don't say it, Sadie," Lily said, tossing her napkin on the table. "I know exactly what you're thinking, but please don't voice those thoughts. I'm going to pay the bill, then we're going home."

"That sounds like a plan, Lily. I say we sit around in our pajamas and have ourselves a rip-snorting girls' night."

"Yeah, a plan," Lily said, handing over her credit card to the waiter.

The ride back to Lily's apartment was made in virtual silence.

"Deep in my heart, I have this fear that Matt is not going to show up for the wedding," Lily said, a catch in her voice.

"Of course he's going to show up. Stop thinking like that. He called and said he was delayed. Delayed, Lily, does not mean he won't show up. This is New Year's Eve. I guess his people would rather be home with their families. I can't fault them for that; nor should you."

"I was on my last nerve back there at the restaurant. No one really ate. It wasn't just Betsy. Did you notice that?"

"I ate everything on my plate, Lily."

Tears rolled down Lily's cheeks. "I have this awful sick feeling in the pit of my stomach. This whole thing is a charade. I'm just fooling myself."

"I don't want to hear that kind of talk," Sadie said fiercely. "Matt Starr loves you. I see the way he looks at you. Don't even think such a thing. Okay, we're here."

"What would I do without you, Sadie? God, I'm going to miss you."

"We aren't going to talk about that either. For now we're going to open a bottle of wine and talk about old times. If need be, we'll open two bottles. Okay?"

"Okay."

The organist looked questioningly at the minister, who merely nodded. Her signal to keep playing.

The groom was an hour late.

"I'm sorry, Reverend," Lily said in a choked voice.

"My dear, I have all day. Perhaps something unexpected came up. We can wait a while longer."

"No. He's not coming. I'm . . . I'm going to . . . leave. Would you mind telling the guests. . . . I can't . . . I'll fall apart. I need to leave here with whatever dignity I can muster. Even if it is by the back door."

"Lily . . ."

"How could he do this to me, Sadie? How could I have been so blind? I knew. Dammit, I knew, and I still put myself through this. I can't bear to face those people. Reverend, is there a back door?"

The minister led the way to the back door and held it open. "What do you want me to tell the young man if he shows up?"

Lily squared her shoulders. "Reverend, you truly do not want to tell him what I'm thinking. Don't worry, he won't show up. I guarantee it."

"My dear, is there anything I can do?"

"Yes. Tell that organist to stop playing. Thank you."

Lily started to sob the moment she got into the truck. "Do I look like a fool to you, Sadie?" she asked.

"Of course not. If I ever get my hands on that guy, I'll choke the living life out of him."

"Oh God, oh God, he did it to me again. Twice, Sadie!"

"Lily, I have to go to Dunleith Plantation to cancel the reception. I don't think anyone will show up after the minister makes his announcement, but you never know. Will you be all right? I won't be long. It's the right thing to do in case some of the guests do show up.

Sometimes people don't go to the church and go straight to the reception. Your guests won't know what to do."

"I didn't think about that. Go ahead. I'll be okay. You don't need to stand around and watch me bawl my eyes out. I hate him for doing this to me. Do you hear me, Sadie? I hate him. I will never, ever, forgive him for this. Never!"

It was ten minutes past eight on the cold, rainy evening of his rehearsal dinner when Matt Starr swung his Jaguar off Highway 20 at Vicksburg and headed south on Highway 61. He whistled as he drove, knowing he was going to see Lily soon. He continued to whistle as Gracie, his dog, laid her head on his lap. He drove through the small community of Washington on his way to Natchez. He pulled to a stop at the first intersection and waited for the light to change. He could see the truck scales where Highways 61, 84, and 98 merged. He was almost into town when he noticed the AmSouth Bank's ATM machine in Magnolia Mall. "See, Gracie, everything is working out and coming together. We were in such a rush this morning, I forgot to hit the ATM. A bridegroom needs some money in his pocket. This is just perfect."

Matt stopped the car, left the engine running, and climbed out. He walked the ten feet to the machine, looking back once to see Gracie watching him. A chill washed over him. The place was deserted. The ten-foot walk to the ATM machine set his nerves twanging. He looked at the lush shrubbery surrounding the bank, knowing he couldn't be seen from the street. Of course it was deserted, it was New Year's Eve. The thought made him feel better.

He stood for a moment, shivering in the light rain that was still falling. The temperature had dropped, too. He could feel the wind through his flannel sweatshirt and light windbreaker. His big toe felt cold, too.

Lily was going to be so happy to see him. Sometimes things just worked out right. He'd finished up all his work and at the last second decided to drive instead of flying, so he wouldn't have to put Gracie in the cargo hold. Besides, he loved driving with the big dog sitting next to him. He could see it now. After the tumultuous greeting, Buzz and Gracie would romp about Lily's apartment while he snuggled on the couch with his soon-to-be bride. And then they would toast in the New Year. He couldn't be happier. His thoughts soured when he thought about how disappointed Lily probably was when she played his message saying he was going to miss the rehearsal and the rehearsal dinner because he made the decision at the last minute to drive instead of flying. He crossed his fingers and made a wish that she would welcome him with open arms.

He looked back at the car to see Gracie watching him through the window. Sweet Gracie, so full of love and devotion. She was in fine fettle tonight. She'd been to the groomer the day before and now sported a pink polka-dotted neckerchief. He smiled at the picture she presented. He remembered how he'd laughed aloud when he'd fastened her leash and she'd pranced around, knowing she looked good. Just like a woman. He didn't know who he loved more, Lily or Gracie.

Matt slid his card into the slot, punched in his code, and waited until the bills slid out. He marveled as he always did at how crisp and clean the new twenty-dollar bills looked. The only problem with new money was it stuck together and he had to spit on his finger to separate the bills. There was a lot to be said for dirty, wrinkled money.

He felt the man's breath on his neck, but before he could turn around strong hands cupped his neck in a vise. "Behave yourself, Mister, and you won't get hurt. I just want your money. Now, pretend I'm your best friend and shove that card through the slot again. Do what I tell you."

Matt half turned but felt a light, warning squeeze to his neck. He could hear Gracie barking inside the car. Anxious but obedient, Matt did as he was told. It was only money, and he had plenty of that. Out of the corner of his eye he saw two more men appear from the back of the bank to stand alongside his car. One of them was antagonizing Gracie. His blood started to boil. "Keep getting money until the machine won't give you any more. How much money you got in that account, Mister?"

"A couple of thousand," Matt answered truthfully as he stared at the man's hands under the ATM light. No need to tell him how many thousand. Squared-off nails. Clean hands. Paper-pusher hands. Not the hands of a thug.

"Hey you guys, come here. You're never going to guess who this guy is."

The two men stepped out of the shadows and came closer to peer at the ATM card Clean Hands was holding out for their inspection. None of the three *looked* like they had ever been within walking distance of a computer, so how could his name impress them? He smelled tobacco, an ever-so-faint scent of aftershave, garlic breath, and something else he couldn't define. As far as dress went, they looked better than he did. He started to shiver again but not with fear. He suddenly felt icy cold. He'd read hundreds of stories about people being at the wrong place at the wrong time. He was being mugged. Under a bright light at an ATM machine in a deserted shopping mall on New Year's Eve. This end of town was not where the action was tonight. Let them take all his money and the car, too.

"Hand over your wallet, and we'll take the Rolex, too." The ATM machine had notified him he had reached the one-day limit on withdrawals.

Matt peeled off his watch and tossed his wallet to the man standing closest to him. He told himself again that it was only money and a hunk of steel sitting near the curb. He'd stopped at this machine on four different occasions on his trips to Natchez and all four times there had been people going in and out of the bank, shoppers going to the big Super Wal-Mart. Tonight the area was empty of cars and the lone security guard. Once he'd actually seen a patrol car. Ten o'clock wasn't that late. The law of averages said there should be at least one person out and about. The rain was light and didn't pose a problem. A chill ran up his spine and then down his arms. He cursed the fact that he'd refused the services of his security team. His competitors all walked around with a bevy of pistol-packing security guards and drove in bulletproof limousines. In his opinion, all they did was call more attention to themselves. He preferred to keep a low profile and blend in with the crowds. Maybe he'd made a serious mistake. If he could just get to the car and his cell phone. It didn't look like that was going to happen. Gracie was barking furiously.

"Headlights approaching," one of the men hissed.

"Shut that damn dog up and take him out of the car. Don't do something you'll regret, Mr. Starr."

Matt opened the car door. Gracie lunged against him. Her huge body trembled. He called her to his side and hooked his thumb and forefinger inside her collar. "Shhh, don't make a sound, Gracie," he said softly. The big dog pressed against his thigh as four young people whizzed by in a pickup truck giggling and laughing, their arms waving in the air. They looked like they were having the time of their lives. They also looked like they were more than a little inebriated. They were probably on their way to a New Year's Eve party. He took that moment to look down at the sidewalk and noticed the shoes on the men's feet. One of them wore expensive Cole Haan shoes. He recognized them because he owned a pair. The second man, who had yet to speak, wore Brooks Brothers wing tips. He recognized those, too, since he'd worn Brooks Brothers shoes since his college days. The third man wore pricey, high-end sneakers. He himself wore Converse high-tops. With a huge hole in the right toe. His eyes narrowed. Maybe this wasn't just your run-of-the-mill ATM hit. Maybe this was something else.

Matt started to jiggle, shifting his weight from one foot to the other as he tried to keep warm. The wind was kicking up, and the rain was starting to blow in all directions. "Get in the car. I'll drive," Clean Hands said.

"Take the damn car. You have my wallet, ATM card, and my watch. You don't need me. My dog is sick, I'd like to get her home. I won't call the police if that's what's worrying you," Matt said.

"I-don't-think-so. Get in the car and keep that dog quiet."

Matt climbed into the backseat and sat down. "Carjacking and kidnapping are serious offenses. You could go to jail for a very long time," he said tightly.

"So's murder. Now shut up."

"Tell me what you want. This isn't about taking twenty-dollar bills out of my account. It isn't about stealing a Jaguar either. Let's save us both a lot of trouble. Tell me what you want and let me get the hell out of here."

"This is the last time I'm going to tell you to shut up," the high-end sneakers man muttered as he steered the car onto Business 61. He made a left turn at the light, drove a half mile on Wilson Road before he hit Highway 555, the Old Pine Ridge Road, then made another right that would take him north to Anna's Bottom.

It didn't look like he was going to make his cozy evening with Lily after all. Matt felt his insides start to shrivel when he pictured Lily making explanations at the rehearsal dinner. The vision of her waiting for him a second time at the altar made him sick to his stomach. Why hadn't he waited till morning to hit the ATM machine? He could have done it at anytime tomorrow. Oh, no, he had to do it tonight. Now look what happened, you sorry son of a bitch.

Where was the damn cell phone? On the front seat? No, Gracie had been sitting on the passenger side. He would have seen it if it was there. It wasn't in the console either. It must either be on the floor or somewhere on the backseat. Shit, maybe he was sitting on it. Gracie whimpered next to him. He patted her head just as something pricked his arm. At first he thought it was a twitching nerve in his arm, then the world turned black.

"Now what?"

The driver turned to look over his shoulder. "You tell me. That guy is one of the richest software giants in the country. Yeah, he looks like a bum, but maybe he's just eccentric. I've seen pictures of him plastered all over the place. He always dresses like this."

"If he's that rich and that famous, someone is going to come looking for him. He was right, carjacking and kidnapping are serious business. Why don't we clean out his account and let him go? The most we planned on getting tonight was a few hundred each. You have his PIN number. I wouldn't do well in prison," the man sitting on Matt's right side said.

"Look, do you want a few paltry hundred or do you want *thousands?* People like him have more than one account. I say we stash him somewhere and clean out as much as we can. Let's take a vote."

"Okay."

"Okay."

"So where are we going to stash him?"

"There's an abandoned shack at Anna's Bottom. I know how to get in and out. I'm banking on this guy having a line of credit. We'll just tap into it."

"I read something about him in the *Wall*

Street Journal the other day. I read the headline at the newsstand while I was waiting in line. Damn, I can't remember what it was. Yeah, yeah, he's getting married on New Year's Day. It said something about one of the world's richest men was tying the knot and there was no prenup. They made a big deal out of the prenup. The chick lives here in Natchez. I think he'll cooperate."

"Looks like he's going to miss his wedding. We're probably doing the dumb *schmuck* a favor. What about the dog?"

"We dump the dog first chance we get. That gives us two bargaining chips, the girl and the dog," Sneakers said. "He'll play ball."

"How long is that shot going to last him?"

"Six hours, maybe a little more. I have one more on me, and that's it."

"We'll worry about that later. I'm going to pull over. Put the dog out on the side of the road. Don't hurt the animal. I like animals."

"Settle back, gentlemen, we have a long ride ahead of us. And you guys said this little enterprise wouldn't work. Who in their right mind would think three highly respected brothers with their own business would be out robbing ATM customers in the middle of the night? If we play our cards right, we might be able to kiss that business of ours good-bye and head to the islands and lead the good life. You gotta admit, this is better than insider trading. The SEC always catches up with those guys. I don't see anyone catching up with us. Once we get his money, we let him go and split. It'll take him weeks to find his way back. We'll be long gone before he manages to get to the authorities. We're not talking murder here. We feed him, too, let him do a little exercising. All we want is his money. Do we all agree?"

"Yeah."

"Yeah."

He woke with a hammering headache, then opened his eyes to total darkness. Where was he? Gingerly he felt his arms and legs. One leg and one arm wouldn't move. It took a full minute to realize he was tied to something. "Gracie, where are you?" he whispered. When there was no response from the shepherd, he started to struggle until he realized it was an exercise in futility.

It must be night. How had he gotten here? Where was here? He remembered the prick to his arm. Drugged. Son of a bitch! "Gracie!" he called, but this time his voice was louder. "If you bastards hurt my dog, I'll kill you. I'll track you to the ends of the earth." The silence told him he was alone.

41

He closed his eyes because there was nothing else to do.

They woke him by poking a stick at his chest. "Where's my dog?" he demanded.

"You hear that? He's more interested in his dog than he is about what's happening to him. Commendable. We're going to untie your foot so you can sit up. Your dog got away when we stopped for gas."

"Lying bastard. My dog would never leave me. Tell me what you want."

"We want your money. That's it, your money. Pure and simple."

"How do you propose to do that? A letter isn't going to do it. My bankers aren't stupid. It won't work. My accounts have safeguards in place, fingerprint I.D., stuff like that. What that means is I have to offer up my fingerprint to withdraw any sum over five hundred dollars at any one time. It's not the same at every bank or branch. In some instances, it's an eye identification or voice I.D. They are new safeguards we put into place last year for just this reason. I'm not doing it, so forget about it. I want my dog."

"Oh, you'll do it, Mr. Starr. If you don't, we'll pay the little lady you're supposed to marry later today a visit. Do you want to change your mind? We aren't talking about going into a bank. We're talking about wire transfers, and don't even think about telling me it can't be done."

"You bastards. Lily has nothing to do with this. You touch one hair . . ."

"Yeah, yeah, yeah. Like you're really going to do something. Look around, Mister Starr. What do you see? Four walls, a sturdy door, no windows, and that board you're sleeping on. It's four-thirty in the morning in case you're interested. I think what we're going to do is clean you up and drive you to New Orleans so we can go shopping for money. One wrong move, and you get dumped in one of the bayous. You'll be dead in an hour. Now, what's it going to be?"

"If I do all this and you get your money, what happens to me?"

"We stash you someplace. When we get to where we want to go we'll call the police, and they'll come get you. We're not murderers. Let me put it to you another way, you don't have any options. Get him up, tie his hands behind his back. Let him take a leak first."

Matt gritted his teeth. "Where's my dog?"

"I told you, he hopped out of the car when we stopped for gas. The dog was alive. I like dogs. That's the truth. Come on, move."

"The dog is a she, not a he."

"Whatever."

He was right, there were no options.

It was just turning light when Matt was shoved into the backseat. He felt something hard nudge his thigh when he landed against the back door. The cell phone? It felt like it. One of the men climbed in next to him. "Wake me up when we get there," he snarled.

Matt worked his bound hands around the hard square he was half-sitting on.

"What the hell are you doing back there, Mr. Starr?"

"Trying to get comfortable. Can't you just tie one of my hands to the door handle or something?"

"No."

It was the cell phone. Now the problem was, how to get it into his hip pocket, and he had to do it before it became full light. He sat quietly, his mind racing. Without stopping to think, he brought up his knees, one leg outstretched. He shoved the leg into the driver's neck, knowing he was going to get clobbered for doing it, but it gave him precious seconds to jam the cell phone into his hip pocket. The Jaguar careened to the right and then the left as the driver struggled to control the powerful car.

"Try a stunt like that again, and you're dead meat. Get on the damn floor and don't move. Keep your foot on his neck and don't go to sleep."

Matt felt himself being shoved to the floor. His leg swung out again and clipped his seat companion smack on the mouth. He felt something warm splatter on his face. Blood.

The Jaguar came to a screeching halt. Strong hands yanked him from the car. He inhaled deeply of the crispy pine-scented air and wished he had a cup of Starbucks coffee to welcome the new day.

"Put him in the damn trunk!"

"No. We want him alive and well. The trip's too long. Find something to tie his ankles with and give him another shot of that stuff. Do it now, you idiot. He'll sleep the rest of the way. Am I the only one with any brains around here?"

A moment later, Matt's ankles were tied. For the second time in under an hour he was shoved into the car. He thanked God for the hip-length windbreaker that covered his hip pockets. The needle stung, then his world went dark.

Two

The mirror said she looked like a beautiful bride, but it was all a big lie. In order to be a beautiful bride, one had to go through a wedding ceremony, preferably with a groom in attendance. The stunning Demetrios original with matching veil and the requisite blue garter just wasn't cutting it. Especially since the groom had been a no-show.

Lily Harper gritted her teeth. By God she wouldn't cry. She absolutely would not cry. Dumped at the proverbial altar on her wedding day for the *second* time. Not just any day. Oh, no, he had to do it on New Year's Day. Jilted twice and by the same man both times. What kind of fool was she? A lovesick fool who believed a man's lies. She remembered now how bad it had hurt that first time. How devastated she was. So devastated, she trashed the gown and veil and ran as far and as fast as she could. She'd ended up in Wyoming and signed on as an outdoor survival guide with a company that planned Extreme Vacations for wealthy businessmen. With her degree in forestry, she'd aced the rigorous training program and managed to hide out until Matt Starr came back into her life. Sweet-talking Matt Starr and his dog Gracie. Oh yeah.

Her face burned now when she remembered how eager she'd been to swallow the lies he'd fed her. With no family to fall back on to guide her, she'd had to rely on her friend Sadie, who thought Matt Starr was the neatest thing since sliced bread. Sadie was a bigger fool than she was.

Lily looked around the sunny apartment. Her home away from Ozzie Conklin's survival camp for the rich and famous. Right now she couldn't bear to think about her first real estate venture, the white elephant she'd purchased from Sadie last April at Ozzie's insistence. You need to put down roots, he'd said. And, he'd gone on to say, owning a house is a tax write-off. Since that time the project had grown legs. The house was supposed to be her wedding present to Matt. For the past year she'd racked up huge telephone bills talking daily to the contractors, who specialized in restoring antebellum mansions. While she wasn't a native of Natchez, having grown up in Florida, along with Sadie, she'd been coming here for years for visits with Sadie. Four years ago she'd leased an apartment in the Bienville complex on South Commerce

Street, returning every winter with Sadie when Ozzie closed down the camp for three months. She preferred the laid-back life of Natchez to life in Fort Lauderdale, but coming here to soak in the milder temperatures during December, January, and February when Ozzie closed down had never really made her happy. Maybe that was because she was incapable of being happy. Maybe it all had something to do with Matt Starr and the fact that she'd signed the lease on the apartment, along with Sadie, after she'd finally given up hope of ever seeing him again.

Lily kicked off her satin heels and watched them fly across the room as she burst into tears. "Damn you! Damn you to hell, Matt Starr." She hooked her thumbs into the delicious V of the Demetrios gown and felt the material give way. Thousands of tiny seed pearls created a blizzard as they sailed about the room. She continued to rip and gouge until the elegant gown was nothing but shreds. When she realized she was still wearing the matching veil, she ripped it from her head and stuck her foot through the fine netting. Breathing like a racehorse, she hiked up her strapless bra and peeled off the lacy blue garter. She made a slingshot of it and watched it ricochet across the room to land near one of the white-satin shoes.

She sat down on the colorful green-and-yellow sofa and cried because she didn't know what else to do.

Sadie Lincoln opened the door and cautiously entered the living room.

"Go away, Sadie. I don't want to talk. There's nothing to say. Please don't try to cheer me up."

"I wouldn't think of it. I came up to commiserate with you. Everyone's gone except Matt's best man. I think it's safe to say it was one pissed-off crowd. The Digitech crowd that is. You know, they missed the New Year's Eve bash back in New York for your rehearsal dinner, then the wedding that didn't come off on New Year's Day. As Marcus put it succinctly, the wedding from hell that didn't come off. Dennis is waiting downstairs. Why, I don't know. My blood is boiling, Lily. I thought Matt Starr was one in a million. It looks like we were both wrong. I need to know what you're going to do, Lily. I can't go off to Australia tomorrow knowing I'm leaving you like this."

"Don't worry about me. I survived the first time, and I'll survive this time, too. The worst part of all this is I *knew*. I knew, Sadie. Something in my gut, my heart, my head, whatever, told me this was going to happen. When he called to say he wouldn't make the rehearsal

49

and the dinner last night, I knew. Even though he said he was probably going to be late and might not make it at all, something told me he was going to make a fool of me again. I played that stupid game of pretend, the way I used to do. I ignored what my heart was telling me even though I knew better. Ozzie taught us always to heed any warning, no matter how slight. Did I heed his warning? No, I did not. The fact that I haven't seen Matt for a month should have been my first clue. Spending Christmas alone should have been my second clue. Why didn't I think that was important? A smattering of phone calls in one month should have been my third clue. Not only am I dumb, I'm stupid as well. Look, don't worry about me. Go to Australia. Meet Tom's parents, enjoy your two-month leave. I'm a survivor. I'll be okay."

Sadie hiked up the hunter green gown and sat down cross-legged in front of Lily. "Are you going to go back to camp?"

"No. Even I know you can't go back. I need to wallow in my misery for a little while before I make any decisions. I think I'm going to sell my parents' condo. I never liked it. That's a concrete decision. I won't have to pay the maintenance if I sell it. I'll save three thousand a year if I get rid of it, not to mention the utilities. I hate going back there. There are just too many memories attached to that condo. With that in mind, the logical thing for me to do is stay in Natchez and make my life here. Thanks for being my friend, Sadie. I'm going to miss you."

Lily stared at her friend's earnest face. Sadie was the kind of friend everyone deserved. She was honest, loving, caring, and fiercely loyal. Right now, her piercing blue eyes pleaded with Lily.

"I need to know you're going to be okay, Lily. This is going to be the first time since we were six years old that we're going to be separated. Do you think it will work for you, staying here?"

"I suppose it's all . . . doable. Right now I can't think straight. Maybe I should just move on. Go somewhere new, different, start a new life. What in the hell will I do alone in Natchez, Mississippi?"

"Finish restoring the house. In another few weeks it will be done, and you can move in. Or you can sell it if you want to. You can teach school. Besides your degree in forestry, you also have a degree in education. Use it. Get over this rough patch. Get grounded, then make decisions. Living here year-round, you could very well come to love Natchez. Just because it isn't for me doesn't mean it won't be right for you. In time you'll adjust to the brutal humidity. We can talk it to death over dinner."

Lily's head whirled. "If . . . if I decide to stay in Natchez, that isn't like running away, is it, Sadie? That's what I did the first time. I don't want to live like that again."

"No, Lily. It's called moving on and getting on with your life. You're thirty years old. This is supposed to be the best time of your life. It can be, too, if you open up and embrace it. You're tough, kiddo. Ozzie made us tough. We're survivors. That means emotional as well as physical. Listen, the guy was a dumb shit to do this to you. It's his loss. You would have made him a hell of a wife. Now, I have to go downstairs and tell his best man something. Does anything come to mind?"

Lily peeled off her thigh-highs and headed for the bathroom. "Tell him to go back to wherever it was he came from. Don't tell him anything else. I'm going to get dressed and drive over to the Emerys to pick up Buzz. If you like, we can get a bite to eat or we can sit here and you can watch me bawl my eyes out. Your choice."

Sadie stared at her friend's retreating back. *Pick up Buzz, get a bite to eat.* The girl had just been left standing at the altar in front of fifty of Matt Starr's associates, and she wanted to get a bite to eat. She blinked. "That sounds like a plan. I'll run downstairs and tell what's-his-name to . . . to do whatever he wants. I'll be right back." She waited for a response and when there was none she wasn't surprised. She let herself out and walked down the steps to the first floor.

It was like all apartment lobbies — slate floor, a mirrored wall, rattan furniture with artificial flower arrangements on the tables. Even with the sunlight filtering through the bamboo blinds it was depressing. This whole place was so unlike either one of them. They'd moved there because she'd told Lily she would learn to love the town and the people. She was usually right about most things. What she hadn't figured on was Matt Starr leaving Lily standing at the altar a second time.

"Dennis, can I talk to you for a minute?" Sadie said, sitting down across from him. Her first thought was he was handsome in a *nerdy* kind of way. He had beautiful eyes and an even more beautiful smile. Her second thought was he probably looked better in tweeds or jeans than he did in his tux.

He was on his feet in an instant, his face a mask of worry. "I don't know what to say. Matt wouldn't . . . I know about the last time but . . . The last time I talked to him was two weeks ago, and everything was a go. I thought it was strange when there was no one to pick me up at the airport. I think something happened to him. How is Lily? Jesus, this must be like a scene in a horror movie for her. Twice and by the same guy. Dammit, this is not something Matt Starr would do. You should understand, Sadie. You and Lily have been friends since you were little children. You know everything there is to know about each other. That's the way it is with Matt and me. I know I sound like a broken record, but Matt simply would not do this. Something must have happened to him."

"Something happened all right. Your buddy got cold feet like he did the first time. Don't try to defend him. This is unconscionable. How much time does it take to make a phone call? Seconds. If your buddy didn't have the guts to talk to Lily, he could have put a note under the door. I think the guy is gutless is what I think. I really don't care to hear anything else about him. As to how Lily is, she's . . . she's none of your damn business. You can tell that to your buddy, too. She'll do just fine because she's a . . . *fine* person, unlike some people I would rather not mention. This whole thing was so humiliating. I was only in the wedding party, and I was humiliated. Who does that man think he is? Because he's rich and the media has him snapping at

Bill Gates's heels doesn't give him the right to do this to my friend. It's beyond cruel. You tell him that for me," Sadie said angrily. "Wherever you're going, have a safe trip."

"Why are you yelling at me? This isn't my fault. Sadie, listen to me. I'm telling you, something must have happened. Matt isn't anything like what you said. He loves Lily. All he wants to do is talk about her, day and night. In my opinion, he's never been happier. He told me all about their plans, their hopes and dreams. I'm telling you, *something happened to him*. Why don't you believe that? I think I'm going to file a police report," he said, jerking at the bow tie at his neck.

"You do that! You have to wait forty-eight hours before the police will even talk to you. If you do file one, don't bother either of us with the results. Read my lips, we don't want to know anything about Matt Starr. Not now, not ever. I don't want you calling Lily and upsetting her any more than she is already. Are we clear on that?"

Sadie stomped off to the elevator. She didn't look back.

Sadie opened the door in time to see Lily stuffing her wedding apparel into large trash bags. She looked grim and brittle. She stepped aside as Lily drop-kicked the trash bag in the general direction of the door.

"I'm sorry about the expense of your gown and all, Sadie. I'll pay you back."

"You will not. I'm taking this gown to Australia with me. I'm sure at some point there will be a dinner party I can wear it to. Give me ten minutes to change, and we can be on our way. I know this is a stupid question, but are you okay?"

"No, I'm not okay. I feel like someone ripped out my guts. My head feels like cotton candy, and my heart is beating way too fast. I just want to get my dog and curl up with him so I can bawl my eyes out and have him lick my face. I need to do that, Sadie. You know, get it out of the way. Damn, the house was supposed to be this big surprise! I know Matt would have loved your old house as much as I do. It was going to be our getaway place or maybe our home base. I'm just now beginning to realize I didn't know Matt Starr. How can that be, Sadie? I was going to marry a man I know nothing about. Let's go to Pearl Street Pasta before we pick up Buzz. I'm not saying I'm going to eat. I just want to get out of here so I can *breathe*."

Forty minutes later they were seated at a cozy table in back of the bar area perusing the menu. It was warm and comfortable, the lighting dim. As the hour wore on, Sadie watched in horror as Lily downed one drink after another. She didn't try to stop her.

"Dennis said he's going to file a missing person's report. He said he thinks something happened to Matt. Do you want to hear this, Lily?"

"No. You have to wait forty-eight hours before filing a missing person's report. You know that as well as I do. I don't care what he does. Tell me something you haven't already told me about your old house. Just talk to me. I don't care what you say, just talk. Oh, Sadie, I hope you like what I did to your grandmother's house. When you come to visit, it won't look anything like you remember it. The outside is the same, but the inside is all open and airy. The kitchen is so modern, state-of-the-art, the bathrooms are elegant with sunken tubs and big gorgeous garden windows. The architect is worth every cent I'm paying him."

"I think staying in Natchez is going to be the best thing for you. Take as much time as you need to get squared away. Soak up the town, take pictures, go for walks, visit the library, and read everything you can. Ask for a tour of the grade school if you think you might want to teach. Hire a housekeeper. That's going to be a mission in itself. You know you can't cook, and you're no great shakes at keeping house. You'll need to check out the vet in case Buzz needs shots or something. Staying here a few months out of the year never gave us time to do the ordinary things other people do. We were here, we were in Fort Lauderdale, then we'd go to New York, and then Wyoming. It wasn't like either one of us actually *lived* in Natchez. I imagine you'll be busy for a few weeks. Whatever you do, don't go playing sad songs on the stereo and don't read any sad novels either. Deal with the here and now."

"It was supposed to be for *us*. Not just me," Lily said, peering across the table at her friend. "There is no *us* now."

"You're going to do this because it's the thing to do, and it's just you and Buzz. You can handle it, Lily. Later you can do whatever you want. You have to get through this period of time the best way you can. You can't go back to Ozzie and the camp because you need to go forward. To go back would be courting disaster. Who knows, old Matt might come to his senses and start looking for you. Some guys get off on crap like that. You're way too vulnerable now."

Lily didn't speak for a long time. When she looked up at her friend, there were tears in her eyes.

"Do you think something happened to Matt, Sadie?"

"No, I don't. I think he's still afraid of commitment."

"Then do you think that million dollars he put in my bank account was a payoff? Do you think he did that knowing he was going to dump me a second time? Was that his way of easing his conscience? And what about all those stock options he gave me? I guess he wanted to be sure I didn't starve. Actually he made me a multimillionaire. The last time I looked, Digitech was around $160 a share. He just kissed me off in the blink of an eye, didn't he?"

"Yeah, that's exactly what he did. Oh, Lily, I'm so sorry this happened. I wish there was something I could do to wipe away that horrible look on your face."

Lily swallowed her glass of wine in two long gulps and held it out for a refill. "What *is* this?" she asked, pointing to her plate.

"Chicken something or other. It's what you ordered. It's good. Try eating something, Lily. Listen, I think I'm going to delay my trip a few days and stay here in Natchez with you. I don't feel right leaving you."

"No, no, no. I walked into this with my eyes wide-open. I have no one to blame but myself. I'll be okay. When you stop to think about it, a million-dollar kiss-off plus stock options isn't so hard to take. I'm going to enjoy spending every single penny of Matt Starr's money," Lily said, tears rolling down her cheeks.

"Lily, don't cry."

Lily gulped more wine as she stared at the busy waiters rushing about "He's not worth my tears is he? How much did I pay you for your house? My brain is numb. I can't seem to think or remember anything. I don't think I'm going to sell the condo. I'll just close it up. I'm not in any condition to make decisions that involve large sums of money right now."

"Good thinking, Lily. There's no hurry to sell. Consider it a sanctuary in case you ever feel the need of one. Eighty thousand, and I robbed you. It's costing you five times that amount to fix it up. That monstrosity Mom willed to me was just sitting empty for twenty-five years. I'm glad to be rid of it and the taxes that go with it. I'll remind you of that tomorrow when you're sober. You said you were using all your inheritance to refurbish it. That's not counting your kiss-off money and all those stock options," Sadie said sourly.

Lily nodded as she poured more wine into her glass. "You don't think he's lying dead somewhere, do you, Sadie?"

"No, I don't think he's lying dead somewhere. Eat something, Lily."

"What did you do with the food from the reception?"

"I told Rene Adams to take it to the nearest homeless shelter or soup kitchen. She wanted to know what she should do with the flowers. I told her to send them to a nursing home. I hope that was okay, Lily."

"That was nice of you. People say their hearts break all the time. I always thought that was impossible, but it's true. My heart feels like it was shattered. How am I going to get over this?"

"One day at a time, Lily. The same way you did it before."

Lily wrapped her arms around Sadie one last time. "I'll miss you, Sadie. I don't know how to thank you for everything. This is the second time you've . . ."

"Shhh," Sadie said, placing her index finger on Lily's lips. "We're friends. I'll call every chance I get. I'm going to miss you so much, Lily. You should leave before we both start to cry. Buzz is waiting for you in the car. If you need me, all you have to do is call, and I'll be on the next plane back here. Deal?"

"Deal."

"They're calling you to board. Call, okay?" Lily said in a choked voice.

"Yeah, you, too. Oh, God, I almost forgot.

I've been meaning to give you this forever. I kept forgetting. It came with the house. It's probably just a trinket of some kind. I found it wedged in the back of one of the closets. It always helps to have something from an old house. You know, an antique or something to let you know someone real lived there before you. It's called a Wish Keeper. I remember hearing my mom talk about it one time. Don't ask me what that means. Dip it in that silver cleaner stuff or just carry it in your pocket. I think it's a good-luck charm. For you, Charming Lily. Remember now, I'm just a phone call away."

"Don't worry about me, Sadie. I'll be okay. I'm going to be busy for the next day or so returning all the wedding presents. Maybe I'll just hire that wedding place to do it for me." She looked down at the tarnished silver chain and pendant before she closed her hand into a fist. It felt warm and comfortable. She stuck it in her pocket and a moment later forgot about it.

"Sounds good. Bye, Lily. I love you."

Lily bit down on her lower lip. She didn't trust herself to speak. She turned to leave, tears burning her eyes.

The sudden urge to run after Sadie was so strong, Lily found herself running through the concourse to the escalator that would take her to the parking lot outside. To Buzz. Buzz was all she had left now.

Inside the Range Rover, Matt's birthday gift to her, she reached for the golden Lab and held on to him so fiercely the gentle giant yelped in pain. When Lily relaxed her hold on the dog, he snuggled down next to her, his big head in her lap. Hot tears dripped onto his head.

"You know what I think, Buzz. I think we should go home, put all our stuff in this fine vehicle, and head for our new house. We can stay in the little cottage. There really is nothing to keep us at the apartment except convenience, so there's no point in hanging around. As Sadie would say, it's a plan. I just want to get out of there. Oh, God, Buzz, how could I have been such a fool? Why didn't I see this coming? Not only was I dumb and stupid, I was blind in the bargain."

Buzz whimpered as he pawed at her legs. Lily sniffed, blew her nose, rolled down the window, and backed out of the parking space. She tossed the wadded-up tissue over her shoulder onto the backseat as she headed for the exit sign that would take her away from the Baton Rouge airport and back to Natchez.

It was five-thirty when Lily stacked the last of the wedding presents on the dining-room table along with a list of instructions. She'd called down to the management offices earlier and was assured everything would be taken care of in her absence.

She eyed the pile of suitcases in the small foyer. She was going to need a dolly to get them all to the parking area and into the truck. Buzz at her side, she took the steps to the ground level where she rummaged for a dolly in the storage area. She smiled when Buzz hopped on top for his ride up in the elevator.

The Rover's clock said it was 5:47 when she peeled out of the parking area to South Commerce and crossed State before making a right on Main and a left one block later onto North Union and her new house. She didn't look back once. She hadn't fed Buzz yet, so she needed to stop to pick up something for his dinner and some coffee for herself. She turned around in the middle of the road in front of her house and headed for the Pig Out Inn, where she picked up some shredded beef on a roll for the Lab. Until tomorrow, it was the best she could do.

Lily sat behind the wheel, coffee cup in hand. She realized suddenly that she was tired. She'd had so little sleep the past few days she knew she was going on pure adrenaline. She watched as a travel-weary family walked across the road toward their car. They, too, must have traveled all night to be with their family for New Year's and now they were heading home. A husband and wife and three small children. A family. She craned her neck for a better look and saw the wife bend down to pick up a fluffy brown-and-white dog. Picture complete. A towhead dressed in a denim romper waved to her. She waved back. A perfect little family. Would she ever be blessed with a family of her own? She shook her head to clear the cobwebs. She emptied the coffee in the cup. She felt like her eyeballs were snapping to attention.

"You know what, Buzz. I don't feel like going anywhere right now. Let's go for a ride. I need to roll my windows down and let some air blow over me. Let's take a spin across the Mississippi River Bridge. Oops, they don't really call it that anymore. They call it the Natchez Vidalia Bridge. You know, like the onions. Sadie told me that."

Lily drove across the bridge, then turned around and did it again. She had no idea why. There was nothing appealing about Old Muddy at this time of day. It was just something to do. On her return she made a right on South Canal Street. She barely glanced at the Visitor's Reception Center as she looked for landmarks to guide her to her house. Following South Canal, she crossed Washington Street, the prettiest street in all of Natchez when the crepe myrtles were in bloom. She craned her neck, struggling to see the street signs. When South Canal turned into North Canal she kept her eye peeled for the railroad tracks and then made a right on Madison, a left on Union, and drove until she came to the house she'd purchased from Sadie. She did love the chinaberry trees in her yard, she thought as she cut the engine and stared up at her first real estate venture. Her new home! She glanced down at her watch: 6:45. She was paying heavily for a second shift of workers. She'd contracted for the second shift to work inside so that the house would be finished when she and Matt returned from their honeymoon. She could hear the construction workers banging away inside. Well, she wasn't going to disturb them. She'd head for the cottage in the back and sack out till morning. Then, with a good night's sleep under her belt, she'd walk around and admire the house and grounds. But not now. If she did it now, she'd burst into tears. This was the moment she had longed for, the moment when Matt would stop the car and she'd shout, "It's all ours, honey! I want us to raise a family here, to grow old together in this big old house. I want you to hang a swing on one of the live oaks for the kids. We'll get a dog run for Buzz and Gracie. We'll picnic under the trees with the kids, play ball in the yard. I'll plant flowers and bring them indoors. Every day we'll have fresh flowers on the dinner table. I did it all for you, Matt, because I know how you like old houses and trees and backyards. We could even build a brick barbecue so we can have weenie roasts with the kids." Now you're never going to know what you missed, you . . . you . . . bastard. Buzz and I are going to do all those things. Me and Buzz. So who needs you, Mr. Software Giant! Not me.

"Let's go, big guy," Lily said opening the truck door for the dog. The golden Lab waited patiently, unsure where he was supposed to go in this strange new place. Lily led the way up the drive and around to the back of the house and down a path to a small cottage. It wasn't pretty or outstanding in any way, but it would be someday. For now it was just a white-clapboard building with a white stoop and two steps. Inside there was a bed, two chairs and a huge fireplace. There was a working kitchen, but the appliances were ancient and rusty and in need of replacement. The bathroom was a disgrace but usable. She could survive there for a long time, provided she ate out.

She knew exactly how she was going to decorate the little house. In the small kitchen she was going to use wallpaper with big clusters of strawberries. The appliances would be a soft white and would match the white table and chairs. If she was lucky, she might be able to match the place mats and curtains to the wall-paper. The heart-of-pine floors would be sanded and then varnished. Perhaps a small rug here or there but nothing large to mar the beauty of the old floors. Maybe she could do it all herself. Why not? She had nothing better to do. How hard could it be to scrape paint, sand, and wallpaper? It could be her own pri-vate little nest. A cozy room like the one she had at Ozzie Conklin's Survival Camp. A small private place to lick her wounds.

Lily reached into her pocket for a tissue, knowing she was going to cry any second. Her fingers touched the pendant Sadie had given her. She pulled it out and looked at it. A warm, delicious feeling washed over her as she fastened it around her neck. Her own good-luck charm. There was nothing wrong with a little luck along the way.

She flopped down on the old bed and was asleep in an instant. Buzz, ever watchful, stretched out in the open doorway, his eyes on the main door. He knew his job was to guard his mistress. His big head dropped to his paws. Only when he heard Lily's light, even breathing did he relax.

The dream, when it came, was so beautiful, Lily sighed in her sleep. She was back in Wyoming with Matt at her side.

"All right everyone, open up your backpacks and let's see what we have to throw away. Oh, Mrs. Larkin, no, no, no. You know the rules. No candy, no gum, and no cigarettes. The forest is too dry. No tobacco of any kind. I'm going to pat you down so don't even think about stuffing your pockets. We eat what we bring with us and live off the land for the rest. Mr. Sebastian, did your instructions say you could bring a cell phone? No, they did not. Put it on the pile. You'll get it back when we return. No firearms of any kind. I don't care, Mr. Oliver, if you are a homicide cop or not. The gun stays behind. Did *any* of you read the instructions?" she demanded, as the pile of objectionable material mounted.

"I'm not keen on having a female guide," a voice in the back chirped. Matt grimaced as he watched Lily for her reaction. "We leave in five minutes. Make up your mind. You can, of course, stay behind and eat all this junk, make calls on this cell phone, and shoot at the trees. There's no way you can get off this mountain for the next twenty-one days. You better make up your mind real quick. It's starting to rain."

"We're going in the rain?" a frizzy redhead whined.

Lily laughed at her designer outfit. "Yep. Single file. Step lively, or you'll be drenched before we hit the woods. Hiking in wet clothes is very uncomfortable."

Lily gave two short blasts on the whistle hanging around her neck. She waited just long enough to see a young man rush out with a basket to pick up all the loot on the ground.

"Move out!"

"Yes, ma'am," Matt said smartly. "I have this sudden urge to kiss you. Do you think we could lag behind so I can hold you in my arms and kiss you till your teeth rattle?"

"Unfortunately, no. I'll be happy to give you a rain check, though. Better yet, we could zip our sleeping bags together tonight. These people don't need to know we aren't married."

Matt grinned. "I love you forever and ever and even then."

"Move! We're supposed to be setting an example for these prairie flowers."

"I still can't believe you do this for a living. What do you do if someone gets sick?"

"You mean really sick? Or do you mean pretend sick to get out of it?"

"Both I guess."

"It's a judgment call. I have a radio. We don't take chances, Matt. I thought you knew that."

"I don't know the half of it. That's why I'm here. I want to know every single thing about you. I want to see you every minute of the day. Our future is something we can't see right now. I'm sure it's going to be wonderful and happy. I want the picture complete. In order to do that, I need to know all that came before. I'm putting my life in your hands, Lily. I'm as green as the others. I trust you."

"I'll be trusting my life to you when we get married. I think that says something about both of us. Like you said, I will love you forever and ever and even then. Now, hustle your ass, Mr. Starr, you are lagging. The rain is going to slow us down, and we can't stop until we get to the ridge."

"I love it when you talk tough," Matt grinned.

Lily burst out laughing. "Oh, Matt, I hope you still love me when we get back to camp."

Matt grimaced. "I hope I don't disappoint you, Lily. I don't know one tree from another and don't know how well I'm going to do foraging for food, but I'm game to try because this is your world. I don't expect you to cut me any slack. If I'm not measuring up, tell me."

"You could never disappoint me, Matt. When you love someone, you love them for who they are, not what they can and cannot do. I think you're going to do just fine."

Matt crossed his fingers as he shouldered his backpack and fell into line.

Three

Lily woke but didn't move. She knew instantly that something was different about the room she was sleeping in. She didn't feel threatened or alarmed, because she knew Buzz would protect her with his life, but she did sense that someone was watching her. She could feel the presence. She cracked one eyelid and peered through her lashes before she bolted upright. "Sadie!" she squealed. "How long have you been standing there? What happened? Why are you here?"

Sadie gurgled with laughter. "This dog of yours wouldn't let me cross the threshold even though he's known me every day of his life. I tried to coax him to wake you, but he wouldn't budge. So I've just been standing here. I guess I've been here about twenty minutes."

Lily was off the bed in a flash to wrap her arms around her best friend. "What *are* you doing here? You're supposed to be on your way to Australia. Sit down, tell me everything. I'm so glad you're here. God, I missed you so on the ride home from the airport. Tell me everything."

"You know me, Lily. When things go awry, I always say there is a reason. I pay attention to stuff like that. We were all on the plane. Then we had to get off the plane because there was a short circuit of some kind in the cockpit. That turned out to be a little more serious than they originally thought. Someone came on a loudspeaker and said we would board another plane in two hours, but only if it arrived at the terminal in time. On top of that I heard two of the stewardesses talking. They said they had to replace the copilot because he was hung over from too much New Year's partying. That was all I needed to hear. I started to think about this trip and about Tom. I never really wanted to go to the Outback. Somehow or other I let him talk me into it. I realize now I only agreed to the whole thing because you were getting married, and I didn't want to be alone. I'm not in love with Tom Bendix. I love him as a friend, but I'm not *in* love with him. Now, do you want to hear something *really* screwy? When I was talking to Dennis Wagner in the lobby yesterday, something happened to me. This is corny so don't laugh, okay?" Lily nodded solemnly.

"I looked into his eyes, and I thought to myself, this man is my destiny. Yeah, he's nerdy and wrapped up in computers, but then

74

Matt is that way, too. I saw a spark in his eyes. Plus, are you ready for this? I just went to the apartment, and he was still sitting in the lobby with all kinds of folders and papers and stuff. When I realized you were gone, I knew you had come here, so I told him he could use the apartment. He absolutely refuses to believe Matt stood you up. He is convinced something happened to him. He said he wasn't going anywhere until he knew for certain. I believe his plan was to rent a hotel room or find a furnished apartment for the time being, so that's why I told him he could use our apartment. I hope that was okay. That's not all, Lily," Sadie said breathlessly. "I saw a stray dog that looked like Matt's. I chased him for two whole blocks, but he got away. We can go look for him now if you want. Gee, this is like old times. Tom pitched a real fit over the phone when I called him to tell him I changed my mind. We both said things, so there's no going back. Now I'm stuck with a round-trip ticket to Australia. God, all I'm doing is babbling. Are you okay?"

"More to the point, are you okay?"

"Yeah. Thanks for not laughing," Sadie grinned.

"There is the little matter of the woman Dennis had with him at the rehearsal dinner and then at the church. Have you given that any thought? She didn't seem his type, but then what do I know. Guess we're going to be bunk mates again. You get the bottom of the bed, I get the top, and Buzz gets the middle. Welcome home, Sadie."

"Perfect. Lily, I couldn't go off and leave you at a time like this. I just couldn't. Are you sure you're okay?"

Lily smiled. "I am now. It is so good to see you. I couldn't stay in the apartment. I had to get out of there. This is so weird, Sadie. Before I fell asleep I was thinking of how I would redo this little house. It was all for you. Everything I thought about doing was to your taste. You know, so when you came to visit you would have your own place and be comfortable. I was going to do it all myself. All I did was dream about Matt. Wonderful, sweet dreams. One right after the other. Your destiny, huh?" Lily said shifting her thoughts to her friend. "Now who's babbling."

"I say we go outside to gather up some firewood. We'll clean out the fireplace, get it ready for later. We can go for some takeout, get some wine, and snuggle in, just the two of us. It will be almost like old times. How does that sound, Lily?"

"It sounds wonderful. There's a woodpile in back of the house. And a wheelbarrow. I'll start to clean the fireplace. Take Buzz with you. He needs some exercise, and he probably has to do his business. That was a long nap I took, so he hasn't been out for a while. I'm going to be all right, Sadie." She almost said 'now that you're here,' but held her tongue.

An hour later, Lily set the shopping bag full of Chinese food on the floor of the backseat of the Rover. Buzz sniffed and growled but didn't attempt to paw through the white boxes that were giving off such tantalizing aromas. Three bottles of Luna de Luna wine rested next to the shopping bag. Their night was set.

"Look at that dog!" Sadie shrilled. "Oh, he's limping. Stop, Lily. I think he's hurt." Lily slammed on the brakes and hit the door the same moment Sadie did. Both women sprinted after the dog, but he was too fast for them. He ran off and disappeared into the shadows.

"We'll call Animal Control in the morning. They know how to catch strays. If they're successful, we'll claim him and take him to a vet to get him fixed up. If we can't find his owner, I'll take him. Buzz needs a companion. He looks like Gracie, Matt's dog. She's such a sweetheart. Buzz got along well with Gracie when Matt brought her down last year. It was so nice watching him share his food and toys with her. Dogs are supposed to be good judges of character. How is it Gracie doesn't know what a weasel her master is?" Lily asked, getting into the truck. Buzz threw back his head and howled. Lily reared back in surprise. "What's that all about, big guy?" she said, stroking his huge head.

Buzz barked and barked as he threw himself against the door in his struggle to get out.

"He probably knows there's a cat out here somewhere, prowling around," Sadie said as she buckled her seat belt.

"Guess you're right. Settle down, Buzz. I don't want you catching some poor cat. We're going home and have some supper. You're having beef tips and rice. Tomorrow it's back to dog food for you when I go to the store."

It was well after midnight when Lily eyed the two empty wine bottles sitting on the floor. Buzz nudged her arm. "Okay, I'm in no shape to walk you, so go out and you get right back in here. You hear me, Buzz. Ten minutes. Don't make me come looking for you. Find your place and get back here."

"What's up?" Sadie demanded. "That is one ugly bathroom, Lily."

"I know. I was talking to Buzz. I let him out. Usually I walk with him, but I'm more than a little tipsy. He's real good about coming back."

"Did you say I get the bottom or the top of the bed? What are you going to do about the apartment?"

"You get the bottom. I get the top, and Buzz gets the middle. The lease was up in December. The management company extended the lease for the month of January because I was getting married. There's a new tenant waiting to move in February 1. Why?"

"Just curious. I wonder how long Dennis will stay. He's kind of cute, don't you think?"

"If you say so. I was supposed to be starting my honeymoon. If things had worked out, we'd probably be making wild, passionate love right now."

"Was Matt that good in bed?" Sadie twinkled.

"He is. Was. . . . Sex was great. Matt was a considerate lover. He could be wild, and then he could be gentle. We were a perfect match in every way. I hate men. I'm never going to look at another one, and I'm never going to get married either," Lily said, flopping down on her end of the bed. "Call Buzz."

Sadie opened the door to call the dog, at the same time turning on the outside light.

Both women waited, but the Lab was nowhere in sight.

At two o'clock, hoarse from calling Buzz, Lily sat down on the front stoop and huddled into her thermal jacket, Sadie at her side. "We can't even go after him because we're too drunk to drive. Let's walk."

"What makes you think either one of us can walk down the driveway, much less around the block, looking for a dog who doesn't want to be found? Buzz knows his way. It's the middle of the night, and there's absolutely no traffic. In case you haven't noticed, my voice gave out at the same time yours did."

"Oh, God, Sadie, what if he doesn't come back? What if he runs wild like that dog we've been trying to catch? He's all I have. First Matt, and now Buzz. What's wrong with me, Sadie?" Lily wailed.

"You have me, Lily. Buzz will come back. He loves you. He's just stretching his legs. Dogs are loyal. Men aren't. That's the difference."

"Do you like men, Sadie?" Lily said, slurring her words.

"Sometimes. Not all the time. Mostly on the weekends I like them. During the week they stink. It's a nice night. Cold, though. It's always about *them*. I hope I never get so desperate for a man that I *settle*. Women do that all the time."

"I didn't know that," Lily mumbled.

"Remember that time the chick from AT&T took Ozzie's survival course with all those men. She was their boss. She came loaded down with all her designer duds and gear trying to prove she was better than all those men working under her. Until it came time to cross Big Red at the gorge. She buckled then, and the little fat guy who chugged all the way had to help her. She sent Ozzie a wedding invitation. She married the fat little guy. Not one of the tall, rugged ones. They either had wives or girlfriends. Guess she figured she wasn't going to get anyone else since she was forty-three. She damn well *settled* is what she did. I saw it on her face when they were leaving."

"What time is it, Sadie?"

"Three o'clock. Has Buzz ever stayed out this late before?"

"Never. Something must have happened to him. We have to go look for him."

"No. We're staying right here. He'll be back when he gets tired. Make sure you give him a good swat when he does get back. I'm going to give him one myself. I can do that because I'm his godmother."

It was four-thirty when both women heard the dry leaves on the ground rustle. Buzz appeared out of the darkness and barked as he pawed the ground. When he was satisfied he had their attention, he ran off to the driveway.

Lily was on her feet in a heartbeat, running after the Lab, Sadie in her wake. They both skidded to a stop when they saw the big black-and-tan dog lying on his side in the driveway. "Oh, God, Sadie, look! Buzz went back to find this dog. Help me get him into the house. We have to call the vet. We need to do something. Good boy, Buzz. I'll swat you later."

Within minutes they had the big shepherd inside. Gently, they lowered the dog to the carpet in front of the fireplace. Sadie raced off for a blanket. Lily ran to the kitchen for water. He isn't a he. He's a she!" she called to Sadie's retreating back. She's got a collar on, too." Buzz hovered, then he lowered his big head to lick the dog's face. Lily felt her heart melt. "It's okay, Buzz. She's going to be okay. She really does look like Gracie. Guess you think so, too. Oh, good, she's taking the water. Easy, girl, easy. Just a little bit at a time. Do you think she's dehydrated, Sadie?"

"If she's been on her own for a while, that's a safe bet. I'll cut up some of the leftover meat and mix it with the rice. You can hand-feed her. First thing in the morning, we'll take her to the vet. I think she's going to be okay, Lily. Buzz seems to think so, too."

"Shouldn't we check her collar and call the owners before we do anything? I wonder why no one has been looking for her. She's beautiful. Buzz got her here. Isn't that amazing, Sadie?"

"It sure is. Guess she trusted him. Dogs really are uncanny."

"I can't make out what it says on her tag. Guess we'll have to wait for morning. I don't know why, but I don't want to take her collar off now. She might not take kindly to a stranger removing it. Buzz would go ballistic. His collar and tag are *his*. How's that food coming?"

Sadie handed over a small bowl. Lily took a pinch between her fingers and fed it to the dog, who ate it gratefully. "Make some more, Sadie, she's starving."

The sun was creeping over the horizon when the shepherd finally closed her eyes in sleep, Buzz at her side, Lily and Sadie curled next to both dogs.

The winter sun was high in the sky when Lily opened one eye to see Buzz staring at her. Should she get up? Was Buzz waiting for her to make the first move? She craned her neck. The shepherd was awake, too. Waiting. "Wake up, Sadie," she said, nudging her friend. "Let's see if this pretty baby can get up on her own. Make some more food, and let's see if she'll take some more water. You get her from the front, and I'll hoist her from the back. If she can't stand up, we'll put her on the bed and see if we can get a vet to come here. Oh, good, she's wobbly, but she's up." She wanted to cry when the big dog licked her hand. She hugged her. "Bring the food, Sadie."

Both women watched while the shepherd gobbled down the entire bowl of food, then drank greedily. Buzz waited patiently for her to finish before he headed for the door. The shepherd followed.

Within minutes both dogs were back indoors. Lily stood rooted to the floor when the big black-and-tan dog lunged toward her and started licking every available inch of her skin that was exposed.

"Whoa, girl, easy, easy. Yes, yes, I love you, too. Look how grateful she is, Sadie. I think she's going to be okay, but we're still taking her to the vet. Then we're going to clean her up. She's a mess."

Sadie smiled. At least for a few minutes, Lily was her old self. Why was it that an animal always brought out the best in everyone? "I think you got yourself another dog is what I think. At least for the time being. It looks to me like Buzz agrees. Let's see who she belongs to. You look, Lily, she's next to you. I don't want to confuse her."

Lily dropped to her knees until she was eye

level with the big dog. "This dog looks so much like Gracie it's eerie. Shhh," she said, when the shepherd started to bark. "I just want to see who let you get away from them. Whoever they are they should be horse-whipped."

Sadie sat down on the chair by the fireplace, her gaze on Lily and the smile on her face. Idly she scratched Buzz behind the ears. The moment she saw Lily's face turn white she was off the chair. "What is it? What's wrong? Talk to me, Lily. You're hyperventilating. Drop your head between your knees and take deep breaths. Okay, okay. What? What's wrong?"

"This . . . this . . . this is Gracie, Matt's dog. That's why she was so happy to see me. She recognized me, and she remembered Buzz. That's how he was able to get her here. Look at her tag. Gracie Starr. Owner, Matthew Starr, and his phone number in New York. Matt would never let this dog out of his sight. I used to wonder who he loved more, Gracie or me, and it was always a draw. Where is he, girl? God, if you could only talk."

"How'd she get here?"

"Good question. Listen, call Dennis and ask him to come over here. My cell phone is on the kitchen table. Matt would never dump this dog, and, by the same token, Gracie would never leave him. Never. That's a given. Oh, Sadie, maybe something really did happen to him. Maybe he didn't jilt me after all. You don't think he's dead, do you, Sadie? He can't be dead. Sadie, say something. Did you get hold of Dennis?"

"He's on his way. He said exactly what you said. He said Matt would never, ever, leave the dog. He said it was like Gracie and he were joined at the hip. He's more convinced than ever that something happened to him. I don't know what to say other than she's a beautiful animal. I wish she could talk."

Lily stroked the big shepherd's head with one hand as her other hand fiddled with the Wish Keeper hanging around her neck. She sighed. At the same moment she felt a hundred lightbulbs go off behind her eyelids. A rough-hewn building among a stand of hardwoods assailed her. A second later the vision was gone.

"What's wrong, Lily?" Sadie said shaking her shoulders. "You're scaring me. What's wrong, dammit?"

"I don't know. I closed my eyes and saw this . . . this . . . I don't know what it was, maybe a shack. It looked old, and it listed to the side. There were these big monster trees everywhere. It was just a flash. Am I losing my mind?"

"Of course not. You were staring off into space. That happens to me all the time. You've been through a rough time, Lily. Anything you experience now can be chalked up to your emotions and finding Gracie. I think I hear a car. Maybe it's Dennis, or maybe one of the workers. I told him we were out here in the cottage. He's nice, Lily, and very concerned about his friend. Please don't go off on him. I know you don't like Marcus, but I think Dennis is okay. He's to Matt what I am to you. Remember that."

"I will, Sadie. I promise. I'm feeling better already. You know what I mean."

"It's Dennis." Sadie ran to the door and threw it open. Gracie barked happily at the sight of Dennis, the guy who had tussled with her on more than one occasion back in New York. She made no move to go to him and waited for him to bend down and cup her head in his hands. She almost purred with the attention. Buzz growled. Dennis backed off.

He looks a lot like Matt, Lily thought. He was dressed like his boss in jeans, sweatshirt, and well-worn sneakers. There were no holes in the toes, however. They were also minus shoelaces. Idiosyncracies of the male species.

"How are you, Lily?"

"I'm okay. We need to sit down and talk. I

want . . . no, that's not right, I *need* to believe Matt didn't dump me at the altar. Finding Gracie like this is telling me maybe you're right, and something has happened to Matt. We're all in agreement that Matt would never let Gracie out of his sight, much less dump her alongside the road. We've seen her for days now, but didn't realize it was Gracie. We thought she was a stray dog just wandering around. We even tried to catch her. That means she's been running loose for two days. Whatever happened to Matt, if something did happen, happened three days ago. Maybe even before that. There's no way to know for sure. Trails grow cold in that span of time. Matt really doesn't know Natchez all that well. The few times he's been here, I did the driving. We were so busy talking, I know he didn't pay any attention to the scenery unless I mentioned a particular landmark or some point of interest. He knows *about* Natchez, but he doesn't know it if you know what I mean. Hell, I'm a transplant, I don't even know it. This property was once owned by Sadie's great-great-grandmother. Her mother inherited it when we were all living in Florida, but none of her family wanted to come back here. Sadie doesn't know much more about the area than I do. It looks like we'll all be learning about it as we go along. Is there anything you know that you haven't told us, Dennis?"

Dennis smiled, but the smile was directed at Sadie. "Nothing that would have anything to do with Matt leaving you standing at the altar. All kinds of things are going on at the office. When someone like Matt decides to take the plunge, it's big news. Everyone starts to scramble and jockey for position. Some pretty unhealthy and ugly rumors started circulating about a month ago. Matt changed then. At first I didn't know what was going on. When things like this start happening, people choose up sides. It was my side, and then there was Marcus's side. We're going to be unveiling some new software that will change the industry. Big stuff. We were all waiting to see whose side Matt was leaning toward, Marcus's or mine. To this day, I don't know, and neither does Marcus. At least he says he doesn't. I'm no Marcus Collins fan. I want that known right up front."

"Duly noted," Sadie said quietly.

"What were the ugly, unhealthy rumors that were circulating?"

"That someone high up in the company, someone like Marcus or me, was selling our software secrets to competitors. I think Marcus convinced Matt it was me. My family, all my friends, called to tell me people were coming around asking questions about me, my income, did I buy anything new, you know, big-ticket items, that kind of thing. They ran checks on me at my bank. I don't mind telling you I was pissed off big-time. I didn't mind the scrutiny because I have nothing to hide. I was pissed at the secrecy of the whole thing. What I did mind more than anything was that Matt would even listen to something like that. We played in the same sandbox when we were kids. I'd lay down my life for him. I thought he felt the same way about me. Obviously, he didn't . . . doesn't."

"Did Matt investigate Marcus Collins?" Lily asked carefully.

"I don't know, Lily. If he did, nothing filtered back to me. I have to make a decision here. We're unveiling the new software four days from now. Do I go back and stand in the limelight, or do I stay here and hunt for my friend? We know he made it this far because of Gracie, so it's logical to start the search here."

Lily shrugged. "I think you were right, and we should call the police. Maybe even the FBI."

"Jesus, God, no! Matt would have a fit if we did that. The place will be swarming with agents, cops, and who the hell knows who else. That's when things could really get skewed. I say we try to do this ourselves. Marcus is back in the New York office. He can handle everything. He knows how Matt feels about this kind of thing. It will be interesting to see if anything is leaked."

"Why? You're implying that Matt was kidnapped. That is what you're saying, isn't it?" Lily demanded.

"Yes. No. I don't know, Lily. I'm no sleuth. It could be as simple as Matt being at the wrong place at the wrong time. Or, it could be something more serious. I'm like a duck out of water. I'm having a hard time getting past the idea that Matt could think I would betray him and the company."

"Maybe that's what he *wanted* you to think, Dennis. Do not ever make the mistake of thinking Matt is a fool. He isn't. Where his business is concerned, he's right there. It's all in his head. I know because he talks in his sleep. Maybe it was just a show to throw anyone else off the track. For instance, let's just say it was Marcus he was suspicious of. He wouldn't want Marcus to know, so he picked you. Unlikely choice since you've been friends all your lives. It makes sense, doesn't it, Sadie?" Lily muttered.

"It makes a whole lot of sense. Matt loved you . . . damn, we have to stop talking in the past tense. Matt loves you like you are his brother. He's told me that hundreds of times. Tell us about Marcus," Sadie pleaded.

"For starters, Gracie hates Marcus. She snarls at his wife, too. Betsy is high-maintenance. That means she likes expensive things. Marcus has a house in the Hamptons that's worth seven or eight million. He owns a big boat. He calls it a yacht. I don't know anything about boats. Every year they go to Europe for a month with the kids in the summer. They go again to Switzerland in the winter, too. Usually around the holidays. Marcus loves to ski. He drives a Porsche, and his wife drives a Benz. His kids go to fancy private schools. Betsy sports a lot of pricey jewelry. They have a ritzy apartment at the Dakota with a live-in housekeeper and nanny. Marcus makes good money, but then so do I. I always have the feeling he wants more. How many houses does one person need? How many cars? He says he likes Matt. Maybe he does, and maybe he doesn't. I see his envy, his distaste at the way Matt thumbs his nose at the establishment and the way he dresses. I'm trying to be fair where Marcus is concerned, but I don't like the son of a bitch."

Lily leaned back trying to absorb everything she'd just heard. She felt like crying and didn't know why. She continued to stroke Gracie's head as she played with the Wish

Keeper around her neck. Suddenly, her head jolted forward and a vision flashed behind her eyelids. Matt's Jaguar parked under a tree in the dark with only the moon for illumination. Her eyes snapped open.

"Did it happen again, Lily?" Sadie asked, her voice full of concern. "Tell Dennis about how it happened before."

"It's nothing. It's just . . . I sort of see . . . something. First it was a shack that was leaning over, and this time it looked like Matt's Jaguar parked under a tree. It was dark with only the moon shining down. I don't believe in stuff like this, so don't go reading something into it that isn't there. I'm probably overtired, and I'm kind of tense right now."

"We have to pay attention to it, Lily, because nothing like that has ever happened to you before," Sadie said.

"You two talk it to death. I'm telling you, it means nothing. I'm going to take Gracie to the vet. I'll just show up and that way they won't be able to turn me away or give me an appointment tomorrow or something like that. Watch Buzz for me, okay?"

"Betsy didn't want to come to the wedding," Dennis went on. "I heard Marcus talking to her on the phone. There was some big gala going on in the Hamptons she wanted to attend. Then when the wedding didn't come off, she was like one scalded cat. I didn't envy Marcus, that's for sure. She referred to the dinner and the church as a ricky-ticky, down-home affair. She called it an embarrassment for people like them."

Lily winced. "It was what Matt wanted, Dennis. He was the one who wanted the dinner at King's Tavern because it's supposed to be haunted. He was hoping one of the spirits would show up over dinner and scare everyone half to death. That's where we were going to stay on our wedding night. He was really into that spirit stuff."

"I know all about it. He talked about it all the time. I told the story to Betsy myself. She had the good manners to shut up after that, but she looked like she was sucking on a lemon. Listen, this place doesn't look too comfortable. Why don't you come back to the apartment and we can set up our command post on your dining-room table. Ooops, in the living room. Your dining room is full of wedding presents. I'll sleep on the couch if that's okay with you girls. The dogs will be more comfortable in the apartment, too."

"Yeah, let's do that, Lily. I'll ride with Dennis, and you go straight back there when you finish up at the vet's, okay?"

"Okay. I shouldn't be long. Take care of Buzz."

As she ushered Gracie through the door, she heard Sadie say, "Now who was that lovely lady with you at the wedding?" She grinned when she heard Dennis's response. "My sister's best friend. She didn't have a date for New Year's Eve, and I didn't have a date for the wedding. It worked out for both of us. I only met her that one time."

"How wonderful for you both," Sadie trilled.

Gracie sat comfortably on the ride to the vet's. She didn't react to anything until they were a mile or so out of town when she reared up and her ears went flat against her head. She growled and then she barked so loudly, Lily pulled to the side of the road. From long years of habit where Buzz was concerned, she'd learned to pay attention to a dog's strange behavior. She reached for Buzz's leash before she climbed out of the car and fastened it to Gracie's collar.

The moment Gracie's paws touched the ground, she started to howl and bark. She pawed the ground in a frenzy as Lily led her up and down the side of the road. "Someone dumped you here, is that what you're trying to tell me? Let's go back. No, huh? Okay, let's see what's around here. A road. Trees. Dirt. Weeds. There's nothing here, Gracie. This road will take us out to Anna's Bottom. But, you headed back to town. I don't know what that means. If you were in the car, you'd want to go forward if they dumped you out here. Instead you went the other way. Unless the car went back that way, too. I don't know, baby. We're going to find out, though. That's a promise. Come on, hop in the truck. We need to get you looked at."

Two hours later, Lily ushered the clean, groomed shepherd out to the truck. The vet had hydrated her, given Lily a small bottle of pills in case Gracie's legs started to bother her with all the walking she'd done. He pronounced her right as rain considering the circumstances. He went on to say, do your best to let her rest for a few days. Lily sighed in relief at the vet's words. The big dog had no serious injuries and would be all right within a few days.

Now all she had to do was try to figure out how the shepherd got loose and where Matt was.

If only the big dog could talk.

Four

She was running for her life, from whom or what, she didn't know. Matt's name was on her lips, and her throat burned from screaming and shouting. She knew she was in the bayous because she could see the thick cane and the buckvine, not to mention the ancient cypress leaning out of the slimy water at crazy angles. She swatted the insects swarming about her face and arms, cursing the cold, slimy water, wondering if a cottonmouth, water moccasin, or copperhead would find her ankles. She called his name again as Gracie and Buzz stood on the bank barking furiously. She needed to get back to where the dogs waited, needed to get to the south and the piney woods and the huge live oaks dripping moss and the reed-thin conifers. If she followed them, she would land in the grassy marsh because that's where Old Muddy bent toward the sea. In the piney woods she could use her survival skills. In this swamp she was the proverbial duck out of water.

"I'm coming, Matt. I'm coming! I'll find

you. I swear I will. You said you trusted me just the way I trusted you. I won't fail you. I promise."

"Lily, wake up. You're having a bad dream. Shhh, it's okay. We're all here in the apartment. Go back to sleep, Lily. It was just a bad dream," Sadie said soothingly as she stroked her friend's hair back from her forehead.

Sadie waited until Lily rolled over on her side and her breathing evened out. When she saw Dennis standing in the doorway, she crept out of bed and joined him in the living room. "It was just a bad dream. What time is it?"

"A little after five. If you show me where everything is, I'll make us some coffee. There doesn't seem much sense in going back to sleep now. This is a nice comfortable apartment you have here," he said, looking around.

"I'll make the coffee. Would you like some toast? It's about all we have. Lily pretty much cleaned everything out before the . . . you know, before. The apartment came this way. Nothing here belongs to us. When I look back now, I have to wonder why we ever came here."

"Why did you?" Dennis said, flopping down on one of the kitchen chairs. *He looks adorable,* Sadie thought, with his rumpled hair and his silk pajamas. His feet were bare.

Big feet, she noticed.

"We needed a place to come back to during the winter. Neither Lily nor I have any family left. We've been friends forever. Working at the survival camp nine to ten months out of the year didn't warrant buying property or keeping up an apartment and paying rent for those nine months. Then a few years ago we decided if we shared an apartment and split the rent, we could have a place of our own to call home during the winter months. It worked. We weren't crazy about Florida. Too many sad memories. Generations of my family used to live here, so it was logical for us to come here, I suppose. As a child, I came here summers for a few years and as I grew older, the visiting stopped for some reason. I inherited the old house and sold it to Lily. She's having it renovated, and it was supposed to be her wedding present to Matt. A place to put down some roots. A place to come home to. Now I don't know what's going to happen. Do you have any ideas, any clues, or are you just going by gut instinct here?"

"Not a whole hell of a lot, Sadie. Like you just said, I'm going by my gut instinct. I've known Matt forever, and I know he wouldn't do this to Lily. I know all about the first time. That was different. He wasn't ready for such a big step back then, and he had worlds to build, mountains to climb, and oceans to swim. He's done all that. He was more than ready for home and hearth. Now with Gracie in the picture . . ."

"Are you going to stay here, or are you going back to New York?" Sadie asked as she reached into the cabinet for cups and saucers.

"I'm going to make some calls as soon as the office opens, but I would like to stay on here if you and Lily don't mind. The sofa is quite comfortable. Did I misunderstand Lily when she said you were going to Australia to meet your fiancé's parents?"

"Yes and no. That's all over and done with. He wasn't my fiancé. We were just very good friends. I'm a free agent," she said pointedly. "That means I can see or go out with anyone I want to."

Dennis grinned. "I assumed that's what it meant. I'm pretty much a free agent myself these days," he twinkled.

"Imagine that," Sadie said, setting the coffee in front of him. "I hate computers," she blurted. "I always press the wrong button, lose stuff, other stuff freezes, the mouse won't work, yada yada yada."

Dennis threw back his head and laughed. "I hate the woods, getting wet and cold and trekking up mountains, crossing skimpy bridges that sway back and forth with your weight. That's just another way of saying I could never in a million years do what you and Lily do. Are you going back?"

"I don't know. I took an extended leave. Lily resigned outright. I'm going to stay around long enough to see her over this rough patch, then I'll make some decisions."

They stared at each other across the kitchen table. It was Sadie who finally broke the silence. "Do they always kill you when you're kidnapped?"

"Jesus! Don't even think that. I don't know. What do they do on those crime shows?"

"I'm not much of a television watcher myself. If Matt was kidnapped, who would get the ransom note? The company or someone in the company like you or Marcus?"

"I don't know. I've never come up against anything like this before. Life was routine, no surprises. Just same old same old. Hell, I don't even know where to start. I'm thinking about going to the police to file a missing person's report after I call the office. Matt had this . . . thing about involving the authorities if anything like this ever happened. Gives the company a bad image. I have to think it through."

Sadie leaned across the table. "Tell me about Marcus Collins. You know, the guy stuff. And the business side of him, too. I want to know all about his relationship with Matt. I know Lily doesn't care for him, and maybe her opinion of the man rubbed off on me and has colored my opinion. I don't care for him either."

"You aren't trying to tell me you think Marcus had something to do with Matt not showing up for the wedding? Or are you?"

"I think it's highly suspicious," Lily said from the doorway. "Marcus didn't seem the least bit concerned about Matt's absence. Like me, and unlike you, Dennis, he was very quick to assume and believe Matt was doing an encore, and I could tell he was getting a perverse kind of pleasure out of it. Do we have a game plan here, or are we just going to flounder around?"

"Want some toast, Lily? Dennis?" Both heads bobbed up and down.

"I had this really bad dream. I dreamed I was in the bayous searching for Matt. If someone took a person out there and left him there, he could die. If we're going to report his disappearance to the police, we have to know what's going on at Digitech. I could tell that Marcus doesn't want this reported to the police. So what if Matt gets upset. I know that's what the police are going to think. I say we look for him ourselves. Sadie and I are very good at tracking. Now if he's in and around the Natchez Trace or out by Anna's Bottom, we have a chance. If he's in the bayous, we're in trouble. Assuming he didn't go off and dump me. Gracie pretty much cancels that theory out. I'm not feeling good about this, but I don't feel quite so devastated. Do you think I'm being a fool?" Lily asked.

"No, of course not," Sadie said. "Hope springs eternal."

"Absolutely not," Dennis agreed. "Look, if Matt was kidnapped, and we don't know that he was, there should be a ransom note soon. Marcus has my cell-phone number, and there have been no calls. I have to assume there hasn't been one. Matt made us all swear that we wouldn't involve the authorities. To a point we have to respect his wishes. We could hire some private dicks. We have plenty of those on our payroll. I don't know how quiet you can keep something like this. The FBI has to be called in, things like that. Marcus will bust a gut if that happens. That means his nice, orderly, obsessive, expensive life will grind to a halt. Marcus cannot function in chaos. Matt, on the other hand, thrives on chaos and somehow manages to bring order to everything at the end of the day."

"I'm going to take the dogs out, then shower," Lily said. "By the time you two get dressed you should be able to call the office.

Depending on what you find out, we can decide then what we should do. Is that okay with you? Good. I'll see you in a bit then."

Sadie twirled a hank of her hair between her thumb and forefinger as she stared across the table at Dennis. "Why do I have this feeling there's something you aren't telling? There's something going on at Digitech, isn't there?"

Dennis squirmed in his chair and tried to look everywhere but at Sadie.

"C'mon, spit it out. We're all in this together, and that means we have to share what we have with each other even if it seems unimportant. What you know might be a clue or something we can work at."

"Look, it's just little things. I could be so far off base and talking about it might give you and Lily the wrong idea."

"Think of me as your shrink. Talk," Sadie ordered.

"We . . . Matt, Marcus, and I work out of the New York office at least a week out of every month. Marcus is there most of the time because his kids are in school there. And because of his wife. She doesn't like Oregon, where our main headquarters is located, and she refuses to relocate. I don't know why because Oregon is so beautiful it takes your breath away. The Digitech campus is magnificent. Marcus is on top of everything. Nothing gets by him. Man, he was pissed to the teeth when he found out Matt was going to be named High-Tech Man of the Year again this year. He wants that honor so bad he can taste it. Betsy does, too. Actually, I think she wants it more than Marcus does. Something happened about six weeks ago. Nothing important, but if you link it with some other weird things, then it does make sense in a cockamamie kind of way. Marcus took it upon himself to change our trash pickup. He just decided one day the company that had been with us from the beginning wasn't good enough. I thought they were fine. It was a family company run by the father and two sons. They were pricey but dependable. This new company is for the birds. They show up when they feel like it. They're sloppy, inefficient, and the workers are dirty and slovenly. I saw Matt raise his eyebrows when he got a gander at them, but he didn't say anything. Matt never overrides anything Marcus does. The new company bills twice as much. Before you can ask, we shred everything."

Sadie stared at her coffee cup, her mind racing. "Okay, he's ticked off because he isn't Man of the Year, he doesn't like working in Oregon because his wife doesn't like it there, and he changed trash collectors. It's not much to go on. What else?"

Dennis bit down on his lower lip. "We're supposed to unveil our new software in a few days. But, there was to be a really big announcement following the unveiling. He wants to go ahead with it, but I'm voting no."

"Because . . ."

A deep frown etched itself between Dennis's brows as he stared at the thin, winter sunshine filtering into the kitchen from the window over the sink. He eyed the straggly plant hanging from the ceiling with its yellowing leaves. "I think your plant needs to be watered. Because . . . because I think Matt would want to put a hold on it. At least for now. I'd explain it to you, but you wouldn't understand. What we've developed is going to change the entire industry. Marcus was to make the announcement about the new software, and I was going to make the *big* announcement. Then we were going to do a hookup so that Matt could say something from wherever he was going to be on his honeymoon. I think someone sold us out. Marcus won't look me in the eye. Matt had some difficulty back in early December when he went on the road. I think Marcus convinced him I was leaking secrets. I absolutely refused to defend myself. My loyalty to Matt and Digitech is and has always been one hundred percent. That's all of it in a nutshell."

Upstairs, Lily stepped from the shower, aware that both dogs were watching her. She dried off, rubbing the towel over the Wish Keeper hanging around her neck. Her head snapped backwards as a vision rocketed in front of her. A hypodermic needle and Matt, asleep in the backseat of his Jaguar. Stunned, she reached out to the towel rack for support as she struggled to take deep breaths. The dogs circled her ankles, their tails between their legs. "Shhh, it's okay. Everything is okay, I think," she said soothingly as she scratched each of them behind their ears. Gracie whimpered before she flopped down on the cool tile. Buzz continued to growl.

Lily's body trembled as she stepped into her underwear before pulling on a warm sweat suit. Her fingers itched and shook as she tried to tie her shoelaces. She finally gave up as she rummaged for an old pair with Velcro strips in the closet.

Lily leaned her back against the vanity, her eyes closed. What did it all mean? Why was she having these visions? *Why me?* She wailed silently. *Why me?* Once or twice she'd read articles about people claiming to have visions after a bad trauma or a head injury. Being stood up at the altar, even if it was for the second time, wasn't exactly a trauma that would support something like this. A knot of fear formed in the pit of her stomach. If only she knew what it meant. She'd never been good at puzzles. Sadie was worse than she was. Maybe Dennis would know. Maybe a lot of things.

"Okay, let's go! Everyone in the truck. A romp in the yard, then we're going to go inside the *big house* to make pests of ourselves. We need to goose that contractor a little. I think he's taking advantage of us."

Lily breezed through the kitchen, stopping only long enough to grab a cup of coffee and tell Sadie and Dennis about her latest *vision*. "You two try and figure it out. We're going for a romp in the gardens on North Union Street. Then I'm going to walk Gracie up and down the street to see if she can pick up on anything. It's a long shot, but you never know. I'll be back by lunchtime. Let's go to Fat Mama's Tamales for lunch. Tell Dennis about Mama's Naked Margaritas, Sadie. He needs to get one of her stickers to put on his baseball cap."

"Sounds good," Sadie said. "Be careful in that backyard, Lily. You should start thinking about having some of those vines cleared away. God knows what's underneath them. They're choking off the real plants. If I remember correctly, there were some prize hybrid camellias in that yard you might want to cultivate later on."

"I'll be careful."

Twenty minutes later Lily stopped her 4-by-4 in the driveway and let the dogs out. They immediately raced off. She looked around, her eyes misting. Her wedding present to Matt stood directly in her line of vision. One day it would be as beautiful as the six hundred antebellum mansions, houses, churches, and other structures in Natchez, her testament to a long-ago time. All done with love for Matt. She swiped at her eyes with the sleeve of her jacket. Her shoulders straightened imperceptibly.

Her eyes dry, she stared at what she called the house on North Union Street. She looked first at six live oaks scattered across the winter lawn. They were ancient, the gray moss thick and long, swaying in the brisk January wind. She couldn't help but wonder who it was that originally planted the magnificent trees and was it their intention for the trees one day to shield the house from the winter winds and to frame the old house or hide it from prying eyes? Did young children play on the wide expanse of lawn or did they play in the backyard? She wished she knew.

The outside of the house had been painted back in September, when the days were still warm and dry. It glistened now in the winter sun, the front pillars sentinels to the large mahogany door with the stained-glass fanlight overhead. A treasure, the contractor had said. And it was. In the early-morning light the colored glass cast mini rainbows all over the front rooms of the house. Matt would have loved it.

The structure was two stories high with a cupola on top. The first floor fanned out to the left and right, probably additions as the family grew in size. The shutters were the originals, patched and repatched, and then painted a rich hunter green. The ancient hinges had been rusty but restored. Now she would be able to close the shutters to ward off the brutal late-afternoon heat. But it was the porch that she loved the most. She'd had so many dreams where the porch was always visible. It was bare now, full of strips of lumber and Sheetrock and all manner of saws and building supplies. When it was all done, the porch was the last thing she would do. She already had her mental list of furnishings. Six cane rockers painted white, wicker tables set among the chairs, green fiber carpets on the gunmetal gray floor. Huge clay pots full of colorful flowers she would water every day would be all over the porch. The oscillating fans would whir softly as they stirred the delicate fronds of the ferns that would hang from the rafters. A place of serenity and peace. A restful place to sip ice tea or lemonade, perhaps coffee in the morning or a beer with Matt in the evening when the sun went down. She added clay flowerpots for each side of the six steps to her mental list. Maybe deep pink or pinky red geraniums and some inkvine trailing down the pots. A sob caught in her throat. Would she ever sit here on the porch with Matt?

Lily swiped at her wet eyes again as she ran down the steps and around to the backyard. She called the dogs. "Now, Buzz!" she shouted. Both dogs came on the run. They looked at her expectantly before they streaked off again. She followed them to the far end of the property. She'd never walked this far back simply because of the thick undergrowth. Now, however, the dogs had flattened a path of sorts. She gasped at what lay before her. "A cemetery!" she said in surprise.

She ripped at the vines to expose tiny stone tablets. A children's cemetery. She continued to attack the vines, yanking and pulling until she saw a row of larger stones, eight in all. It was the last one that brought her hand to her throat. She leaned over to run her hands over the letters. MARY MARGARET, and underneath the name, the words, THE WISH KEEPER.

Lily's hand involuntarily went to the pen-

111

dant around her neck. She clasped it in her clenched fist. A moment later she was on the ground, her body rocking back and forth, her vision blurred. The golden Lab reared back and howled, a mournful sound, as Gracie pawed at her legs. Lily knew where she was, but she couldn't focus. She knew the dogs were close and no harm would come to her, but she couldn't see. Where had the sunlight gone? A blinding light attacked her as she stared forward at banks of computers and electronic equipment. Mumbled voices, the words unintelligible, ricocheted about her, causing both dogs to bark fiercely. Her eyes snapped open a moment later. The winter sun was back, the dogs vying for her lap. Her hands lashed out at the grave marker bearing the name, Mary Margaret. "What does it mean?" she wailed. Then she was on her feet running, the dogs nipping at her heels. She herded the dogs into the truck before she got behind the wheel. The only word she could think of to describe her condition was *spacey*. She reached down inside the console for her cell phone. Sadie picked up on the second ring. She started to babble incoherently.

Good, Sadie and Dennis would be there within minutes. She forced herself to take a deep breath. She almost jumped out of her skin when the contractor tapped on the truck window as she was replacing the cell phone in the console. She pressed the remote and the window slid down. She wondered if she looked as frazzled as she felt.

"Just wanted you to know we'll be finished a week from today. The painters are finishing upstairs today and tomorrow. The appliances will be installed tomorrow morning. All five bathrooms are completed. The fireplaces are working, all six of them. We tried them out yesterday. Good draw on all of them. We finished the windows last night. Your drapers will make them come alive for you, wavy glass and all. The stained glass throughout the house has been repaired so expertly it's impossible to tell where the damage was. We left the beams exposed, just the way you wanted. The wooden pegs are all intact. Everything is bright and airy. When you furnish the house to your taste, it will take on a life of its own."

Lily nodded. "Do you know anyone who would be willing to come and clear the grounds? The dogs found a cemetery in the back a little while ago. I didn't even know it was there."

"You'll find all kinds of things once the undergrowth is cleared away. I'll make some calls and get some estimates for you. I'm assuming you want this done yesterday," he grinned.

Lily forced a smile to her lips. "Yes. Several crews if necessary. I want to move in as soon as possible. Choose someone who can do the job quicky and properly."

"You can't walk through the house for a few more days. The polyurethane on the floors isn't dry. They need a few more days just to be on the safe side. I'm running your heat for that purpose. I hope you don't mind."

"No, that's fine. I'm looking forward to the grand tour."

"You're sure now that you don't want me to work on the cottage?"

"Actually, Mr. Sonner, I'm not sure at all. I rather thought I'd do it myself, little by little, but I'm afraid I wasn't being realistic. When we do the walk-through, we can discuss it. I'll make some notes. I want it to be cozy and comfortable. You know, real homey."

"I think we can handle that. I'll see you in a few days."

"Mr. Sonner, you've lived here all your life. Do you know what a Wish Keeper is? On one of the gravestones it says, Mary Margaret, and then underneath her name are the words, *The Wish Keeper.* Her last name isn't on the marker."

"I can't say that I do, but I'll ask my father. He's eighty-four, and he was born and raised here in Natchez. He knows all about the folk-lore and the ghost stories, and he does love talking about it to anyone who will listen. I'll let you know what I find out."

"Thanks, Mr. Sonner. I'll see you in a few days then."

Matt would have liked Bill Sonner. He would have considered him to be a man's man. Matt admired anyone who could make something from nothing. She was so glad the contractor had insisted on before-and-after pictures. If Matt was ever able to see them, he would be so pleased. Damn, she was tearing up again. Buzz nuzzled her neck just as Dennis and Sadie swerved into the driveway to park behind her Rover.

Sadie ran up the driveway. "What happened?"

"Follow me, and I'll show you. This is so weird I'm starting to get really spooked. I . . . Wait, see for yourself. Buzz and Gracie found it."

"It's a cemetery," Dennis said in awe.

"Brilliant statement," Lily snorted. "Read what it says under Mary Margaret's name. See, The Wish Keeper. No last name. This thing around my neck is a Wish Keeper. I had another one of those visions. That's two in one day, Sadie. I'm really jittery. I wish you could have heard these two dogs howl. God, it gave me goose bumps."

"What did you see?" Dennis asked quietly.

"A room full of . . . computers. Electronic equipment. At least that's what it looked like. It's fuzzy, my vision wasn't sharp. Plus, my heart beats like a trip-hammer when it happens. I think my first conscious thought was I was seeing the inside of a Radio Shack. I don't understand. Does Matt work in a room like that?"

Dennis narrowed his eyes. "What kind of electronic equipment?"

Lily shrugged. "I don't know. I'm not a computer person. I did see computers and a wide screen. I think it was a wide screen. Do you know of a room like that?"

"No. Do you think you could make a rough sketch of it when we get back to the apartment?"

"I can try. Mr. Sonner, the contractor, is going to ask his father tonight if he knows what a Wish Keeper is. He's like us, completely clueless."

"I wonder who Mary Margaret is . . . was?" Sadie said. "If you don't mind, Lily, I'd like to borrow your truck and go to the library. I might be able to find something out about this property. I wish my mother had told me more about this place. For some reason she didn't like it. I can't remember why we stopped coming here, if I ever knew at all."

"Maybe you'll find something that will trigger a memory. On the other hand, maybe your mother didn't like the hot, humid weather in the summer. It could be something that simple, Sadie."

Lily turned her attention to Dennis. "Did you find out anything when you called the office?"

"Just that Marcus is like a wild hare. All he did was snap and snarl over the phone. He also told me to get my ass back to New York. There's been no ransom note, so that's a good sign. At least I think it is. I told him to call the press and cancel our announcement. We argued a bit. I won because both of us have to be there. I'm acting CEO when Matt is gone. That's about all I know. Oh, he did say he thinks Matt is on some South Sea island sunning himself and having a high old time. That's Marcus for you. I did remember something else that I had totally forgotten. I was checking through my briefcase and found a memo Matt sent to all our top people which said everyone needed to get on the same page and permanently relocate to Oregon. There's only going to be a skeleton crew in New York from April on. By year's end he wants corporate to be in Oregon. I totally agree. Marcus totally disagrees. April 1 is the deadline for relocating. It might mean something, and then again it might mean nothing."

"Do you live in Oregon?" Sadie asked as she fell in behind Dennis for the walk back to the cars.

"Yes. I keep an apartment in the city for when I'm up there. I much prefer Oregon. So does Matt. I love trees and grass and crisp air. I really like the winters because I love the scent of pine, and I love to ski when I get the chance. I have air-conditioning, but I've never had to use it. At headquarters it's different. Everything is climate-controlled. You'll have to come for a visit someday."

"Hmmm," Sadie said as she sashayed past Lily and pinched her arm to show what she thought of Dennis's comment. Lily was too busy with her own thoughts and herding the dogs into the truck to pay attention.

"We'll pick up something from Fat Mama's for lunch and bring it home," Sadie called from the car. "We can do King's Tavern tomorrow or tonight if you like." Lily nodded.

In the kitchen of the apartment, Lily cleaned out the coffeepot and put on a new pot to brew. Sadie, like her, guzzled coffee all day long. She wondered if Dennis was a coffee drinker. Probably, since Matt had coffee running through his veins. Matt. Everything always came back to Matt. *Where are you?*

Wherever it is, are you thinking of me? This whole past year you and I were on the same wavelength. Tap into me, Matt. Try. I need to know you're alive and well. If you changed your mind about marrying me, I need to know that, too. I just want you to be alive. *Please, Matt. Close your eyes and concentrate. People say that works.* When nothing happened, Lily in her agitation, yanked at the Wish Keeper hanging around her neck. Her head snapped forward, and she thought her eyeballs were going to pop right out of her head. Both dogs pawed at her legs. She wanted to move but felt like she was glued to the floor. A blizzard of images rocked past her eyes. Matt's shoe with the hole. Matt's sore arm. Lulu's Bait Shack. Charming Lily. Sound. Humming.

When she was finally able to move and open her eyes, she had no sense of time. How long had she been standing by the sink? The coffee was done perking. How long did that take? Two minutes? Three? Maybe five? Longer? She simply didn't know.

Lily walked on wobbly legs over to the kitchen table. She needed to get a grip on things, get grounded as Matt always said. Matt said so many things. How could you do this to me? Where are you? She felt tearful, anxious now. Something beyond her control was happening to her. What? Matt always used to say, throw it out to the universe and see what comes back. *Throw what out? My thoughts? My worries? Maybe I need to go to the doctor's to see if I have a brain tumor.* "What's happening?" she wailed.

"We brought all kinds of good stuff," Sadie bellowed from the doorway. Sadie always bellowed now. She said it had something to do with shouting and yelling at the newbies at Ozzie's camp. Lily didn't believe it then, and she didn't believe it now. She stared at her friend. "It happened again."

"What happened? You mean you saw something else. That makes three times in one day. Maybe we should talk to a shrink or something."

"What brings it on?" Dennis asked.

Lily shrugged. "Nothing. I was just standing by the sink waiting for the coffee to finish. I was thinking about Matt. I'm always thinking about Matt, so if that's a trigger, then that's my answer."

Lily watched as Sadie pulled plates and silverware from the cabinets. The food smelled wonderful. She realized she was starving. She shrugged as she reached for one of the white cartons. "This is what I saw this time, but there was something different. I heard noise. Humming actually. I saw Matt's sneaker, the one with the big hole in the toe. He would no more part with that sneaker than he would part with Gracie. He's had those same sneakers since he was in high school. They smell so bad. He wears Odor Eaters inside, but they don't help. I saw the words *Lulu's Bait Shack.* That's the lettering on his baseball cap that he always wears. He'd never, ever part with that cap either. I thought I heard the words Charming Lily. Then the humming. Matt always called me Charming Lily. That's it. Can either one of you make sense out of this? Dennis, you're closest to the coffeepot, so pour us a cup."

"I'm sorry to say I'm not up on this *otherworld* stuff," Dennis said.

"Me either," Sadie said, biting into a fat tamale.

"You both know how Matt always said, let's throw it out to the universe and see what comes back. That's what I did and then I had that . . . that . . . whatever it was."

"Yeah, yeah, Matt always said that and it pissed Marcus off big-time. When Matt would do it, he'd sit down and contemplate his big toe and wait for things to happen. Something always happened. Usually it was related to work. Matt would laugh and give Marcus the evil eye. I don't think Matt liked Marcus very much. He never *said* he didn't like him, it's just my own impression.

Marcus's contract is up in April. The same time he has to relocate. I think that's pretty meaningful considering all the things that are going on. Don't you?"

"Marcus has a contract. I didn't know that," Lily said, her eyes round with surprise.

"We all have contracts. Mine is the only one that is different. The others are your standard three-year contracts all the companies use. Mine reads *lifetime*. That means I'm part of Digitech until the day I die. Marcus found out a while back and from that point on, he put out a hate on me. Subtly but insidiously if you know what I mean. Matt knows because we talked about it. From the time we were little kids, we confided in one another. No secrets to our friendship. That's how I know he loved you, Lily. With all his heart. He told me he dreamed about you every night. He wouldn't leave you standing at the altar. That simply is not who he is today. He was beside himself that he couldn't spend Christmas with you, but he accepted that because he had the rest of his life to be with you."

Lily struggled with her emotions. "I learned something about myself today. All I care about is that Matt is safe and well. Yes, I was hurt, yes, I was humiliated, but that no longer matters. Love is wanting the other person to be well, happy, and, above all, safe. If he did stand me up, I'll live with it. Does that make sense?"

"Absolutely," Sadie and Dennis said in unison.

Five

It was a bedroom worthy of a centerfold in *Lifestyles of the Rich and Famous*, designed by Kathy Molizon, an interior decorator Betsy had met while vacationing in Hilton Head, South Carolina. She'd thrown tantrum after tantrum until her husband agreed to fly in the designer to decorate their apartment. The bedroom suite was the room Betsy bragged about to her friends, making sure to include the fact that the Charleston designer had come all the way from South Carolina just for her. "Just give me European flavor," Betsy had said. "I want to be the envy of all my friends." The designer had done just that. The walls were painted in a warm stonelike finish to give off a castlelike feeling, right down to the large medallion that was delicately stained in the middle of the floor. The bed tucks inside the recessed wall were detailed with triple cast-stone arches that echoed the arched shape of the windows and doors. The windows were hung with elegant silk that bunched at the floor, where inlaid detail abounded and surrounded the room.

Luxurious button-tufted dupioni silk bed-coverings were accented with silk pillows that rested against a quilted chenille headboard. Deep pile carpeting, a shade darker than the stone-colored walls, hugged the ankles and rose up to meet the even darker brocade draperies in the dressing room. The swags themselves were works of art, as were the coverings on the chaise longues. At first glance it looked like a woman's bedroom. On second glance it looked like it didn't belong to anyone and was just waiting for the right occupant to enter. Nothing was out of place, not a hair, not a speck of powder, not a hair-pin. The furniture was pecan and polished to a high sheen, with mirrors on the sides of both extra long his-and-her dressers. Betsy Collins wanted to see the *all of her* from every angle. Kathy had argued that it was too much, but Betsy held firm since, she said, she was the one signing the checks. Kathy had also expressed serious doubt about the sculpture in the left-hand corner of the master suite — a mermaid rising from the sea. Betsy's response was, the antique dealer had said the mermaid bore a striking resemblance to Betsy herself, and she was keeping it, again reminding Kathy who was writing out the checks. The same checks Kathy was still waiting for, thirteen months later. The bottom line: Betsy Collins didn't pay her bills.

Marcus looked at his beautiful wife and felt faint stirrings of desire. He did his best to squelch them since the bed was already made and his wife was wearing makeup. Those two things plus the calculating look in his wife's eyes told him he would need to look elsewhere if he wanted his desires fed. Betsy Collins liked her sex standing up so she wouldn't mess up her hair, her clothing, or her makeup. The words *trophy wife* ricocheted inside his head. Weird as it was, he did love Betsy. He jerked at the tie he was trying to knot around his neck. "When will the girls be back?" he barked.

"Not till the tenth. You know that, Marcus, so why are you asking again? Is this a prelude to another fight?"

Was it? Probably. He stared across the room at his wife and sixteen other images of her in all the mirrors. Where in the hell was she going at seven o'clock in the morning? he asked.

"To the Golden Door, sweetheart. There's nothing to keep me here. The girls are on the school ski trip, you work till midnight. Why should I sit around this apartment twiddling my thumbs? I've put on two pounds during the holiday, so I need to take them off. Do you have a problem with this, Marcus?"

Her tone clearly said he better not have a problem with it.

"Actually, I do, Betsy. You aren't going to the Golden Door. Where you're going is Oregon to pick out a house for us. This is not negotiable, so get that through your head. We need to be moved in and settled before April 1. Like it or not, we're going to Oregon."

Betsy stamped her feathered mule on the floor. Two feathers shook loose and flew upward. Marcus watched them with clinical interest. He knew his wife would bend down and pick them up the minute they landed. She wouldn't want her perfect carpeting to have feathers on it. "I told you, Marcus, we aren't moving. You can go if you want to, but I'm staying here."

"No, that won't work." He adjusted his tie, then stretched his neck. "Digitech stresses family. If we want to remain a part of the company, then this family, of which I am the breadwinner, must relocate. You knew this was coming. Now it's official. I'm selling this apartment. The Hampton house is mortgaged to the hilt. We have to sell it, too. The boat will have to go also. It takes megabucks to operate, bucks we don't have. If Matt doesn't renew my contract, we are out in the cold, sweetie. Since it looks like he's taken a powder, that leaves Dennis in charge. And since Dennis hates my guts, I'd say it's safe to assume things could go either way. Moving to Oregon will show I'm a team player as well as a family man. What's left of my stock options won't last forever. You won't be able to live this lifestyle. That means the kids come out of private school. We buy down on our cars. I can see you in a Honda Civic, Betsy. No more fifty-thousand-dollar vacations. You'll be shopping at Wal-Mart pretty soon." Her horrified look pleased him. "It won't be so easy to find another job. New employers want to know why you left your previous job. Are you getting the picture, Betsy?"

"Don't threaten me, Marcus. You know what will happen if you do that. I'll walk right out of here and half of all those stock options and half of your pension will be mine."

There it was, the thing he most feared. He could feel his insides start to shrivel. He backed down, his voice contrite. "I'm not saying it will happen. I said it could happen. I'll look for properties on the Net today. They have videos available. Maybe we can buy it that way." He wondered what he was going to use for money for the down payment. They were so far in hock he felt light-headed each time he thought about it. At one time their bank accounts had been robust. Now their nine credit cards were maxed out. All Betsy did was buy, buy, buy, spend, spend, spend. He looked at his gray hair in all the different mirrors.

Desire flooded through him again when Betsy let the satin robe drop to the floor. She had a beautiful body. High, rounded breasts, narrow waistline, flat stomach and gorgeous legs. Chiseled. Sculpted. Cold and frosty. Where did all that hot blood that ran in her veins in the beginning go? "How much did that underwear cost?" he blurted. "It's very sexy."

"Two hundred dollars."

Marcus gasped. There was so little material in either the bra or the panties he could stuff them in his ears and still have room. It also occurred to him to wonder if someone other than himself ever saw her underwear. He didn't mean to voice the question but somehow the words tumbled out of his mouth. He apologized immediately. Then he said, "We're broke, Betsy. That's the reason you can't go to the Golden Door."

"Well, if we're broke, then you better find a way to get some money because I'm going. Cash in those options of yours. I'm not changing my lifestyle. This is what you promised me, and this is what I expect. Don't switch up now, Marcus. I will ignore your previous comment and pretend you never said it. If I have to acknowledge it, then you won't like the results. Why don't you do some consulting work? I understand the rewards are handsome. You do see where I'm coming from, don't you, dear?"

He bit down on his tongue so he wouldn't have to tell her how many of his stock options he'd already turned in just to keep her happy. Suddenly he felt sick to his stomach as he watched her image in all the mirrors. She would be the death of him yet.

Would the end justify the means? He started to feel sicker, so sick, he rushed to the bathroom and lost his breakfast. He brushed his teeth, aware of his wife's eyes on him.

"Don't forget to leave the housekeeper and nanny their checks, Marcus. I hate it when you forget."

Shit. Now he was going to have to stop at the safe-deposit box and cash in some of the kids' savings bonds meant for college, deposit the money, and come back home to pay the help and write out a check for Betsy and the Golden Door. How had he been reduced to this? Stealing his kids' college money made him a thief. The end *would* have to justify the means. He couldn't keep on living like this.

It was ten-thirty when Marcus climbed into a taxi for the second time in as many hours.

He started to shake when the cell phone rang. He broke out in a sweat but managed to pick it up on the sixth ring. He deliberately made his voice brisk and professional sounding. "Marcus Collins," he said by way of greeting.

"And how are you on this fine, wintry morning?" the voice on the other end of the phone asked politely.

"As good as can be expected. And you?" Marcus queried, stalling for time.

"Just fine. I heard on the news this morning that Digitech has postponed their announcement. Do you mind telling me why, since I have a vested interest in this information?"

"As you know, Dennis Wagner is acting CEO when Matt is unavailable. I guess he decided to wait. That's all I can tell you. I might know more when I get to the office."

"And the other . . . we still don't have the last part of the . . . transaction. We were very generous in our up-front gift."

Marcus felt his stomach start to roil. He thought he could taste his own bile. "Dennis has the last . . . what you need. I can't force his hand. The timing is all wrong right now. I told you this just the other day."

"Then perhaps we should cancel our business. You refund the advance, and we'll call it a day."

Like he had half a million dollars. He'd just

stolen his kids' college money to pay for their nanny, and this asshole expected him to cough up half a million dollars. He almost lost it then. He forced a laugh even though he felt like crying. What the hell, he had nothing to lose now. "If that's what you want, it's fine with me. I realize now my price was far too low. Savarone offered me three times as much. I was going to call you later today to tell you that. What's it going to be? I'm almost to the office. Match Savarone, give me some extra time, be patient, and it's yours. I'm too old to dick around like this."

"How much time?"

"At least a few days. Matt's out of touch right now. Three days, maybe four. Maybe I'll only need one. I just don't know. It's the best I can do. You willing to match Savarone?"

"Yeah. Same deal."

"Okay."

Marcus paid the driver. The minute he got out of the cab, he took great gulping breaths of air to ward off the dizziness he was feeling.

What the hell kind of monster had he turned into?

A thirty-million-dollar one. *And, how long will that last? Provided I get away with it.* He started to feel sick again as he stomped his way through the lobby to the elevator that would take him to the eighteenth floor.

"This is all your fucking fault, Matt," he grumbled to himself as he jabbed at the elevator button. "It's all your stinking fault."

It was dark again. He could tell by the smells around him that he wasn't in the same place. He lay perfectly still, straining to hear the voices from the next room. He wished he didn't feel so *woozy*. He was too tense, too wired, too out of it to know what he was feeling other than scared that his life might suddenly come to an end. He needed to relax and turn his head. Maybe shaking it would clear it. He also needed to breathe normally. All easier said than done. He wished he knew what day it was, how long he'd been out. When were these jerks finally going to make a decision as to what they were going to do? Who the hell were they anyway? They didn't act like professional criminals, even though they had found and confiscated his cell phone, but more like bungling, we-make-the-rules-as-we-go-along amateurs. Just his damn luck. He thought about Lily and Gracie. The two loves of his life. How were they dealing with his absence? He felt himself relax. He was also able to breathe a little easier, or so it seemed, and his ears didn't seem to be so clogged up.

"That was the last of it. Did you think it was going to last forever? Look, the nurse left the drugs in the drawer after Pop died because it was paid for. We can't keep giving the guy that stuff. Who the hell knows what it will do to a normal person. As it is, if we ever get caught, there's a little word called *premeditation*. Now what? We've been riding around for over four days now. Isn't it time we made some concrete decisions? People in town are going to start asking questions as to why the store is closed. Four days for a death in a family is about it. We're going into five days now. This is making me nervous."

"This is it," Matt heard another man say. "When it gets light out, we'll fetch him in here, feed him, and get down to business. Another day, two at the most, and we're outta here. So far there hasn't been anything on the news or in the papers. I'll pick up today's paper when I'm in town. For someone as rich and famous as he is, it doesn't seem like anyone cares about this guy. I'm going back into town now. I'll spread the word we inherited a sizable amount of money and are going to close the store for the winter months. I'll put a sign on the door, pay the utilities in advance for a few months. Same thing for the house. We walk away and don't look back. We stay away a year, maybe two, and then it will be safe to come back. *If* we want to come back. We leave clean, owing no bills, casting no suspicion on ourselves. Look, we've been robbing people at ATMs for three years. We never got caught. There's no reason to believe we'll get caught now either. If he gets frisky, all we have to do is tell him we know where the chick is."

"Hey!" Matt bellowed.

"What do you want?"

"I want to talk to you. Now!"

"Later, Mr. Starr."

"My ass, later. Now means now!" Matt waited, his head pounding. "In case you forgot, I'm the guy with the money. Now, goddammit!"

"All right, all right. What is it?"

Matt strained his eyes to see in the darkness. "I want to cut a deal with you."

"That's pretty funny, Mr. Starr. Look around. You're tied up. We're walking around. What kind of deal could you possibly offer us?"

"More money for my freedom. More money than you will be able to suck out of my private accounts. If it's your plan to head off for some banana republic and live happily ever after, it ain't gonna happen, gentlemen. There isn't that much money in those accounts. I know how you can get a million dollars in minutes. It will be a simple matter to transfer it electronically. I can do that. Only if you let me go."

"That's not going to happen, Mr. Starr. Now that we know you have an extra million, we're going to want that, too. No deals."

Matt sucked in his breath. He felt like his head was swimming in Jell-O. "A million dollars is a piss in the bucket when you have to divide it three ways. How long do you think it's going to last you in that banana republic?"

"Then what the hell did you bring it up for?"

"Because I want you to let me go."

"Go back to sleep, Mr. Starr. Tomorrow is a whole other day."

Shit, had he just done what he thought he had? Stupid is as stupid does. How was he going to get the million dollars he put in Lily's account? Hell, for all he knew she could have taken the money and split when he didn't show up for the wedding. Maybe he should go back to sleep and let the rest of the drug wear off. That was the easy way out. He needed to stay alert in the hope of hearing something that would help him later on.

"Where are we?" he demanded.

"Even if we told you, you wouldn't know. This is the last time I'm going to tell you to keep quiet."

Matt clamped his lips tight. He wished he knew how long it was since his abduction, if Dennis and Marcus had announced Digitech's Open Door 2001, and what reaction it generated if they had. That thought forced him to think about Marcus and his betrayal. He felt heartsick that a friend, a man he'd brought into the company because of his knowledge and expertise, would turn on him for money. He'd paid him a staggering salary, given him stock options, all manner of perks, company-paid car, a Porsche, astronomical bonuses at year's end, and, as of last week, the man had nothing to show for it except maxed-out credit cards, overdrafts at three banks, piles of debts, mortgages, and a demanding, greedy wife. Marcus Collins had sold him out. Or he thought he had.

Little did Marcus know that Matt had been onto him from the minute he'd heard he was slowly, little by little, cashing in his stock options. That had been the red light, all the warning he needed to start looking into Marcus's private life. He wished now that he had taken Dennis into his confidence, but he hadn't. Instead, he'd let the rumors flourish that Dennis was leaking company secrets so he could lull Marcus into a false sense of security.

Considering his present circumstances,

there was nothing he could do but go to sleep. Maybe he would dream of Lily. He always dreamed of Lily because he loved her. Would always love her. Forever and ever and even then. Such a silly little phrase, but it was one the two of them came up with years and years ago, before he'd lit out on her.

Matt closed his eyes, and she was there, the love of his life, asking him if he was going to break her heart again.

He cradled her head to his chest, and whispered, "I'd break my own before I broke yours, Lily. It won't happen. You're my reason to get up in the morning. Nothing on this earth gives me more pleasure than to wake and see you lying next to me. You are my life. I love you more each day. I didn't think that was possible, but it is."

"I love you just as much. I don't know what I would do if anything ever happened to you. I wouldn't be able to go on, Matt. You've become a part of me. I can't wait to have babies so we become a family. I'm going to be such a good wife to you. I don't know about that corporate-wife thing, but at home you won't have a thing to complain about. I'm going to make love to you every single day. I promise to tell you I love you a hundred times a day, and I will mean it each time I say it. I can't wait for January 1. Mrs. Matthew Michael

Starr. Would you mind if I keep my name? I'd like to be Lily Harper Starr. Legally that is."

"Whatever you want," he said, nibbling on her earlobe.

"Ooohh, that feels so . . . delicious. Do it some more."

"If I do, what will you do for me?" he teased.

Lily whispered in his ear.

Matt groaned. "Show me."

Matt kicked off the spread. Earlier the sheets had been crisp and white and unwrinkled. Pristine. Like Lily. Now they were damp and wrinkled. He didn't care. The instant Lily rolled over, his body covered hers. There was a wild mating possessiveness to his embrace when he gathered her in his arms.

For one split second he felt a head rush and a small speck of alarm and didn't know why. He felt like he was embarking on unchartered waters which was silly because he'd made love to this incredible woman hundreds of times and each time it was better than the time before.

His lips found the pulse at her neck. He licked at it with slow, tantalizing motions and was rewarded with Lily's sigh of pleasure. She curled into him so his lips could trail down to her breasts. She snuggled deeper, her fingers curling the wiry furring on his chest, felt her involuntary tremor. He could feel her shiver in ecstasy when his tongue slid into the warm nectar of her mouth.

"More," she murmured. "More, more."

He felt powerful with her words and marveled at how she suddenly took the initiative, sliding smoothly on top of him. He felt her smile when he groaned with pleasure. The heat of his body mingled with hers, setting off a banked fire he'd been holding in reserve.

She teased him then, nibbling at his ears, whispering wondrous things in his ear while she explored the wet, slick length of him. "You're so beautiful," he murmured. Her hot breath seared his skin making it impossible to think. All he wanted was to feel, to taste, to live.

Her body was warm honey, her mouth a raging volcano he sought to conquer. "Do you like this?" he moaned.

"Oh God, yes, yes, yes."

His hands moved, sliding up and down the sides of her body. Needing the closeness of her, he drew her hard against him as she moaned, arching her back. He kissed her eyes, her lips, fiery kisses that trailed along her jaw, down to the valley between her breasts. The burning heat from her body transferred itself to him, scorching his skin. She was a brushfire gone wild, a raging forest fire that only he could extinguish. Her bright eyes were burning, the only bright color he could see in the dim room.

"*Now,*" he whispered fiercely.

"Yes," Lily whispered in return.

Her body was exquisite, her responses delicious, but it was the expression on her face, the rapture and pleasure he saw there that drove him forward. He read total joy and a hint of wonder in her clear gaze, saw a lone tear in the little hollow under her eye. When relief came to both of them, her name exploded from him like a gunshot in the quiet room.

Matt's eyes snapped open. "Son of a bitch," he muttered when all he could see was darkness.

He lay for a long time trying to get the dream back, but it wouldn't come. "I love you, Lily," he said brokenly. "I love you so much it hurts."

Don't think about Lily. Think about something else. Something that won't hurt as much. Think about something that will make you angry and cause your adrenaline to surge. Marcus. No, not Marcus. You don't want to get blind-faced angry. You can always think about Marcus later when you give him his walking papers. Think about business and how you saved the day before Marcus got his hands on the last thing he needed to peddle it to his competitors. Think about your good friend Dennis and his loyal friendship. Think about XML, short for Extensible Markup Language that will add new powers to the World Wide Web. In easy terms it will become the standardized way of storing raw data and text, spreadsheet numbers, employee records, and pricing lists. The "structured data" can then be imported and instantly manipulated by software programs and devices that had nothing to do with creating the stuff in the first place.

XML. Something he and Dennis had been working on for years along with every other software company, the high-tech equivalent of the bar code. Net surfers will be able to excerpt numerical tables and text from a web page and then paste them into a word-processing application on a PC, which will then allow the PC user to edit or annotate the text or manipulate the numbers. Think about where it stands today when a PC user cuts and pastes from a website, text loses its formatting, and spreadsheets become impossible to manipulate. Think about how you got there first. Later you can think about how Marcus tried to steal the software. Later, later, later. Always later.

Damn, he was boring himself to death. He

hoped the world wouldn't be bored when it was finally time to announce XML.

His thoughts drifted back to Lily. He wondered what she was doing and where she was. They had become so attuned to each other this past year, he had to wonder if she suspected something might have happened to him. Would she look for him? Or, would she take the easy way out and believe he got cold feet? His stomach churned at the thought. What about Gracie, the other love of his life. Where was she? Was she roaming the highway looking for him? The thought was so devastating he wanted to throw up.

The only thing left to him was to throw the whole mess out to the universe and wait for whatever would be. When he had been overwhelmed in the past, he had done it, and it worked for him. There was no reason to believe it wouldn't work for him now. Besides, what did he have to lose? Not a goddamn thing. He bellowed at the top of his lungs. "It's all yours! It's out of my hands now."

He listened to the two pairs of running feet. "What the hell was that all about, Mr. Starr?" one of them barked.

"I just threw it all out to the universe," Matt said tightly.

"What? You threw what where?"

"This whole mess. I threw it out to the universe. Now all the forces in the world will come down on you. It works."

"That's a crock."

"Mumbo-jumbo crap. Shut up now and go to sleep. I can't believe a man like you believes in that spook stuff." Matt was pleased to hear the man's jittery voice. He ran with his ball.

"That's exactly why, you idiot." He started spouting words that meant nothing. "I deal in energy fields and the high-tech world twenty-four hours a day. How do you think I got to where I am? When you throw it out to the universe, all kinds of shit begins to happen. You go back to where you were and wait for those things to happen. I'm going to go to sleep now. I have divested myself of your problems. You can deal with it from here on in." To clarify his point, he rolled over and pretended to snore.

"Do you believe that guy? He's as nutty-sounding as all those tech guys. He is, isn't he?"

"Sounded to me like he knew what he was talking about. I'm sorry we got into this mess. It's getting complicated. Clipping some guy for a few hundred was one thing. This . . . He's calling down the whole world on us."

"This guy is the next best thing to a rocket scientist. You know what they say about those guys. They're all fruity. Are you telling me you're really worried?" the second queried.

"We're gonna get caught and go to jail. I just know it. Then Mr. Smart-ass, who is going to take care of the store? Pop will spin in his grave. We swore to him before he died that we'd take care of the store. Well, huh, say something," the first brother said.

"Shut up. I mean it, shut up."

Matt smirked to himself as he continued to make gurgling, snoring sounds. Good, now they were at each other's throats.

Six

Lily stood in front of the bathroom mirror staring at her reflection. She couldn't understand how she could look the same and yet feel so totally different. Something was happening to her. Something she couldn't explain. She really needed to do some positive thinking about talking to a shrink. She continued to stare at her own person as she thought about all the secrets she suddenly knew. Yesterday she hadn't known any secrets. Today her head felt clogged with secrets of people she didn't even know. How was that possible? She found herself starting to shake. Sensing her uneasiness, the dogs started to circle her feet. She needed to get away from the person in the mirror. She sat down on the edge of the bathtub, her head whirling with her thoughts. The dogs crowded closer, whimpering softly.

The need to go home was so strong she bit down on her lip. Home? Which home? Where? Certainly not the green-and-yellow condo in sunny Florida. She had visited her parents there, but she had never actually lived in the lemon-lime two-bedroom apartment. She'd lived at Ozzie's Survival Camp. At times it felt like home but it wasn't. If anything it was a place to hide out from the world and from Matt Starr. This furnished apartment would never, no matter how many plants and knickknacks she bought, ever feel like home. It was nothing more than a stopping-off place.

Everyone needed a home, a family. If you had that, you really didn't need much else. A home and a family, the two most important things in the world. She didn't have either, so what home did she feel like going to? Hot tears pricked at her eyelids. Maybe it was the house on North Union Street. Maybe her subconscious was trying to tell her that house was going to be her new home. A place to sit back and wait to see if Matt Starr would come looking for her like he did the first time.

God, she was tired, and yet she'd slept for ten hours. Ten hours of nonstop dreams she couldn't remember.

"I think we need to go outside and get some fresh air. We're going to do the town, we'll check out Natchez Under-the-Hill, and from there we'll see if Gracie can pick up some clues. You, Buzz, will follow and do your thing. You know Matt. We're going to take one of his socks with us so you can pick up his scent if there is one. We'll stop by the house to see if Mr. Sonner has any news on our Wish Keeper questions.

"It's been three days now. That can't be good. I just don't understand any of this."

In the kitchen, Lily stopped long enough to tell Dennis and Sadie where she was going and why. "What are you two going to do?"

"I'm waiting for FedEx to deliver some discs and my PC. They promised delivery by ten. You girls don't have a computer, so I thought this might make things a bit easier. Maybe, just maybe, Matt sent an e-mail to the office or to me personally. I'm grasping at straws, but straws are all we have right now. On another front, my sister Rosalie is sending me some highly sensitive discs Matt and I made as a backup. Matt had a special computer room that is climate-controlled built into her house. Sometimes Matt was paranoid and other times he was so far ahead of the pack you couldn't see his dust. I've never known him not to have Plan B ready to go."

They look like they go together, Lily thought as she looked across the table at Sadie and Dennis. She felt sad knowing she was going to lose her best friend in the whole world. Now how in the world did she know she was going to lose her best friend? Intuition? The moony, gooney look in Sadie's eyes? The knowledge of her impending loss frightened her. She clutched at the pendant around her neck as though it was a lifeline. Her head jerked to the right and then to the left. For one heart-stopping moment she thought she was suffering a stroke as she was transported to another place, a dark place that smelled of stagnant water and rotten fish. A terrible smell, one she remembered from her dream. She called out asking for help. And then she was somewhere else with millions of stars wrapping her in a giant cocoon. The universe. She was nowhere yet she was somewhere. She heard words again. *It's all yours. It's out of my hands now.* Matt calling on the universe. She screamed his name. Again and again. She saw his hairy leg, the sneaker with the hole in the big toe, the thick marine cord with the knot tying him to . . .

"Lily! Damn it, Lily, you're scaring me," Sadie screamed. "Wake up! Open your eyes. Shake your head. Do something for God's sake. Dennis, do something!"

Dennis reached for Lily's arms and lowered her to the chair. His grip on her hands was strong and tight. Lily opened her eyes and shook her head. "How long was this one?" she whispered.

"A minute, maybe less. What did you see? You saw something, didn't you?"

Lily looked at her friend's ashen face and nodded. "This is going to sound . . . bizarre but I was . . . I was in the bayou, and then I was floating in space. I felt like I was in this . . . this special cocoon and was surrounded by stars. I was out there somewhere in the universe. I heard Matt shouting, 'It's all yours' and 'it's out of my hands now.' I saw his leg and shoe, the one with the hole in the toe. His leg is tied to something with marine cord, very thick and heavy. That's it." She pulled her trembling hands free of Dennis's tight grasp and shoved them into the pockets of her sweatpants. She felt disoriented, frightened, and angry. Angry because she didn't know what was happening to her.

"Here," Sadie said, shoving a cup of coffee into her hand. "Drink this," she ordered, biting down on her knuckles as she stared at her friend.

"I woke up this morning knowing all these secrets about people. It's like I have this giant file folder in my head, and everyone in this town has a page. I don't know the people. I can't even think what the secrets are. I just know I know them. Do you think my brain is going to explode? I wonder if that's the same thing as having a stroke. Something is happening to me, and I have no control over whatever it is. Look, I have to get some fresh air. We'll talk about this later. I need to be by myself for a little while so I can think about all of this."

"Where are you going, Lily? We need to know. Make sure you take your cell phone with you."

"I'm going to the bank first. I want to transfer the money Matt put into my account to my brokerage account. I can do a wire transfer. I'm not comfortable keeping that kind of money in a savings account. I still don't know why Matt did that. See, this is what I mean. I had no intention of going to the bank this morning. I haven't thought about that account since we discussed it last. Now all of a sudden it's paramount I do this. I'll be back by noon. Here's your FedEx guy. I can see his truck. Lunch is on me today. But only if the bogeymen don't get me," she said, leering at Sadie's ashen face. "I'm okay, Sadie. Once these spells are over, it's all back to normal. We need some food for dinner. If you shop, I'll cook." She was babbling. It occurred to her to wonder if she was making sense. Obviously she was, since no one was questioning her.

"You're sure you're okay?"

"I'm okay."

A light drizzle of rain was falling when Lily herded the dogs to her 4-by-4 and helped them into the backseat. She walked around the back end of the truck and climbed into the driver's seat. She let out a mighty sigh. Maybe *she* needed to throw something out to the universe. If she was lucky, what she threw out would collide with what Matt threw out and then . . . *voilà*, the problems of the world would be solved. The thought was so silly, she found herself gritting her teeth in frustration.

Her first stop was Deposit Guaranty National Bank, where she conducted her business in under fifteen minutes. When she climbed back into the truck the dogs greeted her with wet licks to her neck.

"We're going to Natchez Under-the-Hill. I took Matt there the last time he was here, Gracie. You might still be able to pick up his scent. It's really nice, and you can see the steamboat, *The Isle of Capri*, sitting in the water. Sadie doesn't much care for it, but I don't know why. Tourists used to come here to Natchez to see the stately mansions on top of the hill. Somehow, though, those same tourists could never resist the legends or the magic of the name: Natchez Under-the-Hill. It used to be infamous. There are a few shops, some restaurants, and, guess what, they have Miss Floozie contests all the time. I wanted to enter one, and Matt said no. Silver Street used to be the place to be late at night if you wanted to party. Matt doesn't like to party. He said he did Bourbon Street in New Orleans with Dennis one year, and that was enough to last him a lifetime." The dogs cocked their heads and listened intently as Lily's jittery voice returned to normal. When she parked the truck, they waited patiently for her to secure their leashes before they bounded out of the truck.

"Take a whiff of Matt's sock. You, too, Buzz. Good. Now let's see what we can find. We're going to walk up one side and down the other. Then we'll go back to the house and you can run in the yard."

It was raining harder, and the wind was starting to kick up. Lily yanked at the hood on her jacket. She stepped into an empty doorway of John Martin's restaurant. There were very few people around, which surprised her. Maybe it was the rain. If she undid the dog's leashes and let them roam up and down the street, what would they find? It was a stupid idea, and one she rejected the minute it popped into her head. Maybe she should go into one of the shops and buy an umbrella. Bad idea. Holding an umbrella and two dog leashes would not work. She turned around when Gracie started to paw the door behind her. She whimpered, a heartbreaking sound, as she sniffed at the brass plate at the bottom of the door. Buzz growled.

"The store's closed because," she said peering at the sign, "of a death in the family. What's wrong, Gracie?" She cupped her hands around her eyes to peer into the dim store. Stunned at what she was seeing, she could only gasp. The inside of the store was what she'd seen in one of her spells. What did it mean? She stepped forward again and stared through the plate glass. A tidy store with shelves of computers, televisions, printers, copy machines, and VCRs. Was she dreaming? "It's okay, Gracie. We're going to figure this out, but not here." Off in the distance she heard an ominous roll of thunder at the same moment she felt a light touch to her arm. She whirled around.

"Mr. Sonner. I was just going to go out to the house to see if you spoke to your father."

"I just came down to Under-the-Hill to talk to one of the shop owners who wants some work done. By the way, I spoke to my father last night. You need to understand, this is all folklore. My father said he vaguely remembers something about Wish Keepers, but said it was a woman thing. He said every clan had a Wish Keeper. It was usually the oldest female member of the family. The title was passed down from generation to generation. Always to the oldest and then to their oldest.

All the family members told the Wish Keeper their secrets and their wishes and she held them safe. Supposedly she marked them down on a scroll of sorts. This, too, was passed on, along with an amulet on a string. The Wish Keeper wore it around her neck. He said there were those who said it was a silly bit of nonsense, and then there were those who swore by the Wish Keeper. One other thing my father said was that the Wish Keeper would go into a trance from time to time and *see* things. The past, the present, and the future. He scoffed at that, but he said his grandmother told him about such things, and while he doesn't believe in that kind of rubbish, he couldn't understand why his grandmother would lie to him. That's it in a nutshell. I almost forgot. He drew a picture of the Wish Keeper. Understand now, his hand trembles, and his eyesight isn't what it used to be. If it doesn't look like anything you recognize you might try looking it up in the library under old Natchez folklore. I hope this helps you. I really don't know anyone else who might be of help."

Lily held out her hand for the slip of paper that had been torn out of a notebook. "I appreciate your help. Did you ask your father if he knew who Mary Margaret was?"

"I did. I walked to the back of the property

to see those old stones, and I told him what they looked like. He didn't know a Mary Margaret. Since he claims to have known everyone in town, I have to assume she was before his time. He did ask me a rather strange question, though. He wanted to know if you mixed up wish keepers with sin eaters? A sin eater is someone who is hired at an early age to absorb the sins of anyone dying. Usually each family had one. When a person died, the family held a wake and surrounded the room with food, all favorites of the deceased. The sin eater then ate the food and in doing so, absorbed all the deceased's sins, and that person went to heaven. When the sin eater died, there was no one to absorb all those sins, and he or she went straight to hell, taking everyone's sins along. Not an enviable job in my opinion."

"That sounds awful. I never heard that story before. I'm sure the wish keeper is quite different from a sin eater. It was nice of you to take the time to do this for me, Mr. Sonner. I'll see you in a day or so. It looks like this is going to be one of those all-day rains, doesn't it?"

"It surely does. Paint and varnish don't dry well when the weather is like this. You take care now."

"Mr. Sonner, just a minute. Do you know who owns this store?"

"Calumet Laroux did own it, but he passed away six or seven months ago. His three sons decided to keep the store. It's a nice little store, but sometimes I have to wonder how it supports three salaries. Of course none of the boys are married, so that might explain a few things. They inherited the family house, one of those old mansions on the hill, and they live there with Cal's old housekeeper. I think old Cal was well-off. His ancestors made tons of money when cotton was king way back when. The Laroux house is on the Pilgrimage tour in the spring and fall. It's worth going to see. The whole house is full of priceless antiques, as are most of the houses on the tour. This particular store is Natchez's answer to Radio Shack but with more inventory."

Lily smiled. "I was just curious because it's closed, and there's a notice on the door about a death in the family."

"You don't say. Now I wonder who that might be. Maybe a relative of old Cal's from up North. He had some cousins that lived in Syracuse. Saw them at the funeral parlor when old Cal passed on. I took my father so he could pay his respects. That's how I came by the information I just gave you. I imagine they'll be opening up the first of next week."

"I'll see you in a few days, Mr. Sonner. Thanks again for your help." Gracie continued to whine at the door. Buzz hugged her legs. "Shhh, it's okay, Gracie. We'll leave as soon as the rain lets up." She bent down to hug Buzz, who hated thunder and lightning.

The moment the rain eased a bit, Lily ran for the truck, the dogs at her side. Gasping with the hard run, she shrugged out of her wet sweat jacket and tossed it into the cargo hold. It wasn't until she fumbled in her pocket for the car keys that she realized she hadn't looked at the slip of paper Sonner had given her.

Lily's jaw dropped when she stared down at the drawing showing the likeness to the pendant hanging around her neck. A chill washed over her. What did all this mean? She was tempted to rip the pendant from her neck, but she didn't. Somewhere deep inside she knew she was meant to wear it, to keep it safe. She didn't know where the thought came from, it was just there.

Warm air rushed from the Rover's heater. "We're going home, guys. It's too wet and cold to romp in the garden. Tomorrow is another day," she said breathlessly. She could hardly wait to tell Sadie and Dennis her news.

The dogs bounded ahead of Lily to the apartment door that opened as though on command by Sadie. "I heard your truck door slam. Distinctive sound. Plus the dogs of course. Ah, Lily, Dennis has sort of . . . kind of . . . taken over the living room with all his . . . *stuff.* There are wires and cords everywhere. I have no clue what he's doing or how or why. It's Greek to me. You and I are sadly lacking where computers are concerned. I think we need to think of him as Tarzan and we're two Janes. Remember how dumb Jane was when she first met Tarzan? That's us. That's not to say we can't learn, at some point. He's almost hooked up and ready to boot up. Don't ask me what that means."

Lily stared at her friend. *She's really pretty,* she thought. *More so now that she's interested in Dennis.* Sadie glowed, and there was a sparkle in her eyes that hadn't been there before Dennis came into the picture.

"Let's go into the kitchen. I have something to tell you. I don't feel much like going out to lunch, do you? I got soaked before. I don't feel like getting wet all over again."

"I went grocery shopping while Dennis was doing whatever it is he's doing. We have all kinds of food. I can make up a salad and grilled cheese if that's okay."

"That's more than okay. That's wonderful. Look at this, Sadie. Tell me what you think it is."

"It looks like that junky necklace I found in the closet and gave to you. The one you're wearing. By the way, why are you still wearing it?"

"Because for some reason I can't make myself take it off. Every time I have one of those spells, I'm holding it in my hand. Now, I'm going to tell you what Mr. Sonner's father said about the Wish Keeper." As she talked she watched Sadie's eyes widen until they almost popped from her head.

"What does it mean, Lily?"

"You're the one who said your mother stopped coming here, and you didn't know why. Is it possible she was next in line to be a Wish Keeper? Maybe it's more than we know. Maybe your mother didn't want the responsibility. Maybe she's the one who tossed the necklace into the back of the closet. You said you hated it here. Maybe you heard things or saw things when you were little along with maybe things your mother said to you. It's possible you forgot them, and it's possible I'm just talking to hear myself talk. I would like to know if anything happens when you put it around your neck. Grasp it in your hand and see if anything happens. You have to be the one to take it off my neck."

"You're spooking me, Lily. What if nothing happens?"

"Then nothing happens. It's probably all hocus-pocus anyway. Come on now, take it

160

off my neck and put it around your neck. Okay, now grasp it in your hand and wait."

"Abracadabra! Holy Moley! Bubble, bubble, toil and trouble," Sadie chanted. In spite of herself, Lily burst into laughter.

"Nothing's happening. I'm sorry, Lily. I was hoping it would work for us. It's just a junky necklace. Toss it out." Sadie laid the necklace in the middle of the table. Both girls stared at it with unblinking intensity.

"You would have been next in line to . . . to . . . carry on, Sadie. But then if your mother didn't do it, maybe the . . . what's the word, it all skipped a generation or something. Maybe whoever lives in the house is the one to be the Wish Keeper. You gave it to me, then all these weird things started happening. Remember me telling you this morning that I felt like I knew a lot of secrets? I don't feel like that now. I feel like a huge weight has been taken off my shoulders. Why don't we just put it away somewhere and forget about it."

"That's a very good idea. Do you want to test your theory one more time first? Grab it and see if anything happens. Then when nothing happens, you can stop worrying about a brain tumor or having a stroke. You won't have to go to a shrink either," Sadie said, her voice cracking with anxiety.

Lily reached out to pick up the amulet and then pulled her arm back.

"Maybe you're supposed to make a wish. I bet that's it, Lily. Wish for Matt to come back. Do it!"

Lily's arm snaked out a second time. Before she could change her mind she picked up the pendant and chain and closed her hand into a tight fist. Her eyes wide with fear, she waited for something to happen. She closed her eyes and made her wish. "Nothing."

"Then I guess it's just a bunch of tomfoolery," Sadie said.

"Guess so. Maybe it's different when you actually wear it. Maybe it has to be part of your person. I think we're both a couple of morons for even thinking this trinket could mean anything." The words were no sooner out of her mouth when her body jerked forward, and her vision blurred. Her hands reached out to claw at the air around her. She heard Sadie scream for Dennis, felt the pendant slip from her hand to land at her feet. But it was Matt's voice that snapped her to attention. *"If you take my clothes, I'll freeze to death. If you leave me here to die, that will make all of you murderers. You son of a bitch! Take your fucking hands off me!"*

Dennis reached for Lily's hands and held her steady. Lily heard the pendant slide across

162

the tile floor. No one made a move to pick it up.

"I think we should sweep it up with the broom and a dustpan and dump it outside in the Dumpster," Sadie said as she backed away from the spot where the necklace landed.

"We can't do that, Sadie. I have to put it back on. It's how I see Matt. What else do we have to go on? It's not as though it's hurting me. I think we proved there's nothing wrong with me health-wise. It's paranormal or otherworldly, extrasensory something or other. I wish I knew more about stuff like that." Lily walked over to where the pendant lay, bent down, picked it up, and slipped it around her neck. She shrugged.

"While I'm making lunch, tell Dennis about your trip to Natchez Under-the-Hill," Sadie said. "Let's hear what he has to say. By the way, are you all plugged in?"

"I'm good to go right after lunch. Nasty day out there. Cold, too," Dennis said, his eyes on the pendant hanging around Lily's neck.

Lily carefully recited the morning's events. "Gracie kept whimpering and sniffing at the door of the electronics store. I looked in, and it's the same room I saw during one of those spells. At first I thought it had something to do with Matt, but you said you didn't have a room like that. This store looks like a Radio

Shack. Later, if you want, we can go take a look. I have no idea what it means. But, if it means nothing, why would it be a vision? So far everything I've seen has to do with Matt. I think we need to make a plan and actively start to search for him."

"Where? I'm all for anything that gets this show on the road, but where do we start?"

"That store. It's better than nothing," Lily said, craning her neck to stare into the living room at the computers and printers Dennis had lined up. "What do you hope to learn with all that stuff?" she asked, pointing to the living room.

"I won't know till I check things out. I'm going to phone the office now. Call me when lunch is ready." Lily nodded.

Sadie turned to stare at Lily. "He's cute, isn't he?"

"I guess so," Lily said absentmindedly.

"How do you suppose he'd be in bed?" Sadie whispered.

Lily's head jerked upward. "Don't you think the question should be, how do *you* think he'd be in bed?"

"I bet he'd be *spectacular!*" Sadie said dreamily, tears dripping down her cheeks from the onion she was peeling.

"Spectacular is good. But you can't go to bed with Dennis. You just met him."

"I'm not talking about now. Maybe . . . sometime. I get all warm and fuzzy when I'm close to him. Isn't that strange, Lily?"

"Rub your hands under water with a stainless-steel spoon or spatula and the onion smell will go away. You can do that if you cut up garlic, too. I saw that on Martha Stewart," Lily said, eyeing the cucumber in Sadie's hands. "Rub some garlic on the sides of the bowl." Seeing Sadie's surprised look, she said, "I watched the show a few times when I was in my nesting mode. I even watched the Emeril Lagasse and Bobby Flay shows. You're making that salad all wrong. You're supposed to rip the lettuce, not slice it and you score the cucumbers and radishes. Carrots should not be in chunks, they should be thinly sliced or shredded. People don't like to chomp on carrots. Green peppers should be added sparingly because they're gassy."

"Yes, ma'am," Sadie said smartly. "I'll gladly turn this over to you if you want to do it yourself."

"No thank you," Lily said sweetly as she leaned farther back in her chair so she could hear Dennis talking on the phone. She brought her finger to her lips to warn Sadie to be quiet.

"Well where the hell is he, Meredith? You're his private secretary. You're supposed to know where your boss is at all times. Page him. Now!"

"Ooohhh, I love it when a man growls," Sadie whispered. Lily rolled her eyes.

"What do you mean he's not answering the page? It's almost noon. When he does show up, ask him how he'd like to move to Oregon in the morning instead of in April," Dennis snapped irritably. "He has my number."

"Well Marcus isn't in the office. That's so unheard of it's suspicious. He never goes out to lunch for fear he'll miss something. He's always in by the crack of dawn. I have to assume nothing in the way of a ransom note has come in. He'd call me if that happened. At least I think he would. Do you get a news station here at noon?"

Lily shrugged. "I have no idea. I don't watch television during the day. Try CNN. Channel 31. Why?"

"Just a bad feeling I have."

Dennis fiddled with the remote until he had the channel he wanted. He waited patiently for the weather report to finish. The top-of-the-hour news would be on in seconds. Lily gasped when she saw her picture spread across the screen. Sadie dropped the red pepper she'd been slicing as all three of them peered at the screen.

"Goddammit! I knew he was going to do

166

something like this. I would strangle the son of a bitch if he walked through the door right now. Now there's going to be a feeding frenzy. We need to talk fast and come up with a plan. The newshounds will be on your trail any minute now. Matt has always been news, but the wedding and all will make this a major event. I think, and this is just my opinion, you should make a statement the instant they track you down. Say you both agreed to call off the wedding. As to Matt's whereabouts, you know nothing. You both agreed to some time apart. It was an eleventh-hour decision on both your parts. Too much is hanging on the company. This is Marcus's way of pushing for the announcement and the huge bonus that follows it. The bastard isn't answering the page because he knows we're an hour behind New York. He's like Gary Cooper, he likes to do things like this at high noon to get everyone's attention. Too many people are asleep or getting ready for work for an early-morning news flash. Six o'clock is when people are going home. Noon is when you get the biggest audience. He actually paid for someone to do a survey on that. I'll fix his ass. Watch this."

Lily blinked.

Sadie picked up the red pepper and washed it off.

Both girls listened intently as Dennis worked

his cell phone. "Personnel," he barked. He identified himself, rattled off his I.D. number, and said, "Terminate the trash collector and reinstate the old company if they still want the job. If they don't want it, take bids and find a new company. Do it now. Call their office and do not allow them in the building today. The workers all have pagers and cell phones. No, I'm not just talking about the New York office, they have cousins or uncles or someone who collects trash in Oregon, too. Get rid of all of them. Call me back and fax me their response at this number.

"It's a small, nit-picking issue, but it will make Marcus get off his duff. He'll call me just to tell me what he thinks about it. At least it's one way of getting his attention, short of going to New York. Would you like me to make some coffee?"

"Yes, by all means. I think I was supposed to do that, but Sadie and I got to talking. You seem at home in the kitchen, Dennis. How'd that happen?"

"My sister. When we were younger and our parents were working, it was her job to start dinner. On her busy days the job fell to me. It was either learn or starve. You should taste my Chicken Kiev. I love the smell of perking coffee."

Sadie beamed.

Lily smiled. She continued to smile as Dennis managed to rub shoulders with Sadie standing at the counter near the sink. He snitched a slice of cucumber. Sadie swatted him playfully. The smile on Lily's face dissolved. Matt always used to snitch pieces of vegetables from the salad bowl. She'd swat him just the way Sadie did. *Oh, Matt, where are you? Am I ever going to see you again?*

She fought the urge to touch the pendant hanging around her neck.

Seven

Matt was jerked to wakefulness with a hard jab to his shoulder. It took him a minute to realize someone had covered him with a blanket at some point during the night. How considerate of them. What the hell kind of crooks were these guys? He rolled over onto his back but said nothing. He knew they were untying his leg. That had to mean they were on the move again. Then again, maybe not. It was light outside, he could see thin slivers of light creeping under the door. So far everything had been done under the cloak of darkness. Why, he didn't know, since he'd seen their faces clearly at the ATM machine.

"Up and at 'em, big guy. Let's go. You get three minutes to take a leak, then you trot right back inside. Any funny business and you'll regret it. Take his shirt and shoes. That'll get him back inside in a hurry."

The light hurt his eyes. Shit, now he was going to get a headache. He could feel it hammering away at the base of his head. He did his best to check out his surroundings as he unzipped his pants. Lily always said stay alert, pay attention to details. Trees, pine mostly. Ground almost frozen. Damn, it was hard to pee and jiggle from one foot to the other. "If I ever get out of this, you guys are going to pay for this," he muttered.

"Let's go, Mr. Starr. We don't have all day."

Any other time, he would have given the voice an argument. Not now, though. He was freezing. He jogged forward and into the brick building. Deserted. Inches of dust and cobwebs. No furniture. The three men were sitting on thick stumps of wood they must have carried in from a woodpile. A laptop was set up on a fourth stump. Obviously the fifth stump was for him. He walked over and sat down. Someone tossed him his shirt and shoes. He put them on gratefully and hugged his arms to his chest. He looked across at the man opposite him, who was flexing his fingers over a computer keyboard. He knew what was coming.

"Let's have it, Mr. Starr."

There was no point in pretending he didn't know what they were talking about. He rattled off an account number.

"To the best of your knowledge, how much is in this account?"

"Around $67,000."

"Close enough. It's gone. Next."

Matt mumbled a second account number. "How much?"

"I think it's $121,000."

"Close enough. Next."

"There's only one more — $4,500. I don't know what you expected, but in my opinion this is not worth a kidnapping."

"Let's do the million-dollar one. Spit it out, Mr. Starr."

Matt sucked in his breath. He repeated the number of Lily's account she'd made him memorize.

"Were you joshing us about that million dollars, Mr. Starr? There's only $501 in the account."

Matt's eyes popped open. "You must have entered the wrong number. Do it again."

"Oh, it was in there, but it's gone now. It was wired out early this morning to another account. I can't access it. This isn't going to get you any brownie points, Mr.Starr."

"You can't hold me responsible for what she does. She's probably pissed to the teeth that I left her standing at the altar, and she's probably in the south of France lying on some beach with some tanned hunk. And it's all your fault, you son of a bitch!"

"I don't much care for profanity, Mr. Starr. You could be right. So, let's move along here and hit your brokerage account."

Matt licked at his dry lips. He longed for a cup of strong black coffee. Good-bye twenty-two million dollars. He realized in that one moment he would give up everything he owned to be free of these men. He said the number slowly and distinctly. *Please,* he prayed, *don't let them figure out there is more than one brokerage account.*

"That's a nice round sum, Mr. Starr. Next."

"There is no next. Everything else is tied up through the company. You need a six-man approval to hit any of those accounts. If you don't believe me, I'll give you Dennis Wagner's number, and he'll verify it. Don't be greedy, gentlemen."

"If you're lying to us, we'll just pay Miss Harper a visit and take it out in trade. Now, is there anything you forgot to tell us?"

"No, there isn't," Matt said.

"How is it that Mr. Bill Gates made billions and you have a measly few million? Tell me that."

"Bill Gates is number one. I'm only number five. Big difference. Now that you transferred all my money, how about giving me a few bucks for some coffee and let me go."

One of the men dug around in his pocket and withdrew a five-dollar bill. He wadded it up and tossed it to Matt. "Okay, boys, strip him down and we're outta here."

"What do you mean, strip me down. If you take my clothes, I'll freeze to death. If you leave me here to die, that will make all of you murderes. You son of a bitch! Take your fucking hands off me!"

"We're leaving you food and coffee. You can build a fire in the fireplace. Be sure to open the draft. This place has been abandoned for a long time. You won't freeze if you stay put. When we get to where we're going, we'll call the authorities and have them pick you up. It might take a day or so. If you choose to ignore my advice, then you will be killing yourself. To show you how considerate we are of your welfare, we carried in enough wood to last you two full days. Nice doing business with you."

And then he was alone, stark naked, with only a pile of wood and no matches.

He jumped up and down, waving his arms to try and stay warm. What would Lily do? She would say, use your brain, move, don't stand still. He had no clue what he should do next. Would he freeze to death in two days? Probably. If he could find some stones, he might be able to rub them together to form a spark. If he didn't rub his fingers to the bone trying. The Burger King paper bag would catch fire quickly. But would the wood be dry enough to catch fire? Son of a bitch! He was free, but he wasn't free. "If I ever find you bastards, I'll fucking kill you," he shouted at the top of his lungs.

Overhead he heard a flurry of sound.

Bats!

And he was buck-ass naked.

Marcus Collins leaned back in his leather chair and looked at the New York skyline. He was on a short leash, and he knew it. If he didn't do something quickly, it would be all over. It was all going to come down on him and then where would he be? CYA and look out for Number One. Was there a way to bluff his way through it? Was there a way to get out clean and not look back? Just how smart was Dennis Wagner? Pretty goddamn smart according to Matt Starr. He didn't need to be a rocket scientist to know Dennis was onto him. The proof was in the paper he was holding in his hand. Dennis had just canceled the trash pickup firm and reinstated the old company. How the hell was he going to explain that to Betsy? Let's see, what had he gotten for that little favor. Ah yes, stand-up sex in the bathroom for all of thirty seconds. He could picture the exact time, the place, the color of the towels, and the color of the bath mat he had been standing on. He could visualize what he was wearing, at the time and what Betsy was wearing, which was almost nothing. She'd smiled that time. Maybe it wasn't a smile at all but a grimace. He'd given her best friend's husband a million-dollar contract for trash disposal, and he'd gotten a small kickback and a quickie that left much to be desired.

He felt ashamed, and he felt guilty. A time or two he actually felt hatred for himself. All he felt now was stark fear. Because of that fear, he'd gone down to the parking garage yesterday and called the Network News Office and the *Wall Street Journal*, disguising his voice and informing them of Matt's no-show at the wedding and his subsequent disappearance. At best it was a temporary diversion. What he had to do now was find the last sequence to the XML and turn it over to his competitor, collect his thirty million, and split. All he would be doing was taking a page out of Matt Starr's book and disappear. If Matt could do it and get away with it, so could he. He wondered if he would miss Betsy and the girls. He shrugged. The girls were miniature versions of Betsy. No, he wouldn't miss them much. He'd bet his Presidential Rolex she would have some rich guy on the string within a week. The thought bothered him. He knew in his gut his little family wouldn't miss him at all.

Once, when he was young, he'd had ideals. He wondered exactly when they disappeared. Was it when he married Betsy or was it when he realized Dennis Wagner would always be second-in-command? Or was it when his brother approached him to ask for help in paying their father's bills at the nursing home? His chest heaved in anguish when he remembered what he'd said to Owen that awful day. "Let the state take care of him. He's got Alzheimer's and doesn't know if he's in a ten-thousand-dollar-a-month nursing home or one that costs two thousand. He gets his medicine, he has nurses, and they take him for walks. That won't change at a pricey home. The answer's no, Owen."

The shame running through his body was so thick he gagged. Owen had never spoken to him again. Owen was a vice cop in Ridgewood, New Jersey. His wife Margie was a fifth-grade schoolteacher. They had five kids and lived in a split level on a shady cul-de-sac. His kids were active in sports, and Owen umpired Little League. Margie was a Brownie leader and baked and cooked wonderful meals. They were a real family. Owen told him once he and Margie had sex four times a week. Owen had taken a second mortgage on his house in Ridgewood to pay for their father's nursing care. As a family they went to see him every Sunday afternoon.

Marcus wished he could cry. There was no way he could ever make that right.

He looked at the house on the screen of his computer, then clicked the mouse and it disappeared. With things in such turmoil there was no point in searching for a house. He wasn't going to Oregon in April. If his luck didn't change soon, his ass might be languishing in a federal pen in April. The thought was so horrendous, he jumped up, removed his jacket, and jerked at his tie. He rolled up his sleeves, narrowed his eyes, and sat down at the computer. All he needed was Matt's or Dennis's password and he was home free. He pressed the buzzer on his desk. "Meredith, hold all my calls. That means all, no matter who it is. Say I left the building. I have my pager. Order me a corned beef sandwich and don't forget the pickles. I'd appreciate some fresh coffee."

He'd tried this all before and gotten nowhere. He'd never been this desperate before, though. Maybe this time, if he didn't give up, he'd crack the password. He heaved a mighty sigh and brought up the program he'd helped design. He stared at it for a long time. Instead of typing, he picked up the phone and called the Bellflower Nursing Home. When the operator's cheerful voice came on, he said, "This is Marcus Collins, could you tell me how my father is today?"

"He's having a good day today, Mr. Collins. He ate all his breakfast and went for a walk with one of the volunteers. He's scheduled for a haircut later this afternoon. Then around four-thirty he gets to drive the golf cart if he's up to it. He likes that a lot."

"Is there anything he needs or wants?"

"No, I don't believe so. I'm looking at his chart. Mr. Owen Collins was here on the weekend. Mrs. Collins brought a tin of cookies, and the children played cards with him. He's doing as well as can be expected."

"Thank you. That's good to know."

Marcus knuckled his eyes when he hung up the phone.

Now it was time to figure out how he was going to handle his new life. All he needed was one little word that had no more than eight letters.

Matt stomped around the room, cursing and shouting his frustration. At least he felt warmer for the effort. Whatever he was going to do he was going to have to do it soon. Once darkness came and the temperature dropped he was going to be one sorry man.

At least he could see with the light filtering

through the grimy windows. He looked around, trying to figure out what kind of building he was in. An old hunting lodge maybe. Abandoned. Maybe somewhere, possibly upstairs, there was something he could use for clothing. He heard the bats rustling again up under the eaves. They'd probably come out in a flock once it got dark. *Move, Starr, move.* He ran then, coming down hard on his heels, just enough to jar his entire body. He didn't feel so cold when he stomped and ran. He took the stairs two at a time and actually felt his body flush with the effort.

He looked around in dismay. The loft was empty. He gritted his teeth when he heard the rustling again. He pounded his way over to the window. He dropped to his knees to see how high up he was from the ground.

Knees. What was he kneeling on? A box? A window seat? Window seats were always used for storage. Growing up he'd had a window seat in his room right under the dormer window. He'd kept his baseball glove, his bat, his tennis racket, and his hockey skates in the box. His breath escaped his blue lips in little dry puffs. *Please, God, let there be something in here I can use. Please. Please.* He was afraid to lift up the lid, afraid he would see nothing in the bottom. Damn. He thrust up the lid and shouted in glee. Blankets. Wonderful warm blankets. Flannel shirts, corduroy trousers, green Wellington rubber boots. A quilted jacket of some kind. Wool socks. Lots of wool socks someone had knitted. Thank you, God. No underwear. He felt disappointed. Within minutes he was bundled up to his chin. Blessed warmth. He was about to close the lid when he noticed a fat white candle and a tin of matches on the bottom. Manna from heaven. "Thank you, God. I swear, I will do something good when this is all over."

This was what happened when you tuned in to the universe. Let them all laugh. Did he care? No, he did not.

Now what should he do? Should he take his chances and leave this snug harbor or should he wait till morning and get a fresh start? He could build a fire, eat the contents of the Burger King bag, and make a cheerful night of it knowing he was going home in the morning. Home to Lily and maybe together they could find Gracie. His heart fluttered at the thought of his dog and how she might be wandering around, trying to forage for food. Maybe Lily was gone, along with the million dollars he had insisted he put in her account. Her million dollars. Possession was nine points of the law. If she had left with the money, how could he blame her? He couldn't. Well he had the rest of his life to find her.

All he had to do now was figure out where he was and how to get back to civilization. He needed to think about the men who had brought him here, too. They'd transferred his money to bank accounts somewhere. Wherever that somewhere was, that's where they were going. Or were they? His money was probably all over the world by now, being transferred from one account to a hundred others. God alone knew where it was. Two days, they had said. Did that mean it was going to take them two days to get where they were going? Or was that to throw him off? Did they know about the blankets and clothes under the window seat? More than likely. Maybe they thought he was stupid and didn't have the brains to explore the loft. Somehow or other he rather thought they had left the stuff for him to find. From the beginning they said they weren't murderers.

Hot damn, he was sweating. He wished he knew what time it was. Way past noon he thought. Maybe two o'clock or later. Too late to start out without knowing where he would have to spend the night.

He clomped downstairs, the Wellingtons making loud clopping sounds on the steps. They were too big by several sizes, but the four pairs of socks helped to fill them. If he didn't move fast, or run, they would stay on his feet. He heard the bats again. Were they rabid? What would they do when night fell? Did they come out in flocks and fly about, or did they go outside? Maybe they only roosted in the house during the day. He felt totally ignorant. He'd bet anything Lily knew all there was to know about bats. Charming Lily, the love of his life. He reared up suddenly and threw out his arms. *Let her know I love her. Let her know I'll travel to the ends of the earth to find her.*

It was amazing that fast food could taste so good, he thought, as he chomped on the cold Whopper. The French fries were equally delicious even though they were cold, too, soggy and greasy. He ate every single one. The icy coffee was better than the finest champagne. He loved every mouthful.

His stomach full, Matt threw the logs on the fire along with the burger bag and waxed containers that held the coffee and French fries. He struck a match from the tin and watched the dry wood spring into flames. Now the trick would be not to let the fire go out. The moment he heard a high-pitched scream, he whirled around, his heart leaping in his chest. There was nothing to be seen in the dark corners. Where had the sound come from? And then he saw them. Bats, falling down the chimney into the fire. He raced upstairs for one of the blankets under the window seat, galloped back down the steps, and did his best to beat out the flames. In his life he'd never heard such squealing and screeching.

The moment the blanket caught on fire he knew it was time to leave. He bolted and almost lost one of the Wellingtons in his haste to get out the door. *How was I supposed to know there were bats in the chimney? No one said anything about bats. They told me to build a fire.* He sat down on a fallen log and looked back at the building where he'd been held a prisoner. Hundreds of bats were flying in crazy circles all around the house. He ran then because he didn't know what else to do.

When he couldn't run anymore, he looked around for a log to sit on. He had no idea where he was. The moment his breathing returned to normal, he took stock of his situation. He was in the woods, that was for sure. The heady scent of pine assailed his nostrils. It reminded him of his youth and Christmas. He'd always gone with his father to chop down the tree and then set it up in the living room. He loved the smell of the branches and the sap on his hands.

It would be dark soon. He had to think about where he was going to spend the night and how he was going to stay warm. Maybe he could break off some of the lower pine branches and make a bed of sorts and use more of the branches to cover himself. Even though he was warmly dressed, the ground would be cold and damp. His rear end felt cold because the trousers were too big and air rushed up his legs. Underwear, especially jockeys, kept your butt nice and warm. Someday he was going to write all this in his memoirs. If he lived to write about it.

The woods were thick and dark, the undergrowth dense. How was he to get out of there? He had no knife to hack at the vines and thickets. Each time he stomped his foot the Wellingtons came off. It was all going to be an exercise in futility. How long would it take to starve to death? There were no berries or nuts around. No water. How long before he started to dehydrate? Lily knew all these things. Well, Lily wasn't there, and he had to do the best he could.

Was he going north, south, east, or west? Maybe he could tell when the sun set. The only problem was he couldn't see the sun through the thick canopy of trees. Was he going to die out here? How long before his cold, stiff body would be found?

Dennis. Dennis would look for him. His good buddy Dennis would never believe he stood Lily up. Dennis was as dumb as he was about this survival stuff. Give him a computer and he had no equal, but his performance during the Extreme Vacation had been so dismal Matt had cringed. His own had been no better. He had to believe that somehow Dennis would come to his aid.

Lily, I am so sorry. If you truly love me, then you won't believe I deserted you. I can only hope you listen to Dennis and are trying to find me. Don't give up. Please don't give up. I'm going to do my best, but I don't think it's going to be good enough. Me asking for help. That's a hoot, isn't it?

He realized he was tired but knew he had to keep moving, to cover as much territory as he could while he could still see. He took a deep breath and started out again, a little slower this time so as not to use up all his energy. He did his best to calculate the time by counting to sixty over and over and ticking off the minutes on his fingers. He'd walk for forty minutes if he could hold out that long and then try to make himself a shelter for the night. He needed a weapon, a big stick. Just in case. What kind of animals prowled during the night? Lily would know, but he didn't. Suddenly he felt so stupid he wanted to cry.

A smile tugged at the corners of his mouth at the thought. His mother had told him once that big boys were allowed to cry. She'd said,

"When something hurts real bad, Matthew, it's all right to cry. Crying will make you feel better." It was a pity his father wasn't of the same opinion. Tears were a sign of weakness for him. He wanted a tall, strapping son who would take on the world and conquer it. Matt had to wonder if his parents would be proud of him today, had they lived. His mother would have been proud of him if he pumped gas for a living. Not so his father. He remembered how he'd cried at his mother's funeral and even afterward, but he'd been dry-eyed when his father was lowered into the ground. That first year he'd gone to the cemetery almost every day to talk to his mother, pointedly ignoring the other grave. Once he thought he'd felt her presence. And once he thought she'd whispered something in his ear that sounded like, "Enjoy your life, son. You don't need to keep coming here. I'm watching over you."

He'd stopped going then and only went to the cemetery around Christmas and on Memorial Day. The past two years he hadn't gone at all. He raised his eyes and looked upward. "Can you help me, Mom? I don't know what to do, where to go. As much as I miss you, I'm not ready to meet up with you yet."

He couldn't go another step. The damn boots were giving him blisters. A rotten log beckoned, and he sat down, dropping his head into his hands. He did cry then because his mom had told him a long time ago it was okay for big boys to cry. Angry with himself and his circumstances, he started to curse. "Sorry, Mom."

Matt struggled with the piney branches, but they were hard to break off because they were wet and thick. His hands were black and sticky with the resin, but at least he had a bed of sorts. Would the thick pine boughs keep him warm during the night? He'd know soon enough. All the light was suddenly gone. He lowered himself to the ground and pulled at the pine branches until they covered him from head to toe. He struggled to remember one of the prayers he'd learned in Catholic school, prayers he hadn't said in a very long time. "Our Father . . ."

While Matt Starr prayed, Marcus Collins cursed. It was almost eight o'clock, and he was no further ahead than he was when he settled in around noon. Eight hours and nothing to show for it. He yawned and stretched his arms over his head. He needed a break, a diversion. He'd order a pizza and work another hour, then call it a day. He'd go home and think up some lies that would get him some extra time. He adjusted the lamps before he walked out to his secretary's office. He looked down at the mound of pink slips. Calls he had to return. He pawed through them as he called to place his order for the pizza. The guard would bring it up when it arrived, and he wouldn't have to worry about running down to pay the driver. Matt had accounts all over the city for takeout. Once in a while, Matt did something he approved of. He winced at the tone of some of the messages. He had yet to check his private voice mail or e-mails. They were probably just as angry-sounding. Betsy had called five times. Okay, no point in returning her call. He knew her friend had called to inform her about losing the contract for trash pickup. Like he gave a good rat's ass about that. Twelve calls from Dennis. Screw you, buddy. One from his tailor — his new suit was ready to be picked up. Something to look forward to. Another call from the kids' ski lodge saying both his girls had fevers. What did they think he was going to do, rush to Maine and bring them home? That was Betsy's job. Screw that, too. Six calls from Eric Savarone's secretary, Martha. Two calls from two different banks. So he was overdrawn again. Or Betsy was overdrawn. Same difference. Thirty-two different calls from the media requesting interviews about Matt Starr's disappearance. *Like I'm really go-*

ing to return any of those calls. Marcus snorted his disdain. *Let them put their own spin on things.* And then the mystery caller. No name, just a number. Well, he knew who that was. He'd talked to him earlier in the day. No rush on that one either.

Marcus tossed the pile of slips into the trash basket and headed to the executive washroom, where he washed his face and hands, drying them on a fluffy white hand towel. He combed his hair, straightened his tie, and left the room, but not before he turned off the light. He was always frugal about turning off lights, and it was a big bone of contention with Betsy and the girls.

Outside the washroom, the lighting dimmed suddenly, a sign that everyone was gone for the night with the exception of a few hardy souls with no home life. The elevator pinged as the door slid open. Marcus reached for the pizza box, thanked the guard, and headed back to his office.

He felt lonelier than he'd ever felt in his life. He tried to straighten his shoulders, but they remained slumped. The loneliest man in the universe.

Universe! That was it! Instead of going into his office, he raced down the hall to Dennis's office. He looked around in dismay. Where the hell was Dennis's computer? He ran farther down the hall to Matt's office. Some irony here, he grimaced. What he was about to do was something he didn't want to show up on his own computer. Later, when they put two and two together, they would check the logs, the computers, and anything else they could think of. His pizza order would be on file, too. It was so easy to evade the sign-in sheets, it was pathetic. Still, it paid to be cautious.

Marcus slammed the pizza box down on Matt's desk and sat down. His nimble fingers attacked the keyboard. He typed in the word, *universe* and sat back, his heart pounding inside his chest. His fist shot in the air the moment the program activated. "Yesss." He was in. He felt almost giddy as he worked his fingers. There it was, the final phase, the part he'd been locked out of, thanks to Matt and Dennis. He shoved discs in, copied, and recopied. It all took less than fifteen minutes. The moment he finished and exited the program, he shrugged into his jacket and topcoat, totally forgetting about his burning hunger and the cooling pizza. Seconds later he returned for the pizza box and tossed it onto his own desk. He returned a second time for the pink message slips in the trash. He fingered through them until he found the one he wanted from the girls' teacher who was on the ski trip. He laid it on the desk next to the phone. It would buy him some time. Let them all assume he was heading for Maine. He left a note to that effect for his secretary.

Now he was free to leave. He looked back once from the door leading to the elevator. "Fuck you, Matt Starr."

He got off the elevator at the fourth floor and took the stairs to the underground garage. He patted the discs in his inside breast pocket. He walked over to the phone and dialed the all-too-familiar number. The phone on the other end was picked up on the second ring. "If you meet me now in the lobby of the Hyatt, we can do our transfer. It has to be now. I have to leave for Maine right away. My little girls are up there on a school ski trip, and both of them are sick. I have it all. Now. No, it has to be now. I'll be there in twenty minutes."

His second call was to the man named Eric Savarone, Matt's equal in the software game. This time the phone was picked up on the first ring. "I have it all. You want it, it has to be now. I'll meet you in the lobby of the Plaza in ninety minutes. Don't dick around because I won't wait. I have to leave for Maine, my little girls are both sick. Of course you can peruse it. This is it, the whole ball of wax. Ninety minutes."

At eleven o'clock, Marcus Collins stood in line at the Swissair gate, waiting to board his flight to Zurich, sixty million dollars richer. His laptop secure in his hand, he smiled at the flight attendant and took his seat in the first-class cabin. He immediately ordered a double scotch on the rocks.

He settled back. He'd just pulled off one of the biggest software scams in the industry with no one the wiser, and if his luck held, he had a three-day jump on it all. So, fuck you, Matt Starr, Mr. Man of the Year.

Eight

Lily stared out the kitchen window at the parking lot below. She blinked at the gaggle of reporters, photographers, and the television truck from CNN. Matt Starr was news. Big news. That made her news, too. Without a doubt all the men and women standing out there already knew Matt had left her waiting — twice — at the altar.

"They can't call because I have everything hooked up, and the phone line is in use," Dennis said. "Hanging out downstairs is their only recourse. The best thing you can do is go down and make a short statement. That doesn't mean they'll go away. And they'll follow us wherever we go. We need to think of a way to outwit them. Sometimes I really hate the press because they can make your life absolutely miserable. Other times I love them when they act decent and professional."

"What should I say?" Lily asked as she fingered the Wish Keeper around her neck.

"Make it short and sweet. Say calling off the wedding was a mutual decision. Say you both want to think things through for a little while. Tell them you're staying here, and Matt is off somewhere, but though you don't know where exactly, you will definitely be in touch. Period. I'm glad now that we didn't bring the police into this. Sadie and I will watch from the window. Don't answer any questions. Say what you have to say and leave it at that. They'll throw all kinds of stuff at you to get a rise out of you. Don't fall for it. Remember, when you don't say anything they can't twist it and come back at you. Don't let them put words into your mouth. That's Matt's philosophy."

"If that's Matt's philosophy, then it's good enough for me."

Lily was back in the kitchen in seven minutes. "They're like a pack of jackals. God, how does Matt deal with all that?"

"He doesn't. He hates it. Usually he leaves it up to either me or Marcus. Marcus loves giving interviews and being quoted. When they photograph him, he's untouchable. We're Matt's buffers. Now what?"

"Now I'm going back to Natchez Under-the-Hill and take another look at that electronics store. Where's that sketch I made for you, Dennis?"

Dennis handed her a slip of paper. Lily stared at it intently. "I can't be sure. I need to have it with me when I look in the windows."

"And then?"

"And then I don't know. We need a starting place. There's something about the store that is bothering me. Whatever it is, it bothered Gracie, too. Right now it's all we have to go on."

"I'm going with you," Sadie said, slipping into her jacket. "I'll take Buzz, you take Gracie, and we'll pretend we're going shopping. It's pouring rain, so those guys out there aren't going to be that interested in following us. If they do, all they'll see is us shopping with two dogs. Dennis can stay here and do whatever it is he's doing. We'll take our cell phones with us. If anything goes on, or you come up with something, call, okay?"

Dennis nodded.

Fifteen minutes later, Lily parked the Rover and they all trundled out and ran for the street.

"There it is, Sadie. Right between John Martins and the Under-the-Hill Saloon. The blue van that followed us just parked. That means they're going to be watching us. One of us will buy something in that little store so we have a bag to carry. Just pick up some junk. Gracie is getting antsy. She's picking up on something. She did the same thing when we were here earlier. Let's just be nonchalant and peer in the windows. There's a dim light, so we can see fairly clearly now that it's starting to get dark."

"Oh, God, look, Sadie. The sign is different. The one I saw this morning just said the store was closed due to a death in the family. Now it says the store will be closed until further notice. In the few hours since I was here, they came back. Well, *someone* came back. There's a lot of high-end, pricey stuff in there. Who would go off and close a store like this and leave it indefinitely? I don't know what the crime rate is here in Natchez, but this looks to me like an open invitation for serious theft even though the sticker says an alarm company is monitoring the premises. The inside looks just like the picture I drew with the exception of the counter. This means something, Sadie. I feel it in my gut. Quick, run next door to the store and buy something. I have an idea."

Sadie was back within minutes with a plastic bag full of gift candies.

"All you bought is candy!" Lily grimaced.

"Dennis has a sweet tooth. It was a bargain. What's your idea?"

"Head for the truck. Come on, Gracie. Good girl. That's it, jump up. They're watching us. Call information and ask for the phone number for Calumet Laroux. See if they'll give you the address. If they won't, we'll have to stop at a phone booth and look it up. We'll try to lose these guys and head over there if you can get the address. My gut is telling me something is wrong. Always go by the instincts of a dog. You and I both know that. This dog is trying to tell us something. I just don't know what that something is. Yet."

"Got it," Sadie said triumphantly. "Two-oh-seven Jefferson Street. I think it's between Wall and Canal. Same street as King's Tavern, just further up."

"We'll find it, but first we have to shake the blue van," Lily said. "Hang on, we're going for a ride. Keep watching the side-view mirror, and let me know as soon as we lose them."

Lily darted up one street, down another, crossed a third, and then roared back up the cross street before the skies opened and buckets of rain started to fall. "I'm cutting my lights and taking the next cross street. Hang on, Sadie."

"You did it, you lost them," Sadie squealed as she craned her neck to look behind her. "Where are we? I can't see the street sign."

"I think we're on Rankin. I can't read the sign either. I have to backtrack. This rain is something, isn't it?"

"Yeah, it is. What are you going to do when

we get to that house, Lily?"

"We're going to knock on the door. What we do after that is going to depend on what Gracie does. With this awful rain, no one is going to pay much attention to us, that's for sure."

"Okay, here's Jefferson," Lily said, turning the corner. "It's the second house from the corner because the first one is 205. I can see the numbers clearly in the coach light. I'm going to turn the lights off again. Let's get out quietly and walk up to the porch, assuming there is a porch, like we belong here. We have to keep the dogs quiet. Maybe we should walk around back just to be on the safe side. Do you see anyone?"

"Not a soul. There's hardly any traffic either. Do you have a flashlight in this rig?"

Lily laughed. "It has everything. I could live out of this truck if I had to. Shhh, don't make any noise now. Don't slam the doors, ease them shut. You take Buzz. I'll hold Gracie's leash. See, she's agitated already, and we haven't even gotten to the house."

Gracie strained at her leash, her ears flat against her head, her tail tucked between her legs as she dragged Lily forward to the walkway leading to the garden and the back porch. Rain sluiced down as the wind kicked up. An owl made itself heard from deep in the backyard. "It's totally dark inside, not even a glow from a night-light," Lily whispered. "Do you think they have an alarm system?"

"I have no idea. One would think so. Oh God, you aren't going to . . . break in, are you?"

"It depends on Gracie. Atta girl," she said as she let go of Gracie's leash. The shepherd bounded up the six steps to the back porch. She did a crazy dance, running from one end of the porch to the other before she stopped by the door and pawed at it.

"I guess we have our answer. She senses something. You don't see Buzz acting like she is. Something isn't right about this house. I didn't see one of those alarm company signs out front. Give me the flashlight. They usually put the alarm pad next to the door so the glowing buttons alert any would-be burglars. I don't see one, Sadie. We have two choices. We can either break one of the panes of glass and unlatch the door, or we can kick it open. The downside to breaking the glass is the lock might be one of those new things that latch from the top or the very bottom, and we won't be able to reach it. The wood is old. Kicking it open will make noise, but it's raining pretty hard, so the sound might go unnoticed. I'm going to do it, Sadie. You can wait in the truck if you don't want to be part of it."

"No, I'm okay with it. On the count of three we kick, right?"

"One! Two! Three!" They looked at one another as the doorframe splintered, and the bottom hinge on the door shook loose. Gracie raced inside. Lily shouldered the door aside and walked through the opening, Sadie and Buzz behind her. The first thing she did was to shout Matt's name over and over.

"What are we looking for, Lily?"

"I don't know. I think we just need to follow Gracie and see what she comes up with. Hold the flashlight down toward the floor just in case someone walking by spots a light that isn't supposed to be on."

They watched as Gracie zipped through the house, snapping and snarling. She barked once, an alarming sound as she thundered her way to the second floor, where she stopped at the second door on the left of the hallway. They continued to watch as she padded around the huge room sniffing everything before she came to a final stop at the closet. The shepherd reared back, then slammed her huge body against the louvered doors. The doors crashed inward. Sadie pulled and tugged at the door and leaned it against the wall as Gracie disappeared inside the closet. When she backed out of the closet she had Matt's sneaker, the one with the hole in the toe, in her mouth. Lily's face drained of all color as her knees buckled.

"That's Matt's sneaker!" Sadie screamed. She dived into the closet and pulled out a small bundle of clothes.

"He's dead, isn't he?" Lily whispered. Tears rolled out of her eyes and down her cheeks. She crawled over to where Gracie was sitting, hugging Matt's shoe between her paws.

"No, Lily. This . . . this doesn't mean he's dead. It doesn't mean any such thing."

"Yes, yes, that's what it means. Whoever lives here killed him and hid his clothes. They probably stole his car, his wallet, his watch, anything he had on his person. Oh, God. We have to call the police," Lily said, yanking at the Wish Keeper around her neck. She fell backward, her head rolling to the side until her cheek pressed up against Matt's shoe. She felt herself cowering as bats swarmed in all directions around a brick building whose windows were boarded up. Movement to her left allowed her to see Matt running away, green boots on his feet. Pine branches whipped to the left and the right and then darkness, total darkness, the only sound coming from the squealing, swarming bats.

Lily rolled over. "I saw him! I saw him, Sadie! He was wearing green boots, you know, those rubber things that go up to your knees. Bats were swarming everywhere around some kind of brick building that had a chimney. Some of the windows were boarded up. There were all kinds of pine branches. They were everywhere. Then it got dark. I saw him. I saw the green boots plain as day. He was running away. I saw him. I actually saw him. Pinch me, Sadie. I'm not dreaming, am I?"

"No, you aren't dreaming. If you saw him, that means he's alive and well. This shoe and the clothing mean nothing since he's wearing green boots. I wonder what that means. Are we going to go to the police now?" she asked anxiously.

"No. We have to put everything back the way we found it in case these people come back. I know I can't get that shoe away from Gracie, so I'm not even going to try. I am going to take the other one with us. Matt loves those sneakers. Let's prop this closet door back up, toss those clothes back in there, and get out of here. I guess the back door will have to stay as is. We can call the police and say we were driving by and thought we saw a prowler. Mr. Sonner said the house is full of priceless antiques. We don't want to be responsible for them being stolen. I'll find a way to send a money order to pay for the back door and the closet door. I feel so . . . I don't know what the word is . . . elated . . . fearful but elated. We have to find him, Sadie."

"You're thinking he's somewhere on the Trace or maybe out by Anna's Bottom, right? Lily, good as we are, and I say this with all modesty, we don't have a prayer of finding him in those woods. There's got to be around four hundred thousand acres, and it's all federal land now. I know that because I read it in the paper not too long ago. I have no idea how big Anna's Bottom is. I don't even know if you're allowed on the property. Are there parks there? Do you know? We might have a chance if he was at that wildlife preserve. A chance is being real generous. You know the one, Saint Something-Or-Other. I see the signs all the time, but the name eludes me at the moment. I think places like that are closed for the winter. It sounds logical that whoever snatched him took him to a place like that and turned him loose. No one goes to those places in the winter. Did Matt learn anything when he took our course?"

"Not much. For a while he thought it was a game. He knew we'd get him back safe and sound. However, sometimes Matt is like a sponge. He soaks stuff up, and you don't realize it until later when he regales you with the whole thing. I'm going to attempt to draw the building I saw. First thing in the morning, I'm going to go to the historical society and see if anyone recognizes the picture and, if we're lucky, can tell us where it is and how to get there. We're going to pack up and start searching as soon as we have something definite to go on. If you don't want to go with me, Sadie, it's okay. I'm taking Gracie and Buzz with me. I'm not sure about Dennis. He's a bit of a prairie flower when it comes to the outdoors. He might slow us down. What's really worrying me is if Matt really is out there, how long can he survive with no food or water? I'm just assuming he has no food or water. He doesn't know how to forage. Gracie did better than he'll do. It gets damn cold at night. Sadie, I'm worried, and I'm really starting to get scared."

"You have every right to be scared, Lily. So am I. I think both of us are selling Matt short. I think he's going to be just fine. We could alert the rangers. Or don't they have rangers? At least the authorities."

"Let's talk to Dennis about it first. I don't want to cause Matt or his company any problems later on."

Lily's heart melted as Gracie got up, Matt's shoe tightly clamped between her teeth, and walked out the door. Such devotion. Lily hugged the other worn, smelly sneaker to her chest.

Human devotion, animal devotion. It was called love, pure and simple.

Matt woke and knew it was daylight because the forest wasn't as dark as it had been when he lay down hours ago to go to sleep. He wasn't cold, but he was hungry and had no idea what time it was. The moment he stood up, every single bone in his body protested. He did his best to hobble about as he struggled to get his bearings. He looked for a tree to climb, but they were all too high, with no low branches, nothing to get a foothold on. There was no way he could possibly get his bearings if he didn't know north from south or east from west. Maybe his best bet would be to go back the way he'd come, to the building where he had been held captive, but he'd run blindly because of the bats. How had his captors gotten to the house? By car or on foot? People with brains didn't build a brick building in the middle of nowhere without an access road. How had he gotten to the building? Was he driven? Did he walk? Did they carry him? He simply couldn't remember.

He made the decision to go back. He looked around for the path he'd taken to get to where he was. Anything he might have trampled had sprung upright thanks to the heavy morning dew. He felt a wave of panic start to overtake him. Common sense told him panic would get him nowhere. What would Lily do? Notch the trees, mark the path anyway she could. He longed for bread crumbs but knew if he had a fistful of them he would eat every single one. He wished there was a way to sit down to a golden yellow omelette with crisp bacon piled high on the side. At least four slices of thick Texas toast with warm, soft butter and a whole pot of strong, dark coffee. Maybe some jam for his toast, the kind his mother used to make from wild strawberries, the little red ones that were sweeter than sugar balls. He loved eating jam out of the jar when he finished breakfast. His sweet for the day. When he finally got his ass out of there that was the first thing he was going to eat. For the moment he would chew on a stick and pray to God it wasn't poisonous. Stick. He needed a stick to carry. "I will get out of this," he muttered. "I swear to God, I am going to get out of this."

Once or twice during the long morning he called out and didn't know why. Maybe to hear his own voice. There was never a response.

His blisters now had blisters; before long they would get infected. He knew it was way past lunchtime. He thought about food again. The second thing he would order to eat would be a thick ham sandwich with two slices of Swiss cheese with lots of mustard on good, fresh rye bread. Two bottles of Corona beer to wash it down and then a big, as in really big, slice of homemade apple pie, the kind with raisins and nuts in it. Two scoops of ice cream and a huge mug of coffee. He groaned as he chewed on his stick.

He continued to trudge along until he saw a bright shaft of light. His step quickened, and one of the Wellingtons slipped off his foot. In his life he'd never felt such exquisite relief. He took a moment to revel in the feeling. He saw the building then. The same building he'd been in yesterday. He'd managed to get back to the building. He hobbled over to the fallen log he'd sat on the day before. He pulled off the other boot and almost cried with relief.

What the hell was he supposed to do? Maybe if he went back inside the building and up to the second floor he could open one of the dormer windows and somehow get on the roof. If he could get to the roof, maybe he would be able to see over the top of the tree line to a road or a direction in which to go forward. He thought about the bats. Would they attack him?

He clenched his teeth, wishing there was someone close enough to kill.

★ ★ ★

"This is Dennis Wagner, Meredith. I need to speak to Marcus. If he isn't there, tell me how I can reach him. Don't tell me you don't know if you want to keep your job. I called over a dozen times, and he hasn't responded. Nor has he answered his pager. Now where the hell is he?" He listened to Marcus's secretary's jittery voice and frowned.

"Marcus went to Maine? Now I've heard everything. Did he say when he would be back? He didn't say, he left you a *note?* Did he take his cell phone or pager? You don't know? Give me his home phone number, Meredith. I'll call Betsy. She isn't home either, she's at the Golden Door? Yes, give me that number. With both Marcus and me away, who's dealing with the media? Lou Sims. Okay, put me through to Lou. Yes, I have Mrs. Collins's number. Thank you, Meredith. If Marcus calls in, tell him to call me immediately."

Dennis chewed on the end of a pencil as he waited for Lou Sims to come on the line. "Everything okay, Lou? Good. How are you doing with the media? Yeah, yeah, they are a pain in the ass. Just keep saying 'no comment' until you're blue in the face. Sooner or later they'll let up. Do you know why Marcus went to Maine? What's wrong with his kids? As long as it isn't serious. Anything going on I should know about? You have my number, call me if anything happens. Otherwise, it's business as usual. I'm not doing much, just hanging out here till Matt gets back. Nah, don't believe that crap. Matt's a stand-up guy, he wouldn't leave his fiancée standing at the altar. I don't give a shit what Marcus Collins said. Who are you going to believe, Lou, Marcus or me?" He listened, and said, "So Marcus plays racquetball with Eric Savarone, so what? I play chess with some of our competitors once in a while. Hell, I think Matt had lunch not too long ago with Bill Gates. Don't get your jockeys in a wad over this unless you have something more concrete to go on. Ask Marcus when he gets back. Okay, call me if you hit any snags."

Lily and Sadie both started to babble the moment Dennis clicked off his cell phone. Lily held out Matt's shoe as she pointed to Gracie, who was lying on the floor, Matt's other shoe between her paws. "We broke into that house. We're criminals, Dennis. We could go to jail." Dennis waved away the words as though they were of no importance.

"Dennis, tell me again why we aren't calling the police and the park rangers? We're just three people, they have hundreds that could be out there searching for Matt. We're playing with his life here. These visions or whatever it is I'm experiencing aren't really helping us. He could die out there, Dennis."

"It all has to do with the company, Lily. Matt and I talked about this so many times I know the drill by heart. He absolutely refused to have security guards, said he wasn't going to live his life like that. We talked about possible kidnappings and such and he said under no circumstances were we ever to pay ransom if something like that happened. You never call in the authorities unless you have no other choice. He meant it, too. The man's my boss and my friend. As much as I want to call the police, I always pull back because our other option is us. You've got his shoes, so we know he's alive. Okay, we *think* he's alive. You did a B&E and found his shoes and clothes. In your vision he had on boots and other clothes. He's alive, I know it. He's always trusted me to do what we agreed upon. I can't switch up now. Maybe if things get dicey and there's no other choice, then I'll do it. Until I'm satisfied in my own mind, it's the three of us. Now, draw me a picture of the building. Instead of going to the historical society in the morning, run down to the police station, give them some kind of story, and ask if they can recognize the building. I think Sadie should be the one to do it. The less visible you and I are, the better it will be. Do you agree?"

Lily nodded as she reached for a pencil and a sheet of paper from the fax machine. Sadie shrugged back into her jacket and waited patiently.

"I'll stop at one of those twenty-four-hour convenience stores to get what we need. We have enough gear for Dennis, don't we?" Lily nodded.

"I'm going to pack up our gear. Sadie and I agreed to leave early in the morning. Probably four-thirty or five. We can stow our stuff in the Rover tonight just in case someone is hanging around outside when we're ready to leave. Are you definitely coming with us?"

"I'm with you for whatever good I'll be. If you remember, I didn't do so well the time the company went out with you. Where are we going?"

"That depends on the information Sadie brings back. I can't sit here any longer doing nothing. The more days that go by, the worse it will get for Matt. He just isn't an outdoor person. That's not a bad thing. I'm not a computer person, and I don't think that's such a bad thing."

"I wish we knew more about the people that own that store. That's a really fishy deal there. It kind of smacks you in the face if you know what I mean. I know it's late, but can you think of anyone we can call to ask questions about the owners of the store?"

"Only Mr. Sonner. He pretty much told me everything he knew when I saw him outside the store. He didn't seem to have any problem believing the store was closed for a death in the family. The only thing the least bit out of the ordinary was the comment he made about the store paying three salaries since they didn't do that much business. This is the only lead we have, so we have to run with it."

"Marcus isn't around," Dennis blurted.

Lily withdrew from the hall closet to stare at Dennis. "What does that mean?"

"He hasn't answered any of my calls. His secretary said he went to Maine where his kids are on a school ski trip. His wife is at a spa in California. I suppose it's logical for Marcus to be the one to go to Maine since he was the closest parent. Marcus prides himself on being the kind of executive that returns phone calls, chats, and does all that professional bullshit to get ahead. So, it's unlike him not to respond to his pager. I think he sleeps with the damn thing because he doesn't want to miss anything. I was thinking about calling Betsy when you gals walked in. I have a bad feeling where Marcus is concerned."

Lily yanked at the sleeping bags. She unrolled them and then rerolled them, trying to make them smaller and not as bulky. "I don't suppose you have any long underwear, do you?" Dennis shook his head. "What do you think Betsy will tell you?"

"Probably nothing. Still, it won't hurt to call."

"No, it won't hurt to call. Guess you're going to have to wear our underwear. Sadie's might fit you, but they'll be short in the leg so you'll have to pull your socks up high. Your feet are the first thing to get cold, then your rear end. Since you don't have hiking boots, you'll have to double up on your socks. It gets real cold early in the morning and again at night. You know about hypothermia, right?" Dennis nodded.

"How long do you think we'll be out there, Lily?"

"As long as it takes. Call Betsy. See what she has to say. Maybe it will make you feel better."

"That's a lot of stuff you have there," Dennis muttered, eyeing the mound of camping gear.

"What you pack for one day is the same as what you pack for thirty days. The same thing," Lily said.

His eyes on the mounting pile of gear, Dennis dialed from the pad where he'd written the number to the Golden Door. When the connection was complete, he asked to be put through to Betsy Collins. He was almost surprised when she answered on the first ring.

"Dennis Wagner, Betsy. I was wondering if you could tell me where Marcus is or give me the telephone number where your children are."

"Let me be sure I have this right, Dennis. You're calling me here in California to ask me where my husband is? Why?"

"I haven't been able to get in touch with Marcus. He's not returning phone calls, and he isn't responding to the pager. He left a note saying he was going to Maine, something about the girls. I'm assuming something happened. Will you give me the number?"

"I'd give it to you if I had it, but I don't. It's somewhere near Bangor. It's one of those winter resorts that has all kinds of sports, ice skating, skiing, snowmobiling, and things like that. The number should be in the directory. It can't be anything urgent or my housekeeper would have called me. I *am* the girls' mother. Is that all, Dennis?"

"I guess so. If you hear from Marcus tell him I'm trying to reach him."

"All right. Good-bye, Dennis."

"Bitch!" Dennis seethed. "She doesn't know anything. She didn't even know anything was wrong with her kids. What kind of mother is that? Those kids of hers don't know what real parents are like. Every time they have more than one day off they get sent off somewhere. When Matt and I were kids on vacation either his mother or my mother would take us somewhere. They had as much fun as we did. This is a whole new world to me. I don't much like it," Dennis mumbled.

"Everyone isn't like Marcus and Betsy, Dennis. They got caught up in this yuppie, me, me, me thing. It's all about them and no one else. They're selfish and greedy, and one day they're going to look back and wonder how it all went wrong. You aren't like that, neither is Matt or Sadie. Me either for that matter."

"Guess you're right. It's too late to call that ski place now, don't you think?"

"You could try. The worst thing that can happen is you get a recording telling you to call back in the morning."

Lily checked off her list, first-aid kit, topographical map, compass, GPS. Later when she knew exactly where they were going, she would plot in the whole area. Freeze-dried food, power bars, iodine tablets in case they ran out of water, hypothermal blanket, stove, flashlight, extra batteries, sleeping bag, one spare change of clothes, handheld communication radios, toothpaste, and other necessities. Gun. Bullets. The total couldn't exceed one-third of her body weight. She knew to the ounce that her backpack, fully loaded, would be three pounds shy of the allowed weight.

Her pile neatly stacked, Lily started on Sadie's. She half listened to Dennis as she heard the frustration in his voice turn to anger.

"What do you mean he hasn't showed up? You called him and he left the office to drive up there. At least I think he drove. What exactly is wrong with the girls and did you get in touch with the mother? No I'm not a relative and I respect your client's privacy. I'm Mr. Collins's boss, and I need to speak with him. You don't want to be the one responsible for the man losing his job, do you? Yes, I would like to leave a message and yes, ma'am, I know it's late. I wouldn't be calling if it wasn't important. Just tell Marcus to call Dennis Wagner as soon as he arrives. Would it help if I promised to send you a brand-new computer if you tell me what's wrong with the girls? I can have it shipped to you tomorrow if you give me your name and address. Yes, ma'am, it is a bribe, and I'll never deny it." Dennis scribbled furiously. "Now, what's wrong with the girls that Mr. Collins had to rush up there? Lice? Head lice? Both girls? Oh, the whole group. I thought the girls were running high fevers. Never mind. What is it you expect him to do? Yes, yes, I see, he has to be notified so there can be no comeback if the girls are allergic to the stuff you use. Lice, huh? Thank you. No, I won't forget, and no, I won't tell anyone you broke the rules. Be sure to give Mr. Collins the message."

"Lice?" Lily said. "That was his emergency? I can't picture Marcus dropping everything and rushing to Maine to agree to a treatment for head lice. Couldn't he give it over the phone?"

"Go figure." Dennis grimaced. "I'm not a parent, so I don't know how things like that work. I guess he was worried. The whole group came down with the lice." His eyes widened in alarm as he watched his pile of gear mount until it equaled Lily's and Sadie's piles.

Both dogs lifted their heads, then lowered them when Sadie burst into the apartment. "I got it! I really do! I know where the building is. The police didn't recognize it at all. They were young so they're excused. You know, before their time, that kind of thing. But, listen to this. One of the cops had just arrested this old codger for disturbing the peace. He was drunk as a skunk. He heard me talking to the officer on duty and chirped up and said he knew where the building was. And wait till you hear this. An old crony of his owned the building and they used to go hunting and stayed in the lodge. He said they used to take their boys with them and go hunting. He said some of the best duck blinds in the state are right there. The man's name was . . . Calumet Laroux," Sadie said, as though she was announcing an Academy Award winner for the best actor of the year.

Lily leaned back on her haunches, her hand wrapped around the Wish Keeper. When nothing happened she sucked in her breath, at the same time turning away from Sadie and Dennis so they wouldn't see what was happening. She rubbed at the pendant, gave it a twist and then closed her hand into a tight fist. She stared down at her backpack. Maybe she'd used up all the trinket's energy or whatever it was that transfused itself to her person. Maybe Matt was dead, and that's why it was no longer working. Maybe she was ready for the boys with the white jackets. She shook her head to clear her thoughts.

I'm coming, Matt. I'll find you. I promise. Just do the best you can until I get there. I'll do the rest.

Nine

Matt was hungry enough to chew on a doorknob. He looked down at the knob in his hand and had to wonder how many hands had touched it. On second thought, maybe he wasn't that hungry after all. What he was, was pissed-off mad. At himself, at his circumstances, and at the three dudes responsible for his misery.

Now that he had come full circle and back to his starting point, he realized he wasn't quite as confident as he'd been earlier in the morning. A yoke of worry settled itself on his shoulders as he entered the building he thought he would never see again. He walked back outside almost immediately and around to the back of the building, to see which second-floor windows had been boarded over. His shoulders slumped even further when he realized he would have to be a trapeze artist to climb out of the window, assuming he could even get it open, and then somehow climb up to the steep roof. An impossible feat, even if he was fifteen years younger and ten pounds lighter.

"Shit!"

Back inside the building, with the door hanging open behind him for light, he viewed all the roasted, toasted bats from yesterday. His eye fell on one of the bats still flopping around, whose mouth was foaming. So they were rabid after all. Now he didn't feel so bad about the fire. He turned to run, but one of his knitted socks snagged on a splinter just as he came down hard on the ball of his foot. He yelled in pain as the splinter gouged through the socks into the middle of his foot. One eye on his foot, his other eye on the flopping bat that was way too close, he ran, dragging his injured foot behind him. He had the good sense to slam the door shut before he dropped to his knees in the little clearing outside the building.

He hated the sight of blood, especially his own. He yanked at the large, rough splinter and then pulled off his socks completely, forgetting the blisters on his heels and toes. He screamed in agony as blood poured from his foot. His clenched fists pounded the ground in front of him. Now what was he supposed to do?

Get off your ass and do *something*. He looked at his foot, trying to see if there were any more splinters in the open wound. He'd come down hard on his foot, and the wood spike had gone through the three layers of his wool sock and into the fleshy part of his instep. He wanted to touch the wound, to try and squeeze it to see if any tiny splinters were gouged in the flesh, but his hands were black with the sticky resin from the pine boughs. He sure as hell didn't need an infection. Lily had said survival was basically common sense. She'd left out the word *knowledge*. He closed his eyes as he tried to remember what if anything he had learned when he'd taken the course with the other top executives. No one had punctured their foot. He'd gotten poison sumac, and he now knew what those leaves looked like. He itched just thinking of the experience. He'd never touch one of those vines again. Maybe mud. Somewhere he'd learned that if you packed wet mud around a bee sting, the swelling would go down and the stinger would come out when the mud was washed away. What would mud do for an open wound? Maybe leaves on the wound and then the mud and the sock. He was going to have to go back into the house and go upstairs to get more socks from the window seat. Then how was he going to find some mud? The ground was just short of being frozen, there was no water, and he had nothing to dig with but his hands. The leaves, if he could find leaves, would have to do. He was pleased to see the blood was starting to clot. He also knew that the wound would open up the minute he started to walk on it.

Maybe it was time to throw this one out to the universe, too. He did, and didn't feel one bit better.

Matt woke and looked around. He knew the day was going to come very soon when he would start to hate the smell of pine. At Christmas he'd have to get an artificial tree. He moved gingerly, shrugging off the pine boughs he'd broken off yesterday. He must have slept a very long time. The sun was just now creeping over the horizon. That had to mean it was around six or seven o'clock, more likely seven. Something was wrong. He didn't feel right. Then he allowed himself to feel his foot throb. He was warm and incredibly thirsty. Where could he possibly get water where no water existed? Lily would know. Sadie would know. He looked around and felt pleased with himself when he saw the heavy dew on the scraggly bushes. He crawled around, licking as many leaves as he could. It took thirty minutes of licking before his thirst was quenched. He felt proud of himself. He hoped the day would come when he could tell Lily what he'd done. He could picture her smile, see her beam with pride that he'd remembered something from the wilderness journey they'd taken together.

Matt stared around the clearing. He knew the direction he'd come in on because he'd broken and trampled the brush. Which direction should he go now? He tried to look beyond the tops of the pine trees but it didn't help. He had to choose a direction and start out.

He hobbled inside, careful to steer clear of the flopping bat, and made his way upstairs. He reached in blindly, his eyes on the eaves as he grabbed as many pairs of socks as he could. The trip down the steps was agony. His breath exploded in a loud *swoosh* of sound the minute he was outside with the door closed behind him. With the clean socks on his feet, the decision not to wear the Wellingtons was easy. He would take them with him, though, because sooner or later the bottoms of the socks would wear through.

Matt started off, choosing to go west. He didn't know why. An hour into the trek he started to feel uncomfortably warm, and his chest felt heavy. He opened the quilted jacket. The boots were heavy. He thought about leaving them behind, but Lily's words about common sense demanded he carry them. Walking was becoming more difficult even though he was basically walking on his right heel and more or less dragging it along. He tried to ignore the pain.

It was midafternoon when he realized the terrain had changed. The ground was less hard, more springy. Maybe that meant he was near water. Or maybe it meant it had rained in this section of the woods. The trees were a little more sparse, the undergrowth considerably lighter. He could actually see ahead of him for sections at a time.

It was time to stop. His right leg refused to function, and he was starting to ache all over. He was coughing, too. He couldn't carry the jacket and boots any longer.

He looked for a place to stop for the day. Maybe if he slept for an hour or so he would be able to walk another hour, possibly two before total darkness. It had become fairly routine, yanking at the scrub pine and breaking off the branches, layering the ground and then breaking off another layer of pine boughs to cover himself. He sank down on the ground, grateful for the softness of the pine boughs. As his eyes started to close, he wondered if he had a fever. He wanted to touch his forehead the way his mother used to do when he was little, but sleep overcame him before he could do it.

Help was on the way, but it was long hours away.

A light drizzle was falling as Lily led the parade out to the Rover. She carefully stored their gear and the dogs in the deep cargo hold. Sadie took the front passenger seat, while Dennis climbed into the back.

"I can find my way to Highway 61. I can put us in the general proximity of where we want to go. From there you'll have to direct me, Sadie. There's a map light on your right." She turned to look at Dennis. "This could well be a wild-goose chase, Dennis. If Sadie and I decide that's the case, then we're heading back, and I'm going to the police. Make sure you understand that. I don't care about Digitech stock taking a nose-dive or Marcus Collins or even you at this moment. Matt's been out there seven days. That's an entire week. I don't know if he has water or food. I'm hoping he does, but if he doesn't, he isn't equipped to handle an experience like this. The weather alone could do him in. I'm not selling him short, I'm telling you like it is. Do you understand, Dennis?"

"Yes I do, and I agree. Let's just hope for the best."

They rode in silence, sipping on coffee they'd picked up at the twenty-four-hour convenience store. It was full light when Sadie said, "Slow down, Lily. This is as far as you can take the truck according to the map. There might be another way in, but it's not on this map. Normally there is a front end and a back end. I imagine if this place has been deserted for a long time, the back end has overgrown. This looks like a fairly current map. Let's rock and roll, people."

"I'm sorry, Dennis, but since you weigh in at 180, you have the heaviest backpack. Remember what I said about carrying a third of your body weight. That's why. I gave you the climbing gear, the stove, the spikes, and the flare guns. Sadie and I will take the dogs and our own gear. Let's go. It's at least an hour's walk to that abandoned hunting lodge. Don't talk, conserve your energy. Pay attention to the ground. I'll notch the trees as we go along. Let's go."

An hour and twenty minutes later, the hunting party ground to a halt near the abandoned hunting lodge. Lily stooped down to her haunches and slid her backpack to the ground, sighing with relief. Dennis did the same, then sprawled on his back. To Lily's eye, he looked a pale green. "You're out of condition, Dennis."

"I was never *in* condition. Walking up and down the halls at Digitech was my only exercise. I see now where that has to change. I'm okay, I can handle this. If you can do it, I can do it. I might not do it as well, but, by God, I'll do it. Now what?" he gasped.

"We check out the building, then make a decision," Lily said. "Easy Gracie, easy. Buzz, calm down. Stay," she said firmly. Both dogs sat back on their haunches, their eyes on Lily. "I'm almost afraid to open the door," she said tightly.

"I'll open it," Sadie said. Dennis was on his feet a second later, crowding Lily out of the way to stand next to Sadie, who reached down, turned the knob and then kicked the door wide open.

Gracie gave a mighty lunge and jerked free of Lily's hold. Buzz followed and both dogs bounded into the dark building.

"Stay back. Lily, call the dogs! Do it now! This place is full of dead bats and some live ones as well. I can see foam on one of their mouths. God, I've never seen anything like this. Someone must have built a fire, and they were nesting inside the chimney. There are hundreds of them." Gracie threw back her head and howled as Lily struggled to pull her backward.

"I'll wait out here with the dogs. See if there are any signs that Matt was here."

It was nine-thirty by Lily's watch when Sadie and Dennis exited the deserted building. "Well?"

"Someone was here. The ashes are cool, but not cold. The fire was recent, within the past few days. Like I said, there are hundreds of dead bats in there. A bunch of live ones too, up in the eaves. There's a second floor. The top of the window seat was open, and there's stuff in it, old clothes mostly. Large in size. There's no food, no sign of food or water anywhere, and there's no furniture either. Most all the windows have been boarded up. That's it, Lily. I think, and this is just my opinion, if more than one person had been here, there would have been a sign. There's nothing. If they left Matt here, he's gone. Gracie would know. Do you want to trust her in there with those bats?"

"No. I'd let her loose, but I'm afraid she'll run off. We'd never be able to keep up with her. I'll loosen the leash and see what she does."

The retractable leash allowed the shepherd to move forward to the edge of the small clearing where the underbrush was the lightest. She barked furiously as she nosed the ground and pawed at it. When she made a mighty lunge forward, Lily fell to her knees, Gracie dragging her forward in her frenzy. When she backed out of the tangled vines, Lily's jaw dropped at what she held in her mouth.

"What is that?" Sadie screamed.

"It looks like a sock. Let me see, Gracie.

229

Easy girl, I just want to look. It's a sock all right. Actually, it looks like it's four socks all in one. And there's blood all over it, along with a bunch of splinters. The sock was in a layer of pine boughs. Matt made himself a bed. That's good, he's thinking. He did pay attention after all," she said quietly.

"You might want to take a look at this," Dennis said, holding up a sharp, thin sliver of wood with blood on the end.

"You don't need to be a genius to figure this one out," Sadie said. "Remember that spell you had with those green boots? They were probably too big and Matt put on extra socks from that window seat upstairs. He probably got blisters and took the boots off and got the splinter in his foot."

"When? Before or after? If he had the boots, why didn't he leave?" Lily demanded.

"I don't know. It's just a thought. Maybe he got bitten by one of the bats and is disoriented. It's possible, Lily, so don't look at me like that. I hope it didn't happen. Why don't you try yanking that pendant again. Maybe something will come to you," Sadie mumbled.

"I've been doing just that since last night." She gave the Wish Keeper a hard tug, but nothing happened. "See?"

"It's starting to rain harder," Dennis said,

pulling the hood on his jacket up over his head. The girls did likewise. "We need to find some cover."

Lily led the way to the edge of the forest and waited for the others. Gracie sat patiently, the sock firmly between her teeth, Buzz at her side.

"We have to decide which way he went. The only thing we know for certain is, he slept out here, but we don't really know if it was just last night or the night before. The pine boughs are very fresh. He could have slept here as many as three days. This is just a guess on my part, but I think he set out, went round in circles, and ended up back here. This looks like the brush has been trampled, and that would be south. But it's trampled coming in, not going out. So we don't want to go that way. If he took another direction to leave the first time, the heavy dew made everything spring upward. Or else he was extremely careful, which isn't like Matt. He can be like a bull in a china shop. We've got north, east, and west left. I say we split up. Divvy up the flares, Sadie." She spread the map open on the ground. She marked off the areas the three of them would cover. "We'll search till two o'clock and meet here," she said, putting a large red X on the three maps Dennis had photocopied the night before." It will take us roughly an hour from all three directions to get to the X, and that will give us enough daylight time to make camp. The forest is pretty thick but the rain is still going to come down, and that's going to slow us down. If anything goes awry, shoot off your flare. Any questions? Okay, Dennis, you take Buzz. He's very good in the woods. Buzz will always know how to find me. Sadie, are you okay with this?"

"Sure. See you at three o'clock."

"Okay, Gracie, let's go find Matt."

Matt woke and struggled to curl into a ball. He tried to bring his knees up to his chest, but his right leg was too stiff. He knew he had a problem the moment he pulled up his pant leg. An angry red streak was crawling up the inside of his leg. Blood poisoning. He tried to remember the last time he'd had a tetanus shot. Years and years ago. He knew he needed some very strong antibiotics. He wished he was part-Indian so he would know which leaves would work to draw out the poison. For all he knew the ones he'd wrapped around his foot could be making the condition worse. He couldn't ever remember feeling as bad as he felt at that moment. He knew he had a fever, and every time he took a breath he coughed. His chest felt like it was on fire.

It was still light out. He had to move, and he had to move now. Lily's words echoed inside his head. *The worst thing you can do is stay put.* Move, always move, don't wait. Waiting for someone or something can get you dead. Move. Crawl if you have to, but keep moving. He moved, on his hands and knees. His stomach rumbled, and he needed water. He noticed then that it was raining. Thank you, God. Rain meant he could stand still with his mouth open. He would also get chilled and develop pneumonia. Like there was really something he could do about that. He was sick. He knew it and also knew there was nothing he could do to help himself except to pray and keep moving. He wished he wasn't so hungry. He wished so many things. He wished he was a little boy playing outside with Dennis just waiting for his mother to call him in to supper. On Thursday nights she always made chicken with stuffing. Dennis liked the stuffing better than the chicken. His mother always made cherry cobbler on Thursdays, too. His mouth watered. Bread-baking day was Wednesdays. The house always smelled so good, especially in the winter. A late-afternoon snack for Dennis and himself on bread-baking day was a thick slice of bread with a scoop of yellow butter and his mother's strawberry preserves. His mother would always keep track of which one got the heel of the loaf since it was the favorite slice for both Dennis and Matt. On rare occasions, she would slice off both ends and present them with a huge smile and a big hug. He wondered if Lily would ever make bread and jam. He made a mental note to ask her. Lily. *Please, God, let me see her again. I'll do whatever You want me to do,* he thought.

Get off your ass and move. Charming Lily, my ass. Tough-as-nails Lily was more like it. But only when she had to be tough. Most times she was soft and warm. Her smile could light a room and his heart at the same time. *Just because a bird can eat berries doesn't mean a person can eat them. Remember that.* There weren't any berries at this time of year anyway. His stomach continued to growl. He looked around for the stick he'd been chewing on. He bit down on it. A far cry from fresh homemade bread and strawberry jam.

Matt felt the rain trickling down inside the quilted jacket. For a brief moment it felt cool and wonderful. Then he started to shake. *Move. Keep moving. Look for cover.* What did that mean? Move and look for cover. Should he find a spot to get out of the rain or should he keep moving? How could he do both? Just the thought of breaking off more pine boughs and making a new bed made him dizzy. He knew he didn't have the strength to jump up and pull down a branch, much less try to break it off.

It was raining harder, and before long it would be dark. His feet were cold and wet, time to put the Wellingtons on. He struggled to get them on over his soaking wet wool socks. If he lived through this, he was never going to wear shoes or socks again. Never. He felt his forehead. It was hot. Not warm but hot. He checked the red streak going up his leg. "Mom," he said in a choked voice, "I need some help. I should be able to do this myself, but I can't. Are you watching me? Am I disappointing you? I'm trying, Mom. I'm really trying. I'm going to go on until it gets totally dark. Lily said you have to keep moving. Remember that time I had my tonsils out and you rocked me on that big old rocker in the hallway. My throat hurt so bad. You kept putting those little chips of ice in my mouth and singing to me. That's one of my best memories. You made ice cream that day in the ice-cube trays, and that night you let me suck on them. It was vanilla. I love vanilla, Mom. Listen, Mom, I don't want you to worry about me. I'm just talking to you to make myself feel better. If you can . . . you know . . . do stuff . . . that we can't do down here, will you look out for Gracie?

"I made a will, Mom. Did I tell you that? I did. I left everything to Lily. I never told her. I guess I should have. I wonder why I didn't. You'd like her, Mom."

The terrain was really different now. The ground was wet and soggy. He started to shake and couldn't stop. He thought he heard water, but he wasn't sure. Was he near one of the bayous? If so, what did it mean? Would he be closer to civilization, closer to . . . what?

He was soaked through to the skin. He had a high fever. He had blood poisoning and was shaking from head to toe. If he didn't have pneumonia, it was only a matter of time before he got it. He did the one thing he hadn't done before.

He prayed.

"This sucks!" Dennis muttered. "I'm soaking wet down to my underwear. My ass is as cold as my feet. I'd kill for some hot soup. I wasn't cut out for this. I wish there was something I could do, something I could contribute. I feel like a slug. How can the two of you sit there eating that beef jerky?"

"It's dark, Dennis. There's nothing else we can do unless you want to continue searching in the dark. I don't recommend it, but we do have flashlights. If you want, we can start out again. We're pretty close to the bayous now.

It's unfamiliar terrain to Sadie and me. The forest is one thing, we know how to track and take care of ourselves out there. The bayou is something else. It's your call, if you want to keep going, Sadie and I are game."

"Sitting gets us nowhere. Let's keep on going. Isn't Gracie picking up on anything?"

"Yes, she is, but I can't let her loose. I'm basically following her. She has Matt's scent. If he's out here, she'll find him. Okay, Sadie, let's go. I'll lead. Keep Buzz close to you, Dennis."

A long time later, Dennis grumbled as he ground to a halt. "I haven't heard a peep out of either one of you for the past five hours. Aren't you soaking wet? Aren't you miserable? Where the hell are we going?"

Lily turned to look at Matt's best friend. A sharp retort was on her lips, but she bit down on her tongue. She had to remember that Dennis was out of shape, he knew nothing about outdoor life, and while he was concerned about Matt, he was also worried about his own endurance. "We're following Gracie. It's three in the morning, Dennis. We're all tired and yes, we're all wet. Getting excited and angry only uses up energy. I suggest we stop, sleep until it gets light, then head out again. The rain isn't going to let up, that's a given. The ground is exceptionally wet, so that has to mean we're near the bayou. I can see cypress all over. By daylight, we'll have a better idea of where we are and which way to go. Gracie will find him if he's out here. Let's find some shelter and call it a night."

"I'm sorry, Lily. I wish I was better equipped physically and mentally for this search. If I'm slowing you down, just say so," Dennis said.

"You're doing fine, Dennis. No one said this was going to be easy. I'm pretty miserable myself right now. So is Lily," Sadie smiled.

"I guess what you're saying is, suck it up, right?"

"That pretty much covers it," Sadie grinned. "Try and get some sleep."

Dennis closed his eyes. How the hell was he supposed to sleep when he was so cold and wet he expected icicles to form on his nose any minute? He knew he had blisters on his feet, and his back felt like it was sprained with the heavy load he'd been carrying. They were girls for God's sake. Neither of them weighed more than 105 pounds, and he hadn't heard a peep out of them all day long. Talk about sucking up. Maybe if he thought about some-thing pleasant, he might nod off for a little bit. He smiled to himself when he wondered what Sadie looked like in a bikini.

Lily hunkered down between the dogs with

Sadie on the other side of her. Buzz stretched out, but Gracie remained on her haunches, her ears straight up, ever alert. "We're going to find him, girl. I feel it in my bones. I think he knows we're out here. Easy, now, we'll set off again when it gets light out."

Her hand closed over the Wish Keeper, her other hand secure on Gracie's leash. She waited for something to happen. She sighed, and then tugged at it again.

She was here but she was there. It was a place she didn't recognize. A large field or perhaps a large garden area. She watched as a man on a tractor tilled the soil. From off in the distance she watched an elderly lady shield her eyes from the sun to stare at the kind, generous man who helped her from time to time and who never wanted or expected anything in return. Just a loving man who did for others. And then he was gone, the small tractor overturning. The elderly lady ran as fast as she could. The tractor, the kind man, the elderly lady disappeared and a little girl walked over to the spot in the field and looked about. She dropped to her knees and ran her hands over the wet ground. So much blood. She looked at her hands, then at the dirt. Her daddy's blood. Such sorrow in her big, dark eyes. She didn't understand. The elderly lady returned to lead her away, washed her hands and told her to go home to her mama. Such tragic, dark eyes. Such grief for one so small.

Lily jerked to wakefulness and stared out at the darkness all around her. What had she just seen? Was it a dream or one of her spells? Did she just experience one of the secrets entrusted to her? If that was the case, then she couldn't talk about it to Sadie and Dennis. If she was the new Wish Keeper, even temporarily, she had to keep her own counsel. Who was the little girl with the big, dark eyes? Surely there was no secret to the kind man's death. Perhaps the little girl was wishing for her father to return. How was she supposed to know what was a wish and what was a secret? Would knowledge come in time? She felt like the young man in the television show who got tomorrow's newspaper today and then had to act on it. What was she supposed to do in the future? She sighed. Time would undoubtedly give her the answer. She sighed again as she closed her eyes and prayed for sleep to come.

Matt woke to rain splashing on his face. It must be raining harder than it was when he first lay down to sleep. How many hours ago was that? He felt disoriented. It was almost light, so at least eleven or twelve hours had gone by since he'd lain down in his pine bed. He struggled to move, to stretch out his hands to catch the precious rain. He gulped at it from his cupped hands. Nothing in the world had ever tasted as good as the fresh rainwater. He tried to move his injured foot that was swollen to twice its size. A hard cough erupted from his chest that left him gasping for breath. He felt his foot, and it was fiery hot to his touch. There was no way he was going to be able to get the Wellington back on. He was also burning up and shivering inside his wet clothes. He coughed again, his head rocking on his shoulders with the force of the strain.

Lily's words thundered in his ears. *Move. Crawl if you have to but move.* How was he to crawl on one leg? His wet clothes now weighed more and he would be dragging deadweight. He wondered if it was possible to roll along, but where would he get the momentum from? Scratch that idea.

He waited for full light. Twenty minutes later he pulled his trouser leg up to stare down at the red streak going up his leg. It was almost to his knee now. A flurry of panic washed over him.

Move! Dammit, I said move! You have to keep moving till you drop in your tracks. He coughed again as violent chills racked his body.

"I'm going. I'm going." He crawled forward. Once he thought he heard a dog bark.

That's when he knew he was delirious.

As he slogged his way forward on his elbows and one good leg in his best combat crawl, he thought about how nice it was going to be when he could take a shower and fall into Lily's bed. The big king-size bed with the sweet-smelling sheets that had little purple flowers all over them. The pillows all made from some kind of duck feathers would hold his head and caress his cheeks. He grimaced as he tried to figure out how they caught the ducks to steal the feathers. Poor creatures, they must freeze without the warmth of their feathers so people like him could dream about soft feathers. He wondered again how they got the ducks to stand still to pluck the feathers. Someday he was going to ask someone who was an authority on duck feathers. Lily would probably know. Dennis wouldn't know. Dennis slept on some kind of foam that curved into your neck. He continued to cough as he struggled forward.

Move! Faster! Don't stop. Don't think! Move! No matter how badly you hurt, no matter how badly you feel, keep moving. Don't give in. Move, dammit!

"I swear to God, Lily, I can't go any faster. I'm doing the best I can. I'm not slacking. If there was a way for me to get up and walk out of here, I would do it. I would do it for you,

Lily. I don't ever want to disappoint you. I don't want you to think I'm a *wuss*." He fell forward on his face and started to cough, the sounds ratcheting up from somewhere deep in his chest. He wanted to curse his circumstances, but the words simply wouldn't come. Exhausted from coughing, he lay there for a moment before he pulled himself up on his good knee and moved forward. How was it possible to feel so hot and yet so cold at the same time? He thought he heard a dog bark again. "Oh, Gracie, I'm so sorry. I let you down. I promise if I ever get out of this, I'll track those bastards to the ends of the earth, and I promise you, I *will* find you. I will, Gracie. I swear to God, I will find you. You got me through some bad times in my life, and I'm not about to forget that. It was me and you. Just me and you for a long time." He fell again. This time his energy was so depleted all he could do was roll over. He coughed until he couldn't cough anymore. He closed his eyes and was asleep almost immediately.

Ten

"I can't believe you two girls earned a living doing this day in and day out for nine months out of the year. How in the hell do you do it?" Dennis gasped as he slogged forward.

"It was a job," Sadie said quietly. "We rarely had this kind of mud, and it didn't rain every day. I guess my best answer is you get used to it. And we didn't do it in the winter. For the most part the people were nice. I'm not saying you aren't nice. This is a whole different ball game, Dennis. Don't talk, just keep moving. Talking saps your energy if you're walking."

Lily stopped and turned around. "I don't know why but I have this feeling I should let Gracie loose. We need to rest a few moments so we can go after her because she's going to take off like a bullet. Actually, we'll have to run. This mud will slow us down so be prepared. Five minutes," she said breathlessly.

"Okay, on the count of three, I'm going to take off her leash."

The shepherd lunged forward the moment she was free of the leash and sprinted away, the others behind her. Her bark was so loud, Lily cringed at the sound. To her ear it sounded like a joyful bark. *Please God, let Gracie find Matt. And please let him be alive and well. I promise, I will never ask You for anything, ever again. Just let Matt be alive and well.*

It wasn't the rain that woke him. Maybe it was the dream. The best one ever since he'd been abducted. The tremendous weight on his chest and lower body made his eyes snap open. Or maybe it was the loving licks to his face. "Gracie! Oh, God, Gracie, is it really you? I found you. This is the best dream. I swore I'd find you. I was prepared to go to the ends of the earth. Oh, God, I love you as much as I love Lily. How come there are so many of you? You brought the whole army, didn't you. Six, seven, they all look like you. C'mere, baby, let me hug you."

Out of breath, the others skidded to a stop to watch Gracie lathering Matt with her own brand of love. "Matt! You're alive!" Lily screamed, running over to where he lay with Gracie.

"God, Lily, this is the best dream. What the hell took you so long?"

Tears dripped down Lily's cheeks. "I had to tree this bear, fight off a couple of alligators, ford Old Muddy, that kind of thing."

"That's it!"

"I stopped in town to buy a push-up bra before starting out. God, I can't believe we found you. We have to get you out of here."

"I didn't stand you up, Lily."

"I know that, Matt. Sadie, shoot off two flares. That should bring somebody. In case no one shows up, we have to make a litter and get him out of here as soon as we can. Dennis, help Sadie."

"Dennis. Old buddy, are you here? I knew you'd come looking for me. You brought a double, huh? There are three of you, Lily. Which one should I kiss first?"

Lily laughed. "Gracie would rip out my throat if I tried to take her place right now. That's the way it should be. Later, we'll have all the time in the world."

"I don't know if I have that much time, Lily," Matt said, struggling for each breath he took. "I think I have pneumonia, and I know I have blood poisoning. The streak going up my leg is moving pretty fast. I keep seeing my mother. She's waiting for me."

"Shut up, Matt. I don't want to hear that kind of talk. Don't say that again. If you did see her, that just means she's watching over you. We're here now. We're going to get you to a hospital as soon as we can. I'm going to peel off your socks and look at your foot. I'll do what I can with what I have to work with.

We each have a thermal blanket so we're going to strip you down and wrap you up before we put you on a litter."

"Where are you getting a litter?" Matt gasped.

"We're making it, buddy. Just hang on," Dennis shouted as he stripped a young sapling to match the one Sadie had cut. He watched as she wove the climbing rope around and through the three saplings that would carry Matt's weight. It took all of six minutes. His face reflected the awe he felt.

"Okay, help me here. We need to get him out of these wet clothes and wrapped in the thermal blankets as soon as possible. C'mon, people, hustle. Time is crucial here. Move, move, move!"

"I did it, Lily. I kept moving. I did everything you said that I could remember." A violent fit of coughing overtook him before he could say anything else. "I licked the dew off the plants, I chewed the bark. Can you bake bread?"

"You did good, Matt. I'm very proud of you. Don't talk now. We're stripping you down. You'll be nice and warm in a minute. These are some duds you're wearing. I never made bread, but I can learn if it's important to you."

"Push-up bra, huh? How sick am I, Lily?"

"Pretty damn sick. You already know that. Stop talking, Matt. Trust me, okay?"

"With my life, Lily. I love you, Gracie. I really love you. How'd you get here with the army?"

"I found her, Matt. Actually, Buzz found her. She was looking for you. She's fine now, so shut up. I don't want you talking. Talking triggers your coughing spells."

"Okay, buddy, you're snug as a bug now," Dennis said the moment they peeled off Matt's clothes and wrapped him in the thermal blankets. "Do you feel warmer? Of course you do. Don't answer that. Okay, we're going to lift you onto the litter and get you out of here. Did you check that GPS thingamajig, Lily?"

Lily looked down at her Global Positioning System and prayed the batteries wouldn't run out. If they did, she had her compass and her map. With a GPS, even a rat could find its way out of a maze of navigational challenges. "I'm doing that right now. We're on the money."

"Tell me where to buy those things. That's what I'm going to give everyone for Christmas this year," Dennis said.

"Don't give me one!" Matt mumbled.

"Buddy, you are *Numero Uno* on my list."

"Okay, let's go, we're outta here!" Lily said,

taking one end of the bottom half of the litter while Sadie took the other half. Dennis carried both ends from the top.

"Move, move!" Lily said jogging forward.

"That's all you ever say, move, move, move!" Matt mimicked Lily. "Been there, done that." In spite of herself, Lily smiled.

"How long before we make civilization?" Dennis queried an hour later. "I'm exhausted. You two must be tired."

Lily could have been dropping in her tracks but she wouldn't admit it, and neither would Sadie. "You talk too much. Keep moving. We have another hour to go. Where the hell are those people who live around here? Someone should have seen the flares."

"They're probably following their daily routine. The chances of someone actually looking out of their window and seeing the flares had to be about zip. Nor are people with brains clomping around out here at this time of year."

"I heard that," Matt mumbled.

"Can you really trust that gizmo, that GPS thing?" Dennis demanded.

"Sometimes you get crappy reception if it's a bad satellite afternoon. Sometimes you run out of batteries. I carry spares. It's called a low-tech backup for a high-tech solution. Sadie and I both took clinic courses in Arizona before we bought them. We're okay, Dennis."

"She's okay, Dennis. Stop bothering her," Matt mumbled again between bouts of coughing.

"He doesn't sound good, Lily," Sadie whispered.

"No, he doesn't. The blood poisoning has really taken hold, too. That guy of mine is pretty tough, Sadie."

"Yeah. Yeah, he is. I didn't mean . . ."

"I know. We'll get him to the hospital in time. Modern medicine . . ."

"Is wonderful. You wanna bet someone shows up just when we make it to the car? If they do, I'll give them what for," Sadie snarled.

"I'll help you," Dennis chirped.

"Dennis, sign me into the hospital with your I.D.," Matt said.

Sadie looked questioningly at Lily.

"If the press gets wind of this, the stock will nose-dive. That's the main reason I didn't want to broadcast Matt's disappearance," Dennis said.

They continued to trudge their way to open ground. When they finally reached the Rover, Gracie leaped in first, Buzz second. With coaxing and a stern voice, Lily was able to convince the dogs to lie on each side of Matt for warmth. All the heaters in the world wouldn't be able to do what the dogs' warmth would do for him.

"Where's the fucking people?" Dennis shouted.

Sadie swung around and eyeballed the software expert. "When you want something done, always call a woman. She'll make sure the job gets done and done properly. We'll get Matt to the hospital on our own. As for all those people who live around here, they're probably watching television or sleeping. Maybe they're reading the paper or eating. In case you haven't noticed, we did the job and don't need them."

"We're all in, Lily," Dennis said. "Matt's totally out of it now, so burn rubber. Don't worry about red lights, just go."

"I hear you. Don't you die on me, Matt Starr," Lily bellowed.

Gracie howled. A mournful sound.

Buzz whimpered but didn't move, his big head on Matt's chest opposite Gracie's head.

Dennis leaned over the backseat, his hand on Matt's forehead. "He's burning up."

"I know," Lily said tightly. "I know."

At the hospital, it was all Lily and Sadie could do to hold down the big shepherd while the emergency-room attendants wheeled

Matt into the hospital. "There's nothing Sadie and I can do now, Dennis," Lily said. "You do what Matt wants you to do. We'll take the dogs home, shower and change, and come back. Then it will be your turn. Is that okay with you?"

"Yeah," Dennis called over his shoulder as he ran behind the gurney.

Lily held it together until she got into the truck. Sobs ripped from her throat as she fell against Sadie. "What if he doesn't make it, Sadie. My God, you saw him. I'm a far cry from a doctor, but I know he doesn't just have pneumonia, he has *double* pneumonia. What if he doesn't make it?"

"I don't want to hear talk like that, Lily. He will make it. He's led a strong, healthy life, and he's a fighter. You heard him, he was thinking of the company by saying to sign him in as Dennis. He said he loves you, he loves Gracie. He's not going to give that up, he'll fight for it."

"He saw his mother. That's not good," Lily wailed.

"Don't give me that bullshit, Lily," Sadie said. "You've been seeing all kinds of weird things lately. That doesn't mean you're going to die. Not another word. Do you hear me? Now, blow your nose and let's go home. I can't wait to get out of these wet clothes. I want a cup of hot coffee, and I plan to main-line that bag of double Oreo cookies we bought the other day. I'm going to eat the whole bag. Every single one. You can have the Fig Newtons. I'm driving, you're a wreck."

"Okay, okay. I'll sit in the back with the dogs. She found him. Isn't it amazing, Sadie? Oh, wait till Matt sees that we found his sneakers. He's going to be so happy. Did I ever tell you how much he loves those shoes?"

"Only five hundred times or so. Do you think it will be all right to leave Gracie in the apartment? Now that she found Matt, will she do something wild, like going through the window?"

"No. Gracie knows something's wrong. For some reason, dogs always seem to know before people know. Animals really do under-stand, and, believe it or not, they know when a crisis is under way and react accordingly. She has Matt's sneakers to keep her company and, of course, Buzz. Let's go home, Sadie."

"Why do I feel like one of the three stooges?" Dennis demanded.

"Because we *look* like the three stooges," Lily said wearily. "We've been here night and day for five days, and Matt is still on the criti-cal list. I feel like death warmed over myself.

253

There should have been a change in his condition by now."

"We have the best of the best taking care of him. It's Matt, he isn't fighting. This is probably going to sound crazy, but is there a way to possibly bring Gracie here? I know hospitals frown on animals, but if a blind person came in and needed their Seeing Eye dog, wouldn't it be allowed? Just maybe hearing Gracie bark, knowing she's here, might be just the spark he needs."

"I thought I was the spark," Lily said glumly.

"I didn't mean that the way it sounded. Maybe what I should have said was Gracie is the match to light the spark. I say it's worth a shot. It sure as hell can't hurt to ask. Worst-case scenario, we smuggle her in."

"I'd like to see you try that little trick, Dennis," Sadie muttered. "I'm up for anything that will speed things along. Are you sure those doctors are the best of the best?"

"They're Matt's own doctors. They won't give away his identity."

"Listen, Dennis, I don't care about that identity thing. Right now all I want to see is some improvement in Matt's condition. I don't give a hoot about Digitech stock. See if you can get the doctor on the phone. I'm game for bringing Gracie here if he gives the okay. Five days is an eternity. He hasn't said one lucid word in all that time. He's in, and he's out. Something's wrong. I feel it. As much as I would like Gracie to be the answer, I know she isn't it." In a frenzy of impatience, Lily yanked at the Wish Keeper around her neck. For one wild moment she thought her head was going to spin off her neck. She heard Sadie and Dennis arguing as visions flashed behind her eyelids. The little boy was so sturdy and young. Way too young to be covered in blood. Everyone dressed in white scurrying around, their tasks left unfinished as they tried to staunch the flow of blood. So many pills. So many colors. Medicine cabinet vials, bottles, syringes. Too much blood. Someone screaming. Fill the bottles, lock the cabinet. Write everything down. What's his blood type? Where's the mother and father? We need to know. Stat!

"Lily, what's wrong? Is it happening again? She's not coming out of it, Dennis! Do something! Lily, come on, this is me, Sadie. Listen to me, open your eyes. We're in the hospital. Matt's here. Matt needs you. Lily," she said, shaking her violently by the shoulders.

"People are staring," Dennis hissed.

"Who cares. Lily. Ah, good girl. It's over. Lily, talk to me."

"How . . . how long . . ."

"A minute, two, possibly three. I wasn't watching you at first. What did you see?" Sadie whispered.

"A lot of blood. A little boy. They didn't know what his blood type was, and they couldn't find the parents. The medicine cabinet. All kinds of pills and stuff. They keep it locked. There were pills all over the place. You have to write it all down. What does it mean? I have no idea. I had one when we were tracking Matt, but it wasn't a real one. It was old, like a long time ago. There was a little girl in that one. She was so sad. Dennis, go down to Admitting and see if a little boy was brought in here around the time Matt was admitted. Usually they won't tell you stuff like that, so sweet-talk them. See if you can find out where the locked medicines are. Are there medicine cabinets on every floor? Maybe Matt is getting the wrong medications. There were pills everywhere, as though they had spilled. All colors. It's probably nothing. It seemed so real, though. God, this thing is a curse. The first thing I'm going to do when I get to the new house is to put this Wish Keeper back in the closet where you found it, Sadie. I can't handle this."

"We'll deal with that later. Let me nose around a little on this floor and see what I can find out. Stay put, Lily. That's an order."

How hard was that going to be? There was nowhere to go and nothing to do. The only time they could see Matt was for five minutes at the top of each hour. *Please, God, let him get better. He's too young for You to take. Please. Please,* Lily prayed.

It was thirty minutes before Sadie and Dennis returned. Dennis offered up what he had found out.

"There was a little boy brought in the day after Matt. I guess it was all in the newspapers, so it was all right for them to tell me. It was a head-on collision, and the child didn't make it. His parents were pronounced dead at the scene of the accident. That's all I know."

"There is a locked medicine cabinet on every floor," Sadie said. "The charge nurse is the only one with a key. I think Dennis should call Matt's doctor since he's still here and have him check the medicines. The nurses won't listen to us. It's worth a try. If you say there were pills all over, it's entirely possible whoever put them back mixed them up or put them in the wrong bottles. Right now anything is better than doing nothing. Don't stand there, Dennis, see if you can get hold of the doctor."

"Yes, ma'am!" Dennis said smartly.

"I didn't mean that the way it sounded," Sadie said.

"Yes, you did. It's okay. Sometimes my feet don't move real quick. I'll try to get hold of him."

"Do you want some coffee, Lily?"

"My kidneys are swimming in coffee. Thanks anyway. I think I counted every flower, every brushstroke on each one of these paintings at least a hundred times. I even know how many stripes there are on the wall that has the wallpaper. I am so worried, Sadie."

"I know, Lily. Think positive. You count things. I've been thinking these past five days trying to remember things about the old house, my mother and why we didn't come here after that one last summer. I remember bits and pieces."

Her interest piqued, Lily asked, "Like what?"

"My mother had this fight with my grandmother. Maybe it wasn't so much a fight as it was a loud discussion. I told you I didn't remember much about coming to Natchez in the summer, but something triggered something. I loved coming here. It was such a wonderful time for me. It was like I was free all of a sudden. I ran barefoot with the kids, we sucked on ripe, sweet watermelon, and had all these wonderful fruits and vegetables. Everything tasted so good back then, and there was so much of it. There was so much love, too. At night we'd play red light, green light and were allowed to stay out till nine o'clock. Then we'd all gather on the porch and drink homemade root beer. That was the best. They were happy times, wonderful times.

"When I think back now I remember how shabby the house was, but it didn't matter. Old things, worn things, have a special magic to them. I remember touching things and thinking someday I wanted things like that. My mother sold everything. Every single thing. What she wasn't able to sell, she threw away or gave away."

"Did you have a lot of friends here when you were a child? I don't remember you telling me about it when you came back at the end of the summer. All I knew was I missed you and wished I had a place to go to like you did."

"Lots of kids. There was Pam, Johnny, Mary and Caroline and Peter. The year I was eleven Pam's grandmother died, then her daddy died. We all cried with her on the porch. We really didn't know much about death back then other than the person went away and would never come back. We thought we were so grown-up. We would huddle on the porch trying to figure out why no one in Pam's family told her how ill her grandmother was or what it was that was going to take her away. We found out after the funeral that she had breast cancer. While we didn't know what that was, we all felt Pam should have been told. Johnny and Peter hadn't a clue and kept saying girls just wanted to know *everything*. I suppose it was true.

"During my summer visits I was allowed to have sleepovers. Pam and Caroline and I would always sleep in the room where I found the Wish Keeper. I have to wonder now if I had a conscious memory of my mother throwing it in that closet. Stop and think about it, Lily. Why would I go way back in that closet to see if anything was in there? The whole place had been cleaned out; there wasn't even a scrap of paper. That big old room was just full of little-girl secrets."

"Sadie, think now. How did Pam's father die?"

"He was on a tractor, and something happened. We all went to the funeral. It was so sad. Pam never came back after that. And then my mother had that fight, and we packed up and left. I never went back either."

Lily sucked in her breath. "Did Pam have big, dark, sad eyes?"

"Yes. Why?"

Lily described the vision she'd had the night on the trail. "Does that sound like your friend Pam? Did she have a red plaid dress?"

"Yeah, we all had dresses like that. Flour came in sacks with that print, and our parents made us dresses. Sometimes we'd all wear the same one on the same day and we'd laugh and laugh and call ourselves triplets. The boys had shirts made out of the same material, but if they came decked out in them when we were wearing our dresses, they went home to change. All our dresses were made from flour sacks. Two armholes, a neckhole, two pockets, and that was it. I hated it when my grandmother would starch them. Pam was in your vision, huh? What does it mean, Lily?"

"Sadie, I have no clue. You said you girls told secrets in your bedroom. Maybe this was one that took. Maybe she wasn't supposed to go to the place where the accident happened, but she went anyway. I'll probably never know since it was something that happened in the past. I probably just blew the whole thing by telling you. Now, tell me about the fight your mother had with your grandmother."

Lily leaned back, her gaze sweeping the waiting room. She and Sadie were the only ones waiting in the room. It was pleasant enough with the dark blue chairs and Harlequin design carpet. The magazines were old, tattered, and some of the pages were missing. Those who had waited before had cut out the coupons or articles that interested them. There were too many flowers, the scent almost overpowering. Patients probably left the flowers behind rather than carry them home. In the far corner there were two Tonka trucks and a box of colorful blocks. A temporary home away from home for those who waited for news of a loved one.

"My mother's face was red and splotchy. When she looked like that I could always tell she was mad. You know, really mad, not just upset. My grandmother was crying, and my mother was screaming at first, and then she started to cry, too. She kept saying she didn't want to know the secrets, didn't want to go crazy, and she wanted her last name on her tombstone. I thought that meant she was going to die, and I guess that's why I blocked it out of my mind all these years.

"This all took place in the room I slept in. My grandmother took the pendant off her neck and put it on my mother's neck. She ripped it off and threw it in the back of the closet. She kept saying her daughter, meaning me, would never wear that evil thing because there was not going to be anyone to hand it down to her. Then she packed our bags and we left. I didn't get to say good-bye to any of the kids, and my grandmother went to her room and locked the door. She died the following month. My mother came back for the funeral. I heard her tell my father she sold off everything and closed up the house. When I gave you the Wish Keeper I didn't really know what it was. To me it was just something from the house. Something for you to have to show that other people did live there and, oh, I don't know, make you feel like you belonged to the house. I'm so sorry, Lily. I think you're right. Get rid of it."

"But, it helped me find Matt. It can't be evil. When Matt is well again, we'll talk about it, and then I'll make a decision. For now, it is what it is. I'm glad you remembered all that. You never did find out anything when you went to the library, did you?"

"No. It's one of those things people in families talk about, but it's kind of sacred if you know what I mean. Everyone knows about it, but the librarian said it was folklore, nothing more. I thought I told you that when I got home that night."

"Maybe you did, and I wasn't listening. Those first days are a blur to me now."

"Here comes Dennis with the doctor. I can't wait to hear this."

He looked just the way a doctor was supposed to look. Tall, immaculate, professional-looking, with a stethoscope around his neck. His coat cloud white. Tinge of gray at the temples, bright gaze, and a gentle smile. They'd met days ago, but if she'd been asked to describe him at that point in time, Lily would have simply said, he looks like a doctor. She waited now, her gaze expectant to see if the doctor would chalk it up to craziness.

"I have the pharmacist checking the medicine cabinet as we speak. And before you can say it, no, I don't think you've lost your mind. Things happen in hospitals. Dennis told me about your . . . vision. I view this as precautionary. We should know something shortly. In the meantime, I'm going to check on Matt. Why don't you all go home or go for some lunch. I have all of your cell-phone numbers. I'll call the minute I know something. Get some fresh air. Hospitals are just riddled with germs," he grinned. "That's doctor's orders."

"I think that's a good idea. Come on, ladies, let's take a walk. It's snowing. Just flurries, but flurries are snow. We'll stop somewhere for a sandwich and a cup of hot chocolate. Up and at 'em, ladies."

There was no point in arguing with Dennis. Lily stood up and suddenly realized how tired she was. She tried to remember when she'd last eaten solid, nourishing food. Her weary brain refused to give her the answer.

Dennis was right, it was snowing lightly. Lily hunkered down inside her warm jacket and followed Dennis and Sadie to a cozy coffee shop that had green-checkered curtains on the windows. It was small inside, with just nine tables and a counter. It was so clean and fragrant, Lily wanted to stay forever.

"I just love the smell of fresh coffee and cinnamon buns," Sadie said.

"Me, too," Dennis said. "Growing up, our house always smelled like cinnamon and celery and fresh coffee. My mother always had a pot of coffee going. I don't know where the smells came from because my mother wasn't much of a cook. Matt's mother now, she could cook. I ate there at least five nights a week, not to mention lunches and many, many breakfasts. Matt's house was my second home. He had this great old swing in the backyard. Actually, it was a tire from an eighteen-wheeler. That baby could almost reach the sky when we pushed it. One time Matt decided to jump off in midair and landed in his mother's rosebushes. We picked thorns out of his ass for days."

Lily burst out laughing. She loved hearing about Matt's childhood. Her own was so bland compared to his.

Lily eyed the jambalaya and dug into it with a vengeance. She'd just finished sopping up the last of the juice with a chunk of crusty French bread when Sadie leaned back, and said, "What's the scoop on Marcus, Dennis?"

"There is no scoop. He never showed up at the ski resort in Maine. I've called his wife three times, and she knows nothing — or says she knows nothing. He hasn't called the office, and no one knows where he is."

"Maybe the same people who snatched Matt, snatched him," Lily said.

"Not possible. He didn't take any of his things, his bank accounts are untouched, and he didn't leave any instructions at the office. He literally dropped off the face of the earth. I'm going to call Betsy this afternoon to see if there are any new developments. I'm thinking he bailed out. I dread telling Matt."

"I'll have the homemade blackberry cobbler and a cup of coffee," Lily said to the hovering waitress.

"I'll have the same," Dennis said.

"Me, too," Sadie said.

"If I had known this place was here, I never would have eaten all those egg salad sandwiches or drunk that bad coffee at the hospital," Sadie said.

Dennis's cell phone rang just as their dessert was set in front of them. "Okay," Dennis said. "We're just about finished here. We'll see you in a bit then, Doctor."

"Well?" Lily and Sadie said in unison.

"Your vision was on the money, Lily.

They've been giving Matt the wrong medicine. Not just Matt, everyone on this floor. They switched his IVs and are pumping him full of mega antibiotics. One of the volunteers replaced the pills when the nurse dropped them to help with the little boy. She went by the color of the pills. All the blues went in one jar, the whites in another, and so on. She didn't know. She thought she was doing what she was supposed to do. She entered the time, then locked the cabinet like the nurse told her to do. No deaths resulted, just a terrible mistake. Thank God you're wearing that *thing*, Lily. Now, let's eat this delectable cobbler, drink this wonderful-smelling brew, and head back to the hospital. I'm feeling real good right now."

"Yeah, me too," Lily said softly as she fingered the pendant around her neck.

Eleven

The hole was deep and black, with tinges of gray on the perimeter. He wondered what it meant. Where was he? How did he get here and why couldn't he move? He struggled to remember. He had to move. Lily said he had to move. He longed for his mother. She would know what he should do. He called out and waited. *Mom! Mom, can you hear me? I need you, Mom. Will you help me, Mom? Hold out your hand and pull me out of here. Please, Mom.*

I can't, son. If I take your hand, you won't be able to go back. You have to stay where you are. Everything will be fine. This just isn't the time for me to reach out for your hand. When that time does come, I'll be here waiting. There are a lot of people waiting for you. Help is coming. Just be patient, Mattie.

You only call me Mattie when I'm sick. Is that why I'm in this big black hole?

Yes, Mattie, you're sick. I want you to dig way down deep and tell yourself over and over that you're going to get well. You have to believe, Mattie. Can you do that for me?

Sure, Mom. Hey, Mom, did I ever tell you I still have those sneakers you bought me. The ones Dad said cost too much. The right one has a big hole in the toe. I wear them everywhere. I even put some of that electrical tape on the sole because it has a hole in it. I'm never giving up those shoes. Dennis told me he saw you at the pawnshop selling your watch. That night you gave me the sneakers before I went to bed. You told me to scuff them up and make them a little dirty so Dad wouldn't know you bought them for me. I went out in the middle of the night and tramped through the garden and the wet grass. I did what you said. Tell me how to get out of here, Mom.

Do you see the gray edges around the hole, Mattie?

Yeah, Mom, I can see them. What does it mean?

Gradually the gray edges will move to block out the black area. When that happens you'll be able to get out of the hole.

Is that for true, Mom?

Mattie, I never, ever lied to you. I want you to close your eyes and sleep. When you wake up the black hole won't be as dark. Go to sleep now. I'll watch over you until you climb out of the hole.

Thanks, Mom. I love you.

I love you, too, Mattie.

He woke from time to time to see his

mother's smiling face, and she would always point to the gray border surrounding the dark hole. When he finally opened his eyes wide a long time later all he could see was bright sunshine. His mouth was thick and fuzzy and his eyes felt like they had a hard crust all over them. He knew where he was, but he didn't know how he knew.

"I think I'd like a cold beer," he said in a voice he didn't recognize as his own.

"You would, would you? Oh, Matt, you're awake. Hey, everybody, Matt's awake," Lily shouted.

They came on the run, nurses, doctors, Dennis, and Sadie. "He wants a cold beer," she said, happiness ringing in her voice.

"Everyone clear out, we need to check our patient," the doctor said. "Welcome back, Matt," he whispered. "You had us a little worried there for a while. How do you feel?"

"Like someone slammed me against a brick wall. Was that Dennis I just saw?"

The doctor leaned over and whispered in Matt's ear. "So, Mr. Wagner, do you think you're up to a little solid food?" he asked for the nurse's benefit.

"Only if you bring a beer to go with it."

"I think that can be arranged. Lie still now, I want to check the dressing on your foot and take your vitals."

"How long have I been here?"

"A little over ten days. We're going to get you up later on. Don't expect too much. You're pretty weak. The trip to the bathroom will exhaust you."

"Don't forget the beer, Doc. Listen, let me ask you something. Now you've known me a long time. You know I'm pretty levelheaded for the most part. I saw my mother. She talked to me. Was I hallucinating? Was it the drugs you have me on or did I *really* see her?"

"What did she say?" the doctor asked.

"She told me the black hole had gray around the edges and when the gray grew light, I'd be out of the hole. When I opened my eyes I was here. I asked her to hold out her hand, and she said no. Does that mean if I had reached out my hand, and she'd taken it, I would have died? I need to make sense of it all."

"I've heard of things like this before," the doctor said. "You were right on the edge, Matt. It could have gone either way. Later, when you're up to it, Lily and Dennis will fill you in. But to answer your question, it's whatever you want it to be. I, personally, believe in these things since I've seen and heard them so often, and they're almost always identical to what you just told me. Your medication is coming right up, and I'll see that you get your beer. Your buddies want to visit. Be thankful you have such loyal friends."

"Thanks, Doc. For everything. At the moment I don't know exactly what everything is but thanks anyway. Now, do you think I can see my dog?"

"Wait till you get my bill," the doctor twinkled. "I'll see what I can do about Gracie."

"That's one bill I won't mind paying." A moment later his eyes closed, and he was asleep.

Outside in the waiting room, the doctor addressed the trio. "He fell asleep. Right now that's the best thing for him because it's a natural sleep. He could sleep for twenty-four hours, or he could sleep an hour. There's no way of telling. He's on his way to a full recovery. I think it's time for me to get back to my own practice. Matt's in good hands here. Dr. Pinell is a fine doctor. My advice is simple. Let him rest up for a couple of weeks, nothing strenuous. Lots of good food, some fresh air, and easy on the booze. Your boy is golden."

Dennis pumped the doctor's hand vigorously. "Thanks for dropping everything and coming down. Somehow Matt will make it up to you. Have a safe trip home."

Lily and Sadie smiled from ear to ear as

they, too, shook the doctor's hand.

"I want an invitation to the wedding," the doctor called over his shoulder. Lily smiled and nodded.

"Let's just peep in on him," Lily said.

They jostled each other running for the door.

"He looks so white," Sadie said.

"He looks like he lost a good ten pounds," Dennis said.

"He looks so wonderful," Lily said, tears misting her eyes. "He's been to hell and back, and he still looks wonderful."

Dennis reached for one of her arms and Sadie reached for the other. "We're going home now," Sadie said. "We're going to cook dinner, then we'll come back."

"Yeah, that's a good idea. I want to see Matt before I leave in the morning."

Sadie's jaw dropped. "You're leaving tomorrow."

"I have to get back. With Marcus gone, no one is minding the store. Technically, Lou Sims is in charge, but there are things I have to do no one else can do. I'll try to get back on the weekend."

"Are you going to New York or Oregon?" Sadie asked.

"New York first. It all depends on what I find when I get back there. Eventually, I have to return to Oregon. Maybe Matt will bring you out once he's all better."

"Are you going to call us?" Sadie demanded. "I know you're going to be calling Matt, but I mean us, me and Lily."

Dennis shuffled his feet. "Well, yeah, sure. Uh-huh. I will. You could call me, you know."

"I might do that. You're peeling the potatoes for dinner."

"Why do I always have to peel the potatoes?" Dennis grumbled.

"Because Lily and I don't like to peel potatoes. You never said you didn't like to peel potatoes, so the job is yours. We do the rest. It's your turn to do the dishes, too."

"Isn't life wonderful?" Lily sighed.

Matt sat propped up in bed the following morning, his gaze glued to the doorway. The moment he saw her his eyes lit up. She ran to him, her arms outstretched. Tears ran down her cheeks and mingled with Matt's. "Do you forgive me?" he whispered against her hair.

"Yes, yes, yes. I have to tell you, though, that was a bad day. I sliced up my wedding dress and put my foot through the veil. I just wanted to lie down and die."

"I'm sorry. Lily, if it wasn't for you, I never

would have made it. I just want you to know that."

"Let's not talk about any of that. It's all in the past. Where did all these flowers come from?"

"I tried to tell the candy striper they weren't mine, but she said they are. No one but you, Dennis, and Sadie know I'm here. They're probably for the guy next door. He had a bunch of boils lanced on his rear end. I heard them talking. My mother used to have flowers like this in her garden. I saw her, Lily. She talked to me. Do you think I'm nuts?"

"No, I don't think you're nuts. When I tell you my story you're going to think I'm the nutty one, but I'll do that later. The nurse said I could take you down to the lobby in a wheelchair for a few minutes. Keep the blanket on, and we'll be good to go. I wish I knew the words to tell you how much I missed you and how grateful I am that you're alive and well. I'll find the words later, okay?" Lily gave him a bone-crushing hug.

"Everything is okay, Lily. Our world is now right side up. I will never take another thing in life for granted as long as I live. Another thing, you are never going to be out of my sight ever again."

"That sounds pretty good to me. Okay, here we go."

The moment the elevator door slid open and the wheelchair crossed the threshold, the only thing to be seen was a black streak of lightning.

"Gracie! Hey, girl, it's good to see you. What do you have there? Jesus, it's my sneakers! Where in the hell . . ." His mouth open in amazement, the dog half-on and half-off his lap. Matt looked down to see both his sneakers, which Gracie had dropped by his feet. Lily bent over to remove his paper slippers and worked them on to Matt's feet. Gracie yipped her pleasure.

"Yeah, yeah, you can get up here. Dennis, hey, buddy, good to see you. Lift this dog up onto my lap, will you?"

The big dog wiggled and squirmed until she was comfortable before she laid her head on Matt's chest. A lump rose in Lily's throat at the way Matt caressed her head and whispered in her ear.

"I got my girl, my dog, and my sneakers. What more could a guy want?" Matt asked happily.

"Listen, I'm on my way back to New York," Dennis said. "Business calls. I wanted to say hello and good-bye all at the same time. If you need anything, call. I'll try to get back this weekend, but that will depend on a lot of things. It's good to have you back, buddy."

"Thanks, Dennis. I knew you'd come after me."

"Don't thank me. Thank these two beautiful women here. In a million years I could never do what they did. Man, we carried you on a litter for twelve miles. Without them, you'd still be out there. I was worth diddly-squat. We'll talk later. I have a plane to catch."

"I'm glad to see you're okay, Matt," Sadie said. "I'm leaving, too. I'm driving Dennis to the airport. Do you want me to drop Gracie off at the apartment?"

At the sound of her name, Gracie snarled and growled at the same time. Matt laughed. "This dog has no plans to go anywhere. Trust me on that."

"Okay, I'll see you back home, Lily. Don't worry about Buzz. I'll walk him for you."

"What are you going to do about her, Matt? They don't allow animals in hospitals. I can chase down the administrator, but I don't know what good it will do. Do you want me to try?"

"Would you, Lily? I don't have the heart to send her home. If she went through half as much as I did, then she's staying right here with me. Tell him I'll build a trauma unit or a burn unit on this place if they let her stay with me. It's only for today and tomorrow. They said if I continue to improve, I could go home on Friday."

"Are you serious about this, Matt?"

"Whatever it takes, Lily."

Lily turned once to look over her shoulder. She smiled at what she saw, Matt's head buried in Gracie's neck, his arms secure around her huge body. He couldn't be comfortable. Gracie weighed eighty-six pounds. She probably felt like a feather to Matt.

Lily found the administration office and knocked softly. She didn't know what she expected but the cramped, cluttered office wasn't it. Nor was the man, a small, chubby individual with a harried look and worried eyes. She presented her case in a straightforward manner and waited while the little man absorbed all she had said.

"The welfare of our patients always comes first, Miss Harper. If the dog is as important to Mr. Wagner as you say, then I have no problem with the dog staying in his room. I was apprised of his condition the moment he was brought in. I won't downplay the problem that occurred earlier either, and I have no desire to deal with lawyers. It's not necessary to bribe me, Miss Harper."

"Oh, no, sir, please don't take it that way. If I tell you something, will you keep my confidence?"

"Absolutely. I pride myself on my honor. This is a hospital. We are in the business of saving lives. We never do anything foolish."

Lily explained who Matt was and what had happened to him and to the dog. "He wants to do this for you, sir. He can afford it. That dog means the world to him. Please, if you have a moment, will you walk with me to the lobby so I can introduce you to Matt and Gracie?"

Lily smiled from ear to ear when she entered the lobby to see both Matt and Gracie sound asleep.

"Don't wake him. Let him sleep. I'm here every day until eight or nine at night. You can always find me if you need me. What I'm seeing is something quite wonderful. I'll notify the charge nurse. Just take him upstairs. I rather imagine the nurses will fight to walk the dog for you. It was a pleasure to meet you, Miss Harper."

"The pleasure is mine, sir. Thank you. Matt will want to talk to you personally later or tomorrow. It wasn't something he said as a bribe."

Lily waited until the administrator was out of sight before she started to wheel Matt to the elevator. Gracie cracked one eyelid, saw that it was Lily, and closed her eye again. Matt remained asleep.

As Lily wheeled Matt to the elevator she stopped once to realize just how happy she was. Finally. She thought about singing but squelched the idea. Instead she hummed a tune under her breath.

Betsy Collins looked at the pile of unpaid bills and didn't know whether she should laugh or cry. She picked through them, one by one, looking at the totals on each bill. She flinched. The calculator found its way to her hand, but not before she considered what the small keys might do to the pearly white polish of her French manicure. She used the eraser on the tip of the pencil to tap in the numbers. She gasped aloud at the astronomical sum. The balances on the bank statements left her feeling dizzy. The mortgage payments, car payments, and the boat payments that were all way overdue could make a serious dent in feeding a third-world country.

Her hands started to shake. Where could she get that kind of money? Maybe she could use the children's bonds and college money Marcus had insisted on. Damn, where was the key to the safe-deposit box? She rummaged in the antique secretary she'd paid a fortune for. There were two keys; Marcus had one, and she kept the other. Obviously she needed to hustle her rear end to the bank or the girls would be going to public school next week. How was that going to look to her friends? The term, *scale down* socked her between the eyes as she gathered up her purse and coat.

Forty-five minutes later, Betsy carried the large box into a private room and opened the lid. Marcus always said he kept twenty thousand in cash for emergencies, but all she could see were money wrappers. The manila envelope with the words, *Saving Bonds* was empty. The canceled papers for the CDs they had purchased over the years stared up at her. A wave of panic rivered through her. Where were the stock options? Even though she had no clue as to exactly what a stock option was, other than it was valuable, she could find no paperwork to say there ever were such things. Zip. *Nada.* Zero. Not a fucking penny. Betsy slammed the lid on the box.

It wasn't until she was back inside the luxurious apartment that she realized Marcus had left her. He'd taken everything he could and left her with the bills. Knowing her husband as well as she did, she knew his rationale. She'd enjoyed her luxurious lifestyle, and now he was going to enjoy his. "You son of a bitch!" she seethed. "You goddamn son of a bitch!"

In desperation she tried dialing her husband's cell phone, then his pager. There was no response. "You bastard," she continued to curse. She eyed the stack of bills in front of her again. Her face brightened momentarily when she thought about the stack of credit cards in her purse. Cash advances. Magical words. With approximately two dozen credit cards with a fifteen-hundred-dollar cash allowance for each one, she might be able to scrounge up enough money to get by on for a month or so. She'd have to discharge the housekeeper and nanny. She almost fainted at the thought of doing dishes and laundry. Maybe she could keep the housekeeper and give up the health club. Paper plates were good. Damn, takeout food was expensive. The thought of eating beans out of a can drove her into a frenzy. Maybe she would have to sell the antiques, and everyone knew the dealers robbed you blind.

With less than sixty dollars in her wallet, she knew she had to hustle to get to the different banks that sponsored her credit cards.

Betsy upended the Chanel handbag, the bag she'd paid $1600 for. She wished she had the money in her hand. Her greedy hands searched out the cards and put them in order of importance. Platinum first and then the gold cards. Citibank, American Express, Bank One, and twenty others. She even had a

Discover card, but she'd never used it because she considered it tacky. People who shopped in Wal-Mart and Kmart used Discover card. She wouldn't be caught dead in either place.

She hated tapping into her sixty dollars for a cab, but she did it anyway, her first stop the bank she'd just left a short while ago.

She cried all the way home. Every single card was maxed out, and so were the cash advances. Marcus again. She'd never tried to take a cash advance before, so it had to be Marcus who wiped it all out. She had, however, gotten $300 from the Discover card.

Back in the apartment in her bedroom with the door locked, she started to call the various antique stores where she'd purchased some of her treasures. Her story was the same with each dealer, I'm moving out of state and since I purchased this or that from your store, I was wondering if you would like to buy it back. She had a few discreet nibbles, but nothing concrete.

She was screwed, and she knew it.

Plan B. Go back home to her mother and father. Back to Hoboken, New Jersey, one of the many armpits of the world. Back to her parents' small Cape Cod house with three tiny bedrooms. Back to her cigarette-smoking, beer-drinking parents, who played cards with the neighbors twenty-four hours a day. Back to the smelly, dirty house with the smelly furniture and dirty dishes piled high in the sink. Back to the house with the hoard of cats whose litter boxes were never changed. Back to the house she swore she'd never go back to.

Or.

She could go out on the street and peddle her ass.

Betsy Collins threw herself across the two-thousand-dollar champagne bedspread and howled her misery, but not before she turned down the pricey coverlet so her mascara wouldn't damage the fabric.

A long time later, Betsy crawled off the bed and stomped her way to the bathroom, where she repaired her makeup, changed her wrinkled outfit, and left the apartment for the third time that day. She was going to the Digitech offices to make some demands. What did she have to lose? Nothing. Nothing at all.

Dennis Wagner's eyebrows shot upward when his secretary announced Betsy Collins. "Give me ten minutes and show her in."

"She wants to go to Marcus's office."

"Absolutely not. If she gives you a problem, call security. Ten minutes."

Dennis looked down at the rat's nest of problems on his desk. Things he had to take care of immediately so he could call Matt back. He'd been back less than five hours and he had already spoken to Matt four times. He waited the full ten minutes before he rang his secretary. "Send Mrs. Collins in."

She looked terrible, which pleased him. "Sit down, Betsy. I hope you're here to tell me where Marcus is."

"If I knew that, I wouldn't be here. He left. He took everything and left. I have sixty dollars to my name. I have children. I have bills. I thought at first you sent him somewhere on some hush-hush thing but that doesn't appear to be the case. What I would like is for you to give me some money, or cash in some of those stock options Marcus has. At least give me his last paycheck, so I can buy some food for my girls. I don't know what to do. He just . . . vanished. I was in California, and when I got back he was gone. Did you hear what I said, he took everything?"

Dennis felt like he was swimming upstream in a whirlpool. "Marcus cashed in all his stock options, and he cashed his last paycheck himself. He has some sick days he carried over from last year. Plus his vacation pay for this year. That's about it, Betsy."

"What about his 401K plan?"

"He borrowed on it before the holidays. I remember him saying something about the boat. Those monies have to be paid back to the plan. There is, of course, the Christmas bonus, but I can't give that to you until we know more about Marcus and where he is. No one in this office has heard a thing. He said he was going to Maine to see the girls, and that's the last we heard."

"You have to give it to me, Dennis. If you don't, I'll be out on the street. What's Marcus's is mine. We're married."

"I don't have the authority to do that, Betsy. Matt's the only one who can do that."

"Call him. Tell him I'll be out on the street with my daughters if he doesn't okay it."

"Fine. I'll call him. Go into the executive dining room and wait for me. One of the chefs will give you a glass of wine or coffee if you prefer. It might take a while for me to get hold of Matt."

"I prefer to wait right here. He might want to talk to me."

Dennis walked around to the front of his desk. He took her elbow in his hand and escorted her to the door. "Wait for me in the dining room. I'll be there as soon as I reach Matt."

"God, I detest that woman," Dennis muttered as he returned to slam the door to his office. He dialed the hospital and waited for either Lily or Matt to pick up the private line. "It's me again, Matt. Listen . . ."

It took another thirty minutes to have checks cut to Betsy Collins's name. He marched down to the dining room with the envelope in his hand. "Matt gave the okay to pay you Marcus's bonus. This is all there is, Betsy. We wrote separate checks for the sick days and for vacation days. You have a quarter of a million dollars in your hand, Betsy. I would advise you to see a good tax man and an accountant. Taxes are due in April. If for some reason, Marcus doesn't return, you are going to be liable for all the taxes. It's a very serious business. You could very well end up owing all the money you hold in your hand. The IRS takes these matters very seriously. Seek professional help as soon as possible. I'm sorry things turned out this way. Are you sure you don't have even a vague idea of where he might have gone?"

"All I know is he cleaned out everything. His passport is gone, but I don't know if it was in the safe at home or not. He might have kept it in his briefcase. The briefcase is gone, too, but none of his clothes. He just walked away. Kind of like what Matt did at his wedding. By the way, how is he?"

"Matt? He's fine. They're working on a

new wedding date."

"Tell him not to invite me," Betsy said as she slipped into her coat. "I suppose I should thank you for this."

"That isn't necessary," Dennis said.

"Good-bye, Dennis. Happy New Year!"

"The same to you, Betsy."

Dennis watched as Betsy made her way down the corridor to the elevator. He'd bet his last dollar Betsy Collins would not seek out an accountant or a tax man. She would cash the check and continue to live just the way she'd been living since she married Marcus Collins. Well, it was her problem now, not his. Matt always said you could lead a horse to water but you couldn't make him drink.

Back in his office, Dennis stared at the phone. Before he changed his mind he picked it up and dialed the number in Natchez that he'd memorized. He smiled when he heard Sadie's voice. "Hey, it's me. I thought I'd give you a call to see how you are."

The lilt in Sadie's voice was unmistakable. "I'm fine, Dennis. It seems strange without you here. What should we do with all your computer equipment?"

"Matt's going to need it when he gets out of the hospital. Just leave everything where it is. Is it in your way?"

"No, not at all. I'm going to leave as soon as I find a place. Lily and Matt don't need me underfoot. I've been thinking about going back to Ozzie's. The camp is closed for the winter, but there's always something to be done. Fresh paint, stuff like that. I know he'd let me return if I asked him. Are you still in the office? It's kind of late, isn't it?"

"I'm trying to play catch-up. Marcus's wife was just here. She wanted money, and Matt said to give it to her. I think he just cleaned everything out and split. A lot of rumors have been flying around here, and I have to sort them out. Matt's doing okay?"

"He's not sleeping as much, and he's eating well. Gracie won't leave his side. He'll be home in a day or so."

"When . . . when will you know what you're going to do, Sadie?"

"I'll stick around long enough to see if Lily needs me. If not, I'll make my decisions by the weekend. Are you still thinking about coming to Natchez this weekend?"

"If I can wade through all my work, I will. I made a plane reservation just in case. I'd like to take you out if I make it."

"You mean like a date? I get dressed up, you get dressed up and we go somewhere and then, when we get back, you kiss me good night and then jump my bones?"

Dennis grinned. "If that's your idea of a plan, I think I could run with it." He loved the gurgle of laughter he heard on the other end of the phone.

"How's Lily?"

"Lily is on top of the world. I have never seen her happier. When she came home earlier to see Buzz and to shower and change clothes, she was singing in the shower. She deserves all the happiness she can get. I worry, though, about that damn pendant. I wish I had never found it and given it to her. Lately it seems all I do is make empty wishes."

"If you hadn't given her that thing, we might never have found Matt. Lily will handle it. I guess I better get back to work so I'll say good night, Sadie."

"Night, Dennis."

Five minutes later, Dennis was so engrossed in what he was doing he didn't hear the knock on his door until it opened and he heard his name called. "Andy, are you still here? Is something wrong?" Andy was his protégé, a young guy much like himself when he first started working with Matt. A young guy full of promise. Just possibly someone who would be able to fill Marcus's shoes in the not-too-distant future. He was shy, uncomfortable around people, but a whizbang in the computer room.

"I don't know. Maybe. It's Marcus. At least I think it's about Marcus. For some reason I went to the deli for lunch today. I don't know why, I just needed some fresh air. These guys were sitting behind me and I heard them talking. They were from Comlock. That's Savarone's company. He got screwed over for thirty million. And, get this, the guy that heads up BQWARE got stung, too, for the same amount. They didn't say who it was that did the stinging. But, I did hear them mention Digitech more than once. I came away thinking Marcus Collins did the stinging. I didn't hear that, and it's only my opinion. Marcus was here the night it supposedly happened. I know because I was here working late myself. He didn't know I saw him. Actually, Dennis, he was working in Matt's office. I thought that was kind of strange, but hey, I'm low man on the totem pole around here. I don't question people like Marcus Collins. Plus, the guy doesn't like me. I don't know any more than I've told you. If it means something to you, good. If not, that's okay, too. Sixty million bucks is a lot of money, Dennis. A lot of people would . . . do things they wouldn't normally do for that kind of money. I'm outta here. See ya tomorrow."

His head spinning, Dennis could only nod. Sixty million dollars. Son of a bitch! No wonder Betsy couldn't find her husband. He'd taken his passport and split, sixty million richer. Maybe. Well, there was only one way to find out. Go directly to the source and ask.

The big question was, how did Marcus get Matt's password? Guesswork? Did Matt somehow let it slip? On purpose? In the end, did it really matter? The final phase was safe and secure, and only Matt knew where it was. The third and final phase still on Matt's computer was their second effort that had gone awry. Marcus should have known that if he'd taken the time to peruse it. The guy had balls, he had to give him that. When this little story got out, it would grow legs and take off. Comlock and BQWARE would be the laughingstock of the industry. Not to mention what it would do to their stock. Digitech, on the other hand, would *soar*.

Dennis looked at the phone. Even though it was an hour earlier in Natchez, Matt was probably asleep. The morning would be soon enough to tell him.

Time to go home. Time to go home and think about how damn lucky he was to have Matt Starr as a friend and boss and time to thank his parents for instilling honesty, pride, and integrity into his life. And while he was in this thanking mode, maybe he would offer up a little prayer of thanks for Sadie Lincoln. He knew that she was going to become a major force in his life. He knew it as sure as he knew he had to keep breathing if he wanted to stay alive.

Twelve

"This is one of the happiest days of my life," Lily said as she hopped out of the Rover to help Matt out of the wheelchair. "I think it will be better if you sit in the back with Gracie."

"Honey, this is definitely the best day of my life. All I want to do is go home, take a shower, wash my hair, put on some clean clothes, and eat some *real* food. Did you put those sheets on the bed with the little purple flowers on them? You know, for later."

"That was the first thing I did this morning," Lily giggled. "Matt, Dennis left all his computer equipment for you. I won't be able to help you with any of that. I thought I would leave you to do what you have to do while I take care of some errands. I hate leaving you alone, though."

Matt frowned as a worm of fear wiggled around inside his stomach. He'd spent a lot of time thinking about this moment while he was in the hospital. How was he going to feel when he was alone for the first time? Locked apartment doors were just that. Anyone bound and determined to get in would get in. Dogs like Gracie and Buzz could be at someone else's mercy. He'd seen that for himself. An alarm system? Was he going to live his life in fear? How was that going to look to Lily?

He knew what he was feeling at the moment was normal. Just last night the doctor had stayed to talk for an extra fifteen minutes during his rounds. He'd said, "Don't give in to the fear, because if you do, your life will never be the same." And the doctor was right. He knew he was going to have to suck it up and grit his teeth. He wasn't going to look over his shoulder every ten minutes either. He would be more alert, more cautious, and not do dumb things like stopping at ATM machines after dark. He could make it work for him. Still, an alarm system might help.

"Hey, I'm a big boy. I'll be fine. Gracie and Buzz will keep me company. Don't worry about me. Do what you have to do. You and I have the rest of our lives to be together."

"Matt, will you have an extra hour or so this afternoon? I want to take you somewhere to show you something. It's nothing strenuous. Do you think you'll be finished with your work?"

"The hell with the work. Dennis can handle all that. I just want to get a bead on the bastards that abducted me and took my money. I'll probably exhaust all my leads in ten minutes, so the answer is yes, I would love to go with you to see whatever it is you want me to see. By the way, Lily, I never asked you before, but what did you do with that million bucks I put into your account?"

"I moved it. I had this vision, so I moved it. It's safe and secure. Do you need it?"

"No. I'm glad you did that. If you hadn't transferred the money, it would be gone by now. I'm going to find those guys, Lily. It might take me a while, but I will find them."

"I know you will, Matt. I'll help you in any way I can. I still think it was the Laroux brothers. I'm going to go to the *Natchez Democrat* and see if they have a picture of them. Their father was very well-known. I'm sure there's something on file somewhere. Maybe I can even call them. You're the only one who can identify them, though. Okay, we're here."

"I shouldn't be feeling this weak," Matt grumbled.

Lily laughed. "So you won't be moving at the speed of light for a while. The doctor said it would take two weeks before you were back to normal. Think of it as a vacation with nothing to do but sit around and hold my hand."

"I'm up to more than holding your hand, Lily."

"I'll just bet you are."

Sadie welcomed Matt with open arms. He grinned from ear to ear.

"We're going to leave you now. Lock the door behind us. I'm not sure when we'll be back. At least by four this afternoon, maybe a little later. I'm going to cook you a really great dinner, with wine and candles and fresh flowers. Hold that thought, okay," Lily said, standing on tiptoes to kiss him lightly on the lips. "I bought you new clothes and washed them a couple of times to take away the newness. Everything's on the bed. See you later."

"This is going to be the fastest shopping expedition in history," Lily said as she parked the truck behind Webb Furniture. "I'm buying everything off the floor and asking for immediate delivery. I suppose this is an ass-backwards way of doing things, since I haven't been inside the house since Mr. Sonner finished it. Hey, Sadie, maybe the little guesthouse is done. Damn, we should have checked that first."

"It's done, Lily. I took Buzz over to run in the yard yesterday. I thought I could stay there if you plan to move into the big house. I don't want to cramp your style with Matt."

"Really! That's perfect. Now you can pick out your own stuff. That's going to be all yours, Sadie. Forever and ever. For some reason I think you're going to end up in Oregon in this big fancy house nestled in a mountain with all kinds of evergreens surrounding it. I didn't *see* it, but I do feel it." She laughed when Sadie blushed a rosy pink.

From the depths of her oversize canvas tote bag, Lily withdrew her furniture list. She was a salesman's dream as she walked up and down the aisles pointing or saying, this and this, and I want that and that and those two pieces over there and that armoire over there. Out of the corner of her eye she could see Sadie doing the same thing.

Lily wrote out a check the moment the store manager agreed to delivery for one o'clock.

"That gives us time to shop for bedding, dishes, and all the other things we need, and if we have time, we're going to the *Natchez Democrat* to see if they have any pictures of the Laroux sons. I read the paper every day while Matt was in the hospital, and there wasn't one word about the family house being broken into. I even read the back issues that came out when we were searching for Matt. I wish I knew how Matt planned to handle all of this. He's so worried if word gets out, the stock will go down. Here this guy was abducted, robbed blind, left to die, and he's worried about his investors."

"If he wasn't like that, you probably wouldn't love him. Do you really think I'll end up in Oregon?"

"Absolutely. You blew Dennis's socks off. He's about as smitten as a man can be. He called you, didn't he? You have a date. You don't need to be a love guru to figure out where it's all going. I'm so happy for you, Sadie. I didn't much care for Tom, but if he was what you wanted, I was okay with it. I just want you to be happy. You are better than a sister could ever be. Friendship is the most wonderful thing on this earth. I think, Sadie, you are the only person in the whole world I would trust with my children, my dogs, and my money."

"Lily, that's the nicest thing you've ever said to me. I feel the same way. That's how Dennis feels about Matt. My gosh, I almost forgot to tell you what Dennis told me last night about Marcus's wife. Wait till you hear this!"

They talked as they walked through the department store choosing pillows, comforters, sheets, and other household items. An hour later the Rover was packed to the roof. "That was fun, wasn't it?" Lily giggled as she got behind the wheel. "Last stop, the newspaper. If we have to do the microfilm thing, I'm going to leave you there and pick you up later.

Better yet, if you don't mind, I will leave you there. Is that okay, Sadie? As it is, we're cutting it pretty close. My fingers are crossed that the delivery truck will be a little late."

"Sure, don't worry about me. I can walk to the house from here. I need the exercise."

Sadie watched Lily drive away. She felt lost suddenly. Her best friend didn't need her anymore. Maybe that wasn't totally true, but now that Lily had Matt, she would want to spend all her time with him, which was the way it was supposed to be. She needed to move on now and get her own life. She eyed the phone in the lobby of the *Democrat* and made a mental note to call Ozzie when she finished what she'd come here to do. Maybe by then the lump in her throat wouldn't be so big. If it dissolved, there was less chance that she would cry.

She thought about the little cottage she'd stopped by to see yesterday. She could be happy living there. No, she could visit from time to time, but she couldn't live there. She needed to get on with her own life, forge new paths, meet new people, swim a couple of oceans. Meet some nice guy and eventually get married and have a couple of kids. She'd ask Lily and Matt to be the godparents. She wasn't going to count on Dennis, and she wasn't going to sit around and wait for him either. If he was seriously interested, he could find her in Wyoming. It was called taking charge of her life.

She eyed the phone again. Maybe she should call Ozzie now and get it out of the way since she had all afternoon to herself. She fumbled in her purse for change. Satisfied that she had enough money for a short conversation, she dialed the number before she could change her mind.

"Lulu, this is Sadie. Listen, I'm calling you from a phone booth, and I don't have much change on me. I wanted to ask if you could use some help. I can leave on Sunday if that's okay with you. Thanks, Lulu. Lily's fine. They're going to reschedule the wedding. Probably sometime soon. Tell Ozzie I said hello. I'll see you Sunday night."

Damn, the lump was back in her throat. And her eyes were burning, too. Only weak-kneed females cried, and she was not one of those. She squared her shoulders and walked up to the information desk to make her request known. She waited patiently until the Lifestyle weekend editor could be found.

She was an older woman, well past retirement age. She was lively, though, with a spring in her step and a twinkle in her eyes. "I'm Jolene Abernathy, and you must be Sadie Lincoln. I understand you would like to see a picture of Calumet's boys. Well, honey, you are in luck. I have one sitting right on my desk. I miss that old codger. I used to pick him up every Saturday night to play bingo at St. Mary's Basilica. It's the Catholic church Calumet belonged to. That man did have the luck. He won most every time we played. He'd laugh for hours because you see, I never won. It gave him such pleasure. We were friends all our lives. Now, tell me, why do you want to see a picture of the boys?"

Why indeed. "It's like this, Miss Abenathy. I'm a survival guide in Wyoming. I came here for a friend's wedding. It's the darnedest thing, ma'am, those young men sent in a deposit to take our survival course and forgot to complete the most important part of the forms. I thought as long as I was here, I'd look them up and ask them to complete it. I'm going back to Wyoming on Sunday night." At least one part of her bald-faced lie was true.

"I went by the electronics store Under-the-Hill, and the shop is closed due to a death in the family. You wouldn't happen to know when they'll be back, would you?"

"I'm sorry, I don't know. A survival course you say? Mercy. Those boys are forever traipsing off somewhere. Cal was so indulgent with them. Now, don't get me wrong, they did work in the store, and they did take it over when Cal had his last stroke. They took mighty good care of their daddy. They had nurses round the clock. Course, Cal could afford that. He made his money early on when cotton was king, as they say around here. Now, here it is. Striking-looking young men, wouldn't you say?" Miss Abernathy held out a framed photograph.

"They do look . . . sturdy. You have to be sturdy to take our course," Sadie said solemnly. "Is there anyone who might know where I can locate them since time is of the essence? I'd hate to see them lose their reservation since the deposit was quite substantial. You know, close personal friends, relatives, neighbors?"

"I can't say that I do, sweetheart. Did you try any of the other merchants Under-the-Hill? You could try Minnie Figgins. She kept house for Cal and stayed on to work for the boys after he passed on. I think she goes home at night now, though. When Cal was alive, she slept in the maid's quarters. As for neighbors, I doubt the boys have much to do with them. They're as old as Cal was and have live-in caregivers. I suppose you could stop by and ask. I think Minnie is your best bet. I'm sorry I'm not more help."

Sadie stared down at the picture in her hands, wondering how she could possibly get a copy of it when the woman said, "You're welcome to take the picture if you promise to return it. It has sentimental value."

"That's very kind of you. Yes, I would like to take it with me. I'll be sure to return it."

"What exactly will you be doing with the picture?"

"You did say they were bachelors, didn't you?" Sadie twinkled.

"Did I? Yes, they are. Oh, I see, you're single and available. Yes, of course."

Sadie forced a laugh. "Uh-huh."

"Well, I have to get back to work. Take as much time as you need, but be sure to bring the picture back."

"Thank you very much. I'll get it back to you as soon as I can. I hope you win at bingo tomorrow, Miss Abernathy."

"I don't go anymore, child. When Cal passed on all the fun went out of it."

"I'm sorry. Thanks again," Sadie said as she made her way down the hall and out to the lobby where she stared at the picture in her hands. "Bastards," she muttered under her breath.

Sadie buttoned up her jacket and headed down the street. It wasn't that far to the Laroux house. A fifteen-minute brisk walk at best. She slipped the framed photograph into her purse and set off.

She was wrong about the fifteen-minute walk. It took her thirty minutes. When she rang the bell on the front porch she hoped the housekeeper would invite her in and possibly offer her a cup of hot tea. She rang the bell three more times with no response. Well, she'd come all this way so she might as well try the back door. Perhaps the old lady was hard of hearing or maybe she was outside.

Sadie found her sitting on the steps, smoking a corncob pipe, a wizened little woman with steel gray hair tied into a topknot. She was skinnier than a string of dry spaghetti, with faded blue eyes that watered constantly. She removed the corncob pipe and offered up a toothless smile for Sadie's benefit. Sadie loved her on sight.

"What can I do for you, young woman?" the woman asked, tapping the pipe on the corner of the step.

"I'm looking for the boys," Sadie said boldly. "We're supposed to go on a trip together. Do you know where they are?"

"They left without you, honey," the housekeeper said, filling the pipe with fresh tobacco from the pocket of her baggy house dress. Eighty pounds at best. Maybe seventy-five. She also looked to be 105. Sadie blurted out the age question.

"Ninety-five my last birthday. I'm hopin' to make it to one hundred so that Willard Scott will put me on the television with them there jelly jars. That's only five more years to go. I'll be gettin' my hair fixed that day. The president of the United States sends you a personal birthday card when you turn one hundred. Did you know that?"

"You'll be pretty as a picture, and no, I didn't know that," Sadie said. "Are you going to get a new dress?"

"I might. One with a lace collar. The kind you can use on other dresses. I don't know if they still make them anymore. Things keep changing," she said fretfully. "So what are you going to do now that the boys up and left you, young woman?"

"I don't know. Do you know where they went?"

"Far away they said. Might be gone a whole year. They paid me up for the whole year and told me to take care of the house. I moved back in here and let my place go. They closed up the store. Said one of their cousins would come in the summertime and take it over. Can't remember which one. Didn't know there were any cousins left. You don't remember so good when you get old. Closed up the store real tight, in-surance paid up, too. That's why they done it that way. You can't do nothin' these days without in-surance."

She needed their names. She couldn't ask, now that she had said they were friends. "Mrs. Figgins, did you have nicknames for the boys?"

"I didn't, but their pa did. The oldest one was named after his pa and everyone called him Junior. The middle boy now was named after his mama's father's side of the family. His name was Hawthorne. The boys called him Thorny, and so did his friends. The young'un was named Bristol after his mama's mama's side of the family. Every one pretty much called him Tolly."

"Are you sure you don't know where they went, Mrs. Figgins? It's really important. I can't believe they left me stranded here like this. Didn't they say anything at all to give you a clue as to where they were going?"

"The three of them were like magpies, one would say something and then the other would say something different and then Tolly would add his two cents. It made me no never mind. Someplace warm with sand and no humidity, Junior said. They didn't pack much. It don't make no sense to me. They up and buy a new car, one of those fancy ones with the tiger on the front, and then they leave without you. What's gotten into these young'uns lately."

Sadie sucked in her breath. "How many cars do they have?"

"Four or five. They're all in the garage. Mr. Cal had to add on to the garage once they were old enough to drive. They be right over there. Take a look-see yourself."

Sadie trotted over to the garage and opened the door. The housekeeper was right, there were four cars parked side by side. The car on the end caught her eye. A silver-blue Jaguar. Matt's car. She squeezed her eyes shut and opened them again. She wasn't dreaming. It was Matt's car, complete with New York license plates. She closed the door carefully.

"I guess I should be going, Mrs. Figgins. Thanks for all your help. If those boys call, you be sure to tell them how upset I am that they left me behind."

"They won't call. They never do. But I will certainly do that if they should call. What name should I be giving them if they do call?"

A devil perched itself on Sadie's shoulder. "Tiffany Diamond."

"Now that's a sparkly kind of name," the housekeeper cackled.

"I'm a sparkly kind of gal," Sadie grinned. "Bye, Mrs. Figgins."

The housekeeper sucked on the pipe and blew out a stinky-smelling puff of smoke. She waved airily in Sadie's direction.

Sadie ran all the way to North Union Street. She was breathless when she burst through the front door. "Lily, I have news! I found Matt's car! Honest to God! There it was, right in the garage! That old house-keeper didn't have a bit of trouble telling me the boys had a new car, and she even told me to go look at it. Do you believe that, Lily? We have to tell Matt right away! Our first real big break. We should call the police, or do you have to check with Matt first? I bet there are millions of fingerprints all over it. Am I a detective or what? I'm going back to Wyoming on Sunday night!" Sadie blurted. "Say something, Lily!"

"Damn, you're good. You really found the car! Right there on their property! Unbelievable. God, I love you. Matt is going to go over the moon. I just called, and I guess he's sleeping because he didn't answer. I don't think we should rush over there and wake him up. The car isn't going to go anywhere. Let's give him another half hour, then surprise him."

"Sounds like a plan to me." Sadie looked around, noticing the room for the first time. "Ohhhh, Lily, this is gorgeous! I can't believe it's the same house! You did a fantastic job." She flopped down on a wheat-colored sofa with bright plum-colored cushions. "And it's comfortable. You could get lost in this sofa.

Matt is going to love it! Lily, it's beautiful. I hope you and Matt will be very happy here. You should have been a decorator. What an eye for color. I'm glad you decided not to carpet the floors. Look how great they came out. Such character. The exposed beams are stunning. What are you going to do to dress up the windows?"

"I don't know. Maybe just swags. I want to live here a while before I decide. I don't want to make a mistake. Do you think Matt will like it?" Lily asked.

"Lily, he's going to love it. This is a Matt and Lily house. I feel it in here," Sadie said, thumping her chest.

"It all just blended. The easy chairs, the ottomans, the little tables, and, of course, the big coffee table. Matt loves to pile junk on tables, and he also likes to put his feet up. He's going to flip over the big-screen TV. I can't wait for him to see it. What time is it?"

"A little after three."

"Let me give you the rest of the tour before we head over to the apartment. Everything is in place. I even washed the sheets and put them on the beds, and I washed those big fluffy towels I bought for Matt. They're so big they're like sheets. The dishes and silverware went through the dishwasher, and while they were washing I ran to the Natchez Market on

Seargent S. Prentiss and bought dinner. I've got a roast going in my new oven. Get this, I bought a bread machine, and bread is baking! Don't you love the smell? I can't believe you found Matt's car!"

Sadie wrinkled her nose. "Yeah and it looked clean, too. Shoot, maybe they had it washed and there are no fingerprints on it. Damn, I didn't think of that."

"There's bound to be one they forgot. We'll hope for the best," Lily said as she escorted Sadie from room to room.

"Sadie, tell me that was a joke about you going back to Ozzie's."

"I have to get on with my life. There's nothing for me here. You have Matt, and I'd just be a third wheel. I'm not living off you, and that's final."

"What about Dennis? I thought . . ."

Damn, the lump was back in her throat again. She tried to clear it. "If it's meant to be, it will be. If it isn't, nothing will happen. I refuse to sit around here waiting for him to maybe call or maybe say he's coming for a visit. We just met for heaven's sake. I'll do one last year with Ozzie and decide what I'm going to do when the year is up. I need it to wean myself away from you, Lily. You're embarking on a whole new life, and I don't belong in that life except as a friend that you can call on night or day. I'll visit if Ozzie gives me some time off. Remember, you're going to be traveling with Matt."

"But . . ."

"Shhh," Sadie said, putting her finger near Lily's lips. "It has to be this way. Now, how did the cottage come out?"

"Wait till you see it. For sure you won't want to leave. Wait right here. I have something for you." Lily ran to the kitchen for her purse. She rummaged in the depths of it for a crackly blue envelope. "It's the deed to the cottage. It's your home away from home forever and ever. It's my way of saying thank you for all our years of friendship. Don't think for one minute that I don't know you could have gotten $150,000 for this piece of property and yet you sold it to me for $80,000 because it was all I could afford with the renovations. Say something, Sadie."

"Thank you. It doesn't seem like enough. Two words." She hugged Lily, whose eyes were as wet as her own.

"I wish you wouldn't leave. I always thought we'd be together forever and ever. Matt loves you like a sister. He won't care."

"I care, Lily. I can't live in your shadow. We'll always be friends. I'll be your kids' godmother, and, if I ever get married, you'll be my kids' godmother. For sure that will bind us together forever and ever. We certainly were lucky when we found one another. Come on, I'm dying to see what you did with the cottage."

Sadie burst into tears the minute she stepped over the threshold. "It's just like you said, right down to the strawberry-pattern wallpaper in the kitchen. What a difference those gleaming white appliances make."

"Quick, look at the bathroom!" Lily gurgled.

"A garden tub! Where did you get wallpaper with ferns and frogs on it? My two most favorite things."

"Mr. Sonner found it for me. Isn't it gorgeous? This place was done in four days. All the pipes were here, so it was a simple matter to swap out the appliances. Ditto for the bathroom stuff. Sanding the floors and installing the new wiring were the biggest jobs. These floors came out as good as the ones in the main house. Like you said, old stuff has such character. I bet if these floorboards could talk, our ears would ring with the stories. The fireplace was cleaned out, and Mr. Sonner even laid a fire for you. It's ready to move into, Sadie. All you need is your toothbrush and jammies. Your own little place, Sadie, given to you from my heart. This will always be your home. When I had it subdivided, I paid the taxes for the next thirty years. What do you think of that? Don't get carried away; the taxes were minuscule."

"I think you're nuts is what I think," Sadie said, hugging her friend again. "I'll think about this place every day when I'm in Wyoming."

"I hope so. I'm going to miss you, Sadie. I understand, though. I'd do exactly the same thing if the situation was reversed."

"I love these oversize chairs. You can sleep in them. Everybody in the world should have a red plaid chair. Or two red plaid chairs. God, this is just so wonderful. Thank you again, Lily."

"Enough already. We need to get back to the apartment so you can tell Matt what you found out. He's going to flip out! Wow! Sadie the sleuth! Is there anything you *can't* do? Listen, if he's still asleep, we let him sleep till he wakes up on his own, okay?"

"A thing or two," Sadie said, linking her arm with Lily's. "I agree that we shouldn't wake him up. Good sound sleep is important to him right now. Do you think Matt will go to the police now that we found his car? If he can I.D. the picture, that's all the proof they'll need. Finding the car is a bonus and more proof. If they didn't get rid of his clothes in the closet, that's even more proof. I know we broke in, but that doesn't matter. But even without the clothes, we still have the car and Matt's positive I.D. if he recognizes the guys in the picture. The housekeeper is the one who told me to look in the garage."

"I don't know, Sadie. Matt has this thing about the company and the stock. He doesn't want to see it nose-dive. He worries about his investors. He said he dreams all the time about armies of investors storming Digitech's headquarters when something goes awry. They haven't unveiled the new software, and then there is that really *big* announcement. I wish I knew more about his business. I can't even carry on an intelligent conversation where computers are concerned. Little kids know more than I do. Maybe I'll take some classes so I at least learn the basics. I still can't believe you found his car. The chances of Matt and Dennis finding those guys has to be one in a *kazillion.* Even if they do find them, how can they get them back here? I'm assuming *far away* like the housekeeper said, means another country. There are places that don't extradite. I know he isn't going to listen to me, Sadie, if I try to push him into going to the police. If it was me, I'd be singing like a bird."

"Me, too. Don't worry about the computer thing. Only take classes if you want to, Lily.

Do it for yourself, not someone else. Everyone isn't computer literate. There are many people in this world who are totally turned off by computers, and yes, I know it's the future. Another thing, remember where we've been for the past ten years. When would we have had time to learn about that stuff? I have to believe Matt knows what he's doing. I think it's commendable that he puts his investors ahead of himself. Foolish but commendable."

Lily sighed. "We had the winter months. We could have done it then. I think I have a mental block where Matt's business is concerned. I need to get back to the apartment and bring him here. I think the roast will be okay. The bread machine shuts off when the bread is done, and keeps it warm. Are you going to move into the cottage today, Sadie?"

"No. I think I'll stay in the apartment tonight. I want you two to have the whole place to yourselves. Remember, you have no coverings on your windows."

Lily laughed. "I can't wait for the yard to be done and for spring so I can plant flowers and work outdoors."

"Oh, Lily, you are going to have such a wonderful life." Sadie beamed with enthusiasm.

"I know, Sadie, I know. God really did bless me this time around."

Buzz bounded to the door, Gracie behind him, the moment Lily fitted the key into the lock. Her eyebrows rose at their quiet greeting until she looked into the living room to see Matt sprawled asleep on the sofa. She smiled, and whispered, "I could sit and look at him all day long, Sadie. My heart just feels like it's going to overflow. Those first days were pretty dark, and this heart of mine was black and ugly. Why are we so prepared always to believe the worst? Dennis didn't. He hung in there and wouldn't budge. That doesn't say much for me, does it? Do you think I'm insecure or something?"

"You had every right to feel the way you did. I would have felt the same way. What's that old saying, once burned, twice shy or something like that. That's all in the past. This is now, and your future is looking bright and rosy. Enjoy every minute of it. You do your thing. I'm going to start gathering up my stuff and pack everything. Sunday is going to roll around real quick."

"Sadie . . ."

"Shhh, this is the way it has to be for now. I'm okay with this. It's not my time to make heavy-duty decisions. Boy, am I glad I didn't go to Australia. I'd be one cranky girl about now. Lulu said Larry and Annie are there already. Seems Ozzie wants to give the place a face-lift for the new season, and there's plenty of work for everyone. I'm looking forward to seeing the gang. They're like family. Who knows, maybe some of the others will show up, and it will be like old times. At least we'll have some time to enjoy some winter sports. I haven't skied for so long I don't know if I'll remember how to make my feet work. C'mon, Lily, wipe that awful look off your face. I'll just be a phone call away."

"I know but . . ."

"I have to think about me now, Lily. Smile. If you don't, I'm *never* coming back. I'm going down to the storage area for my trunks. I'll try not to make any noise. Do you want me to leave the door ajar?"

Lily shook her head as she shrugged out of her jacket and threw her purse on a chair in the small hallway. "Do you want some help?"

"Nope."

Matt rose up on his elbow the minute the door closed. "Lily, what's wrong? Why are you crying? Come here. What happened?"

"I'm not crying. I was thinking about it, though. Sadie's leaving on Sunday. She's going back to Ozzie's camp. She thinks three's a crowd. It wouldn't be like that. She said she wants to get on with her life. I understand that part of it. She stayed on here to be with me instead of going to Australia. Sadie has always been my one-man support team. I just feel bad. You know, kind of lost. We've never really been apart before. We walked to school together for twelve years. We roomed together at college. We traveled together, then worked for Ozzie for ten years. She hasn't even gone, and I miss her."

Matt stared helplessly at Lily, uncertain as to what he should say. He put his arm around her shoulder. "I think I know how you feel, honey. If Dennis up and left, I'd feel like I lost part of me. You're thinking right now if she leaves, she's taking part of you with her, and you're losing part of her. If it was a perfect world, this wouldn't be happening, but it isn't a perfect world. Sadie's right, she's doing what's best for her. You can't be selfish with your emotions. I remember some very long discussions you and I had last year where we both agreed that when you loved someone totally their happiness came first. Love is being generous, wanting that person's happiness more than your own. I bet you thought I wasn't paying attention, huh?"

Lily sniffed. "No, I knew you were paying attention. I'm going to miss her. It's a girl thing, Matt. I know you understand, but you don't *really* understand. I'll be okay. Hey, Sadie found your car! Do you believe that? I was going to bound in here and stun you with the news. That's the really important news, and here I am blubbering like some silly little girl. I'm sorry, Matt."

"How? Where? How'd she do that? You girls are amazing!"

"Wait, there's more," Lily said, running to the dining room to where Sadie tossed her purse. "Look at this!"

"Holy shit! That's them! They're the bastards that robbed me and left me to die! Son of a bitch! Where did you get this?"

"Sadie got it. I think she missed her calling. She should have been a detective. Are you going to the police now, Matt? I think you should."

"I need to digest all of this. I want to talk to Dennis. I can't believe this. Look at the bastards, they're wearing suits and ties. They look like fucking upstanding citizens!"

"We know for certain now who they are and we have names. The one on the right is Junior or Calumet Laroux Jr. The one in the middle is named Hawthorne and is called Thorny. The one on the left is obviously the youngest and goes by the name Tolly. His real name is Bristol. You have Sadie to thank for all this, Matt."

"I'm feeling kind of light-headed right now. Do you mind if I go outside for a while and get some fresh air? I can't believe this! I thought I'd never be able to find them. You need to tell me how this all happened. Didn't you say you wanted to show me something?"

"I did and I do. How about a ride in the truck with the windows down? We can take the dogs. Otherwise, are you feeling all right?"

"I'm fine. I was waiting for Dennis to get back to me earlier. I closed my eyes, and I guess I drifted off. We didn't make much headway in tracking my money. It all went to the Caymans and from there it's a blizzard of transactions. Even Dennis can't get a handle on it."

"I just have to gather up a few things. I'll meet you by the truck." Lily tossed him the keys just as Sadie opened the door to shove her trunks into the hall. She watched, a smile on her face, as Matt twirled her friend this way and then that way, shouting his thanks over and over.

"I owe you, Sadie Lincoln. Big-time." Sadie flushed at his praise. "Considering all you've done on my behalf, I wonder if I might impose one more time. Do you think you could pick Dennis up at the airport? He's coming in on a seven o'clock Continental flight from New York."

"Of course. I really didn't have anything to do this evening anyway."

"Good. See you later."

Lily trotted into the living room, her makeup case and Matt's shaving gear clutched in her hands. "I heard that," she chortled as she looked pointedly at the two trunks standing in the hallway.

"Don't go down that road, Lily," Sadie snapped.

"I'm outta here," Lily said, dumping the two plastic cases into a Kroger grocery bag. "Keep your fingers crossed that Matt likes the place. I don't know what I'll do if he doesn't. He will, won't he, Sadie?"

"Of course he will. Go on now, make Matt's day!"

"I'm going, I'm going, but I feel all twitchy and jittery inside. If you need me, call, Sadie. Or better yet, after you pick Dennis up, stop by the house and we'll all have a nice glass of wine. Will you promise?"

"Nope. Go, Lily. I have things to do."

A gust of wind blew in the door when Lily opened it. She ran down the steps shouting, "I'm coming, Matt!"

Thirteen

Lily cuddled deep into the crook of Matt's arm and sighed contentedly.

"I don't believe I've ever been happier in my life, Lily. When are we getting married? I want us to have kids right away. You okay with that, honey?"

"Oh, yes, to the kids, but no to a wedding. I'm not going through that again. Let's just wake up someday and say today is the day and go for it right then and there. I can't do it again, Matt, I just can't. If you want, we could go to Las Vegas and get married in one of the wedding chapels or go to city hall and get married by a justice of the peace. That's about all I can handle in the way of a wedding. The question now is, are you okay with *that?*"

"I'm for whatever you want. I like the idea of eloping. Just us. We can always throw a big party after we get back right here in our new house, which, by the way, is something I never expected in my wildest dreams. I don't know what to say."

"It's not finished. It will look a lot different when the curtains are hung. Pictures on the walls make another big difference, and scatter rugs here and there always add something to a room. Not many rugs, though, because I want everyone to appreciate these old floors. Plants in the corners, a few ficus trees, knick-knacks, that sort of thing. That's what makes a house a home. It's called *stuff*. I just love stuff. A couple of more weeks, and it will look really beautiful. Owning an old house is an ongoing project. Something always goes, a leak, a wire, an appliance, the roof, a leaky window, faulty furnace, that kind of thing. I know this sounds crazy, but I am actually looking forward to all those disasters."

"Me, too. We have the dogs and the house, so all we need now are the kids." Matt grinned from ear to ear at his pronounce-ment.

"I wonder what it will be like to have a baby in the house," Lily murmured.

"Damn wonderful would be my opinion. What do you think it will be like living here, Lily? You know, putting down roots, belong-ing to a community. What if the townspeople don't accept us? There are a lot of what-ifs when you take a big step like this."

"I see it all in my mind's eye, Matt. That doesn't mean it will work that way, but it's a place to start. In order to belong, you have to join up as they say. You have contributions to make. I'm sure I can donate time to any number of worthy projects, at least until our babies come along. Oh, Matt, there is such history to this town. So many stories to tell. Sadie and I took a tour of the Natchez City Cemetery last year. Don Estes, a retired banker and amateur historian, gave us the tour, and he was so knowledgeable he boggled my mind. He seems to know everything. There was one grave where this little girl died who was afraid of the dark. The mother wanted steps built in behind the stone so she could walk down there and sit with her little girl. Can you imagine that? And then there was Louise the Unfortunate. If you don't want to hear this, I can tell you another time."

"No, I want to hear it. I want to know everything if we're going to live here. Then when our friends come to visit, I can tell them what you're telling me. Go ahead, Lily, tell me the story."

"Sometime after the Civil War, a young prostitute at Natchez Under-the-Hill died of a disease described as a 'disorganization of the lungs,' probably tuberculosis. As she had no family, no known last name, and no funds, Reverend Stratton took up a collection from the saloon keepers and merchants from Under-the-Hill to pay for her funeral and a small headstone on Jewish Hill. He directed his eulogy of Louise toward her 'sisters' in the oldest profession, with the goal of swaying them from their chosen paths. He's the one who had her tombstone inscribed 'Louise the Unfortunate.' Isn't that sad, Matt? Can you imagine being buried without a name on your marker? It's like Mary Margaret, who was buried as the Wish Keeper.

"Sadie went ballistic once when we went to the cemetery in Florida to visit our parents' graves. There was this big, elaborate stone with a man's name on it and next to it a little stone, no bigger than a tablet with the words *His Wife.* She was buried without a name. After that, every year when we went back, Sadie and I visited that grave and put some flowers on it. When it's time to die the only thing you can take with you is your good name. Both Louise the Unfortunate and the wife of that man didn't have even that. It makes me mad, Matt."

Lily leaned up on her elbow. "I don't want to get mad all over again. One day, I'll take you to the cemetery and show you the graves. Right now, though, I have to talk to you about something really important. But first I think we should talk about what you're going to do. I really wish you would go to the police. If not the local police, the FBI. You were kidnapped, Matt. You were left to die out there.

If we hadn't found you, you'd be dead by now." She shivered at the horrible thought.

"I didn't die, Lily. I'm here, and I'm okay. This isn't as easy as you make it sound. I have to think about the company, the investors, and a host of other things. We're days away from making our big contributions to the high-tech world. I don't want to spoil that. I can file charges anytime. Yeah, the trail is going to grow cold, but somehow I'll find those bastards. If I report this now, it will be plastered all over the papers within hours. We also have to deal with what Marcus has done. Things like that affect your investors. It's like they can't trust the company. That's about all the negative publicity we can handle right now. Even though we had nothing to do with it, we're going to get a lot of adverse publicity. One of our own was a traitor. I'd like to strangle the guy. I suspect he's going to be easy to find because Marcus is too damn arrogant for his own good. You know what, there's nothing we can do. So he snookered a couple of competitors for a big score. Do you think they're going to go after him? I think not. They were trying to steal our company secrets. I don't know if they approached Marcus or he approached them. In the end it doesn't make any difference. He sold out. It will circulate in the industry, and by next week it will be old news. It happens every day of the week. So I lost someone I thought I could count on. We have backup. Dennis has a protégé he's about ready to give some authority to. The kid kind of reminds me of Dennis and myself when we first started out."

"I'll still feel better if you go to the authorities, Matt."

"Lily, look at me and listen to me carefully. I can't prove anything. Think about it. So my car is in their garage. They'll say I parked it there. I'm assuming it wasn't damaged. How can I prove otherwise? I stood you up at your wedding. They'll say I did it once before and I got cold feet again and took off and landed myself in a mess. How can I prove that's not true? So I transferred large sums of money from my accounts to other accounts all over the world. That's done twenty-four hours a day seven days a week. So what if I never did it before? I did it this time. My dog got lost. Dogs get lost all the time. I got lost. You found me. Yep, I almost died because I was foolish and did foolish things. I'll look like a fool, and I don't want the CEO of Digitech looking like a fool. Do you see what I'm talking about, Lily?"

"So they get away with it is what you're saying."

"For now. Dennis and the new kid are going to be working on it day and night. If there's a way to track the money, they'll find it. First rule in business, follow the money. So, can we lay this to rest for now?"

"Yes, but I don't like it. I hate it that they're off spending your money. I hate it that they dumped Gracie and left her to fend for herself, and I want to kill them with my bare hands for leaving you out there to die. I won't talk about it anymore, if that's what you want."

"Okay, it's your turn. How about telling me whatever it is you've been teasing me with. Whatever it is, I can handle it. I can, can't I, Lily?" He sounded so anxious, Lily smiled.

"I don't know, Matt. I'm having a hard time with it. It's this gizmo hanging on my neck. If we move into this house and raise a family here, I officially become the new Wish Keeper. Promise me you'll keep an open mind, okay?"

"I promise."

"You know how you're always throwing stuff out to the universe. . . . It's kind of like that with me and this . . . *thing*. Now listen carefully. I'm going to give you a test when I'm finished."

Matt propped the pillows behind his head as he listened. When she finished a long time later, clearly agitated, he fingered the pendant around her neck. "What do *you* want to do, Lily?"

"That's just it, Matt, I don't know. At first I thought I was meant to wear it to find you. Make no mistake, without it, without the visions or whatever they were, I never could have found you. I feel like I *am* the Wish Keeper. I know secrets, but I don't know what they are. They're just there. Wishes are something different. I don't understand that part of it. What I do know is when I take it off, I feel different, lighter if that makes sense. But something always makes me put it back on. Wishes and secrets are more or less the same thing, don't you agree?"

"Yes," Matt said.

"Isn't this kind of like when you're at your wits' end and you toss it out to the universe and then sit back and wait for things to happen?"

"Yes and no. You touch it, and you see things. Things that are happening or have already happened. That's almost like an instant response. I guess that's the difference. Are you afraid of it, Lily?"

"In a way. It's a tremendous responsibility. What if I see something, and I don't understand it and don't know what to do?"

"Did you ever make a wish on it?"

"No, not really. What I'm asking you is

this. Are you okay with me keeping it and acting on something if I get one of those . . . whatever they are, visions or spells?"

"Yes, I'm okay with it."

"You don't think I'm crazy, do you, Matt?"

Matt's arm tightened on her shoulder. "No, I don't think you're crazy. I think things happen all the time in this life of ours that have no explanation. Either you accept it as it is, or you reject it. I don't see anything evil in it. I think you'd feel that. What do you feel?"

"Sometimes burdened. Sometimes I feel heady, like I can literally take on the world. It's difficult to explain. I feel different when I'm wearing it. There's a gravestone in the backyard that says *Mary Margaret* and underneath her name are the words, *Wish Keeper*. There's no last name. No date. I guess she was the official Wish Keeper here in this house. The job and the pendant were supposed to be handed down to Sadie's mother and then to Sadie herself, but her mother refused to accept it. Sadie found the pendant in the back of the closet and gave it to me. She said I needed something from the house to make it officially mine. Up to that point, she didn't remember any of this stuff, and it wasn't till we were spending such long hours at the hospital that little bits and pieces came back to her."

"If you're asking my opinion, Lily, it would be this. Wear it until you no longer want to. If you feel it affects you adversely, take it off. Everything in life is not explainable. I certainly learned that."

"I wish it was pretty. Actually, it's kind of ugly," Lily said, yanking at the chain to center the pendant.

Matt watched in horror as Lily fell away from his embrace and rolled off the bed onto the floor. Her eyes were glazed as her hands tried to reach out to him. He was off the bed in a second, her head cupped in his hands. "Lily, Lily, what's wrong? Snap out of it. Lily!" He shook her shoulders to no avail. "Lily, it's me, Matt. C'mon, honey, sit up. What's happening here?"

Lily jerked free, sat up and stared at Matt. She struggled to take a clear, deep breath. "It happened. This is the way it always happens."

"Jesus," Matt said, rocking back on his heels. "You scared me. Did you see something? Talk to me. What the hell did you see?"

"I saw the three brothers. And then I saw Marcus in a different place. I don't know where it was."

"What?" The single word exploded from Matt's mouth like a bullet.

"The brothers were at a beach bar. One of those resort places where there's a cabana bar right on the beach. They were together laughing and talking. That's all I saw except their bare feet. One of them was really sunburned."

"Are you suggesting that Marcus engineered the whole thing? I can't believe that! Those guys were amateurs. They didn't know who I was until they looked at my ATM card. Lily, take that damn thing off. If this is what happens to you, then I don't want you wearing it. Take it off, Lily."

"Marcus wasn't with them. He was separate, in a different place." Lily reached up and removed the chain and pendant. She laid it on the floor in front of her. Suddenly she felt like crying and didn't know why. "Where would someone like Marcus go with all that money? You know Marcus, try and think. You said the brothers were amateurs. Would they stay close to home, go far away? This whole thing is so bizarre it's making me crazy. Where would Marcus go with all that money?"

"Lily, I have no idea. I was never really involved in Marcus's private life. Off the top of my head, I'd say he wired the money into a Swiss numbered account, then wired it to a thousand other accounts just like those jerks that snatched me. Maybe the south of France. Spain. He could be anywhere. Hell, he could be in Miami for all I know. Miami is only two hours from New York by plane. It would be

333

just like him to be right under everyone's nose. Wherever he is, he's probably laughing his damn head off. Was it in the past, now, or was it going to happen?"

"I don't know, Matt. Usually it's in the past, like it already happened, and I'm getting a replay. Is that important?"

"Shit, Lily, I don't know."

"If they left the country, they must have traveled with their own passports. Your abduction was a spur-of-the-moment kind of thing. Wasn't Marcus's departure much the same?"

"Yes. Why?"

"Then that means they all traveled with their own identification. You have a window of time here. Can't you hire a detective to do whatever it is they do, bribe people, nose around, that kind of thing? You have names now and a picture. I would think your firm would have some top-notch security. Call them, Matt. Don't let the trail grow any colder."

"It's late, Lily. I'll do it first thing in the morning."

"No, Matt. Make the call now. They can be ready to do things in the morning. Things can be done during the night that can't be done during the day. You certainly have nothing to lose. Please, do it. They can put the gears into motion." Seeing his reluctance, Lily said, "I took off the Wish Keeper for you. You can do this for me."

Matt reached for the phone.

It was two o'clock in the morning when Matt hung up the phone for the last time. "They're on it. Don't get the idea they're going to be out there acting like gumshoes. It's all done with computers these days. We'll probably know something late today. Gracie needs to go out. Looks like Buzz is ready, too. I'll take them."

"I'll go with you. I could use some fresh air. I'll just turn on the floodlights outside. As long as we're going out, I'll show you the gravestones. The dogs are the ones who found them. Bundle up, Matt. We can't take a chance on you getting a cold. That means you put socks on."

"Nag, nag, nag," Matt grumbled with good nature. "Okay, guys, we're going out. Hold on, Buzz, fetch the leashes. I don't care if they do know the yard, Lily. This dog of mine is never going unleashed again."

"Buzz doesn't need a leash. I'm ready. Maybe I shouldn't put the lights on."

"No. Put them on. I want to be able to see clearly. It's not like we're going to be out here a long time."

"This is it, Matt. The stones are very old. They're so worn, the granite is actually shiny and smooth. Feel it."

He didn't want to stretch out his hand, didn't want to touch a gravestone in the middle of the night, but he did it because Lily asked him to. He felt his shoulders slump, felt a tremendous weight settle over him as his fingers traced the letters on the words, *Wish Keeper*.

"Matt, what's wrong?"

"I don't know. Nothing. I just suddenly felt this tremendous weight on my shoulders and then . . . this . . . surge of energy. Like electricity ripping through me."

"Ghosts are energy fields. Wait here. Don't move. I'm going inside for the Wish Keeper. Stay, Buzz."

Lily was back in less than five minutes, breathless with the exertion of running, the pendant clutched tightly in her hands. She draped the necklace over the top of the stone and then stepped back. "We're giving it back, Mary Margaret. I don't think I'm the right person to continue . . . I can't handle it." She reached for Matt's hand and squeezed it tight.

The floodlight attached to the corner of the roof of the small cottage shone directly on the tiny cemetery. They watched in stupefied amazement as the pendant floated forward, then upward, before settling around Lily's neck.

Buzz whined as he squirmed closer to Lily.

Gracie tried to hug Matt's leg.

"I think we should go inside," Matt said hoarsely as he gingerly backed away.

Instead of following Matt, Lily stepped forward, both hands outstretched. "I need to make a wish, Mary Margaret. I want to wish for a peaceful, happy life. If you can't give me that, I'll have to leave," she whispered. "I'll leave this behind for the next owner."

"Look," Matt said.

Lily looked around the overgrown backyard to see it suddenly bathed in warm, golden sunshine. Four small children romped and frolicked with a basket of wiggling puppies, their laughter contagious. Gracie and Buzz looked on indulgently as Lily and Matt flipped burgers and hot dogs on a grill. "Mommy! Daddy! Here comes Uncle Dennis and Aunt Sadie!" More laughter, hugs, kisses. Happiness.

Lily blinked as the overgrown yard came back into view. Her mouth felt thick and fuzzy, her tongue too big for her mouth. Matt, his eyes wild, stood rooted to the ground. "Did you . . . did you . . ."

"Yes. I think we just saw into our future. I

wished for a happy, peaceful life."

"Jesus!"

"Let's go inside, Matt. It really is cold out here. I'll make us some hot chocolate. I don't think either one of us is going to get any more sleep tonight."

"What's the word, Lily? Magic? Supernatural? What?"

"I don't know. We had two boys and two girls, Matt! They looked like little versions of us. And a bunch of puppies. It was this yard, this house. We had a barbecue. Dennis and Sadie were here. They called them 'Aunt' and 'Uncle.' Did you see all that, Matt?"

"Yes. I think I'm spooked. This can't be. How can it be?"

"It is. I have to keep the pendant. That was Mary Margaret's way of telling us it is definitely not an evil thing. I just wish there was someone I could talk to who really knows about these things. Someone who can explain it to me."

"You made a wish, Lily," Matt said, his voice raspy with his words.

Lily nodded. "Minnie Figgins! I know that name. I just heard it recently. God, it's the housekeeper at the Laroux house. The one Sadie was talking to. She's ninety-five years old. She might know something. The name just came to me. We're going there first

338

thing in the morning."

"Fine. But we're going into the house right now. Turn off the outside lights."

Lily reached up to turn off the switch. The yard turned midnight black. Buzz threw his head back and howled. The fine hairs on Lily's arms moved.

"Does that thing open up? Did you ever look inside?"

"No. I mean, no, I never looked inside, and yes, it opens up."

Both Matt and Lily jerked forward when the phone took that minute to ring. They looked at one another as much as to say, I don't know anyone who would call at two-thirty in the morning. Lily's hand snaked out. "Hello," she said cautiously.

"Lily, it's me. I had this sudden feeling you needed me. Dennis and I were just sitting here talking and all of a sudden, the strangest feeling came over me. Did I wake you?"

"Sadie! No, Matt and I just came in from outside. Listen, why don't you and Dennis come over here. I'm going to make some hot chocolate. Bring the marshmallows. We were just saying we weren't going back to bed. I'll tell you all about it when you get here."

"This is beyond strange, Lily," Matt said, sitting down at the table.

"You're telling me. Oh, Matt, I don't think

I want to be able to see into the future. That little scene in the yard was nice. But . . ."

"I know, Lily. I guess it isn't as simple as we thought. I'm not sure you can just take it off. Even if you do, are you still officially a Wish Keeper? Or, do you have to move away? They say spirits are bound to certain places, so it probably wouldn't follow you. I can't get a handle on any of this," Matt muttered. "I like throwing things out to the universe better. There's a sense of *normalcy* to doing it that way. This is kind of like hocus-pocus if you know what I mean."

"Maybe Dennis and Sadie will have some input," Lily said. Her tone of voice said she didn't believe it for a minute.

The dogs didn't bother to bark or get up from their comfortable positions under the table when Sadie and Dennis entered the kitchen through the back door.

"Very nice," Dennis said, looking around. "I like it, Lily."

Lily smiled when the two men grabbed for each other's hands and pumped them vigorously. Friends forever. Lily smiled at Sadie, who tossed her a bag of marshmallows from the shopping bag she was carrying.

They talked into the night, their hands cupped around mugs of hot chocolate.

"We're computer engineers, wizards or so

they say, and we can't figure this out," Dennis said in disgust.

"Reality and the supernatural are two different things. Take off the pendant, and put it in the center of the table. Let's all look at it and when I say go, each of us blurts out the first thing that comes to mind. Not right now, though. So, Sadie, do you think the housekeeper will talk to us if we go over there after breakfast?"

"I don't know. She talked to me. Quite openly as a matter of fact. She's a sweet little lady. Maybe we could take her some flowers or maybe some soft candies. Or a pouch of fresh tobacco. It certainly won't hurt to try. Are we going there mainly to find out if she knows anything about the Wish Keeper or are you going to quiz her on the three brothers?"

"Both. I thought we'd just tell her the truth and see how she responds. I've always believed that truth wins out in the end. Let's just cross our fingers that I'm right this time. So, what have you two been up to?" Matt asked as he winked at Lily. "Go! Dennis?"

"Fear."

"Sadie?"

"Safety."

"Lily?"

"Peace."

"How about you, Matt?" Dennis queried.

"Secrecy."

They looked at one another, their faces registering their emotions. It was Matt who broke the silence. "So, what did you guys do all evening?" he asked directing his question to Dennis.

Dennis burst out laughing. "We spent the evening watching the Weather Channel on television. There's a blizzard heading for Wyoming. Actually it's two blizzards, one sweeping west across Nebraska and one sweeping east across Idaho. They expect both storms to converge on Wyoming around the same time. According to the weather girl it's the likes of which they haven't seen in over seventy-five years."

"Bummer," Lily said, her eyes on Sadie. "Guess you won't be leaving on Sunday night, huh? Unless you want to sit in a Kansas City airport for days and days on your layover. Better call Ozzie and alert him."

"It could blow over. You know those weather people, they always blow things out of proportion. I'll wait till Sunday morning to call. The worst-case scenario is I have to wait a few days. No big deal."

Lily watched Dennis's expression. It was obvious he thought it was a big deal. She thought about the scene she'd witnessed in her backyard earlier. Uncle Dennis and Aunt Sadie. She made a mental note to tune to the Weather Channel to keep up on the weather conditions just in case Sadie decided to go. If that happened, the three of them would somehow derail her into staying.

"What time do you suppose Miss Minnie Figgins gets up, Sadie?"

"I have no idea. This is just a guess on my part but I don't think she sleeps much. My grandmother was like that. She'd sleep an hour at a time and prowl around all night. At least that's what my mother said. My mother said it had something to do with being afraid she wouldn't wake up. You know, long sleeps, that kind of thing. I always thought the older you got, the more you slept, but Mom said it was just the opposite. I think we'd be safe going over there around seven. She might be out on the steps smoking her corncob and drinking coffee. She was quite sociable with me. I suspect she might be lonely."

Lily looked at her watch. "Let's have some breakfast. You guys go into the living room so you aren't under our feet while we cook. Place your order and Sadie and I will whip it up."

"Blueberry pancakes with blueberry syrup and soft butter," Dennis chirped. "Lots and lots of crisp bacon."

"Two eggs over easy, lots of crisp bacon,

white toast, soft butter, and jam. Strong coffee," Matt said.

"I'll have a scrambled egg," Lily said. "How about you, Sadie?"

"I'll have the same as you. Guess you didn't have any luck with Matt going to the cops, huh?"

"None at all. He's got this mind-set, and he isn't budging. You didn't say much about my little revelation out there in the yard. In it you and Dennis were a couple as in Aunt and Uncle. You like him a lot, don't you Sadie? The Weather Channel? That's all you did all night? This is not the Sadie I know and love."

Sadie turned from cracking eggs in a bowl. "He intimidates me, Lily. I'm not the smartest person in the world, but I'm not the dumbest either. I feel dumb compared to him."

"When we were out looking for Matt, did you think he felt dumb compared to you? He did, you know. He even admitted it. That took guts. You need to work on that feeling. Be honest and open. Don't let him get away, Sadie. I think he's the one for you. Matt thinks so, too."

"I think what I do is a worthy occupation. But, Lily, it's a go-nowhere job. So we make twenty bucks an hour. Big deal. We have health insurance and a 401K. That's all we have. Like you, I could teach, but I don't want to. I'm not teacher material. Being in a classroom would make me nuts in three days. Maybe two days. I had myself all cranked up to leave on Sunday. I'm packed. Then this storm. I hate it when I make a decision, and then something goes awry."

"Are you talking about Dennis or the snowstorm?" Lily asked softly.

"Dammit, both," Sadie snapped, as a piece of bacon sizzled and then spit high in the air. She turned it over with a long-handled fork.

"Sadie, look at me. If you could have anything in the world, anything at all, what would you wish for? Wait, wait, don't answer that. Stop what you're doing. Write down your wish, don't tell me what it is, and I'm going to put it in this doo-hickey hanging off my neck. It has to be a little piece of paper, and you have to roll it tight so it will fit. I'm going to ask Matt and Dennis to do the same thing. Then we're going to sit back and see what happens. Will you do it?"

"Why not." Sadie turned off the stove and wiped her hands on a towel before she rummaged in the kitchen drawer for a piece of paper.

"I can't believe I'm doing this," she muttered a few minutes later when she handed over a minuscule piece of paper rolled into a tight little cylinder.

"I am now an official Wish Keeper," Lily said, fastening the top of the little cylinder. "I now hold my first three secrets. Do you suppose they disappear like magic when the wish comes true? If it does come true, do you take the paper out? I need rules and instructions. I'm going at this blind."

"And you're doing a fine job of it, too," Sadie said. "When you were in the living room, what were they saying about the storm?"

Lily giggled. "Dennis and Matt are watching the Shopper's Channel. They're featuring computers for twelve hundred bucks. The first one hundred buyers get a free six-month stint on AOL. They're trying to figure out the profit margin on Dennis's pocket calculator. They're getting nowhere fast." She giggled again. "So what'd you wish for?" she asked slyly.

"None of your business, Lily."

"Testy, aren't we? Want to tell me why."

"I have feelings for Dennis. I don't know where they came from. All of a sudden, he's all I can think about. I know I just met him, but I feel like I've known him forever. I'm afraid to . . . you know, open up. It's that inferiority thing. I don't know what to do about it. I hate feeling this way, Lily, I really do."

"Sadie, when I don't know what to do about something, I don't do anything. I just wait it out. Dennis would be the luckiest man in the world to have you. He knows it, too. Trust me. I'm pretty good at reading people, and I see the way he looks at you. Just be yourself. You don't have to impress anyone. You know that old saying, to thine own self be true. You are so uptight you look rigid. Relax. So what'd you wish for?" Lily wheedled.

"I'm not telling you, so stop asking. You better not look either. If you do, it won't work."

"How do you know that?"

"I don't. I'm assuming. A wish is supposed to be secret. How many pieces of bacon do you want?"

"Three," Lily said. "This is a pretty kitchen, isn't it? I can't wait to hang some green plants in the breakfast nook and over the window. I am going to have a gorgeous view out that bow window once the garden people finish the yard. I can see myself sitting there in the morning with my coffee and a newspaper. Sadie, I am so happy. I bet you five bucks Dennis is in there moaning and groaning to Matt about you. I can go around by the dining room and listen. D'ya want me to do that?"

Sadie's pleasant face worked itself into a

grimace. "I'd love to know, but no, don't do it," she sighed. "What will be will be."

"Boy, is that ever the truth, my friend."

Fourteen

Betsy Collins stared at herself in the beveled-glass mirror. She smiled at her reflection. She did love cosmetics. Where would the women of the world be today without makeup? She waited a moment before she reached for a spritz bottle and sprayed her face. Ah, now the makeup would stay put for twelve full hours. A full day of shopping could play hell with one's makeup. She continued to stare at her reflection, wondering how her husband could have left her. She was so perfect it was positively sinful. They'd made such a handsome couple.

She'd loved him once, and he had loved her. He'd showered her with gifts, made love to her daily, taken her on magnificent vacations. She couldn't have asked for more, and yet she did. Her gaze dropped to the ornate, satin jewelry box and the treasure trove of jewelry she'd insisted Marcus buy her. And now here she sat, alone with her expensive cosmetics, designer wardrobe, and jewelry, with bills that threatened to strangle her. Dennis Wagner's words rang in her ears. *The tax man cometh.* Did they put mothers in prison if they didn't pay their taxes? Probably, since everyone said the IRS had no heart. Oh God, oh God, she'd be reduced to using *Jergens* lotion, maybe even *Noxzema.* They probably issued some kind of harsh soap they doled out to prisoners once a week. What about her weekly waxing? She cringed, knowing they didn't give out razors, much less depilatories. Who would touch up her roots? She'd look like a hag in less than a month.

Get out now. Cut your losses. Take the money and run. Where? How? She wanted to cry until she looked at her perfectly made-up face. "If I ever get my hands on you, Marcus Collins, I will kill you. Cheerfully." Her shoulders slumped. She'd still go to prison. Talk about a no-win situation.

What was it Marcus said . . . scale down, size down, something like that? She didn't have a clue, and she knew it.

A soft knock sounded on her bedroom door. "Come," she called.

"The desk called, ma'am. There's a gentleman named Eric Savarone in the lobby who would like to speak with you. He apologized for the early hour call, but said he needed to talk with you about Mr. Collins. I believe he said they were colleagues. What do you want me to say? I can take the girls to school this morning, Mrs. Collins."

"Tell him to come up. I'll see him in the library. Bring coffee, Mamie. Use the silver service and the bone china. I would appreciate it if you would take the girls."

"Yes, ma'am."

Betsy straightened her shoulders before she cinched the belt on her satin robe. She couldn't remember the last time she'd entertained a guest at seven-thirty in the morning. Her spirits soared, thinking the faceless guest might be bringing money. More than likely he was there to ask for money.

She was every bit a queen as she strolled down the hall to the room she insisted be called a library because of the one floor-to-ceiling bookshelf that held books no one ever read. It was a masculine room with a heavy mahogany desk and scattered tables. The hunter green chairs were comfortable, thick, and deep. She flinched when she looked down at the costly Oriental carpet. If she tried to sell it now, she knew she would get less than a third of the value.

Betsy positioned herself carefully and crossed her legs. The feathered mules on her feet swung back and forth. Another costly item. Maybe she needed to find out how to give her clothes to a resale house. She almost blacked out at the thought.

Who was Eric Savarone and what did he want? The name sounded vaguely familiar. She knew she had never met him nor had they ever entertained him here at home. She would remember a name like Savarone. Italian.

Betsy inclined her head by way of introduction when the housekeeper ushered the man into the library.

"It's rather early for a visit, Mr. Savarone. I was just getting dressed when you called. What can I do for you? Marcus isn't here," she said coolly and smoothly.

"I know that. He's undoubtedly on the other side of the world by now. Look, I'm not going to mince words. Your husband scammed me out of thirty million dollars, and I want it back. Now where the hell is the bastard?"

Betsy jerked upright in the comfortable chair. All she heard were the words, thirty million dollars. "I beg your pardon!"

"Don't play dumb with me, Mrs. Collins. Where is the son of a bitch?"

"Watch how you speak to me, Mr. Savarone. I don't have the faintest idea of what you're talking about. My husband is out of town. You are implying that he stole thirty million dollars of your money. If that's true, you must not be a very smart businessman. I don't think I care to hear any more of this rubbish. I'll see you to the door."

"If your husband is out of town, give me a number where I can reach him or better yet, let's you and I call him together. I thought I was being nice by coming here before I go to the police and the FBI. If you want to pretend you don't know what I'm talking about, that's okay. You can explain, in detail, to the authorities. What's it going to be, Mrs. Collins?"

Just the thought of the police or the FBI tramping through her apartment was enough to give her hives. What was this man talking about? "I was in California when Marcus left. I thought he had gone to Maine to see our daughters, but he never showed up there. No one has heard from him. He didn't leave any messages or instructions at work either. I can't help you because I know nothing. Dennis Wagner from Digitech asked me the same thing, and I told him what I'm telling you. Marcus left me with a stack of bills and sixty dollars in my purse. Dennis gave me a check to tide me over. It was Marcus's Christmas bonus."

Savarone fired up a cigarette as he paced the length of the library.

"Please don't smoke in here," Betsy said, wrinkling her nose.

"Then why do you have ashtrays in here? For looks?"

"Exactly," Betsy said stiffly. When Savarone made no move to put out his cigarette, she looked pointedly at the ashtray. He ignored her and kept puffing. She almost jumped out of her skin when ash dropped on the Oriental rug.

"So what you're saying is your husband dumped you, is that it?"

Betsy winced. "That's a very crude way of putting it, Mr. Savarone, but I'm afraid it's an accurate assumption. At first I refused to believe it myself. Now it looks like I have no other choice. I'd like to know how a man like my husband could scam you, that is the word you used isn't it? Out of thirty million dollars. How did this happen?"

"It doesn't matter how it happened, it happened, and he did it to BQWARE, too. He's off somewhere with sixty million dollars of our money."

Betsy flopped down on the green chair trying to absorb what she'd just heard. Sixty million dollars! If she had sixty million dollars, she could go to the Paris fashion shows and buy and buy and buy. If she played her cards right, she could be on a first-name basis with all the designers. She did, after all, have the perfect body for clothes. They'd fight to dress her. Hell, she could move to Paris. "Marcus is no thief," she said, her voice ringing with bitterness. "Can you prove any of this?"

"I wired the money into a Swiss account that was your husband's account. So did BQWARE. He cut you and your kids out, Mrs. Collins. I'd think you'd want to get even."

"You don't know anything about me, Mr. Savarone, so don't assume anything."

"I know all about you, Mrs. Collins. The industry knows all about you. You're the reason your husband resorted to selling off company secrets. You're referred to as high-maintenance. Any man who cashes in his stock options to keep his wife happy is one sorry son of a bitch. I guess this was his way of getting back at you. If you stop to think about it, it does make sense."

Betsy didn't have to stop and think about it. Everything he said was true. She felt sick to her stomach.

"Let's put our heads together and try to come up with the place Marcus would go. He must have had favorite places. You traveled a lot. C'mon now, let's hear it."

"I have no idea. A vacation was a vacation. Marcus never said he liked one place over another. I can't help you."

"Do you think ten percent of thirty million would jog your memory?" Savarone asked cooly.

"Twenty percent might. Would that be something BQWARE would be interested in also?"

"Possibly. I can make a phone call right now if you like?"

Betsy waved her hand toward the phone behind her on the desk. Ten percent translated to six million dollars. Times two it was twelve million dollars. Invested with a return of ten percent it would give her a million and a quarter to live on. She really could move to Paris. She could sell off what she could and leave everything else for the creditors. With twelve million dollars what did she care about her credit rating? She could pay cash for everything. Except the IRS. Could they force her to return to the States? She could always buy a new identity. People did it all the time. Marcus probably even did it. The kids loved Europe. Kids' appearances changed from day to day. It would work. She just had to think about it a little.

"It's a deal. I want half right now."

Savarone laughed. "That's what your husband said. Actually he wanted it all, *right now.* I wouldn't trust you any further than I trust your husband right now. We pay up when you tell us where he is."

"You're a bigger fool than I thought, then. I don't trust you either. I guess you're on your own. Thanks for stopping by, Mr. Savarone."

Savarone looked at the steely hard eyes, the grim set of her jaw. This was one hard, tough cookie. A greedy bitch who drove her husband into the ground. A hard, tough broad who worshiped money. What was twelve million bucks compared to sixty? He could see her wheels turning. If there was a way to find her husband, this woman was the one to do it.

"I could have the IRS here in an hour, Mrs. Collins. Thirty million dollars is a lot of money to pay taxes on. The Internal Revenue Service likes their money up front. Why don't we sit down like the sensible adults we are and talk about this in realistic terms."

Betsy felt her insides start to shrivel. The IRS would take it all and give her an allowance to live on and she'd be back to using *Jergens* and *Noxzema* again. "Yes, why don't we?"

Sadie led the way around to the back of the Laroux mansion, stepping over the puddles that gathered between the flagstones. She couldn't ever remember a more cold, wet, miserable day. She crossed her fingers that Minnie Figgins would be up and in a social mood. She marched up the steps, the others right behind her. She rapped smartly on the pane of glass on the kitchen door.

The wizened little lady appeared from out of nowhere to open the door. She smiled at Sadie and motioned her to come indoors. The others followed. Sadie made the introductions. "These are my friends, Mrs. Figgins. We'd like to talk to you about something. Is it okay if we sit down?" Minnie nodded, her eyes bright and inquisitive.

Matt went through his spiel, his eyes on hers, watching for her reaction. "I'm very sorry to be telling you this, but they left me to die out there. And then they stole my money. I need to find them. Can you help us?"

The old woman clucked her tongue in sympathy. "They always were a wild bunch. Their pa thought they was just being boys. He made good every time they did something wrong. I knowed a long time ago they was stealin' from their pa. I heard them talkin' up there in their rooms. I wanted to tell him, but he was too sick to be bothering him. Don't think he would of cared much anyway. I knowed they was mean but didn't think they would do something like you jest said. I'm sorry, but I don't know nothin' that will help you. You say that's your car out there in the garage?"

"Yes, ma'am, it's my car. It has my New York license plates on it. Sadie said she saw it yesterday when she came to talk to you.

Think about it, Mrs. Figgins. Was there a place they liked to go to all the time? A favorite kind of place. Maybe a vacation place. Did they hunt or fish? Was there a cabin?"

"They liked to gamble on the boats. They went to Las Vegas pretty often. Most times, though, they just went Under-the-Hill to the *Isle of Capri*. Nothin' else comes to mind. They didn't much talk around me. Secretive they were."

"Can we look in their rooms?"

"Don't see why not. Jest go up the steps. Their rooms are the first three rooms on the right. Their pa's room was the first room on the left. I cleaned the rooms when they left. You won't be finding much. The trash is still on the back porch. The trash man threw his back out weeks ago and hasn't been here to collect it. You can go through it if you want to."

"You go ahead. I'll stay here and talk to Mrs. Figgins," Lily said.

"I'm going to take the car and run to Wal-Mart and have them make a copy of the picture before I return it to the *Democrat*," Sadie said. "I won't be long."

"Would you be likin' a cup of coffee, Miss Lily?"

"Yes I would, if it isn't too much trouble."

"No trouble at all. I just made it fresh a little

359

while ago. I drink lots of coffee."

"Do you think the men will come back, Mrs. Figgins?"

"No. If they did the things you said they did, they won't come back. There ain't no one here now to stand up for them. Mr. Calumet made people listen. Even the po-lice listened to Mr. Calumet. Them boys are cowards I'm sorry to say."

Lily leaned across the table to accept the cup of coffee the housekeeper handed her. The Wish Keeper around her neck shook loose of the buttons on her sweater. It swung into full view.

"Now, young woman, where'd you be gettin' that Wish Keeper?" the housekeeper asked as she peered at the pendant around Lily's neck.

"My friend gave it to me. How is it you know what it is?" Lily asked quietly.

"Lord sakes, child. All us old folk know what a Wish Keeper is. When I was a young girl I worked for Miz Petrie over on Maple Street. My friend Ellen worked for Miz Parsons, and that's how I come to know about the Wish Keeper. Ellen and me, we would talk and compare what Miz Petrie and Miz Parsons whispered about all the secrets. I only come here to Mr. Calumet's house maybe twenty-five years ago. When the second Miss

Mary Margaret crossed over and her daughter took charge of the house and left it to sit empty was the same time Miz Petrie passed over. I came here then to Mr. Calumet. Been here ever since. Mr. Calumet's mama had a Wish Keeper, too. It's upstairs in his dresser drawer. There's no woman folk in the family to pass it on to."

"What does it mean? What are you supposed to do with it?"

"Sakes alive, child, you just wear it around your neck and good things happen. When a soul tells you a secret or a wish, you put it inside. It's not a big job at all. Them that wears it can *see* things. Some say it's magic. Some say it's voodoo and devil's work, but don't you be believin' that. It's only to whisper about. It's not for loud talkin'. How is it you be wearin' it and don't know what it is for?"

"I believe I bought the house where Mary Margaret lived. My friend found the necklace in the closet and gave it to me. Mary Margaret was her grandmother. At least I think she was. Maybe it was her great-grandmother. I've been wearing it ever since she gave it to me. Things . . . things seem to happen. I *see* things."

"Then it's workin'. Some persons could wear it and it would jest be a necklace. Other people with the heart for it will make it work.

Are you afraid of it? Be glad you ain't one of them sin eaters. Being picked to be a Wish Keeper is a happy thing. No one wants to be a sin eater. No one at all."

"Sometimes I'm nervous over it. Don't worry, I won't ever become a sin eater. Do the wishes and secrets always come true?"

"Most times. When Miss Mary Margaret was dying, she made a wish to cross over fast because of the pain. Lickety-split she was gone." The old housekeeper's dark eyes glazed over as she recalled the incident.

"How do you know that, Mrs. Figgins? I thought the wishes were secret."

"The family looked inside after she crossed over. You have to be special to wear a Wish Keeper."

"I'm not special, Mrs. Figgins. I'm just ordinary. I don't belong to the Parsons family. I'm not sure I want this."

"It's too late now. If you *saw* something, it's too late. It took hold. That's the way it works. You can't be givin' it back now. Once it works for you, you be beholden to it. You mind me now. Did you make a wish?" she asked slyly as she puffed on the corncob pipe.

Lily felt a chill race up her spine. "How is it you know so much about this if it's all supposed to be secret? I don't want to know about the future."

362

"It's too late." Lily felt her skin prickle.

"Well, we didn't find anything," Matt said from the doorway. "The only other thing we can do is look through the trash. Did you say it was on the back porch, Mrs. Figgins?" The housekeeper nodded.

Lily locked her gaze with that of the housekeeper. "I don't want to be a Wish Keeper." Her announcement made, she followed Matt and Dennis out to the back porch. The first thing she was going to do when she got home was to remove the necklace and get rid of it. On second thought, she reached up, yanked it free, and tossed it into the bushes. If it kept raining the way it was, the necklace would sink into the soft ground and be lost forever. Her shoulders lighter, she walked out to the garage and opened the doors. Her heart took on an extra beat at the sight of Matt's Jaguar. Satisfied Sadie hadn't made a mistake, she closed the doors and joined Matt and Dennis on the back porch where they were waiting for Sadie to return.

"Did you find anything?"

"Nothing. Several weeks of newspapers. Guess these guys liked to keep up on what's going on in town. That's about it. Damn, it's miserable out here."

Lily looked around the garden trying to find the spot where she'd tossed the Wish Keeper.

She felt her insides start to tighten up when she thought about the housekeeper's ominous warning. Well, it was too late now. Rain poured down on the bushes. She watched as a bedraggled wet rabbit scurried under a spreading yew and disappeared.

They stood shivering on the back porch for another thirty minutes until Sadie swerved the Rover into the driveway. Dennis's cell phone rang the moment she stopped the truck. He shrugged and reached into his pocket.

Lily took a moment to wonder what would happen if all the cell phones in the world went on the blink at the same time. The world would probably collapse. She grimaced. She hated everything that was high-tech as much as Sadie did. I would have made a good pioneer, she thought. Just simple basics. Still, she wouldn't want to give up all her push buttons in the kitchen and the big-screen TV or the VCR. Or the directional finder in the Rover. Or the GPS. *Suck it up, Lily, it's called progress.*

They scurried to the Rover, whose wipers were swishing furiously to combat the heavy downpour.

"I have news! Big news!" Sadie said the minute they were all buckled into their seat belts. "In a million years, maybe two million years, you are never going to believe this. It just came to me. Just like that! I knew even before I asked. I'm telling you, this is unbelievable. There I was, returning this picture, and it came to me. Gee, I hope I didn't keep you waiting too long."

"What? Tell us," they demanded in unison.

"The first thing Lily and I did when we moved to Wyoming was to call the *Miami Herald* and buy a subscription. We got it daily but usually a day late. I got to thinking, maybe these guys would do the same thing. Obviously they were born and raised here. If it was or is their intention never to return, wouldn't they be curious as to what's going on here in their hometown? They do own a house and their store and the inventory in it. They might also want to know if Matt survived and went to the authorities. Matt said they were amateurs and not too bright."

"And?" Lily said, excitement ringing in her voice.

Sadie took a deep breath. "And they did! A whole year's subscription! I even have an address! You owe me two hundred bucks, Matt. That's what it cost me to get the address!"

"You've done the impossible, Sadie. You did what Dennis and I couldn't do with all our computers. Where are those bastards?" The excitement ringing in Matt's voice was contagious.

Sadie reached down into the console for a slip of paper and handed it to Matt. "In the Cayman Islands."

Matt leaned back in his seat and closed his eyes. "Now we have to make a plan."

"Betsy Collins called the office," Dennis said. "That was my secretary. She wants me to call her, says it's important. Maybe she got a lead on Marcus. Looks like this is our lucky day, guys," Dennis chortled. "Everything happens in threes. The snowstorm in the West, finding those three cruds, and a phone call from Betsy Collins. Let's head home and decide what we're going to do."

"Yes, let's go home so I can check the Weather Channel," Sadie said.

"The only place you're going is the Cayman Islands with us, Sadie Lincoln," Dennis said forcefully. "I'm not going anywhere without you. I'd never survive. So there," he said gruffly.

Matt smirked.

Lily grinned from ear to ear.

Sadie put her hand over her heart, and whispered, "Oh, be still my heart."

Betsy Collins reacted to Eric Savarone's visit with a vengeance. She ripped off the frilly satin robe, kicked off her feathered mules, and got down to the serious business of latch-ing on to sixty million dollars. In her under-wear and bare feet she trotted from room to room, trying to figure out where to start and what to look for. She had one wild, crazy mo-ment when she thought about getting herself hypnotized to see if she could remember some vague remark, something she'd forgot-ten that would give her a clue to her hus-band's whereabouts.

She needed to be systematic. She needed to go through everything, every scrap of paper, every note, every bill. She would need to go through all the boxes of photographs they'd taken on every single vacation. Maybe some-thing as innocent as a smile, a landmark, would give her a clue to her husband's where-abouts. She sat back on her heels, her thoughts in turmoil. Marcus was never one to do anything on the spur of the moment. He planned everything in advance, right down to the tiniest detail. He even planned his ward-robe for the entire week on Sunday night, right down to the casual clothes he would wear on the weekend. When he acted impul-sively, he made mistakes. At least that had al-ways been his pattern. She crossed her fingers that it would still hold.

She knew she was a nervous wreck, knew she was frightened out of her wits with the thought of the IRS coming after her. The swarthy Savarone and the unknown man from BQWARE weren't exactly warm fuzzies either. Her best bet was finding Marcus and sucking up big-time for him to take her back. She could concoct some kind of story he would believe. She'd say she turned over a new leaf and had tracked him down because people were after him. That would show some wifely concern. If she had to prostitute herself five times a day, so be it.

The girls! What was she going to do with the girls if she had to go traipsing across the ocean? The nanny could take care of them, of course, but she'd have to keep on paying her, plus the tuition. She could see the money Dennis Wagner had given her dwindling before her very eyes. Marcus always said, you do what you gotta do. It was settled.

It was shortly after noon when Betsy picked up a picture of Marcus standing in front of a bank in Zurich, a wide smile on his face, his arm extended toward the bank. She remembered the picture well. Marcus had said that was the bank where the richest of the rich kept their money and no one was the wiser. Her silly response at the time had been, let's go in and open an account in the girls' names. We'll put a hundred dollars in each account. Marcus had laughed his head off saying they would boot them out for even attempting to open accounts with such paltry sums of money, but she'd insisted, and to Marcus's surprise, the account representative had actually smiled and treated them like every other customer. They'd laughed for days over that. Well, she wasn't laughing now. Somewhere, someplace, there was a record of those two numbered accounts. All she had to do was find it. Marcus would never think she would remember such a silly thing. Well, she did remember. She closed her eyes trying to remember what the numbers were. She drew a blank until she turned the picture over and there they were — the numbers — faded but legible.

"Paris, here I come!"

The next hour passed in a whirlwind. Within minutes she booked a first-class seat on Swissair to Zurich. Her next call was to the girls' school. She announced herself as the wife of the CEO of Digitech and said because of a family emergency, she needed to leave the country. She instructed the nanny to see to the girls' complicated schedules. That worry off her shoulders, she mixed herself a drink and placed a call to Digitech and asked to be put through to Dennis Wagner. She sighed impatiently when she was told she would have to wait for Dennis to call her back since he was out of town.

She waited, sipping her vodka tonic, her thoughts on the Paris runways.

Betsy was on her third vodka tonic when the phone rang. She picked it up on the first ring, her voice cheerful. "Dennis. Thank you for returning my call. What would it be worth to Digitech to find out where Marcus is? No, Dennis, I want to know now. Either it is or it isn't something you want to know. I don't mind you knowing I'm scrambling here. You did get through to me about the IRS. On top of that Mr. Savarone paid me a visit at seven-thirty this morning. I'd say he's a bit upset, as is the man from BQWARE. Understandably so. So, Dennis, what's the answer?" She snorted with laughter. "A paltry hundred thousand dollars is a drop in the bucket. Fine, I'll take it. Wire it into my account now. If you hold on a second, I'll give you the number. I'll be in touch first thing tomorrow morning. I think I know where my husband is. No, I'm almost certain. It's amazing what fear will do to a person. It hones everything. You're damn right, I want my pound of flesh. Why else do you think I'm willing to tell you where he is? Of course I can't guarantee he'll still be there. No one can do that. I can, however, tell you where he went as soon as I get my verification. No, this is not a pig in the poke. Look, Dennis, if you don't want to know, that's okay, too. I came to you first since you were so nice to me the other day. I'll give you one hour to wire the money. After that, the offer goes off the table. Good-bye, Dennis."

She moved at the speed of light. She dressed, packed an overnight bag, securing her jewelry in the bottom of the bag, and was ready to go. All she had to do was wait for the wire transfer and say good-bye to the girls. She would need to go to the bank one last time to convert her money into travelers' checks. Once she reached Zurich she could get lost. Zurich, one of her most favorite places in the whole world. She knew it as well as she knew Manhattan.

The minutes ticked by. Exactly on the hour she called the bank. Her sigh of relief was so loud it shocked her. She was out the door in five minutes and back in the apartment thirty minutes later.

Betsy fixed herself another drink. Maybe, just maybe, she could . . . She didn't stop to think. Her adrenaline flowing, she picked up the phone, rummaging for Eric Savarone's business card in the mess on her desk. She punched out the numbers, identified herself. His voice was just as gruff on the phone as it was in person. "I think I might have a very good lead to my husband's whereabouts. You were right, I wasn't being realistic. This is what I want. Two hundred and fifty thousand in cash from each of you. No checks, Mr. Savarone. Bring it by my apartment no later than five o'clock. I have an early dinner engagement. If you were stupid enough to wire thirty million dollars into my husband's account, then you're smart enough to give me what I want. I am your only chance, Mr. Savarone. Take it or leave it. I'm sure Digitech will want to know where he is. That's not going to look very good when they start naming names and can back up those names, now is it? Five o'clock, not one second later. I told you, I'll know by ten tomorrow morning. I'm just waiting for a definite confirmation. I won't argue the point because you're right. I do want my pound of flesh."

Two remaining things to do. Try to figure out if the authorities could track her. Of course they could. Her mind raced. For now the girls could spend weekends at her parents' home. Once she got to where she was going she would call her parents, apprise them of the situation, wire them some money, and they'd be happy campers. They'd never give out any information if there was the promise of money coming in on a regular basis. The moment she felt safe and secure she could have the children join her.

How best to get the money into Zurich?

Since she'd never carried much with her on any trip, she didn't know what the rules were about taking money into a strange country. Marcus would have known, but they'd lived off credit cards while traveling. He had money belts, but where were they? Paper money wouldn't set off the alarms at the security stations. She could stuff her bra, her panties, and wear a money belt. Smugglers did it all the time in the movies.

She thought about the girls again. There was no point in trying to keep that secret. Sooner or later they would grill her trusted housekeeper and the nanny. As long as she didn't divulge any information concerning herself, they couldn't say anything. Leaving with an overnight case, something she did on a regular basis, wouldn't throw up any red flags this evening. What they did or said tomorrow wouldn't matter.

She tidied up the library and Marcus's office. Everything was neat and perfect, just the way she liked it. Nothing suspicious to anyone looking around.

She found the money belt on her third perusal of Marcus's closet. There were two of them in his gym bag. She stuffed one back into the bag and carried the other one to her bathroom, where she placed it on the vanity.

Talk about a plan coming together.

Fifteen

They were like four magpies the minute they walked into the kitchen.

"You are the lady of the hour, Sadie," Matt said, wrapping his arms around her. "Whatever you want, it's yours. Just name it. I can't wait to get my hands around those bastards' throats."

"You can't let them see you, Matt. We need to come up with a plan so we can outwit them. The minute they lay eyes on you, it's all over. When we get there, and I'm assuming we're going to be on the next plane, we'll alert the authorities. Somehow or other I don't think a citizen's arrest will cut it in the Caymans. We can't go half-cocked here if we want to reel them in. Let's sit down and plan this out in some kind of detail. I'm hungry," Dennis said, looking at Sadie. He reached for her hand. "You are coming, you know. Please," he said imploringly.

Sadie pretended to think. "Sunshine is better than snow. At least for the moment. I'm going to have to have a real good offer to give up all that snow when we get back. Real good," Sadie said tweaking Dennis's cheek.

Lily swung around, her face draining of all color. "Look!"

In the center of the old oak table was the Wish Keeper.

"I threw it away. I threw it in the bushes at the Laroux house. I did. I swear I did. How'd it get here? Did one of you pick it up? Please, someone, tell me you brought this with you."

The chorus of denials unnerved Lily. "I don't want it anymore. I made the decision when I was talking to Minnie Figgins. You take it, Sadie."

"No way," Sadie said, pulling vegetables out of the refrigerator. "Maybe you can't just throw it away, maybe you need to *bury* it. You know, in a deep hole. Cover the hole with bricks or maybe pour cement over the hole once you bury it. Back there in the cemetery would be a good place. If you ask me, that's where it belongs."

"Mrs. Figgins said it's too late. She said once I *saw* something it was too late. She sounded like she knew what she was talking about. How'd it get here?" Lily demanded, the color coming back to her cheeks. "This is getting scary."

"I don't think there's an answer to that any more than there was an answer to all the visions you had. If you don't want to wear it,

Lily, put it back in the closet where I found it. If it . . . *travels,* then bury it. For some reason, I don't think it will move from there. I think, though, you have to be the one to put it back. Don't ask me how I know this. I just do. Do it now, Lily, and we'll wait to see if anything happens."

Lily snatched the pendant and chain off the table and raced upstairs to the closet where Sadie had found the pendant. She crawled back into the corner of the dark closet and wedged the necklace between the floorboards. "I'm sorry," she whispered. "I don't want to be the next Wish Keeper. My wish is that you find someone else to take my place. Someone like Betsy Collins. She could use some responsibility. I do appreciate all the help you gave us in finding Matt, but I'm not the one to carry on." On her hands and knees, she backed out of the closet, then closed the door. Tightly. She turned the little brass lock. Maybe she should call Mr. Sonner and have him board up the closet. That's exactly what she would do. First thing Monday morning.

Only time would tell if her wish was granted.

Downstairs she washed her hands at the kitchen sink. "Where is everyone?"

"On the computer. They're trying to get a map of the Cayman Islands so they can pinpoint the address the paper gave me. There's a thing called Mapquest they think will give you a map and pinpoint an address. If not, they're going on the Net to check it out. Isn't that amazing, Lily?"

"It sure is," Lily said, her eyes glued to the kitchen table.

"They're going to make plane reservations on the computer, too. Matt wants us all to go tomorrow on the earliest flight possible."

"What about the dogs?"

"Maybe Mrs. Figgins will come over and watch them. It's worth a try. She's a sweet lady, Lily. I suspect the dogs will like her, and she'll like them. After lunch, I'll run over and ask her."

"I'm okay with that if Matt is. He's pretty fussy when it comes to Gracie these days. But, he wants those guys so bad he'll probably agree. Now, what's with Dennis? Come on, Sadie, share."

"He doesn't want me to go to Wyoming. I like him, Lily, I really do, but I'm not going to run my life by what he wants when he wants it."

"What does he want you to do? Does he want you to stay here? Go to New York, Oregon? What? Are you going to be a kept woman, Sadie?"

"Lily! No, I am not going to be a kept

woman. I feel like I'm torn in all these different directions. I'm going to go to Wyoming at some point. First, though, I want to see these guys caught. I want to spend more time with Dennis to make sure I know how I feel, and I want to see you get married. I absolutely will not follow Dennis to New York or Oregon. He said if I did go to Wyoming, he'd send me a computer and hook me up to e-mail. That's a start, don't you think?"

"You bet. I think it worked, Sadie. The necklace is still upstairs. I made a wish while I was up there. I wonder if it will come true. By the way, what are we having for lunch?"

"Vegetable stir-fry. We should have gone to Cock of the Walk and ordered their famous fried catfish and those deep-fried pickles. Stir-fry pales in comparison."

"Sounds good. Let's have some wine. We need to do some celebrating."

"Lily, after lunch, do you mind if I take Dennis over to the cottage? After I go to see Minnie Figgins."

"It's your cottage. You can do whatever you want. Of course I don't mind. Shame on you for even asking, Sadie."

"Promise me something, Lily."

"Name it," Lily said, putting her arm around her friend's shoulder.

"Promise me that we'll always be friends.

Promise me that we'll never be so busy with our lives that we resort to Christmas and birthday cards. Promise me that we'll always make time for each other. Promise me that when we get old and have white hair and we're sitting in rocking chairs on our respective front porches that we'll still call each other and talk about the good old days."

"Whew. I thought you were going to ask me something tough. Of course I promise, and it's a promise that will be easy to keep. You and Matt and, I suspect, Dennis, are my family now. You know my feeling about family. It's the most important thing in the world. At the end of the day, it's family you can count on. And of course all those four-legged creatures that help make up our families. What kind of dog are you and Dennis going to get?"

Sadie whacked Lily across the rear end with the dish towel. "Stop rushing me."

"Sometimes you are a little slow in the romance area, Sadie. Dennis doesn't look like a speeding bullet either. You gotta make it happen. Use lots of sesame seed, and I like peanut oil for my stir-fry," Lily said, dancing away from the flying dish towel.

They looked like all the other tourists getting off the plane with their floppy sun hats, sunglasses, colorful shirts, shorts, and sandals. Lily stood at the bottom of the steps leading to the plane and twirled around. "This weather is awesome. My bones actually feel warm."

"Oh, I just love this tropical sun," Sadie said happily. "When we're all done here, I want to come back and just do nothing but laze around. Well, maybe a little diving, a little snorkeling. Great honeymoon spot, I'm thinking," she whispered to Lily.

"For me or you?" Lily grinned.

"Whoever," Sadie said flippantly. "What's our game plan?"

"Customs check, rental car, register at our hotels, and then we're going to play I Spy," Dennis said, leading the way into the airport terminal.

Forty-five minutes later, Dennis signed his name to a car-rental lease. "I always wanted to drive one of these open-air Jeeps," he said gleefully. "I'm driving, Matt, you're too pissed off to see straight. Besides, it's right-hand driving. I did a six-month stint in England last year, so I kind of perfected my skill, but I still think it's weird."

"Now you girls know the drill. You're registering where those . . . those assholes are staying. Dennis and I are staying at the Hyatt. It's your job to make contact and see what their game plan is. You're librarians from Bluefield, West Virginia. Give them the impression you're ready to cut loose, but be careful."

"Oooh, I'm so excited," Sadie cooed. "How far do you want us to . . . you know, *go?*"

"Not *that* far," Dennis exploded. "This could take as long as a week, so don't get carried away."

Lily winked at Matt. He stared at her with a blank expression. She sighed. Right now he had tunnel vision.

"The first thing you have to do is make a positive I.D. Once you do that, call us on the cell phone and we'll mosey around so Matt can verify they're the right guys. Don't do anything stupid," Dennis said.

"Are you implying we're stupid or that we might do something stupid?" Sadie said in a huff. "Where are all these glamorous clothes we're supposed to get to vamp these guys?"

"Buy them in the shops and charge them," Matt said tightly. "Whatever it takes, Sadie."

"String bikinis," Sadie said, gurgling with laughter. "We'll need to get some of that stuff that comes in a bottle and gives you an instant tan. If we're going to be babes on the prowl, then we need to *look* like babes on the prowl."

"Aawwk," Dennis said, sliding behind the wheel of the open-air Jeep.

"Matt, pull that fishing hat lower over your face. Just stare straight ahead. We'll do the looking for you," Lily cautioned. Matt obediently pulled the hat with the dangling fishing lures lower.

"Nice, real nice," Sadie said, as they pulled out of the airport. "Can you find your way, Dennis, or do you want one of us to help you with the map?"

"I'm okay. The girl at the rental place marked the route. Sit back and enjoy the ride, ladies."

"String bikinis?" Lily hissed. "I don't have the guts to wear one of those."

"I don't either, but it sounded good, didn't it?"

They passed the time chatting about the scenery and admiring the lush flowers. "We're almost there. You have a pricey villa just two buildings away from the Laroux brothers. Have your carry bags on your laps so you can hop right out. No point in us giving them a chance to spot us."

"I hope Matt doesn't blow this. He's like a wet cat on a satin sofa." Sadie stared after the departing Jeep. She looked around casually. "I don't see them. Let's register and go shopping. It's almost happy hour, and we definitely need to dude up for that. I can't believe we're going shopping and money is no object.

Do you suppose that's how Marcus Collins's wife does it?"

"I don't know how Betsy Collins does it, nor do I care. What do we do if they don't show up for happy hour?"

"We keep our eyes glued to their villa and arrange a chance encounter. Chance encounters are great," Sadie said.

"These guys are going to be wary of everyone and everything. We need to be cool and aloof. But approachable in a dangerous kind of way. Do you think we can pull that off, Sadie?"

"You bet we can. You hooked Matt, didn't you? He's prime stuff. These guys are duds. Of course they have all that money now, so they probably think they're hot spit. Let's go shopping, Lily. I have every confidence in our abilities."

Her overnight case clasped tightly in her hand, Betsy Collins made her way to the taxi stand. She gave the driver the address of the hotel before she settled herself comfortably in the back of the cab. She could hardly wait to get to her room so she could remove the awkward money belt from around her waist. As soon as she showered and changed she was heading to the nearest bank to rent a safe-deposit box. Then she was going to a five-star restaurant. On the other hand, maybe she should stay away from public places and dine in her room. Tomorrow was another day. And she had to call Eric Savarone as she'd promised. She'd do that as soon as she checked into the medium-priced hotel she normally wouldn't have been caught dead in. Intrigue was not something she excelled in, but she could learn, if sixty million dollars was the end result. She also needed to call home to make sure the girls were all right.

She hugged the loose-fitting cashmere coat around her slim body. It was so cold the heater in the cab felt like it wasn't working. January in Switzerland, what did she expect?

When she climbed out of the cab at the hotel she hoped the distaste she felt wasn't evident in her expression. She registered and handed over her passport for safekeeping. She wondered if she should register with the U.S. Embassy. In the past Marcus had always done that even before registering at their hotel. He said it was paramount. She'd bet her last dollar he hadn't done it this time, though. Nor would she do it. What if she was wrong, and Marcus wasn't here at all? Then what would she do? As Scarlett said, I'll think about that tomorrow.

The room was plain and clean, the bed soft and comfortable. A standard hotel room like any room in a Holiday Inn back home. Brown-and-orange spread that matched the drapes. Dark green carpeting, small television, digital clock, desk, round table with two club chairs. The bathroom was even more plain. The towels were white but thin. There was no fluffy robe, no makeup mirror attached to the wall, no blow-dryer. A bare-bones hotel. There was, however, a bar under the television. She popped a cola and swigged from the bottle.

Betsy rummaged in her purse for her cell phone. Marcus had said he paid extra for the phones to be compatible in foreign countries. Marcus did like the best of everything, but then so did she. She sat down on the edge of the bed and dialed Eric Savarone's number. When the call didn't go through she cursed until she remembered she had to dial the country code first and then the number. The moment he said hello, she went into her speech. "Mr. Savarone, my source tells me that Marcus is in the Cayman Islands. He was there as of yesterday at seven o'clock in the evening. What do you mean, where am I? Cell phones are always scratchy-sounding. It might need to be charged. I'm walking in Central Park, not that it's any of your business. I'm on my way to the hairdresser. No, I have no message for my husband. Look,

385

don't call me again. Our business is finished. Let's be clear on that. I kept my end of the bargain. Good-bye, Mr. Savarone."

She kicked off her shoes and flopped back on the bed as she dialed her New York apartment. The nanny assured her that everything was fine and the girls were happy. The cell phone snapped shut and went back into her purse. Damn, she was going to have to get an adapter if she wanted to charge the phone. She couldn't remember the last time she'd charged it. What did it matter? She'd made her two most important calls.

It was noon when she left the hotel, her carryall and purse secure in her grasp. She shivered, her teeth chattering as she waited for a taxi. "Take me to the closest bank, and I'd appreciate it if you would wait for me. I won't be long. Can you do that? I'll pay you in dollars. Thank you."

She was in and out of the bank in less than thirty minutes with two keys to her newly rented safe-deposit box. The Swiss were so efficient. No dillydallying there. Strictly business. She liked efficiency.

Back in the cab, she showed the driver the vacation picture she'd taken of Marcus pointing at the bank. "Can you take me there?"

"But of course, madam. Do you need me to wait there for you, too?"

"Yes, please." Betsy put the picture back in her purse. What if the money wasn't there? What if she was wrong? If it was there, what was she going to do? How could she transfer all that money? Where would she transfer it to? Another bank? Here in Switzerland? Back to the States? Definitely not the States. The Caymans? Possibly, but not likely. She felt a wave of dizziness at what she was doing. What if she screwed up? If only she knew more about intrigue. It wasn't enough to be greedy. You had to be brainy in the bargain.

Betsy felt herself jolt forward when the taxi driver swerved to the curb and stopped the car. "This is the bank you wished, madam. I will wait for you here."

"Yes. Thank you. This may take a while." She handed him a twenty-dollar bill. "I'll pay the rest when I come out. I'll want to go back to my hotel."

"Very good, madam."

Her heart thundering in her chest, Betsy walked through the doors of the bank. She had an instant recollection of the day she and Marcus had entered the bank and opened the girls' accounts. She walked over to the same desk and sat down. She smiled as she wrote the account number for Alice's account. She flinched when a slip of paper was handed to her showing a balance of $196.14. She did her best to conjure up a smile as she filled out the second slip. She knew she was sweating as she waited for Andrea's slip to come back. When she lowered her head to stare at the slip she almost fainted. It was all there and more. *Oh, Marcus, you poor, dumb fool.*

"I'd like a cashier's check for the full amount, please," she said coolly.

"It will take just a few moments, madam." Betsy nodded. She needed to take a deep breath. Lots of deep breaths. Many, many deep breaths. She also needed to get out of there as soon as possible before she did something stupid, like throwing up all over the place. When would Marcus find out? What would he do? He'd come looking for her; that was a given. How long would it take him to figure out that she remembered about the accounts? Weeks? Days? Hours? Not weeks. Maybe a day or so.

Betsy slid the check into the change compartment of the Chanel purse and zipped it shut. She marveled that her legs were steady as she exited the bank and climbed into the waiting taxi. "Take me back to the first bank, please."

Inside the bank, Betsy filled out the required bank forms and waited while the paperwork was processed, which took all of fifteen minutes, thanks again to Swiss efficiency. Now all she had to do was go back to the hotel and decide what she was going to do with all that lovely, lovely money.

"How do we look?" Lily asked.

"I think you look as good as I do. I do love bright colors. You don't think we look like parrots, do you?" Sadie giggled.

"No, not at all. Island wear is supposed to be colorful. I hope that suntan stuff starts working soon. We're fish-belly white. Blue is definitely your color," Lily said, referring to the shimmery silk sheath with the mile-high slit going up the side of the dress that Sadie was wearing. "I hope Matt doesn't choke on the price."

"Never mind choking. Let's hope he and Dennis get to *see* us in these dresses. I never owned a $700 dress before or $300 shoes. That sea-green dress brings out the color of your eyes and does great things to your complexion. I think you're starting to color up," Sadie said, peering at Lily's arms. "Won't it be a hoot if we start to tan while we're sitting there at the bar? I didn't think that suntan stuff worked, but it does. Oh, we are going to be a glorious bronze just like all those beach bunnies."

Lily giggled. "I think we're ready so let's get this show on the road. I hope I remember how to flirt."

"It's instinctive. We're going to do just fine. It's going to be a boring time if they don't show up. For all we know they might have latched on to some babes by now."

"Guys like the free-food bar at happy hour. If they're here, they'll show. What did we agree on? Cool and aloof and accessible but not available, right?" Lily said.

"Yeah. We're definitely turning color now. I can see the difference," Sadie said as she led the way through a maze of shrubbery and short walkways to the outdoor bar. It was crowded with couples and very few singles. "Let's sit at the bar and cross our legs. We have great legs. Guys like legs. In another hour we should be a beautiful golden bronze."

"There are only five single guys here, and none of them are the Laroux brothers. The singles are looking us over real good because we're fresh meat," Lily muttered. "I could never do this bar scene to catch a guy. How about you, Sadie?"

"Probably not. Most of them are married with wedding rings in their pockets. Smile, here come two of them."

It was eight o'clock when Lily and Sadie climbed off their barstools. "What a bust! Now what?" Sadie grumbled.

"Now we go to our room, call Matt and

Dennis, and go to dinner. We'll have to take a cab to wherever it is. First, though, I think we need to stroll past the villa where the brothers are supposed to be staying. There's no point in going through with this charade if they aren't here. We can't ask at the desk because it would be suspicious, and one of the desk clerks might mention it to the brothers. Just a little pre-evening stroll. Everyone is out walking around, so we won't stand out." Lily mopped at the perspiration dotting her brow. "Does this suntan stuff wipe off?"

"It's not supposed to. The brochure said each application is good for three full days. Maybe the brothers party all night and sleep all day. They have all that money now, so they can do whatever they want. One day is just like the next, party and spend. Go slow, we're almost there. Just look out of the corner of your eye. Laugh and smile in case they're outside, and we can't see them," Sadie instructed.

"I can't see a thing but I can hear music. It sounds like it's coming from the back on the patio. Night owls. If we go back to our villa and sit on the little front patio, we'll see them when they leave. They've got to go past our villa to get to the parking area. My guess would be they'll head out around nine. It will be dark by then, so they won't see us sitting there. I can call Dennis to tell him to lie in wait somewhere, so he can follow them. Do you think that's a good idea?"

"Yeah, great. Guess we better keep these outfits on then. Are we golden or are we golden?"

Lily peered down at her arms. "We are golden. Amazing."

"We're just two beach bunnies without tails."

"You're taking this very lightly. Why is that?" Lily demanded. "Damn, I keep thinking about that Wish Keeper. What if it finds its way back to the kitchen table and Minnie Figgins sees it?"

"I'm trying to take this lightly because I'm scared to death. People kill for a few hundred dollars. What do you think these guys are going to do if they get wise to us? As for Minnie Figgins, if it's there, I don't think you have to worry about her touching it."

"They aren't going to get wise because we are going to be supercareful. We're just two chicks on the prowl. Matt and Dennis are within lurking distance. I'll call them to see if they're okay with all of this," Lily said, pulling out her cell phone.

"Okay." Sadie hiked up her dress and sat down on the stoop.

They waited.

At ten minutes to ten they leaned farther back into the darkness as voices drew near. "It's *them*," Lily whispered. "I can smell them from here, and they are *ripe!* You follow them, Sadie, and get the make of the car they're driving. I'll be behind you but at a distance. I'll call Matt and keep him on the phone until you report back. They're waiting right outside the gates to this place."

Minutes later, Sadie whispered, "It's a champagne-colored Crown Victoria. I couldn't read the license plates." Lily relayed the information to Matt.

"Okay, here's the deal. Matt and Dennis are going to follow them. As soon as they land in one spot, and let's hope they aren't in the mood to barhop, Matt will call us and we'll take a taxi to where they are. Hopefully there will be some food there. My stomach is starting to rumble. I'm also starting to get nervous. Matt couldn't get a look at them in the car. It's entirely possible it isn't them."

"Anything is possible, but my gut tells me it's them. I could really go for a good burger right now. With the works and a nice cold beer."

"Stop it, Sadie. Don't talk about food."

"What should we talk about then? Lily, why do you suppose Matt okayed Dennis to give Betsy Collins a hundred grand?"

"He's like that, Sadie. The guy would give you the shirt off his back. He's probably thinking Marcus got Betsy used to the good life, then he left her. They have kids. That's what Matt sees. He doesn't want the kids to suffer because of something their father did. It's going to take him a long time to get over Marcus's betrayal."

"How are you feeling about giving up the Wish Keeper, Lily? Any second thoughts?"

"No second thoughts. I just feel relief. It's really weird the way that thing made me feel. This is nice, isn't it? It's quiet, the air is scented. I think it's jasmine I smell, isn't it? I like the walkway lighting. It looks so cozy nestled in the shrubbery. I don't think I could live here year round, though. I like the change of seasons. I wonder what it's like at Christmastime?"

"Probably just like Fort Lauderdale," Sadie said.

"That pretty much covers our immediate concerns. Do you want to talk about Dennis?"

"Nope. Do you want to talk about Matt?"

"Sure. I could talk about Matt all day and all night. I just know we're going to have a wonderful life together. I can't wait for him to get involved in the community. I hope he joins the Fare Coffee Club. It's a tradition if you live in Natchez. All you have to do to join is show up. They meet at that little shop on the corner of Pearl and Cotton Alley. What if he loses it, Sadie? He's obsessed with those guys."

Sadie shrugged. "Then he loses it. He's a determined man. Dennis seems to be pretty levelheaded. The two of them are pretty much like you and me, they listen to each other. Still, I wish we had gone to the authorities back in Natchez. I'm not sure what, if anything, can be done here. I hope Matt has more than his arm up his sleeve."

Lily snapped the cell phone open the moment it rang. "Matt?" She listened. "You got a good look? You're sure they're the ones? Okay, we're on our way as soon as we can get a taxi."

"They're at a place called Red Tango. Matt says fifteen minutes, maybe less. And, he said it is the Laroux brothers. He got a real good look at them when they parked their car. He's wired, Sadie. I wish you could have heard him."

"Then we better get going. It's just a hop over to the lobby. There might even be a taxi waiting," Sadie said, excitement ringing in her voice.

"I'm a nervous wreck, and you're excited! Sometimes I just don't believe you, Sadie."

"I'm just as much a nervous wreck as you

are. I wonder what kind of place it is."

"Matt said Dennis told him it was pure sleaze. Guess he went inside to check it out. It figures."

"With all that money they stole from Matt, you'd think they'd go first-class. Sleaze?"

"Maybe this is what they're used to. Babes, chicks, whatever the word is today. One-night stands, no commitments, that kind of thing. Fun, fun, fun and the money stays where it is. They spend just enough, have a good time, and they don't draw any attention to themselves. I see a taxi."

Lily looked around for the doorman but didn't see him. She walked over to the waiting taxi, and said, "Can you take us to the Red Tango?"

The driver looked them over from head to toe. "Are you sure you want to go there? It's not the kind of place ladies go to unescorted."

"We're meeting our husbands there," Lily said, climbing into the backseat.

The driver shrugged. He shifted gears and rolled down the driveway. Sadie sighed. Lily took a deep breath as she rolled down the window. "Lower your window, Sadie, so the wind blows your hair all over. We need to look . . . *wanton*."

Sadie coughed and sputtered but did as Lily requested.

Twelve minutes later, the taxi driver pulled to the curb. Music blasted their eardrums as they exited the cab. Two burly men looked them over. Bouncers. "They look like Jesse Ventura," Sadie said.

Lily looked around for Matt or Dennis, but they were nowhere in sight. She couldn't see the open-air Jeep either.

"It's pretty crowded tonight, ladies. We'll take you in. Do you want a table or the bar?"

"A table would be very nice." Sadie reached inside her purse for a ten-dollar bill. "I can't hear myself talk," she screamed in Lily's ear.

"There must be a thousand people here! How are we ever going to find anyone?" Lily screamed in return.

"I changed my mind. We might do better at the bar," Sadie shouted again as she handed the bouncer the ten-dollar bill. "Hold my hand, Lily, so we don't get separated."

The bouncer sliced a path for them that was four deep and ended at the bar right next to where Dennis Wagner was seated.

"Can I buy you lovely ladies a drink?" Dennis leered.

"We don't even know you," Sadie said haughtily.

"I'll have something blue with an umbrella in it," Lily chirped, her gaze sweeping the room. "We're looking for some friends. However do you find anyone in this crowd?"

"I'll have a piña colada, and I want two cherries on top," Sadie shouted.

Dennis gave their order to a scantily clad bartender. He poked Lily gently and let his gaze tell her where to look.

Both women stared across the room where the three Laroux brothers were holding court with a bevy of nearly naked women.

"We're overdressed," Sadie said.

"But we look good," Lily said. "Thanks for the drink. We'll take it from here. Come on, Sadie. I think I recognize those guys in the villa a couple of doors down from ours. Let's introduce ourselves before our eardrums get ruptured." She leaned over and shouted into Dennis's ear, "Wait here to see if we have any luck luring them back to the villa."

Sadie led the way, using her elbows, her hands and once she kicked someone to make him get out of the way. She was breathless when she reached the brothers' table. "Look, Goldie, our neighbors!" she trilled.

"Would you look at that!" Lily trilled in return. She leaned over the table and smiled. "Tiffany and I saw you walking past the villa this evening. Fancy meeting you here. Such a small world. We were just getting ready to go back to our place to party it up. We wondered if you would like to join us?"

"Why would we want to do that?" the one named Junior said as he pointedly looked at the array of skin surrounding him.

Sadie smiled. "Because we're worth it!"

"In spades," Lily smiled.

"Maybe some other time," Junior said.

"Your loss, honey," Sadie said, turning to leave. "See ya."

"Hey, wait, I'm up for a party," another brother said. "I'm sick of sitting here every night. Do you girls have a car?"

"No. We came in a taxi."

"Hold up. I'll come with you. You can stay, Junior. We'll take a taxi, you can keep the car."

"We agreed to stay together," Junior said. "Remember when we made that rule."

"Then come with us."

"You guys decide what you're going to do," Lily said. "We don't belong in a place like this. You guys look like you have too much class for this dump. Are you that hard-up?"

It was all Junior needed to hear. He shook loose from the women hanging around his neck. "This better be worth our while."

Sadie turned around. "I'm up for a midnight swim, how about you, Goldie?"

"Ooooh, sounds good," Lily said.

They pushed their way toward the bar

where Dennis was paying his tab. "Thanks for the drinks," Sadie bellowed. "We're going home now."

Dennis ignored her as he shoved his way to the door.

Outside in the sweltering night air, Junior came up behind Lily, and said, "We can give you a ride back to the villa."

"Well, sure. That's nice of you."

"Real nice," Sadie said, removing the younger brother's hand from her rump. "Stop that! I'm not one of those tramps you left behind inside. I thought you guys were a class act."

"Does that mean you two girls are a class act?" Junior demanded.

Sadie sighed. "Maybe we made a mistake, Goldie."

Lily sighed. "Maybe we did."

"You didn't make a mistake," Junior said. "Our car's over here. Unless you changed your minds."

"Okay, we'll accept a ride home with you," Sadie said.

"Our cups runneth over," Junior said snidely.

Sixteen

Matt Starr paced the path leading from Lily's villa to the one rented by the Laroux brothers. He was so close and yet so far from his goal. Dennis, who was pacing right along with him, placed a hand on his arm. "Take it easy, buddy. The girls are okay. They can handle this. Now what the hell are you doing?"

Matt threw his arms out and raised his head to look skyward at the millions of twinkling stars. "You doing that universe thing again? We should be going to the police now that you definitely I.D.'d those guys. The cops could be here in minutes. C'mon, Matt. Let's make some decisions here."

"I want my money back. The only way that's going to happen is to confront those bastards and make it happen the way they made me give it up. If we break into their villa, we'll be arrested. If we can figure out a way to get in while they're there, we have the upper hand. I have an idea. I'll call Lily and suggest they go to the beach. That means the brothers will have to go back to the villa to get their bathing suits. We lie in wait, and the minute they're inside, we go after them. With the girls, there's four of us and three of them. We can't take a weapon, that's premeditated. We wing it. What do you think?"

"Is that what the universe is telling you?" Dennis muttered.

"No. It's what I'm telling you. I never did anything like this before. It's as new to me as it is to you. Just bear with me, okay? All we need is their computer. I want to do to them what they did to me. I haven't forgotten for one minute what they did to Gracie. Not for one damn minute. They're gonna pay for that. Are we going to do this or not?"

"All right, but I'll call Lily. You're too juiced up. Just stand there, Matt, and be quiet. We can make this work if we all get in sync. You need to be calm, and you need a clear head."

"Okay, make the call."

Dennis dialed Lily's cell phone and waited. Her cheerful response grated on his ears. "Hi. Listen, I'll make this quick. Matt wants you to head for the beach. Send the guys back to the villa for their bathing suits. We'll be in the bushes somewhere waiting to pounce the minute they get inside. Meet us there."

"Well, hi, Carol. I almost gave up on you. Oh, yes, we're up for a midnight swim. We just met some of our neighbors this evening. Do you mind if we bring them along? Great! Hold on a second, and I'll ask the guys."

Dennis waited, the cell phone pressed tight against his ear. He waited until she spoke to him again. "Okay, Carol, we can be there in ten minutes."

Dennis snapped the cell phone shut. "They're on the way. Don't make a sound, Matt. This is your big moment, and you don't want to blow it." Both men stepped into the dense shrubbery. "I hear them," he whispered.

"What are you so worried about, Junior?"

"Doesn't it seem a little strange that those two girls picked us out of all the men in that club? For all you know this could be a setup."

"They're from Bluefield, West Virginia. They can't know anything."

"You also need to shut up, voices carry in the night air," Junior said coldly.

Dennis poked Matt in the arm. "Okay, they're inside. Here come the girls."

Lily rushed up and grabbed Matt's arm. "What do we do now?"

"You girls go in first, through the front door. We'll be right behind you. I'm assuming the door to the rear patio is locked. Surprise is on our side although Junior's not as stupid as you think. He's already suspicious."

"This is like the Keystone Kops," Sadie hissed.

"You two girls home in on the youngest one. He's not the brightest crayon in the box. Dennis, you take the middle one, and I get Junior. Let's go!"

"What's taking you guys so long?" Sadie trilled as she opened the door and stepped through, Lily right behind, Dennis and Matt brought up the rear.

"If that bastard Marcus was here, we'd have a grand slam," Matt hissed.

"Who's there?" Junior called from one of the bedrooms.

At the sound of Junior's voice, Matt broke ranks and raced around the corner. "It's just me, you son of a bitch! Don't move! If you do, I'll blow your fucking head off! Now, sit the hell down and haul out that computer of yours! Now!"

"What the hell . . . how . . ."

Matt heard the bedlam behind him, but he ignored it, his gaze never wavering from the man standing in front of him. Out of the corner of his eye he could see the man's laptop on the desk in the corner. Could he take him? He was in shape, but he wasn't sure. If he was going to stand there and think about it, he might as well give it up. He rushed forward, his right foot shooting forward to land square on Junior's shinbone. Junior's leg gave out, and he went down on one knee as Matt's left foot shot upward to smash against his nose. Blood spurted in all directions. "Dump my dog, will you?" He swung around again, his right leg shooting forward, then upward, to knock Junior off-balance.

"You got me, ease up."

"Like hell. You're gonna pay for what you did to Gracie. You left her out there to die, you scumbag. Nobody does that to my dog. You hear me? You left me out there to die. I'm taking you back there, you bastard, and I'm going to strip you naked and turn you loose the way you did me."

"What the hell are you talking about?" Junior whined. "We left you clothes and we notched the trail for you. At the most it should have taken you four hours to get to the main road. And we didn't dump your dog. We put her in a safe place. I like animals. We stole your money, but we didn't hurt you."

"You made me miss my wedding. You dumped my dog, and you left me to die. I spent two weeks in the hospital hanging on by my toenails. I don't even know why I'm bothering to talk to you. You move even one muscle, and you'll wish you hadn't. Dennis!" he shouted.

"I'm here, buddy. I'm happy to say there

wasn't a scrapper in the bunch. We tied both of them up with sheets. Howzit going, big guy?"

"Take a look! Give him his computer and then call the police. Boot up and log on. I'll do the rest," Matt snarled.

Fascinated, Dennis watched the blizzard of numbers sweep across the laptop screen. The moment the last transaction was completed, Matt picked up the laptop, walked out the front door, tossed it onto the flagstone path. He stomped on it until there was nothing left but a mass of crushed plastic. Then he stomped back inside.

"Did you call the police?"

"Yep. They're on the way. I have a call in to the Natchez police, too. Our work here is done," Dennis said dramatically. "This is going to hit the papers, Matt."

"I know. It's okay now. I made good on it. My investors can't fault me for this. They will view it as a shining example of how I handle a crisis."

"How'd you find us? We didn't leave a trail," Junior asked, a towel to his bloody nose.

"A vision. Your biggest mistake was not believing me when I told you I would track you to the ends of the earth. I would have probably let you get away with it and kissed the money good-bye if you hadn't dumped my dog. I found my dog just the way I said I would, but I didn't do it alone. I had lots of help."

"I want a lawyer," Junior shouted.

"Yeah, I guess you do," Matt called over his shoulder. He put his arm around Lily and pulled her close. Dennis did the same thing to Sadie.

"Can we get something to eat, Matt? We haven't had anything to eat today," Lily said.

"Honey, I am going to buy you the best meal this island has to offer even if I have to wake someone up to cook it for you. And then I am going to give you anything in this whole wide world that you want for a wedding present. Anything, Lily. If it's in my power to do it, it's yours. But first, we have to go to the police station so I can sign the complaint. You guys with me on this?"

"You bet," Dennis said.

"Always," Lily said, squeezing Matt's hand. "I can't believe it was so easy. The two younger ones just . . . gave up and sat down. You're okay, aren't you?"

"Honey, I am so okay it's sinful. I wouldn't want to do it again, though. What's your best guess, Dennis, is the stock going to go up or down?"

"It's going to skyrocket. You're the man!

Investors love this stuff. Next week we unveil Open Door 2001, and it's clear sailing on the really big XML announcement. You're golden, buddy!"

"Except for the black cloud where Marcus is concerned."

"Marcus is history, Matt. What goes around comes around. A month from now if someone mentions his name we'll say Marcus who?"

Betsy Collins stared around her look-alike Holiday Inn room. If there was one color she hated above all others, it was orange. She had to get out of there. She had to go somewhere that was stimulating, someplace that suited her. She could afford it now. She could afford to buy anything her heart desired. Anything. She didn't move, didn't lower her legs from the bed where she'd propped them. Suddenly all her energy was gone as well as the desire to do anything but sit and swig on little bottles of Coca-Cola that didn't even taste like the Coca-Cola in the States.

She thought about her daughters and how she'd left them behind and all because of her own greed. Did they hate her? How could they not hate her? If there was a way to get them on this side of the ocean she would find it. She wasn't giving up her children. Temporarily yes, long-term no. She just needed a bit more time to come up with a plan. She could see her reflection in the closet door that she'd left open. Who was this person sitting on the chair in her underwear with her feet propped on the bed? A greedy, selfish woman who never thought about anyone but herself. The same greedy, selfish woman who drove her husband away with her constant whining and outrageous demands. It was okay to cry now because she hadn't applied her makeup. What was she supposed to do now?

She couldn't go back to the States. That was a given. She took a moment to mourn the loss of Bergdorf Goodman and Saks Fifth Avenue and all the specialty stores where she shopped. "I'm a woman without a country," she wailed. "My husband left me, and my children hate me. Where did it all go wrong?" How and when did she turn into this hateful woman in the closet door mirror?

It happened when Marcus started to climb the corporate ladder. Don't blame Marcus, blame yourself. "I wish . . . I wish . . . I wish I had the answer to all my problems." She moved from the chair and threw herself on the bed, where she sobbed until she couldn't cry anymore. "I wish I had a fairy godmother who would let me wish and wish and wish. Someone who will keep my wishes and dole them out when needed and not one minute before. I wish I could go back to being more like Lily Harper. I was like her once. I could be like her again. I know I could. How hard would it be for the fairy godmother of her dreams to turn her into a clone of Lily Harper? It wasn't so much to ask, was it? All she had to do was say, I wish I was like Lily Harper. I wish . . . I wish . . ."

What was the point to all this wishful thinking? She was simply too tired to think about things like this. She pulled the orange-and-brown spread down to cover herself and was asleep within seconds.

Betsy woke to darkness. She felt disoriented. How long had she slept? Obviously all day since it was now dark outside. She felt terrible, her head ached, and she knew her eyes were puffy and swollen. And she was hungry. Room service again. She dressed and used the phone in the bathroom to order her dinner. She crossed her fingers that there would be something on television other than CNN. She would probably be up all night since she'd slept the day away.

Thirty minutes later, Betsy snapped on the light in the bedroom at the same moment the knock sounded on her door. She stood in the doorway waiting for the waiter to place the tray on the round table between the two chairs. She signed the check, then locked the door.

She looked down at the tray and grimaced. A ham and Swiss cheese sandwich, a salad that looked like it was all lettuce, a pot of coffee, and a bowl of canned fruit. She reached for the napkin, felt the weight as she shook it out to find a silver chain with a pendant. How quaint. How tacky. So tacky her daughters would love it. It must be something the hotel gave to guests to make up for the awful orange-and-brown bedspreads. She shrugged. Because there was no reason not to, Betsy slipped the necklace around her neck.

"My life is never going to be the same again," Betsy whimpered aloud, as she bit into the ham and Swiss cheese sandwich.

"That's the last of it," Matt said, piling their luggage by the front door. "Before you know it, we'll be in Las Vegas and we'll both be saying I do. Someone's here, Lily."

"Oh, it's Mr. Sonner. I'm glad he got here before we left. I'll be ready to go as soon as I show him the closet. You can start taking the bags out. Where are the dogs, Matt?"

"In the limo. They aren't taking any chances on getting left behind again. Take your time. I have to roust Dennis and Sadie. No, I guess I don't. Here they come."

Lily waved from the doorway. "I'm sorry about this, Mr. Sonner, but as I told you, I want the closet closed up. Take all the time you want. We'll be gone a month. Just lock up when you leave. I want to check the closet one last time to make sure nothing is in there." Minutes later, she dropped to her knees, flashlight in hand. Her heart skipped a beat when the minuscule light revealed nothing but the floorboards. Using her hands, she ran them up one board and down the other. The Wish Keeper was gone. She'd put it there herself, had wedged it between the floorboards, and now it was gone. She felt so light-headed she leaned her head against the wall.

"Miss Harper, are you all right in there?"

"I'm fine, Mr. Sonner. Listen, maybe I was too hasty about this. Would you mind not doing this till we get back? Crawling around in here made me realize how much space there is in this closet. I'm not sure I'm willing to give it up. I'm sorry I made you come out here for nothing." *Act normal, Lily. Stop shaking and pretend everything is all right,* she cautioned herself.

"No problem, Miss Harper. Call me when you get back. I can see myself out."

Lily sat back on her heels, staring at the inside of the closet. "So you gave me my wish after all. Thank you." She took the steps two at a time, then whizzed through the door to the waiting limo. "The door locks itself. Let's go! The Wish Keeper is gone. Do you hear me? It's gone. I told Mr. Sonner to forget about closing up the closet. I don't believe it's gone, but it is."

"Good!" Sadie said. "That means life can return to normal. This is a very happy ending for all of us. Las Vegas is going to be such fun. I still can't believe the Thornton family is closing the casino for your nuptials. Babylon is the most famous casino in Vegas. You two are getting married and going on your honeymoon. Digitech stock went up twenty points. Dennis and I have become *good* friends. The Laroux brothers are in the pokey awaiting trial. Mrs. Figgins is happy with the new pipe we bought her, not to mention the two little kittens to keep her company. Our world is right side up. Life is wonderful!"

Lily squeezed tighter against Matt's side. "Matt, were you serious about giving me anything I wanted for a wedding present because if you are, I know what I want."

"Name it, honey, and it's yours."

The Great White Way.

Lily waved her arms high over her head. "I feel like I should be shouting, Viva Las Vegas!"

"Then do it," Matt grinned.

"Somebody might see me. I can't do that. Here's the deal. In two hours we are having a candlelight ceremony at Babylon's wedding chapel. The whole Thornton family will be there. Sunny's family. You all know about Sunny. After a hard day on the course, Sadie, Sunny, and I would sit and talk way into the night. We know all about that fabulous family. They own a mountain, Matt. Sunny's brother lives on it. When Sunny was diagnosed with multiple sclerosis, her mother, Fanny, with the aid of all the casino owners, built this special place in the cottonwoods for handicapped people. To show you what a remarkable person Sunny is, she gave up her son to her brother Sage to adopt because she couldn't take care of him. That young man is something else. He loves his mother so much there are no words to describe it. Sunny will tell you herself that when she dribbles, he wipes her mouth. There's nothing he wouldn't do for her, but she knew he needed a family and sometimes I just want to cry when I think about it. Her husband divorced her when she became ill. She doesn't give in. She pushes herself and her husband Harry, too. He also has multiple sclerosis."

"I can't wait to meet her. Did you tell her about your idea for a camp, honey?" Matt asked.

"No, not yet. You gotta get her on the side and get her to tell you how she and Harry survived in a snowstorm in wheelchairs. It will make your blood run cold. But, she survived, and so did Harry. That's what this is all about. She's going to go over the moon when I tell her. Well, let's sign in and get spruced up. Sunny told me we each have our own room."

"Isn't the other side of Sunny's family coming, too, Lily?" Sadie asked.

"Sunny said the Colemans from Texas are coming and the Colemans from Kentucky. Let's see, Texas is oil and airplanes. Kentucky is Thoroughbred racing. It should be a night to remember. I swear, Matt, if you stand me up again, I will . . . I will . . . ."

"It won't happen. Trust me."

"It better not. Sadie and I will meet you at seven o'clock in the chapel. Be on time, Matt, or I won't wait!" She waved as he walked off with Dennis.

"God, Sadie, all of a sudden I have this awful feeling. I don't know what it is. Nothing is going to go wrong, right?"

"Nothing is going to go wrong. You are going to be married promptly at 7:10 this evening. Period. Oh, look at the room number, Lily! It's 711. Aren't those supposed to be lucky gambling numbers?"

415

"I have no idea. Okay, here's the room. I hope my suit isn't wrinkled."

"Sunny! Oh, Sunny, it's so good to see you. I didn't know you were waiting up here. I would have moved a little faster," Lily said, bending down to hug the thin, pretty woman in the wheelchair sitting in the middle of the room.

"Harry and I have a room here for the night. Security called to say you had checked in. I'm just two doors away. Harry will be over in a few minutes. So, are you ready for the big step?"

Lily sat down cross-legged on the floor next to Sunny. "Yes, I'm ready, but first I have to tell you something. Okay, here goes. Matt said he would give me anything in the world that I wanted for a wedding present. He meant it, too. Do you know what I asked for? I asked for acreage in Natchez, Mississippi, to start my own survival camp for people like you and Harry. What do you think?"

Sunny squealed her pleasure. "That's a kick-ass present if I ever heard of one. That's wonderful. Sign me and Harry up. Lily, the past two summers were the best for Harry and me. We came back here more determined than ever to push ourselves to the limit. That is so wonderful. I can't wait to tell Mom. Hey, the whole damn family is here. Turn around, Lily."

Lily turned and gasped. "Sunny!"

"Do you like it, Lily?" she asked shyly.

"Like it? It's the most beautiful creation I've ever seen. Where in the world did you get it?"

"My sister Billie made it for you. It's one of a kind. The minute you called to tell me you were going to elope to Las Vegas, I called her." Her voice turned shy again. "She made yours, too, Sadie. Do you like it?"

"You are too much, Sunny. It's gorgeous, it's breathtaking. How did she know what size, what color . . ."

"I might be wasting away, but there's nothing wrong with my brain. Yet. I remembered everything you two said, and I had all those pictures. Billie is an expert designer. She'll be up in a minute for any last-minute alterations. I'll leave you to get ready. I just wanted to be here to welcome you. How much is it going to cost, Lily?"

"What do you mean how much is it going to cost?"

"For people to take the course. Ozzie's camp was expensive. Most of the people at the center have no money. Harry and I were lucky that my family could afford it."

Lily dropped to her knees. "It's free, Sunny. For any and all handicapped. Matt is going to fund it. Maybe not Matt directly, but Digitech will be there, too."

The relief on Sunny's face brought a smile from Lily. "Like your mama said, when God is good to you, you gotta give back. Matt's a good guy. You're gonna like him. If he doesn't stand me up again."

"Not a chance! Can Harry and I call the center and tell everyone?"

"Absolutely! Tell the world."

"Good, then I'll leave you to get ready. Billie will be up in a minute, and she'll take you to the chapel. We'll be waiting. Thanks, Lily. Thanks for everything."

"Lily, I think this is going to be a night to remember," Sadie said. A scarlet-satin maid-of-honor dress. Is this gorgeous or what?"

"It is gorgeous."

"We have exactly ninety minutes to shower, put on makeup, curl our hair, and climb into these fantastic creations. Move, Lily!"

At six o'clock the loudspeakers in every casino on the Great White Way blared to life. The announcement was the same in each one. "The Casino doors will close promptly in exactly thirty minutes. We apologize for any inconvenience. Thirty minutes, ladies and gentlemen!"

Thirty-three minutes later, the Great White Way slipped into velvety darkness.

"The only thing that's going to be missing is Elvis Presley," Sunny giggled as she wheeled herself to the chapel. "What do you think, Harry? Do you think Lily will like Dallas Lord and the Canyon River Band? He's going to sing in public, for the first time, the song he wrote for his wife Sara. It's called 'Sara's Song.' But tonight he's going to use Lily's name. Isn't it a hoot? My brother Sage knows Dallas's wife, and that's how we got him to come here and sing. He's coming out of retirement to do it. Do you wish we'd be able to dance together, Harry?" Sunny blurted.

"Yeah, I do wish that. We can sit next to each other and hold hands. I know it's not the same thing, but we're used to that. I'm hoping, if we keep improving, maybe Lily and Matt will let us help out on some of the courses. Some people are going to be intimidated and scared. If they see us doing it, it might give them the confidence they need to go for it."

"Sure. That's what it's all about. I told Mom, and she was delighted. She's with the Colemans, and they seem real happy about it, too. Look, there's Nealy Coleman. That branch of the family just came to life. Boy, is that a story in itself. She's a jockey. Can you believe that, Harry?"

"I believe anything and everything about your family. They just seem to know how to make things happen. Especially the women."

"Now you're getting it, Harry. Listen, I have a confession to make to you. We snagged Dallas Lord and the Canyon River band for *you*. I know they were always your favorite band. For Lily and Matt, too, but mostly for you. Just because we're in these chairs doesn't mean we lose our appreciation for the things we love. Is it a good surprise, Harry?"

"The best! You did that for me?"

Sunny's head bobbed up and down. "C'mon, let's go. We get front and center because we're *handicapped*."

"My God, Sunny, everyone in Vegas is here! How'd that happen?"

"I called them. This whole town uses Digitech software. You're right," Sunny said, craning her neck to look around, "there must be two thousand people here. Do you think they all brought gifts? Look, Mom's already spreading the word among the owners. About the camp, Harry."

"Jeez, Sunny, here comes Dallas Lord. What should I say? Holy shit!"

"Say hello."

Upstairs, Lily positioned the veil on top of her head. Sadie clapped her hands. "Lily, you are absolutely beautiful. Now, dammit, wipe that frown off your face. Matt is going to be waiting for you when you get to the chapel. He's going to be there, so let's see a smile. How do I look? Am I going to blow Dennis's socks off?"

"Yep! What time is it?"

"We have five minutes to get downstairs. This is not one of those times when you want to be fashionably late. Let's go, Lily."

"I'm so nervous. My legs are twitching. I just know I'm going to trip and fall or put a hole in this gorgeous gown. We don't really know these people. We only know Sunny and Harry, and they're doing all this for us. How am I to accept all this?"

"Lily, look at me. Read my lips. Shut up! Billie is waiting for us by the elevator. It's time to go."

In the suite, one floor up, Matt Starr looked down at his shiny black shoes and muttered, "I hate these shoes. I feel like a monkey in this suit."

"Every groom feels the same way. Suck it up, buddy. This is your big day. The Thornton twins are waiting at the elevator for us. I promised Lily I would personally hand-deliver you to her in the chapel. Time to go." Dennis burst into laughter at the look of panic on Matt's face. He snapped his fingers in front of Matt's face. When his friend didn't so much as blink, he cupped his elbow in his hand and led him from the room.

The elevator door slid open, the Thornton twins, Birch and Sage, entered, followed by a glassy-eyed Matt and Dennis. The door swished shut.

At six minutes to seven, the elevator stopped between the eighth and ninth floor when a buzzer sounded from the control panel. Birch fiddled with it, pressing one button after another until Sage withdrew a key from his pocket and unlocked the phone. He dialed security and wasn't surprised when no one answered. The casino was closed for the wedding.

"What's wrong?" Matt demanded.

"It appears we are temporarily . . . stuck between floors."

"What?" Matt squawked. "What the hell time is it? Jesus, it's almost seven. Lily said she wasn't waiting. She meant it, too. Do what they do in the movies. Remove the panel and climb up the cables. It's just like climbing a rope."

"You gotta be kidding," Sage said.

"I haven't climbed a rope in twenty years," Birch said.

"Don't look at me. I *never* climbed a rope," Dennis said.

"Well, I have. Lily made me learn. Bend

down so I can get on your shoulders. I'll climb the damn cable. Keep calling that number. I'm not standing my girl up for the *third* time. A billion-dollar casino and the damn elevator doesn't work. Someone better tell me why right now."

"It's all computerized," Birch grunted, as Matt's full weight settled on his shoulders. "*Digitech* software."

"No shit! Dennis, write that down. Okay, I'm up here, and it's dark as hell. I need something to wrap around my hands. The cables are greasy. Dennis, give me your shirt. What time is it?"

"Seven o'clock on the dot. I might be a minute fast."

"You better hope to God you're fast," Matt said, shimmying up the cable. "I'm almost there. How do I get the damn door open?"

"Pry it with your fingers. Send help," Sage said, squatting on the floor. Dennis and his brother joined him.

Matt broke into a sweat as he struggled with the elevator door. He finally managed to pry it open enough to use his shoulder to open it wide enough to crawl through. He lost no time in running to the exit sign, where he took the steps two at a time, bellowing all the way. By the time he reached the main floor, he'd lost one shoe and his cummerbund, his frilly shirt was dangling in shreds, his hair wildly on end. "I'm coming, Lily," he shouted at the top of his lungs until he was hoarse.

He careened around slot machines, poker and blackjack tables, and somehow managed to lose his second shoe when he tripped over a money cart and sprawled out on the floor. *Keep moving, Matt. Move, Lily said. If you stand still you're lost.* He moved, doing his best to wipe the sweat dripping in his eyes.

"Hold on, mister, where do you think you're going?" a harsh voice demanded. Matt felt a heavy hand on his shoulder. "Dammit, I'm the *groom*. I was stuck in your goddamn elevator, and I had to climb out between floors. Where's the chapel?"

"Don't know if your bride is still there, mister. Heard she was pissed and stalked off saying she knew it was going to happen. Oh, oh, here she comes. I feel sorry for you, mister," the security guard said backing away.

"Lily!"

"Matt!"

"Lily."

"You said that already. I was just getting ready to put my foot through this veil for the *third* time. What happened to you?"

"Never mind. Where's the minister?"

"I'm right here, son."

"Then let's do it. How late am I, Lily?"

424

"Seven minutes."

"You waited seven minutes. You really waited."

"Yeah. You look awful."

"You look beautiful. I almost killed myself getting here. I made it, though."

Lily grinned. "I would have killed you myself if you hadn't made it. Listen up so you get the words right. You're sure you want to do this, Matt?"

"Lily, I never wanted anything more in my life than I want this. Let's get on with it, Reverend."

While the guests beamed and clapped, the minister said, "I now pronounce you man and wife. You may now kiss the bride."

"Oh, no, not until the ring is on my finger. Where's the ring, Matt?"

"Dennis has it. They're still locked in the elevator. We have to get them out."

"Why? The wedding is over. You really should find your shoes, Matt. What are these people going to think?"

"They are going to think I'm the luckiest guy in the world. Look at me. No one in her right mind would marry someone looking like me. No, no, I didn't mean that the way it sounds. Lily! I didn't mean it that way."

"I know you didn't. Come on, it's time for fun and frolic."

"I do like the way that sounds. Lead the way, Mrs. Starr."

"Will you follow me and be at my side forever and ever and even then?"

"Forever and ever and even then, Charming Lily."

Epilogue

Betsy Collins curled into the club chair, her eyes on the television screen, her fingers twirling the little trinket hanging from her neck. She was starting to like CNN and watching what was going on in the world. She was even starting to like the orange-and-brown bedspread.

A stack of fashion magazines stared up at her. She hadn't looked at them at all. It was weird the way she was feeling. For the past several days she'd barely ventured from the hotel room, taking her meals in her room and going to the exercise room late in the day. All she did was think about her girls and Marcus. Her eyes filled with tears. What was even more strange was she hadn't applied makeup in almost five days. In just a little while she had an appointment to get a wash-and-wear haircut like the one she had when she first met Marcus. She also had to remember to call downstairs to inquire about her laundry.

Betsy shifted her position in the club chair; her fingers continued to diddle with the necklace she'd found in her napkin five days earlier. Maybe she needed some fresh air. If she didn't start to move around a little, she would start taking root here in the hotel room. Or, maybe she should think about moving to a fancier place. She vetoed that idea almost immediately.

She looked at her watch. Almost lunchtime. She hungered for a bowl of thick, hot soup and crusty bread. When was the last time she'd eaten anything so ordinary? She couldn't remember. There were so many things she couldn't remember these past days. It was like she was suddenly a different person. She looked over at the hotel stationery piled up on the dresser. She'd spent hours writing down things. Memories mostly, and then she'd started soul-searching. That list took up two full sheets of paper. Somewhere along the way she'd turned into a mean, ugly, hateful person. With painstaking honesty she'd outlined a list of awful things she'd done not only to Marcus but the girls as well. She knew in her heart she was the one who had driven Marcus to do what he did. "I wish I could do it all over again," she said pitifully. "I wish . . . I wish . . ." Her eyes closed and she slept.

He was waving to her, and then pointing to the bank, a huge smile on his face. She waved back, a smile as large as Marcus's on her face.

She was shaking her head, and he was shaking his. He looked tired, and he needed a shave. He also looked cold. She wanted to take him in her arms and hold him close. She tried to call out, but her lips were frozen and cold. He was walking away from her. "No, No, Marcus, come back! We can make this work. I'm not like that anymore. I just want you and the girls. I don't care about the damn money. Marcus, listen to me. Give me a chance. Everyone deserves a second chance. We can make this right. Marcussssss!"

Betsy's eyes snapped open. She started to cry. Wiping her eyes on the sleeve of her sweat suit, she raced into the bathroom to wash her face. She took a long, hard look at herself. Without the heavy makeup and false eyelashes she looked different. She looked . . . normal, kind of like Lily Harper in a wholesome way. When she got her hair cut, she would look just the way she looked when she walked down the aisle with Marcus. "I'm sorry, Marcus. I wish I could undo all those mean years. I really do." When her eyes started to burn with unshed tears, she sniffed, adjusted the fleece-lined sweatshirt over her hips, and left the bathroom.

Betsy reached for the fleece-lined jacket she'd purchased days ago in one of the hotel boutiques. It was snug and warm. As were the fleece-lined boots. The jacket and boots would keep her warm when she went for the walk she promised herself after her appointment at the hairdresser. Maybe some fresh air would put some color in her cheeks. Maybe the fresh air would clear out the cobwebs in her head. Maybe a lot of things.

Betsy looked into the mirror the stylist held up so she could see the back of her hair. She nodded.

"It becomes you, madam. You look much younger, more vibrant."

And your tip will be in accordance with your compliments, Betsy thought as she opened her purse. She did look younger, and she did look vibrant. The stylist hadn't lied. She exited the shop with a spring in her step. She looked right and then left. Which way to go? She turned left and started walking on the hard, crunchy snow. Sooner or later she hoped she would find a small restaurant that would serve her the bowl of soup she craved.

It was cold, the temperature in the low twenties if she was any judge. She'd always liked the cold weather. The girls loved snow. Marcus loved to ski. She liked to ski, too, but she spent more time on her rear end than she did on her feet. Marcus always laughed, that booming, robust laugh of his. She felt like crying, but knew if she did, the tears would freeze on her cheeks. She continued to walk until she spotted a small restaurant across from the bank that held her children's accounts. She moved against the building to get out of the stinging wind and stared at the building. It was all so long ago. Almost a lifetime ago.

Betsy waited for a break in traffic before she crossed the street to enter the restaurant. It was small, cozy, and smelled heavenly. The windows behind the blue-and-white plaid curtains were steamed up. She tried to identify the smells but gave up. Surely they would have a good hearty soup and fresh, crusty bread. A cup of coffee right now would be perfect. She walked over to the one available table and sat down. She didn't have to ask for coffee, it appeared as if by magic. The small pitcher of real cream pleased her. It took a minute to unbutton the jacket and slip out of it. Just as she was bringing the coffee cup to her lips, she raised her eyes to look across the small room. There, directly in her line of vision, was Marcus. A megawatt smile stretched across her face. And then he saw her. Four long-legged strides brought him to her table.

"Marcus, I am so very sorry. I don't know what else to say. You look . . . you look . . . *awful*."

"I feel awful," Marcus blurted. "Betsy, I can't believe it's you. How did you find me?"

"Before I tell you that, are you glad to see me? I'm glad to see you."

"Hell, yes. How did you get here? Where are the girls?"

"I flew over. That man, Eric Savarone came to see me. The girls are fine. I left them in the care of the nanny and the housekeeper. Trust me, they are in good hands. I miss them terribly. When Savarone left, I started to think. Back then I was working the angles, trying to figure out how I could snatch all that money from you. I figured it out, Marcus. At first all I could think of was the money and what I could do with it. I was going to buy every design Escada could come up with. I was going to be the darling of the Paris runways. Then something happened to me. I can't explain it. This is all my fault, Marcus. I drove you to do what you did. Look, we need to talk, and we can't do it here. I want to eat something first and then if you're agreeable, we can go back to my hotel. I took the money, Marcus, so why are you still here?"

"Waiting for you. I stayed in this general area hoping to find you. I walked these streets night and day. Here you are. I think I knew that sooner or later you'd figure it out and come here. At least I hoped you would. It's a good thing because I'm down to my last twenty bucks."

"I'll buy lunch," Betsy grinned. "Marcus, I cannot tell you how happy I am to see you. I fell asleep a little while ago, and I had this dream. You were in it."

"What did you do to yourself? You look . . . the way you used to look. I like this new look. How in the hell did we get so screwed up? We had it all."

"And I wanted more. I always wanted more and more. It's my fault, and I'm willing to take the blame. Just tell me you still love me and the girls. Please, tell me we can make this work. If I had one wish, that's all I would wish for," Betsy said, her fingers working the pendant on her neck.

"It can work, Betsy. You and the girls are all I've thought about. I turned into this . . . greedy, power-hungry bastard. Maybe together we can make it right."

"I found myself. I hope I found you in time, too. I have so much to tell you. I imagine you have just as much to tell me, so let's eat and get out of here. Marcus, just one more thing. If you don't believe anything else, believe that I do love you. I need to hear you tell me how you feel about me. I can't undo anything, but I will never, ever, become that ugly, hateful person I used to be. Why did it take you so long to leave me?"

"I couldn't leave. I loved you. I kept hoping . . . Jesus, I don't know what the hell got into me. The opportunity was there, and I grabbed it. I haven't had one peaceful moment since all this happened. Damn, this soup looks good."

They ate with gusto until they were full. In between mouthfuls of food, they talked of ordinary things. "Matt got married, Marcus. I saw it on CNN. Not the wedding, just the news. He was abducted and left to die in the woods, but Lily and Dennis and Lily's friend found him. He spent two weeks in the hospital. For a while it looked like he wasn't going to make it. The stock went up twenty points after the announcement. I made them give me your bonus check and your vacation and sick days, Marcus. You earned it."

"I'm the worst kind of thief, Betsy," Marcus said miserably.

"No, I am. Together, we'll make this right. Some way, somehow. I miss the girls, Marcus."

"I do, too, honey. We'll work something out. Come on, let's get out of here. Where are you staying?" Betsy told him. Marcus raised his eyebrows.

"I couldn't bring myself to spend the money. We need to talk about the IRS. Dennis put the fear of God into me where they're concerned."

"I'm square with the IRS. I pay quarterly and am a year ahead. That was the one thing I never messed around with. Hell, I'm even square with the stock options. I can't believe you just up and walked in here. I've been wishing and wishing, and as each day wore on I started to panic." He put his arm around his wife's shoulder and led her to the door, his shoulders straight, his eyes bright.

Betsy woke, instantly aware of where she was and what had transpired earlier. She moved slightly, unwilling to wake her husband. She looked over at him, a smile on her lips before her gaze swiveled to the window. It was snowing outside. A good day to stay in and cuddle. She felt his hand reach out for hers. She'd missed this gentleness, the warm intimacy they'd shared all night long.

"How long have you been awake, Betsy?" he whispered.

"Just a minute or two. It's snowing. Maybe later we can go for a walk and try to find a place to make snow angels like we used to do with the girls when they were little."

"That's too easy, too normal. We need to talk, Betsy. Call down and order us some sweet rolls and coffee. We're going to try and make this come out right for everyone concerned."

Hours later, the coffee and pastries finished, Marcus leaned back on the chair and propped his feet up on the rumpled bed. "Are you sure you're okay with all of this, Betsy? It's going to be a long rough patch until we get past all this. The first thing we are going to do is bring the girls here. We'll rent a little house in the country and I'll finish what I started years ago. You're going to sell your jewelry, and with that money coupled with my bonus money, that's what we'll live on. We'll send back that $100,000 Dennis gave you and the half million you weaseled out of Eric and BQWARE. I can't believe they were stupid enough to give it to you. I'm going to wire all but ten million of Eric and BQWARE's money back to them and sign a note for the balance plus ten percent interest. We'll liquidate everything back in the States, pay our taxes, and with the balance, I will finish developing the software I've been designing these past few years on my own time. I'll cut in Eric, BQWARE, and Matt for a percentage when we sell it. It won't make up for what I did, but it's a start in the right direction. If this software goes the way I think it's going to go, they'll make a fortune. Three years from now, we should be on solid ground. You're sure now you're okay with this? You're going to have to do all the household tasks yourself. There won't be any housekeepers or nannies. No fancy designer duds and no costly vacations. Maybe, if we're lucky, we'll be able to go back to the States someday with our heads held high. Then again, maybe not. We'll always be thieves, Betsy."

"I'm okay with it all, Marcus." Betsy fingered the pendant hanging from her neck. "I wished for this, Marcus. We can make this work, can't we?"

"I think so. I'm going to do my damnedest to make things come out right. Now, did you say something about going out in the snow to make snow angels?"

"I did say that I wish the girls were here. You're right, though, let them finish out the semester, then my parents can bring them over here. It will be something for us to look forward to."

"The jewelry has to go first. What do you call that thing hanging around your neck? I've never seen you wear anything like that before."

"I ordered room service at the hotel, and it was wrapped up in the napkin. I assume it's a souvenir of some kind the hotel gives out to guests. It's rather tacky-looking but also kind of sweet and different. I just put it on and have been wearing it ever since. It makes me feel good for some reason. It's not something I can explain. Besides my wedding ring, it's the only jewelry I will be wearing from now on."

Marcus smiled. "It will be nice to be a family again, won't it, Betsy?"

"Yes it will. Marcus, will we ever truly get past this? What we both did was really terrible. This . . . what we're planning is like . . . we got away with it. We're walking around free as the air. It will always be hanging over our heads, won't it?"

"Yes. That's our punishment. And we deserve it. We'll be living with that punishment twenty-four hours a day. Working together, it might not be too bad."

Betsy reached for her husband's hand. "Let's go make some snow angels."

"Sounds good to me."

"Then let's do it!"